The Dial Press   New York   1972

ACTION

James Guetti

Library of Congress Cataloging in Publication Data

Guetti, James L.
  Action.

  I. Title.
PZ4.G959Ac   *[PS3557.U35]*   *813'.5'4*   *78–37447*

Printed in the United States of America
First Printing.

Book design by Margaret McCutcheon

To Barbara and Nicholas

"Why are you running,
Are you afraid to die?"
"The reason that I'm running
Is because I cannot fly . . ."

—*An old Song*

Action packed account of the life
of Phil Hatcher, college professor
turned gambler, convinced of making
it big.

The special train to Aqueduct Race Track runs through a graveyard. The cars slant up out of the ground into Brooklyn; the train slows—or its rumbling lurch no longer gives the illusion of speed—and on the right the cemetery spreads out. It is not an old cemetery. Most of the stones are not fancy, and none of them appear worn or engagingly tilted. They stand regular and very well laid out, like a little town among all the others where the train, since it is a special, does not stop.

The gamblers on the train watch the graveyard as they watch everything on their way out to the track; it is all part of a trivial and passing scene, as if they were souls, transmigrating. But of course there are a few who cannot ignore the opportunity it presents. They are the ones most dedicated to losing, and they are already mouthing their litanies. For them the cemetery is just one more source of gloomy analogy, full of monuments to their consistent bad fortune, and it calls up all the clipped phrases they will come to use that day: tapped out, bent, broke, dead, dust. The other passengers scarcely listen. With small anticipating smiles they balance on the metal benches, their eyes alert and careless at the same time, like gods' eyes.

The old man who sat across from Hatcher had a foot in both camps. He was an old white bird with a small, handsome face and a cigar stub that had colored the end of his sharp curving nose brown. "Hah," he said as the train coasted through. "Dead man." The he tilted his head back to his *Morning Telegraph*. But when, a few seconds later, he glanced up and saw Hatcher looking at him, he raised his eyebrows sharply and pleasantly; his eyes rounded and he removed, for a moment, the cigar. "You play your horse," he said, "you play your cards. What the difference." He gestured with the cigar end toward the upright stones. "There," he said, making a point. Then he rocked back his head, with his round eyes still on his listener, and opened his mouth wide with all the signs of laughter, though he made no sound. Hatcher nodded, then smiled sternly. The man watched him for a moment, as if speculating. Then he looked away, replaced the black stub, and drawled loudly through it, both contemptuous and encouraging. "Att-a boy!"

Later a conductor made his unnecessary proclamation that Aqueduct was the last stop. Then the crowd hurried to lay down the first two dollars of the day at the turnstile gates. From the subway station down the long incline to the gates they rushed, funneling for the passage and then spreading again as they approached the track, at last running away from each other, as if toward some isolated and secret corner. In the midst of that Hatcher saw the old man again. He shuffled along all by himself, feet set a foot apart and hardly leaving the ground, concentrating on some spot just ahead. But his bird's eye flickered, and he saw Hatcher, too. He raised his head with its fluttering, comb-like growth of white hair and then looked back to the ground, lifting his hand and waggling it sidewise in slow vaudeville fashion. Hatcher slowed, smiled. Then a man stopped in front of him, hacked and spit. Hatcher sidestepped and kept going, going away, swinging through a turnstile, slapping his quarter for a program down hard so there would be no mistake. He flipped the pages to the sixth race, anxious now, but the horse was there, still number nine. For the time everything was as projected, and for the time being he relaxed.

Hatcher had not, of course, meant to come out today—if horse players ever mean to stay away. When he pushed through the heavy glass doors of the apartment house he had felt the day's warmth and decided to walk to school. But on the way he saw that spring had indeed broken out. As he approached the block where the newsstand was, he saw them strung out in his way. Some leaned against buildings or no-parking signs, while others squatted on their heels in the race track crouch. They were in various uniforms—laborers in high shoes and yellow plastic helmets, griddle men in greasy white, businessmen, lawyers, doctors in dark suits, sharpies in wide jackets and open-necked shirts. But still they were all the same. They were all reading or thinking or talking horses, and as he passed the corner, he heard one shout to an unseen friend to lend him a deuce so that at least, for Christ sake, he could play a double.

The horses had in fact come back from Florida a week ago, but most of those who were interested had continued to call their bookies, because they were broke or distrusted the opening days or could not get away. Yet none of that really mattered to them, Hatcher thought, any more than it mattered to him. It was only that they had not decided yet. Now, somehow, because of the new weather or because it was Monday and a fresh week, they were ready. In towns like this one all through New Jersey and Maryland and New York they would have their renaissance. Hatcher heard them talk and laugh to each other over the entries. The dreary earning and spending, budgeting or conniving, cornflakes or steaks—that was forgotten, or, if not forgotten, denied. It had been yesterday, in the winter. They would not go that way again. They all lived now in and under their imaginations' spiritual democracy, the gambler's government, where everybody has a chance. Soon most of them would lie to bosses or wives and go off on the turnpikes to Garden, to Pimlico, or to the Big A.

Which was, more or less, what Hatcher himself had done. Even when he had seen them all out and resurrected and threaded his way through to the newsstand, he had in fact been on his way to work, regarding those clustered gamblers with envy and disapproval. He paid for the scratch sheet, the *National Armstrong Daily*, and turned uphill. He would have seemed to be going uphill, or into a wind, anyway. He walked bent slightly forward at the waist through eagerness, or purpose, or some other excess. But he was bent over the sheet now, too.

As he scanned the crude black print, the horses' names touched off little flares of recognition and fantasy, taking him back to the last time he had studied the past performances, or to a winning parlay of two weeks ago, or to a three-horse photo finish he had been involved in at the autumn meeting at Garden State. Even so, he read quickly, until he got to the railroad station corner and the sixth race at Aqueduct, and then he stopped and read that one again. Far down in the rankings for the race—four-year-olds and up, seven furlongs, non-winners of three since January 7, $12,-500–10,500 claiming—was the name "Insulator."

Deliberately, Hatcher covered the race again, and the other horses in it did not impress him. He reversed for three steps and swung into a phone booth. "Joey? Hey. This is Phil. Yeah, how ya doin'. Listen, Joe. The sixth at New York. Sixth, yeah. Insulator. *Insulator.* He's . . . number nine on the sheet. Right. Eighty win. Right?" But then he imagined catastrophe: lightning, a plane crashing on take-off from Kennedy, a jockey's conspiracy, his horse running second. "Joe? And forty to place. Thanks." He blew out his breath as he put the telephone up, relieved to think of the bet in and later himself here in a classroom talking while in fact there the horses were pounding for the wire. But then to see that in mind suddenly was not enough. Too many things were right—the day warm, the players out, and one of his own running. He went back to the booth and this time was more grammatical, as he made his short explanation and arranged for his classes to be dismissed. Then he was free and he crossed the street to the bus station and bought his ticket to New York.

When the bus crept irrevocably up onto the turnpike at last, Hatcher became anxious. Perhaps he should have studied the race more carefully before making a move. So he took out the *Tele-graph* he had bought thinking he would not need it, and he peered down into the past performances for the sixth at Aqueduct and especially at the block of abbreviations that somehow stood for all of Insulator's recent life and, at times, for parts of Hatcher's own:

12Jun64–6Suf	fst 6f	.22$^{4/5}$	.46$^{1/5}$	1.12		Clm 4000	10	7	10^{12}	7^7 4^3	1^{nk}	JGorse	122	9.40 81–19	Insulator122^{nk}Brierly Babe119^{3}Liable119^1		Just up 10
1Jun64–3Suf	fst 1^{70}	.47$^{3/5}$	1.13	1.44		Clm 2500	5	1	2^1	2^2 2$^{1/2}$	3^2	JGorse	116	*2.20 80–15	Blue Bucks114$^{1-1/2}$Warmonger112$^{1/2}$Insulator116^1		Bohrd Str 9
17May64–1Suf	sly 1	.47	1.12$^{4/5}$	1.39$^{1/5}$		Md 2000	5	3	3^3	3^1 1^1	1^5	JGorse	118	3.60 72–17	Insulator118^{5}Ollies Red115^{no}Kin Run108^{nk}		Easy score 11
10May64–2Suf	fst 6f	.23	.47	1.13$^{2/5}$		Md 2000	7	7	6^5	4^4 4^3	5^4	JGorse	122	4.00 69–14	Hooker110^{1}Joe N.119$^{1/2}$Banana Boy121$^{1/4}$		No threat 11

Hatcher's first time with the horse was on that twelfth of June at Suffolk Downs. All the letters and numbers had been the same then as now, save that the line of code for that day itself had not yet been supplied, that race not yet enacted. Before it had been, Hatcher had hunkered against a pillar and, needing a winner badly, penciled Insulator out of consideration. As the chart shows, he had come from far back for the win, paying $20.80.

The next time for them both was two months later at Atlantic City Race Course. Hatcher had been irritated by the new coincidence, by something more to consider, but no more than that. "The pig just barely won up *there!*" one of his friends had cried. "What's he been doin' since then, huh? He's gonna beat *this* field?" That seemed to be right, though just before the bell, with thirty dollars riding on the favorite, Hatcher thought again and looked again and saw that Insulator was five to one, too low. When the horses went the bay gelding rushed suddenly, easily, into the lead as they turned for home, winning by two lengths and a half, with speed, as they say, to spare. As the bus skirted the refineries at Elizabeth, Hatcher saw that again:

14Aug64–4Atl	fst 7f	.22$^{1/5}$	.46$^{2/5}$	1.24$^{3/5}$	Clm 5500	4	5	4$^{3-1/2}$	3^1 1$^{3/4}$	1$^{2-1/2}$	TMayo	116	5.40 86–12	Insulator116^{3}Jay Rod119^{1}C U Alley114^2		In hand 12

But the tracks had closed before he ran again. It snowed, and Hatcher went back to work. So that it was December before he had discovered the horse once more, down in the second half of the daily double at Tropical. This time Hatcher had made a bet, a good bet he thought, and he had hung in his chair at six thirty as the voice of WHBI gave the results. He did not hear the horse's name. But the next time he saw that it had just been bad luck:

7Dec64–2Trp fst 6f .22 .45¹/⁵ 1.11 Clm 7000 4 10 7⁸ 4⁴ 3³/⁴ 5³ RClapp 120 13.10 82–10 Boat Job114¹/²Live One117ⁿᵏJimgee110³/⁴ Slow st, blkd 10

The bus rumbled through the thick air of the tunnel, and Hatcher was still convinced of it, the bad luck. A slow start, he thought, from an inside post, and he made up all that ground and was there at the stretch with no running room. So he had been confident, and waited, and five weeks later at Hialeah Insulator was entered again, again higher up the scale. Hatcher had had twenty dollars in his pocket when he found out; he bet it at Shoemaker John's strictly cash establishment:

15Jan65–4Hia sl 6f .22²/⁵ .46 1.12¹/⁵ Clm 8500 8 6 4⁵ 4² 2¹/² 1³ RClapp 118 15.90 79–24 Insulator118³Uncle PaulⁿᵏJointure111²·¹/² Rid'n Out 12

Which came, he said to himself, to three hundred and thirty-eight, and more coming today. That was the topmost printed line. Insulator had not started again, until today, but Hatcher was not worried. He kept singing to himself: he runs good fresh, on any kind of track, against any kind he's met—to his fancy, there were no limits. Some coltish injury had healed; he had got on his feed; his trainer had somehow figured him out. Whatever it was, each time he ran he was a different animal, always better than the time before, a changeling whose tattooed lip was all that was left of a three-year-old bay gelding that could not beat two-thousand-dollar maidens at Lincoln Downs.

As he climbed down into the Port Authority Terminal, Hatcher folded the *Telegraph* away. The form no longer mattered. He was sure once again that he knew more about Insulator than the racing paper could tell him. What he knew—and had known that morning at the newsstand, and would know on the train, with the snow dying in streaks between the gravestones and the old man laughing silently opposite him—was what he did not know. He knew that the horse was unlimited, all potential. So he multiplied the world.

8

When it came time for the sixth, Hatcher had seen five races and bet ten dollars for the entertainment. The two hundred dollars for the car payment and grocery bill in his pocket was reserved. On the big board flashing the odds, as the people bet and the odds changed, Insulator was number nine. It may have been that they thought he was too cheap for his new company; perhaps it was that he had not started in two months. For those or other reasons he began at twenty to one, dropped in two or three changes to seventeen, and held. With ten minutes to go the horses were on the track, and Hatcher walked down the long, sloping asphalt, putting the concrete and the machinery and most of the crowd behind him, to have a look. On the nearly orange strip of dirt they minced along, big barreled and thin legged, corks on toothpicks. Their coats shone as they usually do at Aqueduct; the silks, too, were bright. They were well strung out and the lead pony was beginning to make the turn when Hatcher saw Insulator as he had remembered him: the dark bay almost black, colors still blue and white, with the round-faced, dark Cuban hunched high on him, gently rocking forth and back. Hatcher was satisfied. He turned and weaved back through the thickening crowd, who had already blown their money, he thought, and would chew themselves for seven or eight minutes more before they found it out.

He stood near a ten-dollar window and watched the odds. That was merely his habit, since not only did he know what he was going to do but, all but in fact, he had already done it. With three minutes to go, when he got himself in line, Insulator dropped in a single flicker to thirteen. When he came away from the window with his twenty tickets, it was twelve. Then eleven, and then a two point drop to nine. Hatcher swore because every change cost him money, but then it was all right, for the bell rang, the ticket machines stopped their chopping, and the high, thin, precise voice of the Big A said that they were off.

They were off from the seven-furlong chute. The crowd-noise rose, and Hatcher saw a flash of color, a bright wave, moving slowly up the faraway rail. After three sixteenths of a mile they were into the main track, and he began to look for Insulator. But he did not find him for another furlong, and then another, and the pack had begun to string out with the markers flashing by them all too fast. Hatcher dropped his cigarette, groped for another, and strained to look over all the heads at the horses perched out on the far turn, listening, too, to catch the name they were screaming, of some horse who was on the lead. Three lengths of lead they were crying. Who could catch him now? But just then Hatcher heard the other name, the right name, and there he was, black against the rail, driving up from fourth. As if through a thin mist, he could see sharply his number, Hatcher's number nine.

The home stretch at Aqueduct is one thousand one hundred and fifty-five point six feet long, and in March the track is very deep with the added sand that keeps it from freezing. The people who bet speed horses, the front runners, have the worst of it, for those animals use their energy early and tire in the slow going, and when they make the last turn, they seem even more than usual to be running in place. In that long, straight drive home the stretch runners often catch them. Hatcher knew all that. Insulator was moving strongly toward an opening between the second and third horses, as two lengths away the leader shortened his stride. The mob around Hatcher was cheering for the front runner to stay, and his rider bounced wildly on him to keep him there. But Insulator was closing the gap even faster now and, with a happy and arrogant smile, Hatcher turned away. There was little more to see, and he wanted to be first in line at a cashier's window, as he had been the first, he thought, to know.

Then he heard it. The demanding and outraged cries stopped, and the other sound rose and fell in pure, almost abstracted astonishment. Someone on the subway, not the special, told him later that the second horse had stumbled and gone down, and that the horse behind—that was his, Hatcher's, Insulator, though the teller did not know—had fallen over him. In the *Telegraph* the next day it was said that Insulator had broken his left fore cleanly and had to be destroyed. Hatcher had seen that kind of injury before; the horse staggers up and looks amazed and stupidly around. His foot and ankle wobble at the end of his sporadically upheld leg like some child's toy. The journalistic end to it was usually "had to be destroyed," which means a quick and surreptitious needle to spare the feelings of the crowd.

When he turned back toward the track, it looked as if all the other horses were down, and the one on the lead could not have quit now if they had wanted him to. Hatcher could not see any number nine, but he knew that he was there, in it, under it. There had been nowhere else for him to go. The crowd was quiet now as the winner scampered across the finish line, except for a grizzled man in sagging pants who jumped a few inches in the air, screamed "Atta baby!" and "I got 'um!" and held up some blue-bordered tickets.

"I got *'um,*" he said again, quiet and sincere this time. Then he saw a tall, sallow-faced man a few feet away regarding him. He strutted over, brandishing his tickets. "How about that," he said, pointing at the tote board, at the horses cantering back, at anything. "I *gotta* get at least seven dollars."

"Six," Hatcher said, spitting.

"At least six dollars. He win it *easy!* You have 'um?"

Hatcher swayed forward toward the man; he was trembling slightly. The other looked back at him cheerfully vague and grinned slackly. "Huh?"

Hatcher swayed back again and half-turned away. "Go get paid."

"Aw," the other said. "What're ya talkin' about?" Hatcher had begun to walk away from him, and so he called out, "I ain't had a winner in three days."

Hatcher stopped, turning slowly. "You didn't have—" he began, but stopped. It did no good for him, for the horse, for all the ones who had bet losers. The other man hitched his pants, looked dimly at the tickets in his hand, and then smiled. He staggered away through the people to collect.

Down on the turn lay two horses. Three men were wrestling one of them onto a wide skid, trying awkwardly at the same time to keep it covered with a canvas. "Jees Christ," a low, smooth voice said at Hatcher's shoulder. He looked around, and the small, thin, dark man repeated it, "Jees Christ. One, two days a month I get out to the track. That's all. I don't expect to make a lotta money. I *expect* 'em to lose when I bet 'em. But now they gotta *die?* What a fuckin' black cat I am."

Hatcher looked at him blankly, empty now even of irritation, cleaned out. The other took Hatcher's placidness for incomprehension. "Me, I'm talkin' about," he said. "You ever see a goddamn black cat like that?"

"Who did you have?" Hatcher asked, hoping for some company.

"That fuckin' *two* horse! I bet the poor son of a bitch, and down he goes. Yeah, buddy, That's me. That's my luck." He tossed his last sentence out and swaggered away as if proud.

Hatcher turned, too, toward the long passage out under the stands. On his way he heard other accounts of the accident: whose fault it had been, what jockeys had been hurt, and most of all who would have—ah! would have—who would have won if it had not happened. Someone told him, too, that number nine had not fallen at all, that he had bolted to the outside rail and stopped. Another said that two horses had jumped the outside rail and run wildly through the parking lot. None of it was what he wanted to hear. No one said that Insulator had been a cinch. No one could confirm what he, Hatcher, had known; that, after all, that morning, had been the point.

He came out beneath the pastel-checkered façade and walked up the ramp to the trains. Ahead, another early leaver picked up Lawton's orange handicap card—Clocker Lawton—from the ground and played results with himself. A man in a long thin coat asked for Hatcher's program and paper. He handed them over and then saw the birdlike old man from the special already slouched on the elevated platform. He nodded resignedly at him.

"You lose your money already?" the old man said.

"That's right. You too."

"Yah," he said, fluttering his hand in the air and moving off in his shuffle down the platform, as the Far Rockaway-Euclid Avenue train came creaking and rocking to meet him. "Lose all the time."

The trip back to the city, on the regular train with its change at Euclid, was long. Some of the people had got an early paper and were checking tomorrow's entries. Down the car three men were arguing loudly, a new-born and faltering syndicate, about how to split up the forty-seven dollars they had left and how they would have won except for Charlie. Soon they came up on the graveyard again, and a few, becoming quieter, peered at it as the train slid by. The stones marched off in one radius after another, with mud between them where the snow had been, and a harsh green rug of artificial grass lay close to the tracks.

Hatcher changed trains, then dozed, then started and sat staring. He got up well before the stop at the Terminal, leaned against the door, and squinted for the lights. He had fifteen minutes for the bus and would not be home late. Below and beside him a fat woman with red and frizzing hair spoke to her seatmate, a man dressed very neatly in very old clothes.

"What a day, huh? I got two an——"

"Wha? The track?"

"I had a nice one for place. In the third race, you know. Twenty-four and change."

"Eh!" he blurted. "How can you beat 'em."

"And that one in the sixth was easy. He had the best time of anybody. I'm glad they ran at least one race to form today, even with that accident."

"Yeah?"

"Quite a day. I only come out once in a while." Hatcher imagined her hanging day and night over the two-dollar place windows. "It's so hard now," she went on. "Not like——"

"How you gonna beat 'em," the man said. "It's all fixed anyway, probly. Everybody says——"

"Well, I don't know. For me it's an outing. I take what money I can afford to spend. It makes a nice day for me." The train hissed to the stop; doors jerked open. Hatcher looked at his watch.

"Yeah? Yeah but you can't beat 'em," the man was saying.

Chapter 2

The key to their apartment lock was misground, so Hatcher fumbled and adjusted until the door swung in. Margaret's legs were stretched out from the black leather chair pointing toward the television. On the glinting, unstable screen of the old set the last in a series of news programs was winding up. One of a team of commentators was intoning heavily of oilslicks, dying seabirds, pollution, but speaking as if of something else, sounding some grim moral without the words.

"Hi!"

"Hi!" Hatcher threw down his jacket and stared back for a moment at the screen. The captain of the team had now appeared, to confirm, and again there was that suggestion of some gloomy message too obvious to spell out, but no one could escape the knowledge.

"You all right?" she asked.

"Huh? Yeah, I'm O.K."

"You look awfully tired."

"No." He had turned toward the kitchen, toward the ice and the gin.

"Me too." She half-rose and stretched out to him a glass that held a few melting chips of ice and a strip of lemon peel. "What happened today?" she called up after a moment.

15

"Not much. The same." He smiled as he handed over the drink. Margaret grinned back, and all at once he felt very sorry for himself, for them, for her. He leaned over and kissed her wide, still smiling mouth, feeling teeth. "Hi, Mag."

"Hi. Did you forget your exams?" The pile of blue-covered booklets lay on an end table.

"No. I just didn't do them." He went over and slumped down into the couch, snatching a handful of the books and flipping through them impatiently. "Yeah. Maybe after supper. What's for supper?" He pulled out his cigarette pack and poked around in it with a forefinger.

"Just a steak." She shrugged apologetically. "I guess I didn't think much about it."

"Hell, that's O.K." His gaze drifted to the television; a man on a horse was riding over a mountain.

"What time shall we eat?"

"No hurry."

"But about what time? So I'll know when to put the potato in."

"All right. Say eight." He thought about that prospect for a moment. "You know, it would be a lot better if I charcoaled it. Why don't I?" He knew why, but kept on. "Sure. We'll open the door and all the windows and charcoal the son of a bitch."

Margaret laughed. "We could burn down the building, too."

"Only if we got very lucky."

The night was overcast and windless, and the thick air seemed to press down upon whatever rose from below. The too fat steak sputtered and flamed on the grill and filled their three rooms with yellowish smoke. Through the propped door, too, came the smells of other cookings, and through the windows faint signals from the dumps and refineries to the east. Twice Hatcher flapped around the rooms with a copy of *Esquire*. By the time they had finished eating, the apartment was almost cleared, and he closed it up again.

"That was a pretty good steak."

"Not bad," he judged. "A little fat."

"Well, you could've done better with him. Butchers don't like girls."

"He just thought he could get away with it." He probed at a tooth with his tongue. "I'll talk to the son of a bitch."

"It was cooked just right, though."

Hatcher smiled at her. "At guesswork," he said. "I could be the best there is."

"You think that's why I married you?"

He laughed, "I don't know." Then his voice sank as his eyes swung to the pile of examinations on the table. "The other thing I don't know—that I really don't know—is why I gave this fucking exam in the first place."

Margaret laughed and Hatcher went over and turned up the television's sound and then sat down with the booklets. As he scanned the barely legible, stiff prose, the earth was being infiltrated by alien life. In the frequent interruptions of the program's story the vacation commercials, which had begun in November along with the cooking smells, had reached their peak: up, up and away—come on down—I love Trinidad—your place in the sun —best years are now—get away. Hatcher was smug to recognize their hammering strategy. At the same time he was tempted. Though he had not even worked off last summer's bills, still, a boyish, freckle-faced announcer assured him, it's just so much a month.

He kept on with the examinations, and occasionally he shouted in disgust or derision to Margaret, rattling dishes in the kitchen. "Oh, Jesus Christ," he said. "I asked them to write a little about the last few images in this poem. You know? The *last few images?* Listen to this, "The *lost flew imogies* in . . .""

"I don't believe that," she cried, coming over wet-handed. "Let me see—oh, it is. Isn't that pathetic." She shook her hand and flapped her arms once and turned away. "Sad."

Later he muttered, "The little bastard." She was reading, and looked up.

" 'The essential quality of Keats' verse is, paradoxically, an imaginative laxity that seems—only seems—to result in a logical ambiguity.' How the hell did he think he'd get away with that?"

"Is he smart at all? Do you know where it's from?"

"C minus. No, I don't know where it's from, and I'm not going to find out either. They can't even cheat right." He scribbled a failing grade on the paper and threw it on the floor next to his chair. He counted the books left: fourteen, not including the last two, which he had saved for last because they would probably be good. From there he plowed on, fighting the temptation to stop and count them again, until he reached the two good ones. On both papers he labored over long comments. At last he flexed the cramps out of his hand and checked the time. It was half past ten, and the papers would surely have arrived. "Do you want a magazine or anything?" he asked.

"Um. Yes. A magazine'd be good."

"Which one?"

"Any one."

"I'll be back." It was no more than fifteen minutes. The no-parking area in front of the stand was clear, the usual policeman leaning against the sign and reading the back pages of *The Daily News*. Hatcher assumed he was checking results like anyone else and ran in and out and threw the magazine and the *Telegraph* into the back seat. As he passed by the side street to the Greek's on his way back, he craned to see how many cars were outside, but the street was too dark. He had no cash left anyway, after Insulator.

He tossed Margaret her magazine and headed for his chair. He said, as if he had just discovered it, "A horse died today at New York."

"Sad."

"Yeah. A horse I liked." He read her the whole story of the sixth race, of the fearsomeness of so many horses piling up. There was one sentence about Insulator. Margaret's small, oval face lengthened. She had been taught to ride in boarding school, and she liked horses.

"I won on him before," Hatcher said. "He was really getting good. Not many people knew about him either."

"That's so sad, that he broke his leg. Do they always kill them?"

"Not if they're worth a lot. He wasn't. Besides, he was a gelding."

"Oh." After a moment she tried to brighten. "At least it's history now. Just think if you'd had to see it."

"Oh well. They don't let you see that much."

He had begun staring at nothing, and Margaret let him alone. The next time she looked up he was into the racing paper. He read all the columns for inside information. Then he turned to the latest workouts hoping that he would remember a fast time in some future when he glanced at the entries. More news came on the television, another cycle: a captured United States ship was still captured, they said, though it had been for eight months and had gone unmentioned for the last four. Now they would get excited over it again, Hatcher supposed, and write letters to newspapers. And that day some more reporters had asked a governor again if he might run for president, and he had said no again, and so they reported that, still, it was not impossible. Also there were too many knee injuries in pro football. Which meant, he thought, that the coverage was louder and fuller, and so people knew to worry.

He folded his paper to the past performances for the next day's racing and got up, pointing at the television. "I'm going. You want this?"

He was quicker undressing as usual, and as she finished, he admired her from his bed. She noticed. "You want to come over here?"

"It's a good thought," he smiled, "but I feel lousy. Catch you tomorrow?"

"If you can," she yawned. "I don't know. I might not want to —or you might be too tired. Still, we *might.*"

"You watch it or you'll get raped."

"Ha." Margaret turned off her light and flounced over to face the wall. "Good night."

"G'night, baby." His light was still on, and he worked through Aqueduct and Pimlico before he thought he could sleep.

But after shifting and adjusting in the dark for a while, he decided that he couldn't sleep. He was thinking of the game at Jimmy's, of it going on. After a few minutes he switched the light on again.

She awakened as he rustled into his trousers. "You all right?"

"Oh, yeah. But I couldn't sleep. Might stop by the Greek's for a while."

"Ah-h." It was more protest than acknowledgement, but she was too sleepy, and fell off again, and Hatcher crept out on the balls of his feet.

Chapter 3

Hatcher first met his wife in school. For years, it seemed to him, he had done everything in school. Still, even before they had mailed him his Ph.D. papers, he had decided to stay on through the summer. He would teach a class and pay his loan from the First National Bank of Ithaca. That was what he said to himself, though he knew also that he was taking pleasure in staying at a place he had hated, now that he didn't have to stay, anymore.

He had had a fine time in college, a wonderful time. He had played football, and partly because of that his teachers had thought him very smart and also somehow their own discovery, since nobody had imagined he would be much of a student. Before he knew it, his position was so strong that he could afford to be absolutely polite and soft-spoken without losing any ground. He found he could do anything he wanted, and the more interests he admitted the better everyone liked him. He was seduced by all the things he could do and say and think and have thought of him in that one place, and so he wanted it—the Sundays after games, the papers he wrote, the fraternity and the jokes, the good long talks about books, all of it—to last. He decided, with the help of certain of his teachers, to go to graduate school, not thinking, of course, that that would be college, but that it was the only way to get back to college.

The first difference he could see was the girls, who didn't know about him. Nobody knew about him, but it was the girls' not knowing that he noticed. They were all around him, but not available. They had their own football players and bright boys and well-known campus characters. By the time a teacher—an old fool of a teacher, Hatcher thought—had first failed him on an oral examination and then suggested he try out for the New York Giants, he had been ready to leave. Twice, later, he almost took the same bus out of town, because he was finding out that the old Philip Hatcher would not do. That was what he understood them all to be saying. The old, wide, unexercised power, the relaxed playing with various kinds of life, was no longer enough. It was time to commit himself, they were saying, to specialize.

Still he had stayed, largely because staying was the only way to get out without quitting, and he had been prejudiced by football and other things that one should never quit no matter what. He tried also to continue to think that college would still be there to return to when he was finished, but with each year he doubted it more, until in this last summer he was in no hurry, hoping only for some nice girls in the course he was teaching. But he was halfway through it before his awkward sense of his latest status —graduated and officialized adult, the teacher—allowed him to move. And even then he did not do much.

She seemed, as usual, to be surrounded. Not as he was now, by brown-nosers asking their academic questions, but by the presence that lolled near her now and swung his green bookbag against his leg. Hatcher knew from calling the roll that her name was Margaret Francis Miller. That was his only connection. She had spoken for the first time in the course minutes ago. As he watched now, she appeared to consult with the blond boy with the bookbag. He nodded, made a satisfied turn away, and the girl came toward the front of the room.

Hatcher felt strained anticipation. He kept answering questions and only glancing at her behind the little group. But his concentration must have been obvious; the others melted away. Then he distracted himself more intently, pushed in his chair, gathered his books, picked his jacket off the back of the chair. When he looked up she was watching with a faint smile.

"Oh. I—um—appreciated the last line you gave me." Margaret Francis Miller nodded without changing her expression. "I needed it." He chuckled and swung for the door. She fell in step.

"It was about time I said something."

She walked slowly, steadily beside him and said nothing more. Her hair coiled thickly at the level of his eyes, between blond and brown. He reminded himself to report to himself about her eyes. She walked as if concentrating on it, with an odd, long stride, advancing a foot and then gliding forward and past it, as a child stepping out some game, or as if playing with the ideas of walking. Or of walking with him, he thought. They went down the steps of the classroom building and stopped in the hot afternoon. She turned to face him and took a short backward step. Her eyes were large and almond shaped, set wide apart, blue. Hatcher thought she meant to leave him.

"Listen——"

"You want to have lunch?" she asked.

"No, but I want to have a drink." She laughed.

When they were sitting in the only place he could think of, he still could not decide what she looked like, could not think of the words about her he would want later to use to himself, because she had already changed. Only vaguely he remembered how she had first appeared, her head and face too small for her tall figure, and all strangely single-colored—tanned skin and uncolored lips and light brown hair blending. She was smiling at him now. He reached for a cigarette, then looked for an ashtray. She was already out of the booth to reach one and slid it quickly across the formica table. He caught it as it fell.

"What do you drink?"

"I don't, usually. Whatever you have." She had a martini while he had three. She liked jazz; he did not, except for old rhythm and blues. She liked marijuana; he said he did not care for it, but drank a lot. Both of them liked the new supermarket in town and became excited at that mutuality.

"Isn't it wonderful."

"It's great," he said. "Amazing."

He remembered against the grain that he was the teacher. "Do you like horses?" he asked her.

"Oh yes. Do you ride?"

"No. But I bet on them once in a while."

She shook her head and smiled at him. "You're quite an English teacher."

Hatcher was very pleased. So as not to show it, he began to talk. "Well, you know. They say if you teach literature you're supposed to know about everything. Everything counts—fishing and football, and old records and the kind of weather you like—" He stopped. It had occurred to him that this was not what they were saying about literature at all, not lately.

"Where were you raised, anyway?" she asked, as if it meant something.

"Florida," Hatcher said, happy to be able to give that answer. For a moment they were silent.

Then she said, "It's easy to see that about you."

"What?"

"That you try to be different—from what you have to be. As if anytime you said or did something, you were thinking of saying or doing something else."

"You've got me down pretty good," Hatcher said a little gruffly. He was very flattered.

"Oh, a couple of us were laughing about it one day—"

"Us?"

"There was one day, when it seemed that every time you said something was so, you'd turn around and sort of raise your eyebrows and argue another way, or act as if no argument mattered."

He was flushed at the attention she had given him and that she was giving still. "That," he said. "That was just weaseling."

"I don't think so. It wasn't. It was like you didn't want to get caught in one place. Or for people to see you just there. No. It was you saying, 'There's more to me than this.' "

Hatcher fell back against the cool wood of the booth. He looked into his drink and then took some of it. The room was much warmer than it had been, and his throat felt tight.

"That's the smartest thing anybody ever said about me," he said, gazing at her.

"Oh, I'm smart," she said.

Again they quieted, as if embarrassed at admitting so much —she so much knowledge of him, and he so much pleasure at hearing about it.

"Oh," she said, "I'm going to lend you some records."

"I really don't like saxophone at all."

"Three Coltrane, that's all, early, middle, and late. I'm drunk."

"Not possible. Want to take a walk?"

They went up the hill along a gorge, with the sun very bright after the cool dark of the barroom. Strips of yarn-like clouds drifted across the sun, and as they turned to cross a footbridge, the lightest sprinkle of rain fell around them. He stopped and looked up into it, weaving slightly. She went on a step; her long legs under the short dress were bent slightly, pleasantly outward.

"That's a sun shower," he said. On the other side of the bridge she turned downhill.

"I have to go this way."

"No you don't. I'm taking you to dinner."

"I'd like to. I can't. I'll bring the records tomorrow."

"This is desertion. Why can't you?"

"My roommate."

"So?" But he saw without wanting to, the gin acid in his throat again, remembering the green bookbag. The day that had been moving so easily settled down. "So." The world was that dense; never a girl without someone there, around her, already, always this standing in line that the impromptu afternoon had seemed, only seemed then, to cut across.

"Let's go to the races tomorrow," he said.

"Oh. Well. If I can. I'll try. What time?"

"Oh, I don't know. Noon?" He was almost apologetic. "Post time is one thirty."

"Right here," she said, and went downhill.

Her apartment was on the third floor of a pink frame house. Where the stairs twisted abruptly near the top, she stopped for a moment, thinking, then deliberately mounted two more steps and went in.

"Well, hello."

"Hello, Tommy."

"Did you get the extension on your paper? It took long enough."

"It was O.K. He's a nice guy."

The boy ruffled his long, light hair and got up from his sprawling seat in the canvas sling chair. He looked out over the green-painted fire escape. "You're just a sucker for teachers."

"No, I'm not."

"No, huh?"

"That he's a teacher," she said, "is more important to you than it is to him. He's interested in a lot of things."

He snorted. "Oh. I see."

"He just wants to do a lot of things, Tommy. He's no different from you—from the way you talk, about being flexible and not settling in and——"

"You're certainly taking my advice," he broke in. He flopped heavily back down into the cloth chair.

"Oh, bull."

"Well, aren't you?"

"What?"

"Aren't you taking my advice?"

"Somebody ought to," she snapped.

"What does that mean?" he cried. They glared across at each other.

The next day she was there wearing the wrong clothes. Hatcher was surprised by the roundness of her legs, the heaviness of breast, that he had not composed with her tallness and her small face. But as he was drawn, he was disappointed at the faded blue shorts and the heavy knit, pink pullover. Still, he thought, maybe she dressed that way to go racing.

"Well? O.K.?"

"I'm sorry. I can't."

"Come on!" The pretense at gruff authority barely covered the pleading. He knew where he was. The irritation at not being the first in line, with his plans of waiting her out, had vanished. It was her game. For the moment he supposed that she wanted a good grade or something from him, so that she could go to graduate school with her boyfriend.

They never got to the races that year. The first day Hatcher went himself, saw the patrol car parked behind the sign, but hurried on anyway to get there and to bet, to make something out of his losses. The stop at the country judge's cost him ten dollars, but he missed the daily double, too, and so was even. He spent the rest of the day and twenty more trying to make long shots out of the favorites that kept coming in first, the first-in-liners doing it to him again. After that he suggested the track to her only once more, and took another postponement as final.

All he thought he could now do was to take her to drinks and lunches, so he spent the next few weeks watching her eat. He sat back with some beer or gin, and she used both hands to reinforce what he was sure was a usual diet of hamburgers and worse. She cut the pink meat with absorption and purpose, and dabbed at the mint jelly—that he disliked the stuff gave the moment more charm—with her knife and lathered it on the meat, and repeated. She did not talk until she had finished, only looking up from time to time.

In his old car they drove out into the green and tedious country, unbroken, smooth, always green. She told him once that she was from Ohio, that she had been to school in Norway once, that her parents would give her no money now. But that and whatever revelations he himself might have made were only conversation. They gossiped about other students, about teachers. They traded brands of cigarettes with deliberation and argued about music.

She said once that she could not help their being on this kind of schedule, but the apology was unnecessary. Hatcher had long since dropped the idea of measuring his progress with her or of suspecting any strategy of her own. He was too happy in her company to worry about it. He was grateful, too, because he was reconfirmed in his self-conception as an outsider, someone who automatically and rightly had no claim. Once they passed an Indian student on a corner, who smiled vigorously under his turban and waved. Then Margaret told Hatcher that she had borrowed five dollars from the fellow a few days before.

So he teased her. "You conned that poor Indian. Didn't you? Took advantage of him."

"I'm going to pay him back!"

"Sure. And how much are you going to get from me?"

"Nothing. Yet." She laughed shortly and then paused, as if reflecting. "Do you think I'd try to con you?"

"You couldn't con me," he said as he drove. He knew he was going to say something awkward and fixed his stare away, out through the windshield. "Because I'd let you."

Margaret was not embarrassed. "I know you would." Then suddenly she seemed irritated. "You would."

They had stopped at a traffic light. "What?"

She squared around at him. "Look, Phil. You're no different."

"Huh?"

"What do you expect from me?"

He pulled over to the curb, along a plywood construction fence, and shifted into neutral. "Nothing. Why should I?"

"You've got to. You're not *that* different."

"I thought you were all tied up. Besides, we have fun."

"Nobody's that tied up. Yes, we have fun. Eating and drinking and talking."

"Well? Don't we?"

"Yes! But what do you do it for?"

"I don't do it *for* anything!" He defended himself. The one thing he could not afford was the idea that their afternoons had been a substitute or a slow preparation for anything else. If that were so then he had been either too timid or too conniving.

Margaret reached across the seat and put a hand on his arm. It was the first time they have ever touched when they were not joking. "Listen. Would you mind not having a big lunch today?"

"No," Hatcher said loudly. "Whatever you want." He was seeing now that he had been mistaken, and that he must have seemed slow to her. Just like some college professor, he thought.

"We could just have a sandwich at my place."

"Your place? I thought your place was crowded."

"Not this weekend, it isn't." She faced front again and got ready to ride. "Come on. You've never even been there."

When they arrived, Hatcher felt the strain. He did not want her to do any more, to initiate any more. Besides, he felt he was on someone else's ground, and kept shifting in the biggest chair and looking around. The living room had two twin size beds strung along the slanting wall made by the roof. Margaret sat on one of them and looked at him.

"Where's your friend?" he asked.

"Gone for a few days."

"Oh."

"Phil. I'm not married you know."

"I thought it was worse than that."

"I know you did." She smiled at him. "But even if it was, you didn't have to be so—respectful."

"I didn't want to bust in on anything. And I didn't want to chase, I guess."

"Uh-huh." Margaret had raised her eyebrows and tilted her head toward him. She puffed one cheek, teasing.

"All right," Hatcher said. "I didn't want to look like a jerk." She stood up and came over to him, not smiling now. "No," she said. "That isn't fair. You didn't want to look like anything or anybody. You wanted to be some kind of original."

To Hatcher that sounded as if it might be true. Certainly it made him feel better. "Yeah!"

"Yes. But you can't. Even you can't." She was looking at him so openly now that, without planning it, he put his arm up for her and she sank down on him. She was wearing a knit dress, which stretched and came off easily. Her skin was very brown.

She got up and held out her hand. Hatcher stood and held her but could not think how to get over to the beds. Everything he had ever imagined about her at night, and put aside in the day-time, washed over him. He tried to sort it out. Then it was as if he were looking down from some height, and he had picked her up, and laid her down, and got out of most of his clothes, quickly. But then, as he propped over her, looking at her, he began to tremble and could not stop. He flopped over on his side and stared at the angled ceiling. "Wow."

"It's just that you've been waiting a long time," she soothed him.

"Yes?"

"Sure."

He reached out, holding her easily at first until she strained against him, then he pressed against her hard, as if trying to get through, to the other side of her. Before he knew or even wanted to, it had begun, and he tried to think of what he was doing and to slow himself and could not. Still resisting, moving only impercentibly, he felt himself and fought himself and at the last just froze, rigid on her, groaned, finished. He dropped his head over her shoulder and whispered into her hair. "God damn it."

Margaret, with her hands in the small of his back, gazed at the ceiling, and smiled. "Rest a minute," she said. "We have time. The first time won't count."

It was a fine three days. When they awakened on Saturday, it was almost midday, and Hatcher, surer of himself, asked her about it.

Margaret turned on her side and propped her head on her arm. "There was no reason not to."

"I wasn't pressing, you know." That had to be clear.

"I know you weren't. You just misunderstood." That seemed to exhaust the subject. He would have said more, to lend it the importance he thought was due, but Margaret was apparently not interested in such extensions. Nor did she appear unsettled, on Sunday afternoon, when they knew he would have to vacate. Now he compared it to her having to get back after one of their lunches; there seemed to be no difference. But he wanted some commemoration.

"You're awfully good."

"It was you."

He laughed, pleased. "No. But when can we——"

"Oh," she interrupted. "I don't know when we can." That was still where they sat three days later, after the last class, the last lunch. He parked down the street from the pink house. She was still going to New York City with her friend. Those plans had not been changed.

"You never borrowed those records," she said. "Are you sure you don't want them, to take to Jersey?" It was an opportunity, but Hatcher was toughening up now and would not take it. Live and let live.

"I guess I might not see you," he said, shrugging, awaiting a protest. "I can't expect it."

"Don't expect it. You'll see me.

"Listen. Can you get down to the city all right? Do you need some money?" He knew that she did. When she said she did not, he assumed she was avoiding any future commitments to him, and he tried to be graceful.

They said good-bye easily, as if there were no pressure toward anything more, kissing lightly, and finally shaking hands through the car window. Then at the last minute he dropped his pretense.

"Now listen," he said. "In October. When the meeting starts again at Aqueduct. I'll meet you at the paddock, clubhouse side."

"All right," she smiled. Then she nodded, clipped, firm. "I'll see you."

"All right?"

"I'll see you."

If, two months later, it had not been October, if he had said September and Belmont instead, then perhaps he might not even have gone. Through the first month without her he ran the obstacle course of strange people and schedules, establishing himself. Besides, he was half-willing to be content with just the summer, and reluctant to take chances. He said to himself that she probably would not be there and gave himself no time to remember, the morning after, what he might have felt in the night. Yet by the time of late October, when the horses made their short southwest migration on Long Island, the new diversions had flagged. His colleagues were no longer so solicitous; the secretaries had begun to call him by his first name; and he had found some people he could admit things to. Twice in one week, then, he thought he recognized her from behind in the New York bus terminal—the tallness, the flat hips, the hair—and once he had been wrong, and once he had been stepping up into his own bus and so never knew. Still, when he determined to go out to Aqueduct for another opening day, he made up his hope on the horses, forcing his anxiousness onto them. He took with him much more money than he could afford, so that he would think about that too. But he did not use it. He handicapped badly that day and bet only twenty-two dollars, because, when he let himself slowly down the inclined apron toward the fence around the walking ring, looking up at the clouds blowing out to Jamaica Bay, looking everywhere else, too, but at that fence, he saw on the periphery of vision her tall, round figure hunched on elbows over the rail, her chestnut hair in a narrow, thick stream loose down her back, talking caressingly to number three, Duke's Romance, as the horse with his embarrassed eye paced by her.

Chapter 4

When Hatcher knocked, the peephole lightened, and he heard a whinnying laugh. The door swung in, and Jap's head appeared from behind it. "Look who's here," he said in a voice pitched just below hysteria. "Back for more, eh, Phil? What'd you do, blow it all back? Hey, Jim, look who it is." In the right corner of the narrow room the players sat disgruntled—Hollywood, Big John, Sam the Maniac, Abe, Pip, and Jimmy himself. Jimmy got up to meet him with a large, soft hand.

"Hello, Pheel," he said, his eyes liquid. "What's up today?"

"New York. I had a hot one."

"I mean, *how* you go? A horse? From here?"

"No. One of my own. He died."

Jimmy jerked his head back and forth, as if shaking off sleep. "Them hot horses. They're never there."

"He was there. He was going to win it. I mean he really died. In a pileup."

The Jap was hunched at his seat beside an empty table, but at that news his head snapped up, and his narrow eyes crinkled smaller. "He died?" he blurted, high-pitched. "He *died?*" Hatcher nodded seriously.

"You sent it in on him and he died! Hey, Holly, call the S.P.C.——S.——whatever it is. He—oh!" He buried his head in his folded arms atop the table, laughing as if uncontrollably. The poker players looked up, some of them nodding contemptuously at him, others with recognition at Hatcher.

"You want a seat, Pheel?"

"I wouldn't mind for a while, Jim. But I tapped out today over there."

Jimmy shrugged; his voice dropped. "How much you need?"

"A yard?"

"Whatever you want." Under the cover of his great belly he slipped Hatcher some folded twenties. "Where you going to sit?"

The players made room on Jimmy's right, and the game went on. The boy who had been dealing got up, and Jap took his shift. As Hatcher sat down, he felt the night was safe, taken care of. He looked happily at the first hand of cards dealt to him, and when the bet came to him, he turned them over and threw them in. He remembered when he would have played.

On his first weekend at Jimmy's coffee house—the Greek-American Social Club—he had lost four hundred. Frankie had not wanted him to go. "I'm afraid that game's a little rough fer ya," he had said. But what game could be? How could he have known, springing as he was from a lifetime of occasional and friendly poker? Why should it have been any different?

The first hand that first night he had thrown away too; it was too bad, even for him in those days. The second he had received with pleasure; the first three were ace, queen, and jack. The game was, of course, seven-card stud poker, always the same, because it makes big pots to keep the players happy and strings the game out long enough for the 5-per-cent house cut to take hold. Ace, queen, and jack, and the ace and jack were diamonds. He called a fifty-cent bet and drew the nine of diamonds. He had thought, having then a nice eye for beauty of that sort, it was a pretty hand. He had remembered the less aesthetic facts, too; with three cards to come, two of them had to be perfect if he were to have anything. Still he had called four dollars, and someone had raised and

35

then someone else. Hatcher had finished with a pair of nines and dropped out on the last bet. Twenty-four dollars, he thought, still ashamed of it now, turning over his cards again, for a suck hand. Someone with kings and threes had won it.

For weeks he had played that way, in a poker storybook; he bet insistently, aggressive, as if the bets were blows to knock the other players out. Maybe these people played all the time, but he was brave and smart. The cards he was playing did not matter, save as his stage to strut on. He bet on anything, and when all the possibilities he had loosely imagined had died in the dealing, he told himself that he had been bluffing anyway and turned his softness into futile daring.

The others had gone along. He was having a little bad luck, they said, but at least he was not afraid to bet. Hatcher had thought that that was praise. When the delusion of his innate superiority lapsed in the face of so many losing nights, he persuaded himself that he was one of a group. He chewed Greek coffee grounds and cursed bad luck. The rest clucked and sympathized and said they had never seen anything like it, so many bridesmaids, second bests. Sure. You had to play. How could you have thrown that hand away. They had known, he thought, when they had a live one.

"Jesus Christ, teacher," John growled, as Hatcher turned another hand over. "Play a hand, will ya, you cozy son of a bitch."

There was a pounding on the door. Jimmy got up from his hand, peered out through the peephole, and opened. A small dark man with a long scar on his face, Hatcher remembered him dimly, swaggered in and began cursing each player, by name, around the table. When he got to Hatcher, he slapped him on the back, shouting, "How ya doin', kid?" He sat down on his right. They called him TJ, and he was a harness-race driver who had lost his license, whether for incompetence or thievery Hatcher did not know. Hatcher threw in another hand and mused on about how far behind he was.

The cards had not always been bad, and then for brief times the world had seemed righted. There were, at times, cards that anyone had to win with, and Hatcher had, though later he succeeded in giving the money back. For when the cards had changed, as they may, he had not. It was so natural that his cards were good, that when they lapsed they became unreal. He had gone on betting, seeing other cards that he did not have but knew were coming.

It could not have lasted. As his money dwindled, he had begun, slowly, to learn something. As he sat throwing his cards away and trying to shut out TJ's bellowing, he concentrated on a simple, single idea. He did not imagine the other players' thinking, nor did he conceive of elaborate and tricky betting schemes. His only thought now, the lesson he had learned in weeks of losing, was that this was a game of cards, and the cards were all that mattered. On the next hand he was dealt a pair of sevens, back to back, with a jack. He called a dollar. On the next round Abe raised with a queen-seven showing, and Hatcher threw the pair into the pile in front of Jap. TJ raised loudly through the hand and lost.

Hatcher had reversed, from loose to tight. He looked at the cards lying in front of the players and gave credit, trusting everyone else's hand, mistrusting his own. He had learned to believe, and to be afraid, and that money was money. Perhaps that is not so much of a lesson to glean from more than two weeks of nights and almost a thousand dollars. But poker is a simple game, even if not so simple as Hatcher had made it. He went on dropping out, throwing his first three away in fear of being sucked in, doubting his ability to drop out later when he had a hand that was not quite good enough.

"You little shit, Japanese. You motherfucker." This from the old man they called Hollywood, a bad player all his life. Hands shaking, he tore his three hole cards in pieces and flung them over his shoulder. The Jap, who was in fact Italian, cried out his surprise.

Hollywood made as if to strike him with a trembling fist. "Aw, you fuckin' Japanese cocksucker, you been givin' me shit all night. I oughta—I quit! I quit this fuckin' game. You'll never see me again." He seemed about to rise, and the sharp voices around the table immediately became soothing. Jap had tears of laughter in his eyes; his face was stiffly straight.

"Take it eas-zy, Wood," Jimmy said.

"Come on, Holly," said Pip, "he's just the dealer. Ain't I losin' too?" This was the wrong strategy; no one could be losing as much as Hollywood.

"Fuck it," he said, staggering to his feet. "Three hundred and sixty dollars without a fuckin' pot, from that little Japanese."

Jap was struggling openly with his laughter, and Jimmy was frowning at him for it. "I just sat down, Wood," he pleaded then. "For Christ sake! Billy's been dealin'!"

"Woodie," growled John, "get some coffee. Take it easy."

Hollywood sat down again. "Jimmy! Can't we get some new decks in this fuckin' game!" Jimmy jerked his head at young Billy, who ran back to the kitchen for the cards. Jap began to deal again, straightfaced, trying not to look at Hatcher. Wood went on mumbling, "Kamikaze bastard. Every fuckin' hand Pearl Harbor or sothin'? Fuckin' risin' sun!" Jap could stand it no longer. In the midst of his deal he slammed the cards down in front of him and exploded into his wheezing laugh. Hollywood looked at him furious, but then Pip laughed too, and Abe.

"Kamikaze! Pearl Harbor!" Abe said in apparent awe. "Jesus Christ, Wood, take it easy on him. How'd you come up with that?" He shook his head admiringly. "Kamikaze!"

"Well, what the—" Hollywood began, but then his face cracked slowly, and he smiled, too, at his invention, and then everyone was laughing, the Jap howling, convulsed.

After a long moment of it, Jimmy shouted, "Come on! Jap! *Dil!*" And the game went on. On the next deal, Hatcher drew a pair of kings buried in the hole, with a five showing. Across the table Abe, who everyone said was a good player, bet fifty cents on his showing ace. TJ raised to four and a half with an eight up, in case they had forgotten about him. Hatcher liked his concealed kings, and he raised too. They lost some players, and Jap dealt again: an eight to Abe—and TJ cursed at its missing him—then he caught a five ahead of Hatcher, who got the three of clubs, and no help.

"Check," Abe said.

"Fuck it." TJ bet the limit, and all called.

The cards fell again, from Abe through TJ to Hatcher: ten, queen, and the case eight. TJ swore again.

"Well, what the shit have *you* got?" Abe scoffed, staring pointedly at the eights lying around the board. "Eight dollars!"

"I got *you* beat, is what!" TJ howled. "Sixteen!"

Hatcher wanted to play. TJ, he thought, had no more than a middle-sized low pair, but he was afraid of Abe. Still, there were no kings showing anywhere. He called, and Abe looked at him and called himself. His last card up was Abe's ace.

"You had to play, huh, kid? You had to play and catch that."

Hatcher peered at his hole cards again, but they had not changed. He thought he would be beaten, but when TJ bet he called. Jap dealt the last card. It was a king, and that made three of them, all in the hole.

"Eight dollars, you bastards," TJ said. "If youse got sothin', then raise." Hatcher was ashamed to have his entire hand hidden, caught on the last card; he called.

Abe called. "I dunno what you guys got," he said. "Aces up."

"Shit!" TJ snorted. "Eights and fives first four, and that fuckin' Jap don't help 'em." Hatcher turned over his three kings without speaking.

"Last fuckin' card?" TJ shouted.

"You got a lot of nerve, kid," Abe said.

Hatcher jerked his thumb at TJ. "He's bettin' out of his ass. Sixteen dollars on eights. Kings are no good?"

"I had two pair—I had two pair!"

Abe sneered. "I guess you don't worry about me, huh?"

"You got 'em, *bet* 'em!" Hatcher cried. "But you want to sit on the goddam things and then bitch."

"Oh. I didn't bet, huh? Right, kid. Just play like that all the time."

"Next hand, boys," Jap said.

"He's third best all along," Abe said, "and he wins it on the last. I had his luck——"

"Next hand."

"Don't listen to 'em, buddy," Hollywood said in his phlegmy, quivering voice. "When they don't win, they cry. It doesn't matter when you get 'em." Considering the source of this advice, Hatcher was not so sure, but at any rate he was over a hundred dollars ahead. He remembered all the times he had been that much ahead, and more—times when he had come away losing. He began again to turn his cards over, throwing them back as they came. It did not seem worth it.

As the game continued, he watched the others betting loudly, saw them win with single pairs, small two pairs, broken hands, while he had nothing to do but watch. Occasionally a new man wandered in and was told at careful length by TJ or Abe of the biggest pot of the night, and how the teacher had drawn out on them at the last. Hatcher believed it. The only hand he had won, he thought, he had played badly. He continued his caution.

Some time later the young dealer Billy gave him a pair of aces, wired. He called the weak betting through the hand, caught another small pair, and saw a final eight-dollar raise.

"Aw, teacher-r," cooed Big John. "I got a little straight."

Without looking at the straight Hatcher threw his cards in. "That's all for me." As he rose, he passed Jimmy a hundred in chips and cash. Jap said good-night at the door, letting him out. Over his shoulder as he left he glanced at the faces in the corner, settling grimly down toward the green felt where the chips and cards lay. The seventy-three dollars he had won did not seem very much.

He came awake suddenly and staring, grabbed in reflex for the electric clock and jarred his wrist against the corner of the table. Then, finding it, feeling the thin metal protrusion, he lay still again with his hand nestling the vibrating plastic box, waiting. After a moment he heard the low, moaning sound that pre-signaled the alarm. He stabbed with his middle finger just as it broke into full cry, then slumped satisfied back into the damp pillow and the new silence.

His eyelids fell slowly down and snapped open. Hatcher swung up and sat, feeling his eyes hot in his face and his breath hot over his numb and sour tongue. He pushed off the bed toward the clothes closet, smelling dry-cleaning fluid and feeling the light itch of the wool.

Margaret grunted and rolled over. In a slurred voice she asked him what he wanted for breakfast. With a vision of juice and eggs and bacon set out inexorably before him, in the need to ask for it and to wait for it and to eat it, he did not answer. Leaning for a moment on an elbow, Margaret watched his back in the wide closet doorway, then turned over and seemed asleep again. In trousers and undershirt he gathered the rest of his clothes, his shoes, his *Telegraph,* and closed the bedroom door behind him, relieved.

As Hatcher went through his paces, from kitchen to bathroom to kitchen, his face, with its lean, underslung profile, was curiously set. As he came more and more awake, its expression seemed to seep downward, so that finally it showed a kind of empty sternness, a gratuitous potential for severity. Though it may be that he was irritated at the open can of rusty vegetable juice that he got rid of down the sink, or the coffee cream just on the passing side of sourness. For a while he sat at the table and stared out into the concrete courtyard and its straggling shrubs. The *Telegraph* lay before him opened to the handicappers' page, so that he could check the probable odds of the horses he had marked the night before. But he did not bend to it; he only sat, eyes faintly smarting, looking out.

He could not think how long they had been there, in their three-room place on the right side of the shallow river. He could no more feel the time—and it had been almost four years—than he could see the rooms themselves and the furniture in them. It had all become invisible, and he tried to imagine what it had been when he had last seen it, when he and Margaret had begun to live there. Back beyond that beginning he dimly conceived a past full of anticipation.

Hatcher often imagined some past point or moment when there had been many choices, when he could have gone one way or another, where the world had seemed open. It was that contrast, half-dead and real present, half-live and fancied past, that moved him so easily. All the possibilities, then, had funneled down to this. Not that this was so bad, he thought; that was not it. It was that there had been the narrowing itself, the reduction, to a settled life. His face stiffened again, and he rose. He collected a poetry anthology, the blue examination papers, and his racing paper. He laid his cup in the sink and went out.

The *Armstrong* showed that John's Dream had been declared out of the first at New York, so there was no daily double problem; he could put in his other bets after he saw Frankie. He parked in his numbered slot and picked up the scratch sheet from the seat beside him, folding it smoothly and sliding it into his inside breast pocket. The *Telegraph* he shoved down behind the seat. He hiked up to English II.

Because he was five minutes early, Hatcher delayed in his office, scanning textbook circulars to see what he might get for free, and reading again a month-old letter requesting him to review a book, which he had never answered. After that he looked into his desk drawers. He did not want to be there in the front of the room as they filed in, to feel their awkwardness as well as his own while he tried again to work up into the air a poem that once, hundreds of classes before, he had liked. Now he did not even admire his own tricky remarks about it. It was time. His shoes sounded loud and careful over the waxed floor. With eyes purposefully out of focus he swung through the door, and there they were.

A few in the first two rows nodded or raised eyebrows or faintly smiled. Others gave him a quick look and went on with their muttered conversations. One or two looked and shrugged. "Good morning, sir," said someone too brightly.

"Yes," Hatcher said to his tabletop. "Good morning." He fanned out the examination books like cards on the table, beckoned, and the boys straggled up to retrieve them, checking grades quickly and, as if carelessly, sliding them from sight. When they were all seated again, Hatcher looked back at them, sighed loudly, and shrugged. "What can I say?"

A hand waved, and he nodded at it.

"Sir," said a smooth, blond fellow, Carter. "Sir, I'd like to know why we have to keep on with these questions. I mean, it ends up we always write about the stuff from somebody else's point of view. Aren't we trying to learn to express ourselves in this course, or——?"

"What do *you* think?" Hatcher interrupted. Bohannon in the left front corner snorted in deep, dull laughter.

"No," Carter said. "Really. Come on. I really think . . ." He went on in his B-minus voice, the sentences measured, suitably qualified, politic. ". . . And that's the only way that we'll learn."

Hatcher looked at him as he finished, then out the window at the back of the room. "Mr. Carter," he said to the window, "we have talked about this before." He looked around the room at some of the others. "Is it necessary to go over it again?" There were half-smiles, half-shrugs. "Right. Then let's turn——"

"Sir?" said Barnett, sharply. "Sir, I think that's right. We should be free to express our own opinions here, about this. We're . . ." Hatcher blanked out the rest of the speech. It was their favorite and weariest issue. He felt as often the urge to stop it, to plug it up or cut across it with a phrase, to go off to anything else. What did they want? Had they not done the reading again? Or was this so much a game to them that it did not matter what was used to fill the time? Or was there someone among them there interested in this, who depended on it somehow? Through that indecision, old momentum carried him.

"But look. Look. It can't be a question of expressing your-selves, not of expressing your *selves,* because what selves you have are already there, already known, even already expressed. I know. They're what you have and maybe you like them—but where do you get going over them again in the same old ways? That's just *safe.* Now. The whole point—the whole point of exercises like this one is to push you, to push you over or on to something else, something more. All you're saying is that you don't want to be pushed, to be bothered." As he spun it out, he thought he should have been doing something else. He should have been running them, herding, performing for them and building some smooth and carefree surface they could sit back and enjoy. Why not make it a show; when they ambled out, they might give each other short confirming nods: good teacher, good course. He had done it before. But now they seemed at once not worth it, and worth more.

"In other words—" he began again, and stopped. Another boy, small and sharp-eyed, was shaking his head in the second row. Hatcher liked him. He was from Newark and seemed to have spent his life in alleys pitching quarters. "What's the matter?"

The boy laughed uncomfortably. "Well, nothing," he muttered toward his chest. Then he lifted his chin. "It just seems pretty simple to me."

"Yes?"

"Well, look. This is a course. And we're taking it. So we take it, learn the moves. And that's all." It was not quite enough, but at least one of them had said it, and Hatcher settled for it.

"Yes. I think that covers what I was saying." Barnett and Carter shrugged at each other. "So. The poem you wrote about with such small success is on page one seventy-six of your anthology."

There was the usual rumble and buzz as they leaned over for their books, dropped pencils, and as the good many who had no books with them slid their chairs over to look on. "Now," he said. "See how odd the language of this thing is." And they went at it for almost half an hour and did not get beyond that first vague direction.

Hatcher leaned back in his chair, puffed out his breath, and threw down his pencil. "I can see why those papers were bad," he said, rising and going back to the window, looking out, "since the exercise asked you to talk about the inconsistencies of the poem and now according to you there aren't any."

"It's a pretty straightforward poem," Bohannon growled.

Hatcher spun around at him. "Yeah? It is, huh? Straightforward? Then tell me"—he walked around to him, smiling—"tell us what it's about."

The large boy was unperturbed. "It's about reading Chapman's Homer."

"Good. Who was Homer?"

"Greek poet."

"Who was Chapman?"

"*George* Chapman. He——"

"Right, right. It's all in the footnote, isn't it? But now this question is a little tougher: how many times are Chapman and

Homer mentioned in the poem?" Hatcher was standing close to his student now, looking down. Bohannon's eyes slitted.

"I guess you mean besides the title?"

"I guess I do."

"Once, then. Once each. But what does that——"

"And how many lines in the poem."

"Fourteen. It's a sonnet."

"That's in the note, too. But what do you think of that percentage?" Behind him there was a laugh.

"What percentage?"

"Well." Hatcher gestured widely and turned away, walked to his table, turned again. "What are all those other lines doing? What's all this about traveling—and discovery?"

"That's just a metaphor."

"A metaphor? How do you know?"

"Because," Bohannon said, as though his patience were dwindling, "the title says that——"

"That the poem is about reading Chapman's translation of Homer?"

"Yup."

"That's not good enough." Bohannon shrugged, and looked away.

"Anyone can see that," a boy said in the corner of Hatcher's eye. "That it's a metaphor."

"But *how?*"

"Because—well—it's so *fake*. All this stuff about 'goodly states' and 'realms of gold' and—"

"Yeah," said the rest of them. "Right. Yeah." A few of them began to talk. They said that the travel stuff was phony—it was too much—it made you think that the poem was really about something else.

"Good," Hatcher said. "Exactly. That's one of the ways a metaphor can work." He smirked at them. "And if you're taking notes, you can write that down." They laughed.

"But look. What do you get in the last three lines of this? What happens there?"

"Just more of the metaphor," Barnett piped from the back. Something had been approved, and he was reluctant to move from it.

"But something else happens. The focus narrows, the—does this seem as phony as the rest? What's the difference? What do you expect at the end?"

"He's supposed to get back to Chapman's Homer *sometime,*" Hatcher heard, among three or four simultaneous answers.

"Good. Very good. But he doesn't, does he? Well?" But now they were waiting for him. They had become aware of some change in his tone, some new inflection that made it obvious that he knew the answers to the questions he was asking. It was academic. Answer it yourself, since you know already.

"What happened to Keats and Chapman and Homer, then?" Hatcher pressed. They waited still.

"You quit now?" Hatcher chuckled. They laughed too and shifted in their chairs, and remained silent.

"This is a hard poem," he said, rambling now, sweating under his shirt. "This question"—what question—"about the metaphor, about the end of the poem, has bothered a lot of people." More loudly, gaining speed, he continued. "It's a problem. Look." He summarized for them what they had said so far. "And yet it ends all on Cortez, his men, the Pacific. It *is* confusing." He paused, and he thought the curse was lifted. "Do you think it's possible that this confusion is deliberate, that it has something to do with what's going on, with what Keats is trying to do?"

"Well—" he heard from the back.

"Yes?"

"Na-aw."

"Go *ahead.*"

"Cortez's men—"

"Yeah?"

"*They're* excited—and confused. They——"

"Good!" Hatcher cut it off. He looked covertly at his watch: five minutes. "If there's anything to this," he said, gesturing. "If what we've been saying means anything, then maybe the poem, the way the metaphor gets real here—" But he would have simply to say it. "That *imitates,*" he declared, "a kind of confused excitement, the excitement of a discovery, and the confusion of it. Just like at the end of the poem, where you don't know how to read that final image, whether it's part of the same old metaphor or something else."

He did not think they got it. But some were smiling, perhaps to assure him that they understood, and that it was enough, and time to go. "I think," Bohannon abruptly but slowly gurgled, "I think Keats was pretty confused himself."

"You do, huh?"

"Well. Don't *you?* Making that mistake about Cortez discovering the Pacific when everyone knows——"

"The mistake is yours, Mr. Bohannon."

"I don't think so. Even in the notes it says——"

"Yes. The editor made the same mistake. Lots of them have." Bohannon laughed, as if there were no dealing with anyone who would say something like that.

"Keats knew, of course," Hatcher preached, "that it was Balboa who discovered the Pacific"—did he?—"but he wasn't talking about that. No more than he was talking about reading Homer for the first time. The poem is not about the discovery of the Pacific or the discovery of Homer. It's about *Chapman's* Homer, *Cortez's* Pacific, about seeing something you knew about, but seeing it new. Its about rediscovery."

"Wow," someone said, as if breathless, or as if mocking breathlessness. Hatcher could not tell.

"O. K.," he said. "All right. That's all." They went out, some talking lowly, nodding, chuckling. He let them all pass, and then reentered the corridor. It might have been a good class. A few years before he would have been sure of it.

As he squared around the corridor corner, Hatcher saw the chairman. "Hello, *Phil.*" Clough had been walking, even marching, away from his office, but now he turned to Hatcher and grinned to show his small and even teeth. His hand passed slowly over the puffed and shining silver waves on his head. "I haven't seen you, Phil, how are you?"

"Pretty well, *Phil,*" Hatcher said. emphasizing their common name as the other did. "No. I have been busy."

"Of course." They had turned, and with one graceful hand at the small of Hatcher's back, Clough was steering back toward his office. He did not say, "I've been wanting to talk with you," or "Do you have a minute?" There was just the brotherly-fatherly touch at the back, then a muttered joke about a graduate student slouching along the opposite wall, and they were in the office. Clough released, nodded at a chair, looked pointedly at the electric coffee pot on the wall table. Hatcher shook his head. The chairman filled a cup and sat down at his old desk.

"How *have* you been, Phil? How's the book coming?"

"Coming pretty well," Hatcher said. There was no book. In the fall of the year, when he had still thought it might matter, he had passed parts of his doctoral dissertation around. He was forcing himself to write it to get ahead in his job. Only that, he thought: because for him there was no life in the thing. He had had the ideas in it; he was finished with them. He had thought before that he would write them over, say them again, publish them, so that he would be promoted. Now he knew he could not.

"Coming pretty well. You know revising for university presses. One reader says yes with conditions, and you make the changes, and the second reader doesn't like the changes."

Clough barked a short laugh. "First book, Phil. I don't envy you. But I can't say it gets easier either." Stacked neatly in one corner of the desk were the galley proofs of a book of essays Clough was editing. The top page, Hatcher saw, had been finely marked with a very sharp blue pencil. "But that's our job, isn't it?" Hatcher nodded quickly and said nothing.

The chairman swiveled slightly around, framing in the yellowish light from the window his clear profile. He seemed to be smiling. "You want to be a pro, don't you, Phil?" he murmured.

"Yes?"

Clough swung around. "A professional. In this business."

Hatcher laughed, looking around at the books on the wall bound in leather—rare books, some of them, so prettily shiny they seemed varnished. Johnsoniana, he said to himself, and then jingled on, Swiftiana, Popiana—"

"I thought I had. You mean—"

"Of course you have! I only want you to know that I know, that we all know, the pressure that's on you—on any junior member of the department, especially if he's as capable as you are, and as ambitious as you ought to be."

Hatcher nodded encouragingly, and reached into his inside breast pocket for his cigarettes. Clough turned up one of his palms. "And the thing," he said, "is to face right into the wind. You can afford to. I've heard good things about your ms, Phil."

"Good of you to say so."

"Not at all! And of course that piece on *The Good Soldier* will be in the book, won't it?"

"Oh, yes."

"I like that piece." Hatcher had written it four years before, in graduate school, and had published nothing since.

"It's a good novel to write about."

"Yes. Fine novel. Well. I just wanted you to know that you're not being overlooked." He rose abruptly and came around the desk with his hand out. Hatcher stood and took it. "I'm glad we had this opportunity to chat, Phil."

"So am I."

"And good luck with your book. Do you—will there be any news by the end of May, do you think? Perhaps not, eh? A bit soon?"

"Oh, I don't know. There might be."

"Splendid," the chairman said. "Splendid. I look forward to it." He turned to the books on the wall, as if inspecting—not lovingly, but with care—some old edition.

As Hatcher left the office, he saw at the other end of the hall a group gathering for lunch. If he went back to his office for his raincoat, he would have to approach them. Instead he turned left abruptly through the doorway to the stairs. He walked quickly out of the building and down the hill into town, going to see Frankie.

Ever since Frank Buono had bounced a quarter off his heel and caught it, or perhaps since another had turned in the air to the tune of "Double or nothing?" or "You interested in horses?" Hatcher and Frankie had been friends. At first it had been for convenience, because Frankie stood at the center of things: He knew every bookmaker in town and every poker game in the county. But soon Hatcher had been charmed. Frank was a hustler, a fifty-year-old boy whose every word was a strategy, who could not tell the truth about anything, and who was yet paternally anxious to preserve his new and high-class friend from the tricks and schemes of others. "You watch yourself," he would say. "You don't know. This town is lousy with chiselers. Take your last *dime*. You listen to me." And Hatcher would listen, as long as he could between classes or before going home for dinner, to tales of winners lost on disqualifications, of bookmakers' mistakes that had cost a limit double, of bets unmade because Frankie could not get away from his change booth at the parking lot.

When he saw him coming, Frankie stood in the open doorway of the little shack and took off his black rain hat, smoothing a long lock of grizzled hair from one side of his head to the other to cover the recession. His large, almost square brown eyes swam darkly behind the lenses of thick glasses. "Where the hell you *been?*" he said.

"How are you, Frank?"

The mock scowl became a smile. "All right, Phil. 'Bout time you came down to see me. You got the sheet?" Hatcher handed the folded paper over. "That Joe didn't bring it today. No good bas-tard. Hey. Look at what he give me yesterday." He handed Hatcher a soiled paper filled with columns of figures: one-dollar daily doubles, one if two and reverse bets, one-dollar round robins—fourteen bets totaled seventeen dollars.

"How in Christ do you figure a one if two and reverse bet?" Hatcher asked.

"It ain't the *figurin'!* I can *figure* it. It's the same. Two horses—a dollar to win on each. If one wins, two dollars more goin' on the other one, and if the other one wins, two more dollars comin' back on the first one. It's the same."

"So if they both win, you got three lousy bucks goin' on both horses?" Hatcher knew that that must be right, but he was stretching the discussion out to accomodate Frank's outrage.

"Yeah. A course less that extra deuce goin' on each, which hasta come off the top at the end. It ain't the figurin', Phil!"

"But you're supposed to get this in for him?"

"That's it. And what do you think? I sat on it before, and he hit me for sixteen dollars. Why do you think I ain't been relieved yet? Where do you think he is?" Hatcher was silent. "Down the track!" Frank bellowed indignantly. "I guess he thinks I was born yesterday or sothin'. Bastard. Arms me all week and then he goes down to the track."

"I told you you ought to pack him up a long time ago."

"I gonna pack him up!" Frank sat down in the only chair in the booth. "Don't worry! I just wanta see 'im down good, one time. Then I tell him no more arm. You know what I says to him the other day . . ." Hatcher half-listened to the story, like all Frankie's stories probably imaginary, in which Joe was finally and conclusively revealed and condemned. But Frank saw that his attention was wandering and shifted.

"Well, what about it, Phil? You makin' a move today?"

"Too late for the double."

"Forget them doubles! Listen. Those ironworkers give me a hot horse today. In the ninth at New York. He's eight to one on the sheet."

"I'm not gonna start playin' anybody's hot horses."

Frank blinked solemnly at him, then smiled. "Aw, you're right," he said. "You're a hunnert per cent. Why are they givin' it out, you mean."

"Right."

"Ri-ight. Still, their horses do all right, sometimes." He waved at a passing car, at the sound of his name going away with it. "Well, what ya got then? I know you ain't hangin' around here just to talk to the old man."

"No. I just came down to see if you needed half a yard."

"Ha *ha,*" Frankie cackled, reaching over from his chair and punching Hatcher's leg. "You're all right with me, Phil." Then he became severe again. "Half a yard!" he snorted. "Gimme half a gee for Christ sake. You can afford it." A car turned into the lot, and he punched a ticket and collected a dime. At the same time a short, heavily built man with a cigar stuck under his light brown mustache appeared around the corner of the shack. He wore a yellow slicker, and his name was Louie. He had great respect for Hatcher's handicapping because he was the Professor.

"Hey, Professor. Where you been?"

"Where *you* been, Lou?"

"Aw," he drawled through the cigar, "I been chasin' them fuckin' ponies." He took out the stub and eyed his listeners, as if reflecting. "Yeah. Them gee-gees."

Hatcher looked down at the stocky man's boots caked with cement dust. "Not workin'?"

"Naw. I been collectin'—unemployment."

"Yeah," Frankie chortled, nudging his friend. "Yeah. Get this."

"Yeah," Louie said. "They duplicated my card or *son*-thin'. I been collectin' for six months. Again he removed the cigar, and the corners of his mouth dropped. *"Six months,"* he said, slowly. He blinked at them both, puffing again, musing. "But it's no good," he muttered. "No good."

"Why?"

"Aw, it's no good. Chase them horses and where does it get ya? The island of no return."

Hatcher blinked himself then. "What?"

"You kno-o-w. You know that place where all the old people sit—up where the avenue runs off Charles Street. Where them benches are."

"The mall there?" Frankie asked, and confirmed it to Hatcher. "He means the mall."

"Yeah. That's right. The other day I'm sittin' there myself, right alongside of 'em before I even noticed. Me'n them." He gestured and spluttered an indignant laugh.

"The island of no return, huh?" Hatcher said admiringly.

Louie beamed, gap-toothed. "That's what I call it."

Frankie had turned away and was adjusting the dials of his little red radio for the early results. He jerked a thumb when the disc jockey made a remark about everyone out there in bookie-of-the-month land. "Listen to that asshole. Every race, the same joke. I bet he never moved in his life."

"You liked that, didn't ya?" Louie said to Hatcher. "Yeah." He appeared to think for a moment. "Yeah," he went on in slow measure, "I could be right out of Da-mon Run-yon." Then he told a story about sitting on a bench with his friend Pete, and their seeing a very old, very arthritic woman clumping toward them, and how Pete had said, "Louie, if I hold her, will you fuck her?"

"Ain't that *son*-thin'? Ain't he a bitch, that Pete? Well." He gave Frank a folded paper and some money and then left without salutation.

"He's a funny guy, that Louie," Hatcher said, watching the yellow slicker moving slowly up the hill.

"Yeah, he's all right. Dirty, though."

"What?"

"He gets drunk"—when Frank had a single beer he either went to sleep or developed a headache—"he gets drunk, he don't know what he's doin'. I heard one time he shit in his own bath tub." He paused while Hatcher laughed, and then said abruptly. "Listen, I ain't got time to stand here with you. I got a lot to run." He shifted again. "You got anything good today, Phil? I see one horse here I know you ain't gonna let go." He took the sheet out of his pocket and flapped it.

"Which?"

"You know which. That Marlisa, that's who."

"Yeah?"

"What do *you* think."

"Well, you're right. Marlisa and It's Blitz, I'm bettin'. Ten if twenty and reverse."

"Well," Frank said, reasonable now. "That Splitz is a good horse. Don't ever think he isn't. Just hasn't been out though."

"I'm takin' a shot with him."

"We gotta make a move," Frankie said suddenly, "in the next couple days. I'm bent."

"How about Saturday?" Hatcher stepped back out of the booth, walking backwards, toward his two o'clock seminar, as he spoke.

"Has to be Saturday. I don't like it. All the assholes from town'll be down there. Has to be Saturday. Well, I'll see you before then anyway." Hatcher nodded. "Come down once in a while, for Christ sake," Frank called after him. He peered over the top of his glasses. "And have your wife make me a sangwich."

Chapter 7

Two days later Margaret Hatcher discovered in her mail a long and businesslike envelope, return addressed Rankin, Rankin, and so forth. The enclosed letter informed her that approximately six months ago, Mr. Jasper Leonard Wallace had died, that his will had been in order, and that he had left his immediate family thoroughly enriched. He had further, one of the Rankins continued, seen fit to bequeath to his eight nephews and nieces a single block of common stock that had been more or less unproductive for him. Jasper Wallace was one of Margaret's maternal uncles. The value of the stock in question at sale, after fees and commissions, was $30,092.24. The quotient of that amount, dividing by eight, was $3,761.53, which was the amount printed on the yellow check now lying on the floor at her feet.

When Hatcher came out from washing that evening and sat down to dinner, it was his turn. He was satisfied. The race results were in, and although one horse had lost in a photograph, another had won and paid fourteen eighty, and he had made thirty-four dollars. The following night he was going to play poker, and Monday began the week of spring vacation. If his luck held, he thought, he could make Aqueduct three, even four times. So he sat down happily.

The official envelope propped against the wine glass puzzled him, and instead of looking into it he called in to Margaret. She swaggered out of the kitchen, the corners of her full mouth twitching. "*Look* at it."

When he had looked, she began to talk rapidly, rattling and chuckling. But Hatcher scarcely heard her. All the vulnerable extensions of himself, all the debts of money, mind, and time on which he had seemed to depend had dissolved. It was as if some exposed part of him had at last been withdrawn; he felt whole and prepared. When the rhythm of her voice fell, he said, "We're getting out of here."

"Where do you want to go?" Margaret asked, laughing at him.

"Makes no difference. Out. What about the islands?" He said it as if there were such a place, a defined location, and for him at the moment there was: the islands, any island, alone and integral and surrounded only by the liquid sea.

"When?"

"Well. We should take our time and plan. No sooner than— Sunday." He looked at her, sitting calm, her slender hands folded over each other. "What's today, anyway?" he said.

The next day was Friday, when Hatcher, Edmund Spenser, a knight named Guyon, and twenty-three sophomores demonstrated that Temperance was a pretty dull business; and when, in the afternoon, a travel agent with a wall eye suggested the Bahamas, agreeing at the same time that anything was possible and they could go anywhere. But why not—and here his hand ceased its effeminate flapping, then cupped and shook like shooting dice —Nassau, Paradise Island? By dinner time it seemed just the thing.

"See," he said. "Eight hundred to play with. Eight days, a hundred a day. Twelve for the hotel and tickets and food. That leaves over fifteen here."

"Paradise Island." She looked at him, chewing her lower lip.

"Why not? And if we get a little lucky, can't we make expenses for the whole thing?" He paused, and then seemed to decide. "Hell no. If we get lucky, we could make five thousand clear."

The books said, everyone said, that you could do it at dice.

"Paradise Island," Margaret shook her head and repeated, in a voice that mixed eagerness, remonstrance, and sadness.

At Jimmy's that night Hatcher played for three hours without trouble, congratulating himself all the while on his coolness and skill. His hands were either very good or very bad, and he played them as if he were beyond it all already, and the others felt his remoteness, rankled, and called him on two full houses. That was a hundred—he saw it now as plane fare for one—and he closed up and coasted, until his first five cards were hearts and he had to play, and he won. He did not think now of how many ways, for instance, a flush can be beaten. He did not care. He had his new future, his sudden fluidness. He sat in the acrid air of the little room, chuckled at the jokes and the dealers' hysterics when Hollywood tore another deck of cards, drank coffee, and anted up his quarters.

"Hey, teacher," growled John. "You know, you could play a hand once in a while. This game can be fun, you know."

"Hah! What do you think!" shouted a big round Italian boy named Ruggieri. "What a field *he's* got. He's the best," he sneered.

"Listen," said John. "Don't think he isn't." Then they were off, needling, talking sidewise at Hatcher's play, full of praise for him as the complement of their loud contempt for each other. It cost them nothing to say that he was the best. They would have said it of anyone who was winning since they were sure it meant nothing. Anyone could be the best, because so long as they were not winning, it was just a game of dumb luck anyway. Sooner or later the cards would turn, and then they would see who was really best. So they went on with their heckling, and Hatcher went on throwing up quarters and throwing away his cards.

But Ruggieri got tired of it at last. "Fuck this game, *Jimmy!*" he cried as if it were Jimmy's fault. "Let's shoot some crap!"

There was a small, loud chorus of agreement while Jimmy shook his wide, soft face. "Come on, Jim," someone else wheedled, "we got no action tonight. Get the dice."

Jimmy turned on Ruggieri. "No crap games in my *place!*" His voice rose on each word, but then he subsided and muttered, "You tryin' to close me up, you son of a bitch." Then Ruggieri began to shout, too, that he was a stupid Greek, and who was going to close him for just fifteen minutes of crap, and who would talk.

"Besides," he said more softly, his eyes trying to hide their conviction of his cleverness, "you can cut the goddamn game, can't you?"

Jimmy chewed on his cheeks for a moment. "Fifteen minutes then, that's all."

They set up a cardboard box on the poker table, and leaned against it a dirty slab of foam rubber. A small, heavily built man, almost a midget, bounced the dice against it in experiment and one fell to the floor, and so they stood around the table and argued, for the rubber or against it. After a minute Ruggieri shouted something and snatched it away, throwing it into the far corner of the room. Then Jimmy shouted at them all, and they began to shoot.

Hatcher sat down at a table. He was keeping himself pure for Paradise Island, and did not want to play. Yet there was no question of going home. He sat, exchanging a word now and then with his solemn host, watching as they cried out at each other bet or no bet. In ten minutes it was winding up. There had been little money in the game to begin, and Ruggieri, having bet steadily against the dice, had most of that. Jimmy watched the play dwindle and said, "This is no good, Pheel. I got no protection for this. They close me up." At the table Jap cut another 7 per cent when somebody made his pass.

"Then throw them out." Hatcher did not care.

"No good." The folds in his face shook. "In a minute I stop it."

"Listen. Jim. Why don't you come out to the horses with me tomorrow?" Hatcher was thinking ahead, and the circumstances of tomorrow's action had to be set. But the Greek only laughed, and looked fondly up at the oil painting hung across the room. It was a picture of a horse, a filly he had once owned, a filly that had cost him, counting the painting itself, ten thousand dollars. Out of the pallid green background the head of the horse stared, seeming confident that she would be taken care of. With one ear cocked oddly she looked clownish, inconsequent. She had broken down soon after Jimmy had bought her, and now he listened to jokes about her while she looked on with that pathetic, hungry confidence. He continued to stare back at her for a moment. Then he sighed and laughed.

"No Pheel," he said, nodding his head at the quarreling crapshooters. "I got my horses. I got my horses right here." So the next morning Hatcher took his wife to Aqueduct.

They strutted through the morning, isolated from the crowds around them. The people on the train looked at them with resentment, or with fatherly-motherly affection, or with some old conviction that the fall would come. But they ignored it all, and thought of themselves as bright characters. Hatcher got seats in the clubhouse just behind the boxes of the owners and trainers, and after they had seen where the seats were, they went for their lunch to the Kelso room.

Then, like people who could tell something from the looks of a horse, or like people who owned one, they lolled down to the walking ring to watch the obedient animals for the first race swing around. Margaret was excited, pointing at the jockeys, at the trainers with their inevitable snapbrims and sunglasses, and at last at a pretty-colored roan filly named Our Mary Anne, the horse that Hatcher said could be the winner. Then when the post parade ambled by, and the jockey on the roan saw her stare and stuck out his tongue at her, Margaret tugged on Hatcher's arm and pointed again, and then with her thumb on her nose waggled her fingers in the air at the grinning boy.

That settled it. They covered everything; there was no situation too much for them. Hatcher forgot his worries about the favorite and bet all his doubles on the roan filly, who was eight to one because of a poor last race. Back at their fancy seats, they could see everything, especially the green and yellow silks of their horse, tucked in fifth along the backstretch, third on the turn, and then out where the boy took her, in the middle of the track where the going was a bit faster.

"Where is she?" Margaret cried.

"There." He sat back and crossed his legs. "She just made the lead. She's the winner."

She stood and stared, as if trying to draw their filly along to the wire, and as she crossed the finish line, sang, "Atta girl, atta girl."

Hatcher was still sitting back. A heavy man with bushy white brows turned in front and looked at Margaret, then smiled. Hatcher grinned and said, "O.K., baby. There was no question." His wife paid no attention, but watched intently as the horses were unsaddled and led away.

"That was a nice horse," she said then. "How much did we make?"

Hatcher went away to collect thinking what a good woman his wife was. When he returned, he fanned the money out for her, casually. She nodded also, as if it had been expected, and leaned over to stare with him at the past performances for the second. Tipped together in that crowd, with the milling heads of the grandstand only a few feet away to their left and surrounded by boxes full of rich and careless insiders, they seemed a small academy. The ladies of the horsemen gave them little looks.

But the second race was not so easy. Their main horse was Driving Rain, and when they broke, she began to run closer to the leaders than, as Hatcher said, she should. On the turn she was racing in front. Hatcher leaned forward in his seat, then stood to see the favorite begin to make her own run. He thought it was finished for them then, and slumped back down.

"Come on, Driving Rain," Margaret screeched, teetering on her toes.

"She made the lead too early," he growled beneath her. "The goddamn kid got hot pants. She's dead."

But the horse was still running. A sixteenth of a mile from the wire the favorite ranged up alongside her, the jockey whipping and scrubbing, but their own boy was sitting lightly, pushing and pushing again in his rhythm, and his horse and their horse kept on. Hatcher's bitter reserve collapsed, and he jumped to his feet.

"Look at that horse! *Look* at that horse!" A silver presence or two turned again to look at them, amused and patient with youth so easily swayed.

At the wire the two horses were inseparable: right against each other, and nose to nose. As they passed the finish the favorite's hindquarters bunched and kicked for the last jump, and her head seemed to shoot in front. The result board stayed dark, except for the pink sign for the photo.

"Did she get it, did she?"

"Don't know," he raised his voice over the crowd's new roar. "Close. I can't call it." The same bulky form turned in front of them.

"The favorite got up," he said.

"It looked too close to call to me," Hatcher said. "The angle's bad here, remember."

"Not that bad. She got up. She figured to get up. Look at the time of her last. She got it all right." He smiled at Margaret.

"Yeah, O.K. Time!" Hatcher scoffed. "They're still looking at the picture, aren't they? C'mon, Maggie." As they clattered down the stairs he was still muttering, "Time—speed—quack, quack—the son of a bitch. We'll see what the boys on the wire say. Time! That yap."

On the other side of the cyclone fence, opposite the red, yellow, and blue target that marked the finish wire, two men stood apart from the crowd on the rail and argued. Hatcher called across to them, "Who got it?" The tall one, wrinkle-faced and worried, only looked at them and shrugged. The other, in a washy, cracked leather jacket and tweed cap tilted over his eyes, flourished a hand at his friend.

"I *tol'* him. Forget it, Jimmy, I say. The chalk got it." He turned back to Jimmy, his voice raised for the clubhouse couple to hear. "Did I ever call one wrong? And that pig of mine never made a move. Don't I know a boat race when I see one? Believe me. The chalk got it. They wouldn't *let* her lose!" With Jimmy still watching the board, the little one turned away, baring his teeth. Just then the photo sign flicked off, and numbers went up. On the top, first, was number six, Driving Rain. But the first two numbers were blinking, on and off.

"Have your attention, *please,*" trilled the voice from above. "In this race"—the words were spaced and strange, the accents stilted in an incantation—"jockey Jawn Rotz, on number four, Dod-ger-ess, is claiming foul against jockey Jawn Ru-ane, aboard Driv-ing Rain, the *un*-official winner, for inter-*fer*-ence through the stretch. Please hold all tickets." The voice clicked resonantly off. Jimmy's slump became pronounced, and the short one snorted.

"You can bet whose number goes up now," he cried to his friend and the man and woman across the fence and walkway. "Who's gonna win—the outsider or the horse the smart money is on? Hah!" Jimmy mumbled that his horse had run straight, and the other shouted, "Think that makes a difference? Will you smarten *up!* She's comin' *down!*"

"What happened?" Margaret asked.

"I'm not sure. At the end they were both drifting together pretty bad. I don't know."

The crowd was humming and happy at the tension that had come so quickly that Saturday. Scattered through them a few loud voices could be heard hedging their bets: "Ten bucks she comes down—twenty she stays—two bucks they *both* come down." The last of the blanket-draped, sweated horses was far up the track toward the stables.

"Christ," the short man said, grubbing in his pockets. "I musta dropped a double saw somewhere—dropped it right outa my pocket. I'm tapioca for Christ sake. *Shit.* "

"*Your attention please:* the claim of foul is *not allowed,* and the second race *is official.* The winner number *six,* Driv-ing *Rain,* a four-year-old brown filly by . . ." The rest was lost in the conversation across the fence.

"Boy, I thought that pig quit."

"She didn't quit, Smitty. I knew it. She's a nice filly."

"Sure. Yeah, they're all nice when they win." Then he slapped the other on the back. "Well! You won one, huh? 'Bout time!"

"Look at that double. Two sixty. Boy, that's nice."

"Yeah. Listen, Jim. Let me have fifty. I got caught a little short here."

"Whatever you want, Smitty." They walked away from the fence. The short-backed jacket jumped and shook as its wearer talked and gestured. When Jimmy turned for a moment toward him, his face was wrinkled in a smile.

"Did we have the double?" she asked.

"We've got everything," Hatcher smiled, and took the tickets out of his pocket.

They did not return to their seats, but sat for four races more in the dark heavy chairs of the clubhouse bar, watching the races on television, drinking gin. Hatcher was way ahead, twelve new fifties in his left-hand pocket, and on those four races he bet the other money, the two hundred in old tens and twenties that he had brought with him. He was trying to get the money changed, but instead, at fifty and eighty dollars a race, with two seconds, a third, and a six to five winner, he got rid of most of it.

By that time they had had three drinks. They were tired of the *Telegraph* and the racing game. In the dimness of the bar the bright, hard day had dissolved comfortably into old times, and when he went to bet, it was an interruption.

"Let's go, Philip. Let's go to town."

"O.K. One more race, and we'll go to town for dinner."

"Good. Who do we have in this one?"

They had High Hat, a front runner with a world of speed, who had been beaten on the turf only once in his life. The race was on grass, at a mile and an eighth, and that morning Hatcher had thought him the best bet of the day, at even money or so. But when they went out of the bar, crossed to the grandstand, and blinked at the glare through the high windows, High Hat was three to one. If Hatcher had been sober, if he had been still in business, the odds would have seemed too high and frightened him: where was the smart money going? But now everything was simple. Three to one was better than six to five; so much better that at the fifty-dollar window he said, "Four times." Even the new money had ceased to matter now. The day increased and blurred steadily—the frowns of bettors trying to get out of the hole, Margaret's bright smile over the blue and green print of her dress, the stylish outriders down on the track—all the shining parade. He did not see the last flash of the odds, when High Hat dropped to two to one, for when the bell rang and all the gates rattled open a jockey named Hidalgo jumped the horse into a three-length lead before they reached the clubhouse turn.

"He's gonna burn 'im out," graveled a voice beside them as they peered through the glass. "That stupid spic is gonna burn him out." But Hatcher only looked at his wife and smiled and nodded his head down at the horses scampering like big rabbits on the new grass. No dust rose from their feet, and they made only a faint sound as they went by below. Their thin legs were barely visible threshing beneath them, so that the muscles in their shoulders and haunches seemed to work mysteriously in that sea of green with the bright shirts floating superfluously above.

"He's dead," the voice rasped again.

But Hatcher merely nodded once more. "Look at him." As High Hat got round the first turn and into the back stretch, they could see his five lengths of lead and the way he was doing it. The rider seemed far back in the saddle, with his legs almost straight out in front, and the horse was pushing his head out easily between the extended stirrups, seeming never to stride but always coiled for the next stride. Running out in front where he liked it he was running the pack, leading them, back to the barn, out to the fields, where he wanted to be. Then he made the last turn for home, and it was a horse race again. At the crowd's cry he dropped his head lower; his body stretched out; his ears flattened; and his lip seemed to curl back from his teeth as he came on. But his jockey would not let him spend. With seventy yards to go he looked back quickly, once, took another wrap of the reins on his wrist, and the horse coasted in.

"*As the rider pleased,*" Hatcher quoted softly from the future.

"Wasn't he something?" she said, as she watched High Hat crabbing and skittering back to the scales.

"Foul!" a wag cried. "Take him *down!*" People laughed. Hatcher fanned his four tickets like cards.

His wife drew breath sharply, puffed it out, and laughed. "This is easy!" she said. "Why haven't we done this before?"

"It wouldn't be fair to the rest of them."

They took a taxi ride back to the city. At the fifty dollar cashier's window he had not stopped to count, so much ahead that it seemed he did not have to. As well he forgot to suspect the cab driver of voluntary delays and detours. They leaned and slid and bounced together in the slippery seat, occasionally smiling complacently at each other like conspirators. In the softening haze of the afternoon the traffic and buildings and occasional trees glimmered by their windows in a purely visual effect. They measured nothing, as if that passing scenery, the driver's stock misanthropy, and even the presence of each to each—as if all were an entertainment and they the audience, of some show of the world that had no point nor end.

It was early, and they opened the restaurant, feeling themselves proprietors. Like too calm, too powerful children they enjoyed the parade of the waiters, the succession of mussels and lamb and white wine and red. Then, at last, with their coffee and brandy, they were filled, their eyes narrowing toward sleep as the day continued its dissolution. Cigar smoke, brandy fumes, the smells of coffee and chocolate like all the rest lost their separateness, no longer added one to another but merged in a fluid that surrounded them. Sudden money and racing and French cooking flowed into its expectant, unspecified pleasantness.

In the taxi to Pennsylvania Station he turned to her in the darkness and said, "This is what I mean."

Margaret sighed. "What?"

"This is what it's supposed to be."

"Ah."

That night they made love without having to think about it. Still riding the day, they forgot procedures, neglected the usual attention to each other's progress, and even the necessity of climax itself receded, leaving them stretched long against each other, scarcely moving. In that long, extended touch of skin, that light, slow squirming of body to body, at last, murmuring, they fell asleep.

Hatcher was drinking coffee, one page into the sports of the *Sunday Times,* when Margaret asked, "How do you play dice?"

"Shoot," he clipped.

"What?"

"You don't 'play'—you shoot—craps, it's called."

"Craps." Across the table her face, still sleep-stiff, broke into wrinkles. She sniffed, "Craps."

Hatcher grunted approval and went back to the decline of the Giants. He did not notice her leaving the table, nor her rummaging in a closet, until down the center crease of the angled paper rolled the two small, badly spotted dice. He looked up as if irritated, but saw her standing, hands on hips, neat jaw forward, bluffing him.

He laid into a corner of the living room an old dark green blanket, and on and over it wedged the board from the Monopoly set. Experimentally, considerately, he bounced the dice over the blanket and off the board.

"O.K.," Margaret announced. "Who shoots first? What do you bet me?"

"I don't bet you," he laughed. "You're with me. We bet against the house. Wait." He went back to the closet and returned, sorting out the play money. "We'll start with a thousand. The house has the rest. Let's go."

Margaret skittered the dice toward the corner. One of them missed the blanket and backboard. "No dice!" Hatcher said.

"What am I trying to do, anyway?"

"Well, first you're trying to play them both off the board. If you do that, then you want them to come up seven—or eleven. Seven is best."

"Why?"

"Because it's easiest. Seven or eleven win right away." So she threw them out, and they turned seven.

"Hah! I win!"

"No, you didn't." Hatcher was in earnest, appealing to her. "What did you win? You didn't bet anything. You have to bet."

"Well, all right," she snapped, and stripped off a pink five-dollar bill.

"O.K., now shoot." He crouched over the blanketed corner, ready, and Margaret rolled another seven.

"Good, good." From the bank's stacks he picked his pink paper rectangle. "You win. Shoot." She reached for the bills. "No no! We let it ride." The dice came eleven. "Win. Leave it." With the twenty riding, she shot a four.

"Oh-oh."

"It's all right," he urged. "Now. You got to roll that four again, *before* you roll seven."

"Seven wins!" Margaret wailed.

"Not any more," he declared solemnly. "Not after you roll another number. Four is your point now. You have to make it again. Shoot a seven now and you lose." She stared at him, sitting lotus-fashion on the blanket's edge, mouth a little slack. "Go ahead. Shoot."

She did: five—"Nothing, nothing"—then ten—"Go ahead"—and then her four.

"Winner!" he cried, shaking her shoulder with one hand, reaching for the money with the other.

Margaret clapped her hands. "Do I let it ride again?"

"No. Let's take away twenty. And listen; don't roll two or three or twelve—on the first roll. They lose too."

"But what if I do now?"

"Don't. On the first roll. After that it's O.K."

She began again, rolling numbers and making them once more, as required, before she made a seven. "No sevens in the dice!" Hatcher was crowing. "Shoot, shoot."

At last, trying for a nine, Margaret sevened out, sat back, and looked from the jumbled pile in front of her to the neat stacks in the bank. "Boy. How much did I get?"

"About five hundred, I think."

"That's good. Shall we quit now?"

"Well, we *could* quit. But——"

"That whole time I only rolled seven twice. And you said it was the easiest to get."

"It is. That's right. Wait a minute." He staggered up, wobbling on the cramps in his legs, and stumped around, looking over tables, into cigar boxes, through a drawer. "Here!" He held up a black tube, which contained a stick of greasy, white ointment for chapped lips. He came back and with the stick as a marker began to draw numbers on the cloth of the blanket.

"But what are you *doing?*" Margaret shrieked. "The blanket!"

"We can get it cleaned," he grunted. "This is important." He tipped back, surveying the rectangle he had drawn, sectioned neatly into little squares that each contained a number—4,5,6,8,9, and 10. "See up to now we've been shooting like in a street game —just sevens and elevens and make your point and that's it. But in a casino game"—he held up one hand as if preaching, or quoting from a book—"in a casino game, you can bet *all* the numbers every time you shoot, so you have six points going for you every time. You see?"

"You mean, if I make any of these numbers, I win? How can they do that?"

"Because," Hatcher measured it out, "it's easier to roll seven than any of them, and if you roll it after the first shot, you lose. So they even have to give you odds on the numbers, too."

"You want to do this now?"

"Damn right," he said indignantly. "We've got to try to break the game."

She leaned over the blanket. "All right. Let's do it."

"Right. You shoot. I'll handle the money."

Hatcher laid a pale blue fifty in front of her, and she rolled eight. Behind the first fifty then he set another. "Odds on the eight," he explained. "No interest to the house on it. We get six to five free. Now wait." On each of the other numbers drawn on the blanket he placed an aqua twenty. "O.K., partner. Shoot."

She did, and still she rolled no sevens, and next the money on each number was fifty instead of twenty, and then a canary yellow hundred, and, after another fifteen minutes, an orange five hundred. Hatcher was excited. With every number she made he slid more bills from the bank of Monopoly money, where the piles were falling, into a mixed heap in front of them.

"Let's bet more!" Margaret cheered.

"We can't," he muttered as he collected on a number. "The bastards won't let us. The house limit is five hundred. The most we can have on the table is thirty-five hundred. That way they think they can grind us down." His eyes shifted quickly from her to money to dice. "We'll break them anyway."

"I haven't rolled one seven. Can it be this easy?"

"Well, the house thinks it isn't. It's against the probabilities." He grinned. "But it's not against the law." Ten minutes later the bank was down to its stack of white singles.

"Shall we leave the house the change?"

"Would they leave us the change? Shoot a hundred and clean them out." Margaret elevened and that was all.

"I'm sorry, ladies and gentlemen," Hatcher intoned, "the house is broke. The tables will be closed until we get some more money."

"We made a fortune."

"Boy," he said, "if we'd only been there."

With plenty of time for their plane at six, they drove up the turnpike and over the soot-black skeleton of Goethals Bridge, toward Paradise Island. There had been rain in the night, and now it began again—thick, cold rain that slapped into the windshield and slid away. Margaret said that it was good to leave in a storm, and then they rounded a long curve and saw ahead the traffic stacked up and creeping.

"But we have plenty of time, don't we?"

"Plenty." Three quarters of an hour later it was five thirty, and Hatcher was not so sure. For a while they angled and jumped from one lane to another, but when they crested the hill beyond the exit to Rockaway Avenue, the lines of crawling cars seemed to extend to the horizon. After a few more yards they were stopped completely.

"Bullshit," Hatcher said, as if the circumstances were somehow unreal, a lie that someone was telling them. Thirty seconds more and he said it again and pounded the steering wheel. Suddenly, eyes gleaming, he swung the wheels up to the right, bounced over the curb and down toward the bay, and rolled away at twenty miles an hour down an asphalt walk almost as wide as a road. At the bottom of the walk there was the small traffic circle for the exit, with two police cars parked along it.

"Oh-oh." But he kept on, staring through the dark windows at the flat-capped heads hanging over their cardboard cups. He slowed, took the bump down into the road softly, and watched the unmoved police in his mirror as he accelerated away under the highway and the traffic. Rockaway Avenue was wide, empty, and straight. Margaret chuckled. "Can we get there this way?"

"I hope so. You can get to Aqueduct this way. The airport is just beyond." They spun on in the wet and made the turn on Linden, and through the falling dusk ahead they could see the strung out lights of the parkway again and, off to the left, the rearing shadow of the deserted racetrack. There were no cars on the parkway here. At five minutes to six they climbed up into a building like a pagoda, and the flight attendant said he had thought they were not coming. He told them that all the economy class seats were taken, and paused.

"So we'll just have to put you in first. No charge, of course."

Three hours later they stepped down into a moist, warm wind. Hatcher's tweed suit itched on him, and his stomach—full of steak—felt empty. A tall, broad, black man was on duty inside the stucco terminal. He asked disdainfully how long they would stay, and though their return was precisely scheduled, Hatcher said he guessed about a week.

"You come to Nassau to gamble, mun?" He looked up from grease-penciling their baggage tickets, distant, disapproving.

"That's right." The other gave a clipped nod, slapped a suitcase, and made to turn away. "Well, wish me luck then!"

The checker turned and looked at him balefully, then shrugged, and smiled. " *Yah.* Good luck. Mun." Hatcher grinned back, and took it as a sign.

The taxi went on for what seemed a long time. When oncoming cars or bicycles lit up their windshield, they could see the driver's pale, fine hair, long neck, bobbing larynx. They listened to his musical speech as the car wound down through the old narrow streets of Nassau, until they reached the bridge and paid two dollars to cross to Paradise Island. When they passed a large flat-topped building abutting on the hotel, the driver sang, "That the casino, mun!"

"Is it open now?"

"Oh, yes," he said as he took the tip, *"every* day."

In their room he slid back the glass doors to the balcony on the ocean and unpacked while Margaret washed and combed. "O.K.? Let's try it." At half past ten they walked out of the hotel into the misty night, avoiding the connecting indoor passage that he joked must be for the suckers, and into the Paradise Island Casino.

It was a long, dark room, with a darker bar and cocktail lounge at the back, and beyond that the elegant room for baccarat. In the front left corner there were slot machines, brightly lighted, and past them to the right, tables for roulette and black jack, with small groups of lethargic players. But Hatcher's gaze passed all this quickly, sliding toward the rear half of the room where, in two ranks of three, stood the dice tables.

There was a crowd around one of the tables, and occasionally they erupted in noise, mixing groans and cheers. Some of the other layouts had hesitant customers; two were empty. Hatcher chose one of the vacant ones, where the dealers were chuckling, and the pit boss smoking a cigarette in his little balcony.

A bearded dealer bowed to them. "Good evening." Hatcher bought a hundred dollars' worth of chips. "Will the lady shoot?" Margaret shook her head quickly, and he said, "All right then, sir." But when Hatcher put down a five-dollar chip on the pass line he shook his head. "No sir. Ten dollar minimum, sir, at this table and that one"—he pointed across to the other empty table —"on weekends, sir." Hatcher laid down another chip, picked up, for the first real time ever, the red dice, shook and threw.

"Seven! Seven a winner, sir. Coming out again." Two pink chips were stacked beside his first two. He left them there, squeezed the dice and rolled again down into the bearded one's corner. "Ee-leven! Eleven a winner. That's very good, sir—coming out again." Hatcher left the forty dollars. "Six! Point is six. Make six and win." Behind his eight pink chips Hatcher placed eight more, taking the odds on his point. Then he rolled the six right back. Margaret laughed. The far dealer crowed, "Good shoo-ter! Coming out, coming out again, sir."

Hatcher took up the dice, and the natural winners, sevens and elevens, ran from his hand. He pushed, increasing his bets steadily. In ten minutes they were seven hundred dollars ahead, with a small sighing crowd forming around the table. Margaret was silent, standing to his left; the rows of pink fives and green twenty-fives stretched before her. But now—with the other people there—when he lost on a craps or a seven, he also lost the dice, which went tumbling from hand to hand around the table. No one else could make anything, and when the dice came back, neither could he. He thought still that they would turn, for him, and it seemed just a moment later when he looked down in front of his wife at three pink chips in the rack.

"Is it all gone now?"

"All gone," he agreed, but he chuckled then and put a hand on her shoulder. The other arm swept out, over their table toward all the others, all time, all chances.

Margaret nodded, looking toward her feet. "I'm a little tired." She looked up at Hatcher and said, more brightly, "You know I might go to bed."

"You could shoot for us. You could try shooting."

"Oh. Not for real. I am tired."

"Well, then I'll come up too. Of course I'll come with you."

"Only if you want to," Margaret said. "You were doing O.K., weren't you?"

"Yeah," he drawled. "I *was*. Maybe I could stay awhile longer."

"Listen! Why not?"

"O.K." Without more hesitation he extended the room key to her. She stretched out her arm and took it as she backed away, her arm still held toward him, smiling. Then she turned suddenly, and walked up the carpet with that loping, easy stride that Hatcher, now together with the dice and the wet air and the stickmen and the little metallic-skirted girls bringing drinks, loved.

In two hours more he had bought two hundred more in chips and lost them, which made three so far, and he thought passingly of his innocent one hundred a night plan. But still he felt that nothing could touch him; still he was circling, confident, like a fish around a school of bait that could go in any time but held, playing and savoring the appetite and the knowledge that it would be satisfied. Most of the other players had gone. The tables, save two, were closed. Hatcher hung over one of them, betting occasionally and watching. A young man who looked less than twenty shook the dice awkwardly and rolled a seven. Hatcher collected and doubled his bet: another seven, eleven, seven. The boy held the dice for ten minutes, making naturals, an occasional six, an eight, one nine. When he sevened on his third roll for a four, Hatcher had eight hundred stacked in front of him. With that the table closed down; the pit boss pointed them to the last one, in the back, still running.

"How much did you get?" Hatcher asked the new shooter as he backed unsteadily from the table.

"About two hundred, I think. First time." He had dark, slow eyes and hair. He laughed nervously.

"Come on," Hatcher said, steering him four steps to the last table. "We've got twenty minutes. Shoot. And if I were you, I'd bet more."

The tired stickman nodded and drawled, "Comin-n out." The boy's point was five. Hatcher asked him to wait; he took the three to two odds against the five and bet fifty dollars on each and all the numbers. "Five, shoot five and win." His new friend held the dice. One time he was almost five minutes in making his point, and halfway through it Hatcher said to bet the other numbers too, as he did, and he did and the point—"Nine, nine to win"—did not come but they kept collecting. When his partner at last lost them, Hatcher took the dice and took his money away from the numbers. He rolled one natural seven for a hundred and bet the two hundred and lost it.

"This next roll is it, gentlemen," the boss said grimly. "We're open tomorrow." So the boy rolled for two minutes more and they collected four bets, and he sevened. "Good-night now, gentlemen. Good-night."

As they cashed in Hatcher asked, full of sudden superstition, "You coming tomorrow?"

"I don't know. Maybe. I guess so. This was my first time, you know. I won six hundred bucks."

"Then you ought to come tomorrow," Hatcher declared, then

caught himself and laughed. They shook hands; they waved to each other, as if across some strip of mutually held territory. As Hatcher walked up to the room, he slapped his hand occasionally against the sheaf of bills in his pocket. When he entered, Margaret turned dimly in the sheets.

"Hey. I won eighteen."

"What?"

"Eighteen hundred."

"That's wonderful! C'mere." He did, and kissed her. His mouth was smokey and sour. "Ugh," She turned away. "G'night."

Hatcher looked down at her for a moment. Then he went over to the dresser and took out his money, stacking it on top of the glass surface so that in the morning it would be there to see. He stripped quickly and slid into the other bed. But after lying there for a moment, he got up again. He piled all his silver atop the folded bills, so that the money could not be moved silently. Then he crept back into bed and may have slept—he was not sure— for four or five hours, dreaming, or perhaps only imagining since there was nothing of a dream's obliqueness, of the dice bounding on, the chips clattering silently.

He awakened when Margaret rose about nine, not rested but relieved that the night was over. When she had got into the bathroom, he padded dopily around the room. Through the glass door to the balcony it was already dazzlingly bright. He put on his old bathing suit and a plain white T-shirt. When he looked in the mirror, he saw it was not very stylish, and he shook his head once or twice. As he did so, he saw the bills stacked on the glass dresser top. He picked them up and riffled through them. Looking again in the mirror he thought that he still looked all right despite the suit and shirt.

The sound of running water in the bathroom had stopped. Margaret noticed the silence. "What are you doing?" she called.

Hatcher was leaning toward the mirror now, holding the

bridge of his slightly bent nose in thumb and forefinger and wiggling gently. He stepped back, and nodded. "Oh, nothing," he said. "Just counting my money."

"That's nice."

"Why don't I meet you at breakfast?"

The elevators were slow. He trotted down three flights with his money in his fist to the desk, where he rented a safety deposit box and hid away fifteen new one-hundred-dollar bills. In the snack-bar, furnished with white wrought iron and thick plants, he ordered iced coffee against his burned mouth. Margaret came in almost at once, wearing a short, dark cotton robe over a pale brief suit, confident of her long body, smiling at him for the people staring. She ate melon and scrambled eggs and read a newspaper; Hatcher had more coffee and smoked.

"How about the beach," she said.

"Damn right." But they had trouble finding it, doubling back from one corridor, then from another, and finding that the first one had been right. They took another wrong turn through the dining terrace, but kept on through the empty tables anyway down to the glaring cement and got to the place.

The beach at that end of the island was in fact a steep and shifting shelf of coarse sand, and the few people on it were clustered at the entrance to the pool yard, backed away from the blue and purple ocean. Up the beach in one direction was a rock wall and jetty; in the other, the shore flattened and ran along a field adjacent to the hotel, scattered with concrete mixers and a few black workmen. Hatcher and his wife stood awkwardly on the pavement until a young man confronted them. While Hatcher looked down on his stiff swords of bleached hair, he swaggered ahead of them, holding his arms away from his sides, to two padded benches. He spread their towels there, and held out his hand.

Margaret swam in the pool while Hatcher lay sweating under the sun they had been warned about. But soon even some dark

and handsome image of himself was not enough to make him
endure more of that itching warmth, and they threaded through
the supine bodies to the steps to the beach. The water was lighter
now with the climbing sun, and they went into it. Margaret swam
easily and gracefully; he fought the calm water and tired. They
were reluctant to walk the beach because of the jetty on one side
and the cement mixers on the other. Besides, Hatcher was running out of patience. When they had sandwiches and rum drinks
at the poolside bar, he watched the clock covertly.

"What time does it open again?" Margaret asked.

"Oh? The casino? One."

"You want to start now?"

"Well, I guess I might as well. If I don't hit right away, I'll
come out and we'll do something else."

"You go ahead. I'll rest for a while. Then if you don't come up,
I'll come down."

"Right." He turned, and turned back again. "I could wait and
go later," he lied. "You want to do something?"

"No. No, and you couldn't. Come on."

At the room he did not wait for the shower, but changed
quickly into a knit shirt and some shorts, then pounded on the
door over the sound of the running water.

"O.K.," she cried. "Later." Hatcher walked out, ran down the
stairs, walked again through the lobby and down the long corridor to the dark, cool, almost deserted room. With only the slot
machines brightly lighted at the front, it was like a rich man's
penny arcade. He stalked confidently in.

Margaret's entrance, two hours later, was not so happy. She
was beginning to think she did not like it, to think that for her
there was not much to enjoy. It was nothing like horses, nor even
like the occasional poker games at their apartment where at times
she had peered over his shoulder at the stacked chips and ranked
cards on their dinner table. This gambling was pure and uncom-
promising; the people around the tables the night before stank of

sweated, greedy fear. They obviously cared about nothing else.

All that was all right, so long as they, he and she, were not caught in it like the huddled figures she now saw again. But through the morning she had felt him, tightly wound and waiting for where he was now, holding the dice, pale, hands trembling a little, amid the small crowd that elbowed closer and closer and exhorted and cajoled him to make a winner.

Hatcher saw her approach, and he leaned back from the dice, though he kept his place on the rail and smiled. Margaret smiled in turn, widely, and made a mock-gracious sign for him to continue. He threw out a seven quickly, and lost the dice and most of his winnings of the afternoon. He shrugged, picked up his chips, and came over to her. "Feeling better?"

She went along with the idea. "A lot. Winning?"

"In the middle. How about a martini or something?" She looked at her watch. "It's three thirty," he said. "Late enough. It doesn't matter anyway, does it?" A pigeon-shaped girl brought the drinks, mincing in her glittering skirt, and accepted effusively the dollar chips with which he tipped her. They drank two more while he played, losing and winning, losing and winning, and went out for dinner down a hundred and a little drunk. Each of them was determined to be happy away from the game.

But the dinner was mechanical and indifferent, and because of that Margaret was further irritated and emboldened. "Let's not go back in right away."

Hatcher balked, almost imperceptibly and only for an instant. "O.K.," he drew the word out. "What shall we do?" They went for a walk up the road past the casino to the bridge and looked across the bay to the scattered lights of Nassau.

"You want to go over?" The possibility was not real; he was already half-turned back toward the hotel. What could compete with the casino? All the attractions that the hotel seemed to offer in a package, all the potential of the islands themselves, were tinged with the shade of before or after gambling. Any time away was like a time out, a rest between periods of play: it was only the game that was real.

"Oh," Margaret said. "Let's make it tomorrow night. We can think about where to go."

"Good idea. That'd be better, wouldn't it?"

"That would be better." They returned to the hotel bar, where they watched the exotic dancer and had more to drink. When Margaret rose for the ladies' room she took an awkward step. "Wow."

Hatcher took her upstairs, shepherding and fatherly. She giggled and bumped through the door, and he steered her around in the dark and undressed her. When he had got her in bed, he sat down on the edge of it, leaning over her.

She stared at him large-eyed. "I guess I got drunk, didn't I?"

"Maybe a little, Maggie." The fullness of her look and her body against the smallness of her voice misted his eyes. With his hand lightly resting on her stomach he bent to kiss her. She was already asleep. He shook his head sharply and felt dizzy himself. Before he returned to the casino, he splashed cold water on his face for a few minutes.

Hatcher sat at the bar; he drank iced coffee and watched the Monday-night players accumulate. He felt both befuddled and cagey, relieved to be on his own, too, yet confused and sentimental at the thought of his wife sleeping alone in the room. Still in both places himself, he finished his coffee and drifted closer to the tables to see where the dice were passing. He drew the blankly hostile looks that players have for those who calculate on them. But he could see nothing anyway, from where he was, of how the dice were falling—no one ever could. He would have to get into it. At the table with the largest gang of rooters and most noise, he wedged himself in along the rail next to the stickman and threw down money for his chips. Into the midst of his double-mindedness, his hazy, fluid sense of his potentialities, the hard impetus of the dice broke. The game came to him in a rush.

Backing other shooters, he made three bets and lost all three, but that was only what he paid for the dice. They arrived beneath him, and he rolled them out. The stickman, his stick propped in his hand against the table, extending upward almost out of the light, sang. "Four. Eas-zy four. Point is four. How much on the *hard*ways, crap-eleven. How much on the *numbers.* Four the point. Make your bets early." Across the table a man chewed a cigar decisively and bet one thousand to win five hundred against Hatcher's four. The chant went on: "Four, point is four. Make your bets." At the other end a happy face with a lisping cry was betting handfuls of black one-hundred-dollar chips with the four: five hundred, the limit, on the line, five hundred taking the two to one odds. He counted it out; five hundred each on the top three numbers—ten, five, and nine. The stickman was still singing but now reached out with his crooked stick and swept the red dice across the table, flipped them neatly and stopped them below Hatcher, the shooter, so that they showed two and two. "All right, sir," he said more softly, and then, droning again, "Four. Point is four. Make four and win."

"Ten! Hard ten, the other side." Hatcher collected one of his ten-dollar bets on the numbers.

"Same bet, sir?"

"Press the numbers ten." He put down more chips, letting the dealer make change for him. Then everyone was ready again, so he threw them out again, and they bounced and scattered and tipped over three and one.

"Four! Four came easy, four a *winner.* Take don't, *pay* the line. Ma-ake your bets, comin out again. Same good shooter. Comin out." Ten minutes later it was still the same good shooter; four passes later, and now the money on each number was fifty dollars. On the pass line he laid a hundred. The four hundred dollars that he was ahead meant little to him, save as the money he could now bet, money on the table, working and changing. "Comin out." The stick swept across again, angled down again, and Hatcher shot them back. "Four, the *hard* four. How much on the numbers. Make your bets."

Hatcher set another hundred behind the pass line. He shot a twelve, then a three. "No harm done, thooter," called the man at the end.

He paused, then threw a five-dollar chip out into the middle of the table toward the proposition bets. "Hard four for the boys." The boys, the stickman and the dealers, choroused. "Thank you sir; thank you very much; thank you, sir. Good luck, sir. Shoot four and win." He threw the dice away from him, and before he knew to look, he knew, he thought, it was there. At the end of the table a woman squealed and said, "Oh, it's *four.*"

"Four! Came *hard!* Four winner!" the stickman cried before lapsing again into monotone; "Take don't pay line, same good shooter comin out." As he slotted away thirty-five dollars in winnings for the boys, he turned to Hatcher, *"Thank* you, sir. Thank you very much. Comin out, comin out."

Hatcher pressed one hundred on every number, two on the line, two more, if there was a point to take odds on, to go behind it. The stickman chirped, "Comin out," and he shook them quickly and bounced them backhand across into the corner.

"Eee-leven!" someone shouted.

"Eleven winner," came the echo. "Take don't and *pay* the line. Comin out." That was too fast and only two hundred dollars more, and Hatcher rushed the dice out again, into three. People groaned. Hatcher replaced his line bet impatiently.

"Come on, boy," cried the lisping plunger up to him. "Ma' thome numbers!"

And he did: "Five, five, point is five." Then a six: one hundred twenty won; a nine for one fifty more; an eight, one twenty. "At-ta boy!" The ranks of chips were lengthening, mixing. He could not stop to arrange them. He made a ten, collected two hundred. Then, flushed and confident, spinning the dice on the table, squeezing them in his hand, he made the point. "Five! *Good shoot*-er! Pay the line. What a shooter, folks. Make your bets now. Comin out."

Using almost all his winnings, Hatcher doubled the bets again. He rolled ten, five, six, and then eight, and all the numbers won, and he scooped the chips and thrust them into the long mahogany rows built into the table. He bet ten dollars for the boys on five and five, the hard ten, and rolled it easy, six and four his point, and won again. Between his hands sweating patterns on the leather rail there was now a long, solid, single row of greens, filling the rack.

One row of green chips was two thousand dollars, both a row of chips and two thousand dollars. It was a child's collection, like rows of glistening bottles, like sets of stamps gradually, richly filling in an album's page, or like four black bass laid in a row on a bridge, with a line in the water—all becoming always more and more complete. As money it was more than money: not money earned, not the sign of a settled life settling farther for itself, and not money to be measured grudgingly and budgeted and saved.

It was easy for Hatcher to risk bad money for good, money with its finished past for the chance of money with only a future. As he threw out the dice he was throwing out everything—all that he had been and was—in a gamble to gain everything he might be, unspecified. Gamblers have a word for this high risk, for this absolute sense of upset and life; they call it, matter of factly because it so dominates their experience, "action."

But the opposite side, and the sharpness of the risk that the gambler feels, is that he might somehow be thrown out of action, that by attempting to lose time he will be pushed back into it, more bitterly indebted, dependent, and even enslaved than he was before. As winning continues, as the action grows, the fear that it all might end, even for him, grows also. Like all gamblers when they are at last arrived at their private limits, Hatcher had begun to count.

To deny to himself that he was losing his feeling for the play, he bet four hundred, and he left his thousand on the numbers where it was. The stickman sang his song again, and the dice spun out, four and three. Seven the winner, but he did not like it. It was the first seven, the first full stop, in a long rolling time. He collected the four hundred and added one more to his stake on the pass line, betting the limit; he came out eight. The next roll, twelve, was nothing, nor the next two. He threw again, and someone shouted, "Eight right back!" Hatcher gathered up the overflow and shot the limit again.

The new point was six. It seemed to him that his run had been very long. He wanted to stop, to see what he had, and to accept congratulations. He rolled them out ten. "Atta boy!" He stuffed four hundred more blindly toward his rack and threw the dice at the same time. Looking through the moist haze before his eyes, seeking the dice faces among the chipstacks at the other end, he thought he saw five and one. He blinked and looked again: five and two. "Seven loser," the stickman clucked sadly. People sighed. His two thousand on the table, covering everything, was swept away. Hatcher slumped, but his hands fell to the chips in front of him. He began to stuff his pockets.

"What a *thooter!*" cried the man with the rows of hundreds, clapping. Hatcher grinned, sheepish, picked up the last of his chips and backed away from the table. The dice were coming out again; the people cried at them again. As Hatcher walked toward the cashier's booth, he bulged and rattled. People at other tables looked at him curiously. But the cashier was not curious. He had seen more, much more. He smiled only faintly as he stacked, quickly, deftly, sliding everything Hatcher had got into shiny metal counters. He looked up.

"Three thousand six hundred and thirty," he said. "Hundreds?" And did not even wait for Hatcher to nod. Then, with only one pocket bulging, studying his watch irrelevantly, Hatcher went over to the bar to unwind.

He drank bourbon over ice until after midnight, sitting there reserved and feeling the money against his leg. He felt swelled and capable of anything. He listened to the noise at the table he had left proudly, as if he had created it. He saw the faces tinged bright under the lights and was happy to be where he was, isolated in the gloom—and simultaneously he wanted to get back in the game. Instead he distracted himself with the round breasts of the small, brown-haired waitress, the same plump girl he had tipped so well the day before, who smiled, as if bashfully, when she walked by him. He relaxed and felt without definition the rich, popping sound of watermelons as he and his childhood's friends punched into them. He conceived a trial conversation; he thought he might offer to take her home.

He scarcely remembered his wife sleeping, away upstairs somewhere. No more than he remembered that before their excursion —indeed, before tonight—he had thought five thousand dollars much money, that one might be grateful to win it. That and all his other limits were dissolved. The next day, he mused, he would start with a thousand, for the beginning. Fallen back into ordinary life at a bar, Hatcher contemplated the waitress with the usual motives and thought of how much he could bet. He was only held from making his advances to her by the same feeling that kept him thinking of it—his obvious infinite power. It was that confident inertia—anything after those moments at the table was easy—that kept him in his seat, drinking. When he got up at last to their room and crawled unsteadily into his bed, Margaret did not awaken.

When he heard her moving about in the morning, he pretended tensely to be asleep, in fact drifting in and out of a stiff-muscled doze. He listened irritably for the rhythm of her preparations, trying to estimate when she would go out, but when he thought she was leaving he cracked one eye guiltily at her. She was standing before the dresser, looking down, and then he remembered his pile of money there.

"Hi," he said.

"Well, hi! How much this time?"

"Thirty-seven," he grunted, turning on his side to see her reaction to the news.

"Wow," she whispered. "Well, you've got everything you said you would, don't you? You did it." Hatcher was pleased at that, though he shied from the finality it sounded. After all it was not, could not be, over.

"Right," he said, closing his eyes. Margaret went out.

He lay there blankly for another hour or more; if he had had to decide what to do when he rose, he would have remained in the bed. But here there was no choice. There was only the pool, and he dragged himself down to it. Margaret waved at him from the water, and pointed, and he wandered vaguely around until he found her things on a bench. The sun pulsed into his hangover, and he lay aching and wet while a three-man steel band in leopard-spotted shirts played pop music, show tunes, rock 'n roll, all sounding like "Mary Ann." But Hatcher liked the familiar, rippling, enervated music, and he liked watching the players. They stood like all the Bahamians he had seen, with an unformulated arrogance, as if from their height they could afford to treat whites at large as equals. Perhaps not quite as equals, Hatcher thought. In the tolerating eyes of the players he and all the guests of the hotel must have appeared as pampered children—fat, greedy, frivolous. For himself he might have added, aimless. He sat up and smoked and considered the approaching afternoon. He did not want to run back to the casino immediately; his present position deserved some restraint. But that was not to deny his eventual return, sometime that day.

Hatcher now, as all gamblers, was like an athlete in perpetual training. But unlike the athlete, he was not really a winner, nor even someone who could say he was winning. He had won, yesterday, before, somewhere else, in a past that for him no longer counted. For him not playing now had to seem almost the same as losing. In either case he would accept some old pattern; in either he would have to admit that all the action he had wanted was too much for him. So there was the necessity of another trip to the fountain.

But not right away, Hatcher thought, thinking that he was no slave to any casino. When Margaret came out of the pool dripping and sparkling, he asked her how she would like a drive around Nassau.

"Ha. In what?"

"Can't we rent a car? Don't we have the money?" He uttered the last question with august contempt, for all those who might think otherwise. "We'll get a convertible."

"Great. Let's go change."

The man in the car rental booth wanted a hundred-dollar deposit. "Unless you have a credit card," he said.

"I'd rather give you the hundred," Hatcher said, peeling it off.

"Been havin' some luck, hah?" An aqua-blue Mustang, the worse for wear, wheeled to the curb. Hatcher climbed in and reached for the top lever.

"Some."

"You oughta quit, then," said the fellow, "before they get it back. Quit."

"I don't give it back," Hatcher laughed, as the doorman opened the lobby door for Margaret and smiled broadly.

"I dunno," the man was saying when they drove away from him.

There was no toll for leaving the island. With tires hissing they swept over the long white bridge in the sunlight and turned left away from the center of Nassau. Then within a half mile of the bridge he slid to a stop on the sandy road and backed up, toward a dockyard with a sign advertising charter-boat fishing. He was back only minutes after he went across to inquire.

"Shit." He slammed the door.

"What? No boats?"

"I'd really like to go fishing, too. Naw, they don't even go way out here. They creep around in the deep water off the island, the guy said, and when they get nothing there they come in and fish the reefs. *Bottom* fishing, for Christ sake. You know the Gulf Stream is nowhere near here?" he asked indignantly. "It's way over off the Grand Bahama. Too far for them."

"Oh."

"I would have liked some good fishing, too," he said, petulant, snapping the car into drive, spinning its wheels in the sand.

They circled the island of New Providence clockwise, drifting out past stucco villas behind hedges or walls into overgrown country full of saw grass and sandspurs, occupied only by an occasional and leaning tar-papered shack. The light blue sea was always on their left, and once they stopped to skim shells into it. Still Hatcher was marking the time, and as if on schedule they swung down the other side and into the back of Nassau.

As they rode slowly into that end of the town, all the green and blue of the island disappeared. The houses were small, each with its square of dirt yard patted by bare, black feet and combed by chickens. Children stopped their play and stared as the open blue car passed. Then Hatcher and his wife heard band music and ahead saw a half dozen cars stopped in the road. Marching slowly down toward them came a black procession, men, women, and children in dark clothes strutting solemnly behind the band. They were playing "Onward Christian Soldiers."

"Beautiful," Margaret said. "What is it?"

"I think it's a funeral."

"Aren't they grand?" But for Hatcher they were not. The little shanty town and its procession only looked like themselves, separate, impervious to his attention. He felt like an intruder and itched to get away. What had these people to do with some image of an island paradise, with driving in an open car, with a holiday? He sat isolated outside a surface that could not be broken. By four o'clock he had steered his wife, with promises of a fine dinner, back to the musical pool and himself to the casino.

As he approached the tables, a thin, old, gray man—the manager, he thought—greeted him. "You should have been here," he said. "One of the biggest hands I ever saw." Hatcher took the news calmly; he was confident that under his influence there would be other big hands. But he politiely inquired anyway.

"Lot of passes?"

"Wasn't that. Maybe eight or nine, but Christ's own lot of

numbers. Some guy held the dice for forty minutes." He shook his narrow head. "But we didn't get hurt. None of 'em wanted to bet."

"Wish I'd been here."

"I'm glad you weren't," the other smiled. "You know how to bet."

That was right, Hatcher thought as he went away, even happier now with his passage out of the hard sun and into the dark of the gambling room. Here he was recognized, known for what he was; it was like coming home. He stepped to his table of the night before, which was going loudly again, and changed three of his ten hundreds into chips. He began to win.

But he was in a hurry, impatient to reach that crest of risk he now thought his due. Four hundred ahead, he pushed his stacks of green chips over to be changed into black hundreds. One of the bosses shook his head wisely. "No, no," he said. "We can't do that." Hatcher stared. "We can't let you buy the table," the man went on. "If you start with them, all right, but we don't play them unless you do." Hatcher nodded curtly, irritated at discovering this rule. He picked up his chips and stalked down the room to the main cashier.

In the days that followed he was to tell himself many times that that had been the moment, that at that niggling check on his obvious progress he should have quit cheerfully to fly himself and Margaret out with their money. But nothing could stop his ambition.

"Change these," he said to the cashier, reaching into his pocket, "and this. Hundreds." He returned to the table with fifteen black chips in his hand, his change in smaller chips clattering in his jacket pocket. The boss nodded, still wise and now righteous too, as if someone had only begun to behave properly. Hatcher laid two of the pretty chips on the line, and the dice began to skip.

On the first come out they fell seven, and he won. Then the point was eight, and they turned up seven again. He lost. Hit and miss, hit and miss, they turned, aimlessly satisfying their probabilities. But Hatcher was trying to force them or it or whatever it was into some sequence, betting against them and against the chip boss and his rules. He placed all the numbers for a hundred each. On the next roll the shooter sevened out. Then he placed again.

It took only a few minutes. In a few minutes, three green chips were all that was left. He turned, with a furious glance at the boss's impassive face—just doing his job—and walked woodenly away. On his way out to the safety deposit box in the lobby he lost at a blackjack table fifty purposeless dollars in two bets. He forced some delays—an idle conversation with the girl at the desk, a self-conscious reading of the nightclub playbill. But he was steaming, and in less than twenty minutes he was back at the table with another thousand, and in three misses most of it was gone. Then the point was six, and for the first time in his life he bet against the shooter, betting wrong. Two rolls later they came up six. Hatcher walked slowly over to the bar. After one drink of whiskey and two cigarettes, he walked just as slowly out, cursing himself.

Whatever his deficiencies, Hatcher did not want to lose. Some gamblers do, because losing can be as steady as a job, where there are a thousand things to say, and second guesses to be made, and morals to be drawn. The world of the loser is a world of old talk, and for some there is nothing better. Yet even though Hatcher had lost undeliberately, unfortunately, he was tied just as fast and compulsively as anyone to his game. He saw it as a taunting barrier that he had to pass, to get back merely to what he was before he lost, to get even.

He did not taste the fine steak at the restaurant they had both seen in a movie, eating near the very spot, in fact, where a beautiful girl had stabbed someone or been stabbed. He half perceived Margaret's deliberate fun and fought his desire to play again, trying to maintain the easier attraction to the tables he thought he must have felt that morning. But he was not sure he had felt it even then; no more than he really remembered who it was that afternoon who had lost twenty-five hundred dollars in half an hour, who could have done that.

"So it doesn't matter, since you still have over three thousand."

"Right," he said. She wanted him to hold his money. "Sure. Let's not worry about it."

"We are having fun." She was bearing up. She befriended the small boy who brought them water, who was pleased and swaggered. She mocked the people dancing in an ancient style, and she praised the place, the food, and him for thinking of it.

But Hatcher was beyond her model party; he was determined that he should not need it, that all that was necessary was to eat quietly and controlled. For one who is not a gambler, however, such behavior must, of course, appear as sadness, depression, even stupor. Margaret continued, composing the sympathy and happiness and life that he did not want, convincing him that everything was all right when everything, for him, did not matter.

So she went along to the casino. She thought that something was momentarily wrong and could be corrected; she thought her presence might please him, even bring him luck. But she stood stiffly, disliking the game more and more as she saw it take him over. The sun's color had gone from his face, and the trembling of his hands only stopped when he clenched them and struck the leather rail, cursing softly to himself. She saw him squeeze his bets out, hesitate, bet right or wrong, and lose more than he won. There had been ten one-hundred-dollar bills in his pocket when he began, but he was betting in fives and tens, cheaply, waiting for something. The money dribbled away.

Hatcher watched the bland dice with heavy scrutiny, as if they would bear investigation. He was looking for them to turn, to begin that sudden, smooth, rapid course of passes when he would rise with the tide. They obliged and passed. He let the money ride to take advantage of the surely coming crest, and he pressed the winnings with more chips from his coat pocket, and then he lost.

It was like waiting in the surf for a big wave. They said that they came in series, perhaps of three: the third would be the largest, the third third even larger. But where did one begin to count? Hatcher could not begin, though he resolutely bought his chips one hundred at a time and thought about every wager. The dice were rolling, as they may do, pass and pass, miss and miss, and for all his thoughtfulness he lost his third thousand of the day, though it took him until midnight to do it.

Margaret linked his arm then, but he was unyielding, and so she only walked at his side. They did not speak when they reached their room. She did not want to bother him, or to bother herself by seeing how he was. Still she saw too much, all his abrupt and aimless movements. She had to break it up.

"Well," she said, imitating a phrase he had used before their vacation to joke about it, "plenty of action in the Bahamas." At dinner that would have been just right. Now he was anything but in action. He was limp and beaten and trying to stifle his desire to return to the tables before tomorrow.

"Oh," he said, seeing nothing, not the small joke, not the attempt to help him out. "There's action all right." He said that as if the idea were beneath him, and it was beyond him now to see play as play. It seemed an enemy, even a conspiracy of enemies that he had to keep fighting. He was beginning to think that his dependence on the tables was courage.

"Look. If you want to go play some more, why don't you? What does it matter?"

That startled him. "Of course it matters. There's a way of doing it right. I've been betting"—but he could not recall any of the many different, blundering strategies of the day and finished weakly—"too much." He might as well have said too little, or too erratically, or too steadily; he was still looking for the catch that must be there, for the beginning of the mysterious series. Action was not important anymore. He wanted now only to predict and have things come out right. "I've got to control it," he said. "It can be done."

"You can." Margaret thought it had to be simple; he won or

he lost, they came, they went. But Hatcher was stuck fast. He thought her confidence too easy, and it irritated him; she could not know how hard it was.

"God damn it, I don't know if I can. You see that. But I'm going to find out." What was there to find out? What was there to discover in the drone of the croupiers and the pale shaking players and the ranked benches by the pool?

"Well maybe," she breathed, "maybe you could do better alone." Hatcher looked up sharply, but she went on. "Would it help if I went back?" His eyes were hard and alert. Margaret thought it was eagerness, that her proposal appealed to him, and was angry. "There's no reason for me to stay, is there?"

"Of course not. You don't have to go back, for Christ sake. That doesn't make any difference."

"But it's an idea, isn't it?" She was brightly bitter, furious with him for listening to her at all and at the same time hopeful that they both could get out. "You could concentrate."

"No. I'll go with you. What the hell, Margaret. I've won. This is good enough." But she knew it was not, and as he waited for her to answer, she, too, was waiting for him to say it again. It was a decision that, with all the second guesses lying ahead of them, she could not press. Then she lost it. "I'll tell you what," he said, and she shuddered inwardly.

"Look. I know you don't like the place. I know I've been playing stupid. I don't like it either. Suppose we just play it by ear—go along and I'll be careful. And you have the say. The minute you've *really* had it, we go. I mean it. We'll start all over, and do it right." His eyes had become larger, rolling slightly with his excitement, the idea of a fresh start relieving him of all that losing. "Look," he said, and for another hour he talked about his plans, their plans, beginning with a new scheme for the betting the dice and flowering into an idyll of free lives and action.

When he ran down, Margaret whispered, "O. K. But it's up to me?"

"Whatever you decide," he promised, "goes. If I'm not doing

what I said I would, you just stop it." Even then she did not believe it. She suspected that his gambler's reasoning would always find a loophole and that her decision would become too complicated to make. She was tired.

"O.K. Are you going back tonight?"

"Of course not!" He laughed. "Just because I made a few mistakes, you know, doesn't mean—no, tomorrow's soon enough. We have time." He went on talking with her, wheedling, barking, cooing. Soon the rhythms of his speech became hers, the dialogue a game of regular responses. Finally she said that she was tired, and they went to bed.

The bosses, the stickmen, and the dice themselves were not aware, the next day, of any new beginning. Hatcher would win two or three bets, and push and double and bet the numbers, and lose. The betting at the table, at all the tables, was slow, the players quiet. Most of them were temperamentally disinclined to bet much anyway, and so took cheerful refuge in the dice's erratic behavior. The stickman looked around appealing, and a pit boss, up in his little balcony, was driven from his reticence: "Come on folks. They either win or they lose; they pass or they don't. You can bet either way, folks. This is a two-way game."

Hatcher was unaffected by the general air of hopelessness. He concentrated. He told himself that the two hundred he was behind for the day was a lot of money, and he waited for points with long odds before laying down his stack of chips to take them. The dice passed to him. He shot a twenty-five-dollar chip and sevened. He left the fifty there and rolled a five.

"Fifty each, top three." And before he made his five he rolled each of those three members at least twice, the noise at the table growing with each throw, as the people marveled at how it might be done. Twenty minutes later and eight hundred ahead, he quit with his new restraint and went up to Margaret to receive congratulations. He was also checking in, insuring his future freedom, and since with their new agreement there was no pretense at anything else but gambling, after dinner at the hotel Margaret read a paperback mystery, and he went back.

A large, heavy man in a tan suit hailed him from one of the tables as he entered. "How'd you do today?" Without waiting for an answer he continued, "Boy, you should have stayed on. You started something. There was a big run—*big* run—after you left. I made over four thousand."

"Terrific. How you doing now?"

"Son of a bitches turned around and it's gone," he said in a rush. "But we can turn 'em again. You going to shoot?" The last shooter had missed; the stickman pushed the dice, probing, toward them.

"O.K."

"Tremendous, tremendous." The man began scooping chips out of his rack, counting, transferring them to the pass line. "This guy is strong medicine," he explained to the smiling dealer, "strong medicine. Where I get even." The dealer looked to Hatcher and winked, and Hatcher laughed and threw out a nine.

Across the table, a plump young man called for three hundred credit. "What's that name," the boss called down. "Sivler?" The young man nodded solemnly. A harshly pretty and costumed girl stood slightly behind him on his right, looking at the other women around the table. Her man, with eyes staring fixedly, laid one fifty to one hundred against the nine. Hatcher rolled and made it.

"That's throwing it right back at 'em," cried his latest friend. "*Now* we're going." Hatcher nodded and rolled five. Sivler bet against the point again. The tan suit was betting with both hands that Hatcher would make it, and Hatcher himself bet all the numbers, forty each.

"Two ten around."

"Two ten around. A bet, sir." Hatcher rolled a twelve, and then the five.

"Jesus Christ," Sivler said, on the other side.

"Ya-hoo!" cried the new partner. "Dynamite. This boy is dynamite." Hatcher stood there waiting, confident and unsatisfied.

These quick passes that doubled or trebled his money meant little to him; he wanted a run of numbers, and the collecting and collecting, roll after roll.

"Two ten around again." Sivler and his girl friend were looking moodily across at him. Then the man called for three hundred more, and placed a hundred of it on the pass line, with the dice now, with Hatcher, who rolled along in his wishful series, made his points on the fourth try or the seventh, but always took in money, while his companion halloed and cheered and thumped, and at last wandered away with five thousand or so. Across the table Sivler bet cautiously, measured out the chips, and counted them as they came in. Hatcher was not counting; he was working with every roll toward the limit, toward three thousand, five hundred on the table, bet every time.

At one point that evening, with a crowd surrounding him and screaming, he was some eight thousand dollars ahead. The croupiers were laughing, clapping their hands once loudly when they shifted, and the pit bosses climbed up and down, tired and perhaps a little worried. The dealer intoned, for the first time, "Five hundred on the line, yes sir. Five hundred taking odds. Twenty-six twenty-five around. A bet sir." Four was the point. On the third try for it Hatcher sevened. In his flood of luck he thought that was no matter. He bet the limit around again, and the next shooter had to make a six. This time the seven came on the very next roll. But Hatcher could not believe that his fortune, the dice, something, had suddenly and without warning him changed. He bet five hundred on the line.

"Three craps," barked the stickman. "Take the line, pay the don't." Hatcher clucked and bet five hundred again, in admonition. "Nine. Point is nine." He placed five hundred on the odds for the nine, and he brought the seven out. "Seven loser, loser seven. Take line, pay don't. New shooter. Comin out." Not for him. He pushed back from the table, throwing down his three remaining pink chips. For the boys; thank you, sir. He did not feel what had happened, but walked toward the bar still in his dream of winning.

"Hey. You converted me." Hatcher looked at the speaker blankly. It was the man and woman from across the table.

"Whoo," she said.

"You made me a right bettor. How much did you finally get anyway? I win over two thousand."

"Lost eight hundred," Hatcher muttered.

"Lost! Na-aw. You must have been up four or five gees!"

"Seven or eight. I pushed. They turned."

"Jesus," said Sivler. "I get ahead like that, they never see me again."

"Yeah?"

Sivler offered to buy drinks; it was the least he could do, he said, since he had made money on Hatcher's great play. But Hatcher refused, vaguely, and the conversation died. He was already thinking about tomorrow. He had a thousand left. The way he put it to himself was that he had taken his shot tonight, but had not quite got there. His loss was not felt. It had already blurred into another continuum, another illusion of series and progress toward somewhere. As he wandered away, the girl looked meaningfully at her husband.

The next afternoon the dice missed more than they passed, and Hatcher was bled of that final thousand. He was disgusted with them, and with himself for playing when it was not clear that any luck was running. At the poolside, among the other untanned faces of this fraternity of crapshooters, he knew that he should be finished. That should have been it. His gambling money was gone. There was only enough now to pay their bill. Yet he had not mentioned losing or leaving to his wife. What had he lost anyway? The eight hundred he had brought to gamble, another five or six of get-away money. What was that? He had his credit card if things really soured. He was relieved again and boasted to Margaret of the silly bets he had seen other players make.

"Go to it," she said. "I'll write some more letters."

When he cashed his check for two hundred at the hotel desk, the breaking of the rule, the reaching back into their bank account, seemed a paradoxical victory. This money mattered ; now his play would matter too. It was really a clean start this time.

Now Hatcher was grateful for sevens and elevens and quick passes. At first he played the other numbers too, beside his point, but he did it erratically: once on the four, the nine, and then the ten or again the four. He was convinced that the dice were not running, anywhere, and he ignored the shouts from other tables and listened with distrust when croupiers or shooters spoke of big hands that he had not seen. Hopping along this way, winning and losing, he played through the afternoon and evening and into the checking account. At ten o'clock he went out to cash his third check, still queerly confident, sure that this would be it, all he would need. But the night manager shut him off.

"No, no, Mr. Hatcher," the little man in striped trousers said wearily. "We have no connection with the casino, you know. We cash checks for guests merely as a courtesy."

Hatcher was panicked out of any thought of anger, shut out of that magical room where nothing need be permanent, into a world where everything was. He ran up to Margaret and then with her down to the bar. He had four drinks before dinner. Afterward he told her that he had lost three hundred and decided to quit for the night. Then he tried to go to sleep.

Next morning he called his bank, in the presence of the chubby, better-tempered day manager, and established credit with the hotel, a thousand more. In the next two days he returned again and again to his guesswork, a fixture of the casino, there, nibbling, trying to build his stake and always losing a little more of it. On the night before their day of departure, with his last good check cashed, he came up to the dice and rolled four natural sevens in a row, letting his money ride, and with the three hundred odd in pink chips that resulted he plunged sadly—how far he was from the limit—but hopefully into his last chance. He rolled a four, backed up his hundred dollar bet, and placed another hundred on the ten. He made a ten, and then his four. So he extended his range, taking under his growing wings the nine and five, making them too, making them over. He reached for the eight, to encompass the table, but the next roll turned seven. On the next he did not bet. He was a thousand ahead, and he felt his potential. There was plenty of time. He stepped back from the table to survey the room, and he bumped lightly against his waitress.

"I brought you this." She extended to him a short glass full of whiskey. He tasted it; it was bourbon. He had not ordered anything.

"Why, thank you." He reached into his coat pocket for chips to lay on her tray.

"No, no," she said. "You already give me enough." Hatcher smiled at her, at her accent. "I only bring this in my way. I leave early tonight."

Hatcher moved away from the dice table, out into the darkened aisle. He asked her if she were German, and she said no, that she was Swiss, that they spoke German in that part of Switzerland. She went on with her brief autobiography, laughing and shrugging, her face turned upward to him, open.

He looked away from it, around the casino as if from some height, thinking of the game that was waiting for him and this girl below. It seemed that he had it all, that they were all children and she especially. It was all easy. "Would you like me to take you home?" he asked. The waitress said that that would be nice of him, and he said it was nothing at all. "You let me know when you're ready."

When he turned back to the game it had become nothing, too, as if in those moments aside he had inflated beyond it. He played like a man with a million, as if none of it signified a thing. In another few moments he had lost what he had. He threw his last five-dollar chip to the stickman, turned and looked, and was glad when he did not see her. He did not care about that, he thought. He did not care about any of it. He was broke, cleaned out and clean; he had got rid of everything. He walked out quickly.

In the morning Margaret nodded without speaking when he told her he had lost. He supposed she thought he meant their once-defined gambling money, or even all the cash they had, but her thoughts did not matter. Hatcher had begun to realize what being out of money might mean, hanging on his credit card and thinking of all the bills to come, of the one last, small, bad check he would have to cash to get home from the New York airport. He signed for everything at the hotel, and they left their convertible in the airport lot. Its gas tank, against the remembered pleas of the rental agent, was nearly empty.

Chapter 10

Frankie crouched in a corner of his shack and stared at the lightly falling rain as Hatcher drove past him into the lot. When he came up to the change booth, two elegantly dressed Negroes were paying the ticket for their Pontiac.

"That's a dime," Frank said gloomily, but quickly brightened into, "How about double or nothin'?"

The taller black man, in a pale green raincoat that covered a bright suit, nodded wearily. "All right, man."

Frank spun the coin high in the air away from him. "Call it."

"I got heads."

"Heads? You call heads? Hah. I haven't missed one of these in thirty years." The Negroes laughed to each other and bent to look at the coin. It was tails. "Hah!" Frank cried. "See that?" Wisely, the two looked at each other. Frank picked up the dime and held out his hand.

The green raincoat laid a quarter in it. "You owe me fifteen cents, man."

"Right. How about forty or nothin'?" Frankie said, already tossing the quarter up.

"Naw, naw, man," the other said as the coin bounced near him, "I don't flip with you no more." As he spoke, he looked down at the chiming coin lying, heads up, on the asphalt. "Shit," he said, "I would have won."

"Forty or nothin', then?"

"Go ahead, baby," he sighed, "flip it. Heads." The coin spun up again and fell. Heads it was.

"How do you *like* that? First time in thirty years. Huh!" Frank reached the dime over, and stooped for the quarter. The two black men turned slowly and walked swinging and vindicated toward their Pontiac. They were chuckling low-voiced to each other. Frankie winked at Hatcher. "Hey," he called to the swaying backs. "You forget sothin'?" He held up the quarter and cackled at them. "An' don't this belong to you?" He winked at Hatcher again, as the Negroes came back, grinning and embarrassed. Frankie tossed them the quarter.

"Gotta watch that, boys," he laughed, as they made again for their big car. "See that? How I did that?" he asked Hatcher. "They was asleep. I did that just perfick.

"All right, Phil. What the hell do *you* want? Twenty guys put the arm on me today already. My kid comes down with his new car—he needs this month's payment. You know he's gettin' married? You beat that? What a kid I got, uh?" He pushed his rain hat back and stroked his long curl of hair. "And so last week I hadda see my man at the finance, and where does he send the payment book? Home! When Lily saw that, I hadda talk for a half hour."

"What'd you tell her?"

"That I borrowed the money for you! What else!" He continued to stare sternly through the thick lenses, and then broke, slapping Hatcher on the back. "Naw," he sputtered. "Naw, I didn't. I wouldn't do nothin' like that. Still, you was worried though, wasn't you? Listen. How'd you make out down there? Win ten thousand, right?"

"I was ahead good. I pushed it back."

Frank suddenly became understanding, tolerant. "Well," he said. "That *is* rough, them dice. Don't ever think it isn't. You gotta stay away from that shit. You makin' a move today?"

"You?"

"Aw, I dunno. I know I don't work in this"—he gestured up

at the drifting rain—"for them bas-tards. Besides, my tooth—"
With a forefinger he stretched his cheek for Hatcher to look, but
the invitation was declined. "So I might take off for a couple of
races. My brother's drivin'."

"Which one?"

"Domenic! Which one. You think I hang around with them
other *ass* holes?" It was a different one every month. "Soon's I
get relieved," he said, "I meet him at the diner."

"New York, huh?"

"New York!" Frank said, disgusted.

"Well. Better shots."

"Yeah, better shots. What you gonna get on 'em—four to five?
New York. Screw that New York. We go to Canden"—meaning
Camden, Cherry Hill, Garden State Park.

"Are they open now? That's a rough track for me."

"Openin' *day!*" Frankie barked. "Don't worry about it. Plenty
money. I hit the DD right on top, and we start bangin' 'em. Plenty
money." Frank's dispensing with auxiliary verbs was not simply
the sign of imperfect grammar. It was a matter of his choosing
to speak as often as he could in the present tense, so that all his
prospects were always present, and past crises were now, and he
was in action.

"Oh. I see. Opening day. You're sick all right. I see."

"Get off! Din't I show you the tooth?" He tipped his hat the
other way and leered over the glasses. "You comin', Phil?"

"I'm tap city, Frank."

"I can always lend you a half, Phil, you know that."

"Naw, thanks, Frank. I need some cash anyway. Look, I'll
meet you at the diner in half an hour."

"You better be there," Frank warned. Then he chortled and
slapped Hatcher on the back again. "Old Phil," he said. "Philly.
Atta boy, Phil."

Hatcher walked back up the street, toward The Home Finance
Company. He pushed through the heavy glass door, watched his
step on the steps, and was directed to the "second room," a

narrow booth of opaque glass. He settled in with *Life*, but he was a good customer, and was not kept waiting. Mr. McAboy, a very worried, very middle-aged man, gave him a quick nervous smile. "Good to see you again, Professor—Professor Hatcher, isn't it? What can we do for you this time?"

Hatcher explained his needs, a thousand dollars—ah, the full amount, McAboy said—yes, but he did not want to worry his wife about it, and she would not co-sign. That, McAboy said, was not usual. Hatcher agreed. But he had been a good customer, the other said, and Hatcher said that he hoped it would be all right. They were not supposed to. Hatcher hoped they could, and the other went away to call his district supervisor.

In the next booth loomed other presences. He could see little of them through the smoked glass, save that they were black, and many, a family. They were trying to borrow a hundred and twenty dollars more.

"I'm sorry," a girl was saying, "but all your payments last year were late. We can't extend this for any more."

There was a great sigh, and behind the glass a heavy shape reared up. A voice simultaneously high and rich cried, "Come on, then, Cornelius. If they ain't gonna give it to us, they ain't. Come on." Hatcher watched them troop out—a large, heavy black woman, a slender, apologetic, red-eyed brown man, and three small black girls. Then McAboy was back with papers to sign and the money, in old, sweated tens and twenties.

Frankie was already there at the diner, sopping with his toast at the yolks of undercooked eggs. "The finance, huh? Well, that's all right if you pay it back right away. How 'bout sothin' to eat, Phil?"

Hatcher said that he wanted nothing, so Frankie bought him pie and coffee. The short-order man came over.

"Hey, Frankie. Put me in a double? Three and seven?"

"What do you guys think I am?" Frank snorted. "All right, give it to me. I only got about forty of 'em now."

"Thanks, buddy."

"Yeah, yeah." Frank was checking through the scratch sheet to see who the three and seven would be. "Looka them pigs," he said. "Both short prices and not a chance. You know where this goes," he said to Hatcher, stuffing the money away. "Right in my pocket. South River."

"You'd sit on your grandmother's bet."

"Well. Depends on whether they had a shot." Then he stiffened. "Listen, Phil. Don't ever say that. Have I ever cheated you?" Domenic burst through the door and came quickly up.

"*Hey,* Phil," he said, giving his brother a look of disdain. "Comin' down?" They went out and bought another scratch sheet, and drove off in Domenic's tan Plymouth.

Frank was in the back seat, studying; Hatcher was at work in the front. Just as they passed the exit for the Pennsylvania Turnpike, Frank cried, "Guaranteed!" He named the horse in the first race, and said she looked good. But Hatcher was puzzling over a filly named Solarose, who was shipping in from a small track in Maryland where she had won an allowance race.

"What about this one?" he said. "We don't know how good she is—what kind of race that was?"

"Yeah, yeah. She's got a shot."

The favorite in the second race looked, as Frankie said, too good, and Hatcher went on studying—this time over a two year old named Air Gage, who had just been claimed and seemed to be moving up in class, but who had run well in the past against better than he was meeting today. He would be a longshot.

At the track gate Domenic wheeled the Plymouth up to the attendant, handed him a dollar, and then said, "Didn't I give you a fin?" But the man only laughed. All the parking lots were crowded. Ahead of them and to the right there was an empty row that offered a quick exit from the track, but another attendant was waving the cars on past it, shaking his solemn head.

Domenic twisted the wheel and stopped the Plymouth at the head of the empty row. The attendant blew his whistle and started over, and Domenic jumped from the car and threw up the hood, peering into the engine.

"Get that car outa there!" the attendant shouted, still coming. "You can't park there. Get it movin'!"

Domenic and Frank now appeared to be in earnest consultation over the engine, adjusting the distributor cap, removing and replacing the spark-plug wires. The man came up puffing.

"Come on. Come on. Move it. You can't park there. What do you think I waved ya on for?"

"I wish I could," Domenic said. "How do you like this son of a bitch." He turned to his brother. "We're lucky we got here at all in this bastard. Didn't Charlie say it was all right now? I *knew* we shoulda taken your car, even with them tires."

Hatcher had left the car, his face stiff, and retreated across the tramway, where he watched them work it out.

"It's the last time," Frank was saying, "I borrow anything from that son of a bitch." He got back into the car, behind the wheel.

"O.K.," Domenic called, "try it now." He pressed the starter button. "Well, the bitch turns over, but we ain't gettin' no spark."

"Listen," said the attendant, his anger gone, and worried. "You'll have to move it." Other cars were swinging in now, parking alongside them, the drivers indifferent to the attendant's distracted signals. They all looked pointedly at the Plymouth stationed at the head of the row.

"Try it again, Frank," Domenic said. "I wish to hell I could move it," he turned to the man. "What do you think we're tryin' to do? I wish I could move it right to the fuckin' junkyard. Aw," he cried out, throwing down the hood, "that's enough, Frank. How far we gonna go with this. Fuck it. Let the son of a bitch rot there."

"We'll have to tow it away from there," the attendant said, red-faced and bitter. The line of parked cars stretched to the end of the row. Their drivers trotted away to the trams carrying people to the gate; some of them paused, listened for a moment, and laughed.

"Good. Tow the bastard," Frank said. "Save us plenty trouble. *We'll* be rid of it anyway. What can we do?"

"Well. God damn it. I guess it'll have to be all right then." He paused and brightened. "But they might tow it."

"Sure," Frank said. "It's all right for you. Tow it. What. And all these guys too, huh? Yeah. I'll tell you sothin': we couldn't get that *lucky*. It'll be here when we come out." Domenic was already walking away, smiling, toward Hatcher, who was concealed in the crowd awaiting the tram. "And then what?" Frank went on. "All right? Sure. All right for you. Your car works all right, I guess. But how the fuck we gonna get home? All——"

"Hey, Frank!" Domenic cried. "That's enough."

"Yeah," the parking man said, as Frankie turned away. "I guess you did have a rough break, huh? What was it, you think, distributor?"

The odds glittered on the television screens as they entered the grandstand and went up the escalator to the second floor. The horse that Frankie had picked was five to two; Solarose was at thirteen. Hatcher was cautious with his borrowed thousand and set nine fifty aside in his other pocket. In the way of routine he bought four two-dollar daily doubles, linking the favorite and Solarose in the first with the favorite and Air Gage in the second. But as he came away from the window, the odds on Solarose, number eight, had fallen to eight to one. He was interested, but went on down toward the finish line and their seats in the stands. He passed the emptied five- and ten-dollar double sellers, and the horses were at the gate. Then, on the screen in the back corner, number eight dropped to five. Hatcher jumped to the five-dollar window and bought two more doubles on Solarose. They were off before he reached his seat.

"See 'em send it in on that eight horse?" asked Domenic. "Down to three now? That's action."

"I don't play her," Frank growled. She was on the lead, with the favorite on the inside right after her.

"Jesus," Hatcher said. "They'll burn themselves out. We're all dead." But both horses kept on, running as a team. When they turned for the wire the favorite drove through to take a short lead on the inside. Hatcher shrugged in disgust, half-turned to complain to Frankie, and then number eight on the outside came pushing back, coming again, and before the wire the favorite had had enough. Solarose won it by three quarters of a length, but going away. When she trotted back to the winner's circle, the crowd booed because she had been bet down late.

Domenic was bitter. Frankie threw a few ten-dollar double tickets on the floor, and sat glumly while the results were made official, staring at the past performances for the second. Hatcher watched him for a moment and then, abruptly, thrust his two live two-dollar tickets at him. "Here, for Christ sake. Give me four bucks and you'll have something going, stiff."

"Huh! Don't think I won't take 'em! *Thanks,* Phil." Hatcher could not think of a sufficiently acid reply and said nothing more.

The people's choice in the second was Key to Success, one of the horses that Hatcher and Frankie had going for them. When they broke he made a rush for the early lead, bore out at the turn, and had to be pulled up. They were already only half alive. Hatcher was looking for Air Gage, for tan silks, and thought he saw them, close up on the inside, as the horses came around. Then those colors disappeared, and the horses drove down to the wire five abreast spread across the track. Just at the finish a head popped out of the pack—the winner. People were shouting.

"Who was it?" Hatcher cried.

"It was number ten," said a man on his right. "Got it by a head. Didn't you say you had eight and ten?"

"That's me. It was ten? Air Gage?"

"Yeah. Yeah. Maybe even a neck. Ten! Air Gage!"

Hatcher turned to Frank. "I don't wanna hear anything from you."

"Hey, Phil," Domenic laughed. "Got any more o' them free tickets?"

"Phil," Frank said. "You are all right with me."

The daily double of Solarose and Air Gage was three forty-six and change to Frank; eighty fifty plus to Hatcher. He wanted to sit on it for the rest of the day, but in the sixth I'm Smiley looked very good at five to two, and he bet a hundred and finished second. But he got it back when Straight Deal beat Politely, the last time she ever did, fighting it out in the heavy going she liked and winning by half a length. On the way home Domenic craned his head to the back. "How'd you make out, Frank?"

"I win about a hunnert. You?"

"Just seventy-five. But we got the money man with us anyway, right?"

When Hatcher and Frank got out in the middle of town, Hatcher asked, "Did you blow that money from the DD back?"

"Na-a-w. What do *you* think. I come away with over three hunnert. You kiddin'? I don't tell that Domenic nothing."

Margaret was not home when he got there, but after a moment she breezed in, the still drifting rain shining on her. "Look." She held out a small flat jar. "I got us some caviar. To celebrate. Hey. You put in a long day, didn't you? How—"

"Oh, not bad. Better than usual."

When she was pouring drinks in the kitchen, he called, "Listen. We have to talk about something."

"What?" she said, striding toward him with a glass in each hand.

"Well, I was thinking I might play tonight, at Jimmy's. What do you think?"

"Surprise, surprise. Who would have thought different?"

"I know. But after Paradise Island I thought you might have been worried about it."

"Well. How much did we lose down there anyway?"

"Listen. I did go into the checking account, you know. At the end." Her faced changed for an instant. "About four hundred bucks was all," he rushed on, "but I lost more than I said I would." He had got by the only necessary lie now and had begun to confess, his eyes rounding with it. Yet still he was watching his words and her responses.

"You know, I just couldn't handle it. All that money, all that action. It was too much for me."

"Of course." Her blue eyes were leveled on him. "You'd never seen anything like it before, had you? Of course you couldn't."

It should not be so clear, he thought. "But I thought I could. I should have been able to. You know what happened," and he began to tell it, marking the times when he could have, should have quit, the many times that he had changed his mind and tactics, had wanted both the money in his pocket at the finish and the continuing, accelerating process of the play.

"You're doing," Margaret broke in, "what you say you shouldn't do."

"What?" Hatcher was panicked that she meant something about his gambling.

"All this talk about what you did wrong, about the results."

He stopped, and then smiled. "You're right," he said. "But I get one big second guess." He paused again. "Craps is a bad game. I mean it. I say I couldn't handle it, but I don't think anyone can. It's too much, too fast. To make good money you have to go with the dice, be ready to plunge, push. But to take money away, you have to play it close and be an iron man. It's a sucker game, Mag."

Margaret said nothing but nodded, sipping her drink.

"But poker—and I heard about another game today that might be even better. Maggie, I know I can beat these guys. I can work at it. The longer the game goes, you know, the better it is for me. I can wait 'em out. I'll grind 'em. Why not?" He had convinced himself, but even if he had not the speech would have cost him nothing. With more than eighteen hundred dollars in his pocket, he was loose. Work meant only play, and the proposal of some severe and disciplined struggle was merely the prospect of action.

In fact he was not very persuasive. Margaret did not reply because she was thinking of all the sweating faces over the tables and of all the gambling husbands in the world smuggling money for their bets. She did not put him in that class, though she would have had to had she known more. Yet they could not go on losing.

As she was thinking that, Hatcher began to talk about getting their money back. All of it. The figure he had in mind was four thousand dollars. "It isn't that much. This game goes every night." He hunched on the edge of the couch. "It should be easy."

"Easy? Every night? What about school, then?"

"I'm up to here with it. I have to get out. Limping along on ten, then twelve, then fifteen if I'm lucky. For what?"

"It isn't the money, though."

"No. Still. What does a carpenter make, or an electrician or a cop? And why is it my money—mine and stiffs like me—that goes on a plate every two weeks for them to chop up. You know who carries the goddamn country, the tax? Stiffs. Like *me*. Ten to twenty, all of it over the table, and nothing left." She had heard this before.

"I know it's not just that."

"But the money could make it worth it, couldn't it? For good money I wouldn't be asking myself what those kids are doing there. For good money I'd have lunch with all of 'em *twice* a week. For good money I'd even write up the book."

Margaret rose quickly and began pacing in tight circles. "You'd put up with that anyway. Is that what's wrong?"

"No. No, and you know it. It's teaching. I can't give lessons. I didn't know it when I started, but I can't. Once I think something or say something, I can't say it again. And I damn well can't and won't think of something new for every day either. Nobody does that. I just can't go over it time after time after—" He broke off, lapsing into some vision of a single, monstrous and dull lecture that he repeated and repeated. Margaret veered toward the kitchen.

"I'll get us another drink."

"No, no. Not for me. I'm going to play. Will you make some coffee for after?"

"Sure. Coffee is the least I can do for someone who's getting us our money back." For a moment he did not reply, and when she looked around the partition, he was slumped brooding back, staring at the venetian blinds over the bank of three windows. She moved back out of his view and called, "Of course we'll get it back. We always have, haven't we?" She knew the answer to that one.

That was another beginning, and Hatcher, further in debt than ever, though with ready cash in his pocket, was happier than ever for it. After all, he was no longer just trying to get himself even, but had made his chase part of a larger scheme; it would ease his wife's mind and make her happy. And all that he had to do, for that, was what he loved most to do. Only now he could do it more openly and more continually than ever before. He felt it was time to spread out.

In South River, at the Esperance Social Club, there was another, better game. Tiny—the cabdriver, washed-up ballplayer, ex-reporter, and poker player of grim carefulness—had introduced him. Hatcher had won a hundred or so the first night, thought the players easy, and was filled with gratitude.

"Tiny," he had said. "God damn it. If you ever need a favor—"

"Pretty nice, huh, Phil?"

He thought it was, when Charlie from Rahway bet six dollars showing a pair of open queens. "I call," Hatcher said, and turned over the ace high straight he had had since the fifth card.

"Jesus Christ, you *are* tight," Charlie said. "Is *he* tight," he proclaimed around. "No *raise?*"

Hatcher laughed self-consciously. "I thought you had something, Charlie." Then he caught himself. "What?" he cried sharply. "You can't have a full house with those goddamn queens? Was there any on the table?"

"Full house," Charlie chanted back beneath his trim mustache. "Full house! Yeah. I'd like to full house ya." Hatcher laughed some more, and as the nights passed, a sharp reputation stretched before him, long and thin, and he tried to catch up to it. But it was only a simple game, seven-card stud with a six- or an eight-dollar limit. How much could he have done? He merely became more and more careful, as they say, tighter.

When new players came in, they were instructed about him. "That," one would say, pointing, "is who we call the turtle. When he comes out of his shell, watch out. But then he's back in, and you *can not* catch him."

Hatcher liked all of that and later he would turn to Ray who owned the place. "This game is *tight,*" he mocked. "Look at all the granite. Mount Rushmore. I'm the only fuckin' yap." Ray laughed his boy's laugh that jarred curiously with the deep scar that ran down from his forehead across his nose to the other cheek. He thrust his head forward, rounded his eyes, and looked the yokel.

"What, Professor? You mean they're *not* all dummies?"

"Yeah," Willy the dealer said, tipping his head toward Hatcher. "He sits down, plays two hands in three hours, and then he turns around and says"—he drooped his mouth tragically— " 'Boy!' is what he says. 'Is this game *tight!*' "

Hatcher loved this ritual and believed the image of himself that it held. In those weeks he would often begin it himself until all the players, even with their appetite for repeated gestures, were ready for a different joke.

"Come on," they said. "Play cards."

It all made him relatively little money. On some nights, with certain players, the game tightened like a noose, and he could get no action on his bets. A few of the other players, the better ones, who played just as carefully as Hatcher, always took steps to prevent this happening to them. If they were dealt three of a kind, they would check and check, praying for someone else to bet. Or another time they would bluff loudly and obviously, hoping to be exposed, wasting the money so that later, when they had their lock on the hand, they might be called. There were other ways of doing it, too, but not for Hatcher, who thought all such theatrics beneath him.

Still, his style worked while his luck ran, as any style will. He pressed his winners, betting more as he won, and betting the limit, too, on any good hand that might need help, trying to push the others out so that they could not draw to beat him. When what he thought were kings bet, he did not lie in wait with his aces, but raised quickly and, if there was opportunity, reraised, until he and all of them were tired of his voice repeating, "Limit. Limit. Limit." The bets sounded their incantation, a prayer to keep all the cards static, to keep them ranked the way they had been when the hand had begun. That is what the tight player wants. And usually for Hatcher, because of the prayer, or because that, too, is a way the cards may fall, the simple strategy worked. Players dropped out, and the ones remaining in the abbreviated two- or three-man play could draw nothing. Hatcher's bare aces, or whatever high, lonely pair he had begun with, held up. He never considered that that could be lucky, too.

For it did not seem lucky. It was not what he had imagined. Indeed, it did not feel like action at all, but uncomfortably close to the idea he had described to Margaret and himself—dull grinding, hard work. The only gamble in it, he thought, was the largest question: could he keep it up, keep drumming irritatingly away, squeezing money from the game as if playing cards for a living? If the clever players would not bet him, there were the live ones, the rabbits, the fish, always at least one, chasing inside straights and two cards to the flush, and on weekends there were usually three or four of them in the game. And while Hatcher was at this time no better a player than the best of them at the Social Club, he was more tenacious and ruthless than they could ever be. They thought occasionally of jobs, or wives, or health. Hatcher never did; the game was all there was.

The last fish had got up from the table, winning, and all that were left were Rahway Charlie, Al—not Machine-gun Al the sucker, but another one—Willy the dealer, playing to keep the game going, and Hatcher himself. They hated to see the young Greek leave.

"Shit," someone said. *"Four* handed."

"What did Chris win?" Hatcher asked. He was behind eighty dollars and wanted the game to go on.

"Nuthin'," Al said. "A few bucks. He eats like a bird and shits like an elephant." Hatcher threw in his first three cards—six, seven, nine, two clubs—and got up for some coffee. Ray came over, poured some for himself, and spoke from the side of his mouth.

"Might as well pack it in, Phil. I ain't tellin' *you* nuthin'; nobody's gonna get even at *that* picnic." Hatcher knew he was right. In a short-handed game with players like these he risked losing a lot against winning a little. But he only smiled his gratitude for the warning and sat down again, wanting to get even and thinking he could.

Then he had three hands of nice cards, easy winners, and was closer, and on the momentum he bet a pair of queens hard from the beginning and kept betting, and none of the cards that followed helped him, but after the last one he did not hesitate but bet the limit, and Charlie threw away his small two pair and the pot.

Two hands later he began with aces, wired aces and two spades with them. "Four." He bet four more and four again, and his next two cards were spades too, the king and the queen. But the betting had become heavier; Willy and Al raised each other loudly. Hatcher only called. Before the seventh card fell, they had all weakened, and it slid across the table, and for him it was the deuce of diamonds. One pair of aces, four nice spades, and not enough. But when Willy eyed the three open spades and checked,

Hatcher became hopeful again. Then Al grunted and checked too, and he had to try it.

"Eight then!" he cried.

Willy peered at the hole cards cupped in his hand. "So you got the flush," he sneered. "Sittin' on it, wasn't you, son of a bitch?" He turned his cards down as if accomplishing something.

Al jerked his head around to look at him, surprised. "What the hell were you so proud of, then?" he shouted. "*I* certainly can't call him." Both of them felt the emptiness that comes, inevitably, from beginning with good cards and not improving. They had reached for more and had come to think they needed more. The same dull cards they had seen for so long, through so much betting, could not possibly win now. He, Hatcher thought, had known it; he had figured it. Al spun his cards into the pile in front of the dealer, as if glad to be out, and Hatcher took the money.

On the next deal he dropped out early. He counted almost seventy-five dollars in front of him. Milked from the sharks, he thought. He rose. "I got enough," he said, and smiled. "Suckers."

"You're too fuckin' lucky, kid," Al said. "Buyin' that flush."

"Ray," Hatcher called. "Want to let me out?"

"You can't beat him," Willy said. "The best." As Hatcher went out the door and down the stairs, he muttered, "Tell 'em where you got it, Phil."

Hatcher heard Al's low voice again as he reached the street door. "With his cards," it said, "anybody's the best." In the glass of the door he made himself a winning smile. He knew it was more than luck.

For two weeks and more he gambled himself away from Paradise Island, at the poker game every night and the racetrack on his open afternoons. He used the horses as a vacation from what he saw as his evening work. He took every chance he could, on doubles, perfectas, parlays—all kinds of bets he would have avoided at poker—yet his luck held, and he kept winning.

Through those days Margaret's feelings were mixed. That she said nothing was partly from the lack of opportunity, since he was seldom home and hardly awake when he was. For the first few days of it she had even admired him, as if his abstracted comings and goings were the result of some wonderful control, determination, or purpose. He was winning, after all; they were getting their money back. But as always it became too much; he was going too far.

"I hope you know what you're doing." His head jerked sharply up from his dozing on the couch. Apparently the only way to penetrate the atmosphere that surrounded and insulated him was to suggest the possibility of failure.

"*Huh?*"

"Aren't you getting pretty tired? You look tired."

"No. Really." He scrubbed his hands over his face and blinked at her, then swung up from the sofa and sat crouched at the edge of it, hands clasped, forearms on his thighs, head hanging. "I'm just a little sleepy. Not tired. Actually, I'm not that tired. Really."

She knew that somehow he was telling the truth. When he was on his way out to a track or a game, or to pick up the latest *Telegraph* or scratch sheet, he was not tired. He would laugh and gesture quickly and ask her little questions about herself and not listen to the answers but nod and laugh again, always leaning toward the door. What energy or attention he showed her was merely spun off from gambling or the anticipation of it. When a session was over, he fell down from it onto his back, where he was now. Margaret was standing in the middle of the room, girlishly swaying in some pretended lightness, or so that the movement would catch his unfocused eyes. Her hands were clasped behind her, which was the only detail that made it seem to him that she was not looking for some opening.

It may be impossible for another person to understand the gambler, even though she may be close to him enough. But it is certainly impossible to talk to him—to talk to him, that is, about anything other than gambling, and even then the dialogue will die. For he quickly sees that his heat is not yours, that you are not with him. He knows that you do not feel the injustice of being drawn out on the last card or of having a winning horse disqualified. It is easy to see that you do not laugh hard enough at his stories, and even if you do, you will not laugh at the right places because you must guess at rhythms that for him are inevitable and obvious.

As soon as Margaret had seen this, she had stopped finding reasons to be proud of him, but still it had not seemed a problem. All it was, after all, that they were doing, was an experiment with a self-proclaimed and distinct end. It was getting their money back, and it had been agreed upon. She thought—she had to think —that gambling had nothing basically to do with their life. It was separate and temporary, and their life had not changed but merely paused. It was only a question of when it would start again. So, of course, she asked him, "How are we doing?"

"Fine."

"No, I mean how much have we got—back?"

"Oh. I haven't kept close check."

She only looked at him, her mouth tightening. "I mean, not exact. I know we've got at least two thousand."

He nodded shortly, as if confirming some truth. "Pretty good, huh?"

Margaret grinned forcedly back at him. "I'll say."

But a few days later she returned to it, with the immediate excuse that he had told her three times, in three versions, how he had caught the double that day. "Boy," he said, again, "you should have seen the way that Mike's Boy moved on the turn. Christ!"

"Good. We must stand pretty good now."

"What?"

"We must be pretty close to even now." To even, to the end of it.

Hatcher stiffened. "I guess you want the count again, huh? Well it's almost three. That O.K.?"

"No—"

"See, you have to understand one thing about gambling and money, Margaret. Sure, I'm trying to get our money back, a certain amount of money. But I can't count all the time. I have to keep loose, keep playing. I start measuring out the bets, I get tightened up, and we won't get anything."

Margaret sighed from the old leather chair beneath a lampshade shaped like a white paper ball. She looked at him, smiled wanly, shrugged with her hands turned up. Hatcher felt sorry for her. "Oh look," he said. "You see what I mean. It's just that you have to keep *playing.*"

Margaret drew imaginary lines on the floor with one bare foot. "You mean the money doesn't count?"

"*Sure* it counts. You have to count it." He paused, thought a moment, and rushed on, "Just exactly to make sure that you don't have to go back to a life of counting it. You count it to make sure that it really is more than it was before and that you've really left where you were before. And you're not going back to it."

Margaret looked up quickly. "But I thought that that was the whole point," she said. "To get back where we were."

"No, no. I'm not talking about *us.*" But he knew that somehow he was, and lost his drive. "Of course we're going to get back where we used to be."

She swiveled the chair away from him. "You *are* going to stop, aren't you?" she asked toward the wall. "When you get what we had?"

Hatcher barked a loud laugh and fell back into the couch. "*Sure!* You didn't think I was going to keep *this* up, did you?"

Margaret smiled more convincingly to defend herself. "Oh, I guess not."

"I guess not! This is too much. I mean, I'll make a bet now and then—" He could not leave that prospect for long, no matter what he thought he should have done to persuade her. "I mean, there'll be no need to quit altogether. But I'm *cer-*

tainly not going to go on day after day like this. Maybe poker a couple times a week, take a few shots with the horses. That's all. Nothing like this."

"I hope not," she said. She looked at him steadily for a few seconds. "This is a little too much for *me,* you know."

Hatcher rose abruptly and went to her. He bent down and laid an arm across her shoulders. "I know it is. Don't think I don't know it."

She looked up at him, smiled, shook her head quickly as if to dispel her complaint, or his answer to it. He looked at her very earnestly. She did not believe him. "Oh," she laughed like a mother. "Go back to your *Telly!*" He laughed too, and he did.

His pace did not slacken. It did not increase only because it could not. Hatcher had to eat and sleep, and he had to appear at the college twice a week, one morning and one afternoon. But he did not, it appeared, have to make love to her. Still, Margaret was confident about that. That he seemed to avoid any touch or closeness now could not, she thought, be his choice. That feeling, in combination with his obvious physical decline—he had become thin, gray-faced, stupid—made her think of him in terms of illness, obsession, compulsion. His life had become so remote from hers that it was easy and necessary to regard it clinically.

Not that she would have told him he was sick. She did not really want to say that aloud, and she did not think she would have to. She was confident of her bedside manner. "It's kind of primitive, isn't it?" She was sitting on the couch, sidewise, her legs folded under her.

"What is?" His feet were propped on a stool, and the *Morning Telegraph* lay open on his chest. He was waiting for the night's game.

"Gambling. Like the West, the frontier. It gets away from—" She gestured upward, up through the other apartments stacked above them and into the glide paths to Newark Airport.

"That's an idea," he said, looking at the racing form again.

"Well, it's just like it. You do it on your own, set up a little world that doesn't depend on anybody else's complications. You build your own place, by yourself."

"Yeah?"

"Why not? What's wrong with that?"

"Nothing. Except nothing is set up. I don't know how any pioneer felt. But I'm not trying to build anything."

"No, but imagine—"

"You can beat a race," he intoned, "but you can't beat the races."

"I don't understand you."

"It's a thing they say," he yawned and stretched, pleased at himself and at the hint of her irritation. "They think it means that you can't make money playing horses over a time." He paused and savored his control of the talk. "But it doesn't mean that. It means that all you can tell about is what's already finished, the race that's all over, that, sure, you might have beat. But there's always another race. So you never finish and nothing is ever set up or built and you keep going. You see? You can't beat the races because there's always another one." He was satisfied, but Margaret was not completely turned.

"Well, that's what I mean. There's this reaction against anything fixed, this compulsion to——"

"What compulsion?" he asked sharply. "Listen, Maggie. Don't get sucked in by all that horseshit. The goddamn world has had one thought about gambling and that one bad. Every gambler is supposed to be a case. But the fact is only a few of them are, fewer of them than nongamblers, than stiffs." He dropped his paper folded to the floor. "Let's have a goddamn drink."

"Martini. Well what is it, then?"

He called his answer from the kitchen. "You know. I've told you. It's the action. Some want it, and some don't. The ones who don't are afraid of it and call names at the ones who do."

Margaret was annoyed with his smugness. "That isn't what Dostoevsky says."

"Aha!" he cried out in the other room. "I thought so. Dostoevsky! It's between him and the headshrinkers!" He returned with the drinks. "Dostoevsky," he said down to her, "was a sucker. I would have loved to play cards with Dostoevsky."

Margaret laughed despite herself. "All right. All right. But isn't there," her voice softened, "isn't there—action—in anything else?"

"For who? Not real action. Some people go to television shows, or believe what newspapers say, or collect trading stamps and think they're getting a good deal, or stand in line waiting for a towel sale." He rested that case for a moment.

"But they don't gamble," Margaret said.

"They don't, huh? Well, what about the lotteries, the numbers, *and* horses? I'd bet that seven guys out of ten that work in this town bet something every day."

"Oh, all your friends, they——"

"*Not* my friends. What about bingo, raffles, sweepstakes?" He thought for a second, then sneered, "Gas station games. They *all* want action, but they're afraid to try for real action. They want something for nothing, and so they get cheated, robbed blind." He lowered his voice. "The difference between them and me," he said, "is that they have no chance of winning. What they get isn't action at all."

"Our friends don't go for all that."

"What friends? They do too. Don't you count the market? I've heard stories about the way people handle their money in the stock market that would curdle your blood. And it's all inside stuff, besides; the ordinary guy doesn't have a chance.

"Listen, Maggie," he declared at her. "Just because you don't hear about it doesn't mean it isn't going on. But if people don't win, they don't talk it up. Everybody gambles except the ones who are scared to death of it. Oh yeah, and the ones who don't have to, who have made so much stealing they don't have to."

"If that were true," Margaret said, "gambling would have been legal a long time ago. People must not want it."

"Come on, people don't want it! The only people who don't

want it are the mobs, and they're the ones who keep it illegal. That's where the leverage and the pressure against it comes from. Of course they don't want it. Half the bread in their mouths would be gone. But you wait," he held up his hand. "It'll be legal, all right. It'll have to be. There's nothing else for people to do.

"They have to do it." Now it was as if he were talking to himself. "They're stuck in a job, and maybe they don't exactly know that they're being robbed, but they have this dull itch that something is wrong. They're locked in. They pay the taxes and see the money go up in smoke. They make payments to a Christmas Club to put some away, and they get robbed on the interest there. They get sucked in by credit that never should have been offered—that's what should be illegal—for stuff the thieves tell them they ought to have. They're dead, and they know they're dead. Sure they gamble. Who wouldn't?"

Hatcher was caught up in his sermon, and his wife watched him with admiration and distrust. "What are you talking about?"

"I'm talking," he pointed a finger, "about time. Time payments, credit." For him the very air seemed filled with required patterns demanding step after dreary step. His heart went out to America, and he stared into his gin. Then abruptly he looked up and brightened.

"Where are those big scissors?"

She refused to ask him what he was doing. "In the desk drawer, I think."

He moved quickly around the room, holding up the scissors like a prize or a sign, together with some envelopes and one of the marking pens he used at the track. Margaret watched, annoyed and amused, as he sat down again, opened his wallet, and removed his four credit cards. He referred to them then as he addressed the envelopes in large block letters. He took up the embossed plastic cards, one by one, and cut them into small pieces, funneling the pieces into the appropriate envelope. He swore triumphantly as he did it and licked the flaps.

"There. We don't go this way any more. Not any more. Strictly cash." He threw the envelopes onto an end table, rose, and took her glass to the kitchen. "Furthermore," he raised his voice, "I'm not paying them whatever they've got coming, either."

Margaret laughed at his back as the ice cubes clattered. "Windmills," she said.

But she did not pursue him any further then, and for the time gave him the field. She could still be overtaken by his energy and act a partner. This sympathy of hers, this willingness to be impressed, was rather a strength than any weakness.

Hatcher no longer knew that. At times between games he was even saddened, for her existence in their apartment only emphasized her distance from his real life. There was a divide to be crossed to reach her, and he did not have the energy, perhaps not the desire. He could only think of her through some over-deliberate mental adjustment, as of a man talking to a child. A second child, for his game was first in his imagination. He wanted her there, all right, at home to listen to his stories and appreciate his winning, but that was not crucial. So when he was not performing for her, in some diversion, he was merely sorry for her.

Margaret was, perhaps, at last too confident. She could not see how he could fail to notice the sameness of his life, a sameness that the confusion of his explanations of it all did nothing to lighten. Still she thought she could wait it out while he filled his time with her with little stories from the tables or the tracks.

He had been standing, he told her, in the ten-dollar perfecta line at Garden, his sixty-dollar allowance for the last race of that day in hand, waiting for his tickets. There had been a light touch on his sleeve, and he turned to a stocky, apologetic man, with a sweat-shined face.

"Hey, buddy." The man's eyes were dark with embarrassment.
"Yeah?"

"You—uh." In his hand he held a gold-colored watch, which he raised for Hatcher's eyes. The horses were almost at the gate. "Look," he said. "Do you want to buy this watch? It's a good watch. Not junk. What do you think? Twenty?"

Hatcher was sorry for him. "No," he said carefully. "No. I don't need a watch. Sorry."

"No, no!" cried the man. "Christ. You don't want it, you don't want it. It's a good watch." He turned away and walked rapidly off, hunching his shoulders as he made for the escalator to the ground floor. He had not offered the watch to anyone else.

"Oh," Margaret said. "What was he doing trying to sell his watch?"

"He was out of action."

"Yes." But she did not see why that story seemed so important to him—that one, and others.

"They're called 'stoopers,' " he said. "You see them walking around, head down, just after a race. And if there was a foul claim or a disqualification, they're everywhere. They take a few steps, and bend down, and come up with a ticket, and read it. Then they throw it away. Even when they're not working, you can tell them." He paused for the drama. "Their knuckles are all black," he said, "from the floor."

"That's awful."

"Not so awful. Looking for live tickets that somebody threw down by mistake. There are a lot of them. There's one old guy," he said in reflection, "always in a gray plaid suit. He wears a hat with the brim pushed up along one side."

"Ah?"

"He has a cane. Dapper. But if you watch him, and he doesn't see you watching, he stabs the cane at the ticket on the floor. It has something—some kind of gum, I guess—on the end. And then he'll snatch the ticket off, like he was disgusted with the litter or something. As he lets it fall, he looks at it."

"No!"

"Yes. Or he'll just flip a ticket over with the cane end and look down at it quick. He doesn't look at all the ones he sees. Just ten-dollar tickets and up."

For Margaret they were only sad stories revealing unnecessarily the sordidness of his own world. It never occurred to him to explain their special meaning, and perhaps he was not explicitly conscious of it. For every loud or hysterical big winner running through the crowd squeezing a ticket on the largest double in the track's history, or for every dark-suit who sat high in the clubhouse and sent hangers-on to make his bets, there were hundreds, thousands of stoopers, and auctioneers, who would never have thought of selling their watches, until that race on that day, when they make their awkward and futile approach. Any gambler, like Hatcher, is surrounded by ex-gamblers, and he shudders to see them. No bum is only a bum to him, but a possible future incarnation. The image of being out of action for good is always before him, and any stop or respite, no matter how temporary, seems an intimation, a preview of the dead end, whose breathing representation is liable at any time to touch his elbow: "Hey, buddy—" The gambler runs to the windows and makes another bet.

Chapter 12

The Kentucky Derby came and went, and when Hatcher had the winner, May seemed to begin as he wanted, and he did not notice his luck changing. Yet gradually his winnings on what should have been good nights, where his cards seemed good and the players were bad enough, counted no longer in hundreds but in tens. Hatcher shook his head and clucked to himself that he was not concentrating. Just as gradually, too, bad nights became worse. He lost fifty instead of twenty, and then a hundred. At times then he felt grateful to break even, which before had seemed the worst failure of all: coming out as he had gone in.

The nights also became longer; he depended on playing until the sun shined. The other players, who had once muttered, "Hit and run artist" at his receding back, now slapped him on it, and knew that they could count on him until the game dissolved. So if he did not see his change of luck immediately, they did, and the good players were no longer wary of him, and the bad ones saw him as a brother.

Night after night the game at South River was good. They were there: Chris and George the happy-go-lucky Greeks, the kid Frank, Machine-gun Al, who had once held up a candy store with a Thompson and played poker with as much sense, Shaky John —they were all there. But Hatcher could not land any of them and was no longer even sure who it was that was hooked. Aces over queens after four cards, pressed hard as usual, lost to a small straight. Three kings—the first three cards kings and Hatcher checking and counting the pot all along—did not improve themselves and lost, too, to a full house made on the last card, three threes and two fives. Hand after hand he watched it happening as the live ones went broke, cleaned out by others he thought just as soft, and rose immune to him. Frank won sixty dollars and reeled away from the table, eyes narrowed to disguise his astonishment. Chris quit a winner for the first time in weeks, piping what he called his own change of luck. The tighter players shook their heads, but played on. After all, Hatcher would think, they still had him.

For a while, too, his cards were so bad that he could only turn them down, light another cigarette, and wait for the next hand. So that it might take him all night to ante and dribble away sixty, eighty, a hundred dollars. He could see it as a temporary streak then, and he kept waiting. Sooner or later the cards would change. Yet when they did, he was sorry and wished again for hands so poor that he could not have played them. Instead he was dealt just enough, forced, as they say, to play and to lose. In one night he was dealt three aces on four occasions; he lost with them each time. Straights, flushes, full houses would not hold up for him. After each separate and infuriating disaster he pushed away from the table, as if it or he were contaminated, to drink coffee, watch television for a few straining moments, or skim a girlie magazine from the club library. His reputation changed quickly enough. He became known as the man anyone could beat.

Any card player knows that a night at his game is a fantastic network of indescribable, trivial contingencies. The high moments of decision and drama are, in numerical proportion, nothing to all the tiny dependencies of one card on another from which they result. No one thinks of this when he is winning. But those who lose suddenly become sharply conscious in their selective way of the infinitesimal, uncounted chances, for in them lies the cause. If on the third hand of the hour someone stays for just one more card, or two hands later the dealer forgets and shuffles four times instead of three, or if he *had* shuffled four times, or if a player had not skipped a hand to have coffee—so the search for the pattern to it goes. The losers try constantly to transform the endless series of mechanical accidents. They accuse those ahead of them of playing carelessly, those behind of raising without cause. They call out loudly to Willy or Dave or Jap to mix them up a little, or not to shuffle the spots off. They strain to make their fortune personal.

A player in the hole, like Hatcher, aware of how many opportunities for change there are, will try anything to bring about those changes that seem, that should be, important. He calls for a new deck repeatedly. He switches seats a half dozen times in two hours, only to find each new position taking on the characteristics of its predecessor, and the old seat suddenly coming alive. He deliberately stays out of a hand entirely, even two if he has the will. And he becomes more and more outraged to find that from these changes nothing changes. The cards run on, monotonously, hours on end away from him, then days, and weeks. He swears, pounds the felt in front of him, spins the cards hard into the pile in front of the dealer. How, he cries, can it happen? How is it possible? The others cluck in artificial sympathy at his bad luck. Most of them do not remember what it is, do not remember the infuriating absurdity of random minor motions working always to regular result, where thousands and thousands of small opportunities brought only, again and again, losers to the loser.

When the hand began, Hatcher looked at a pair of aces, one up and one down. He narrowed his eyes at the cards; they seemed again only the tools of the other players to make him lose more. Behind him at the white-topped, bright bar sat three or four who had gone broke and whose credit was no good. Beyond, in the far corner of the room, an old Greek, tapped out, stood inches away from the television set and squinted down into its flicker, both suspicious and charmed. He fingered behind his back a fat string of pink beads. Hatcher swung back to his cards feeling surrounded by black cats.

When three more cards had been dealt, the dealer droning as they fell, he still had only the aces alone: ace, ace, three, four, five, ten. He had expected nothing else. "Four," said Red, and Shaky John raised. Hatcher doubted if even aces with another pair would be enough to win, and he had no other pair. He called the bet as if in a trance and cursed himself as the man to his left shook his shiny black hair and raised again. Still he chased the last card and called, and when the last card came it was the deuce of clubs, the lowest card in the deck. It took that, he thought, to help him.

There was only one raise after that, and Hatcher only called it, gun-shy. "Small straight," he said.

"Right in the fuckin' belly," said the black-haired man.

"*Fifty*-six dollars," said Willy, taking the house cut.

"Yeah," Hatcher rasped, feeling guilty, stupid, and lucky. "In the belly. Don't it count?" He took the money and laid it with his little remainder on the worn green felt in front of him, playing table stakes, for what he had.

On the next hand he said to himself that his luck had broken. The first three were the seven, eight, and nine of hearts, and he called a dollar automatically and, just as automatically, was dealt the ten of hearts. There was a bet and a raise, and then, for him, the heart queen. The qualifications of his hand sang in his mind: "All hearts, heart flush, open-end straight flush, all hearts—"

The man on his right, in a pale gray suit, a poor player and drunk besides, bet as usual and broke him from his song. "Limit." Hatcher raised.

Two others called and the bet came around and the other raised again. Aces up, Hatcher thought, the dummy. But he did not want to lose the other players and their money. He called quietly and saw Tony watching him over his *Telegraph* from the rummy table, smiling knowingly as at some shared secret. Hatcher averted his eyes to his money, smiling himself. He had them this time.

His next card was another heart, though not the six or the jack, but what did he need a straight flush for? The black-haired man bet. The drunken fish raised. "I raise," Hatcher said.

"Ya wanna knock me out, ah, bastard! Well, ya did it! Fuck ya! I hope you bote lose!"

"Raise," said the other.

"Raise," said Hatcher. The other laughed scornfully, and called.

When the last card came down it was the queen of spades, but Hatcher did not bother to look at it, only holding it in his hand as if he had. His friend scowled at his upcards, the pair of open sevens and the ace. Hatcher was sure his first three cards had not been aces, and there was apparently only one more ace left undealt.

"Bet."

"Raise."

"*I* raise!" cried the man in the light gray suit.

"You save money," Hatcher said. "I'm all in for four and a half." He pushed the rest of his money into the pot, swearing at himself again that he had not borrowed more before the hand.

"O.K., kid. Save money, huh? I got aces full."

Hatcher's head buzzed. He did not believe it, leaning abruptly forward to scan the other's hole cards in order: ace, six, ace—and the ace on the table, and the two sevens. He smiled and was close to tears of rage. "Motherfucker. Last card Louie."

"That's right, kid," said the other reaching. "Don't it count?"

"Why beat your brains out, Phil?" Frankie said the next afternoon. "Take a break, for Christ sake."

"Break, shit, Frank," Hatcher said. "How'm I gonna take a break? I got to make a goddamn winner."

"Well, I hate to see you go down to that joint Ruggieri opened up. Those guys might be too much for ya."

"You mean they move?"

"Ain't *that*. That game is legit all right—but it's *iron*. They play too tight. But—"

Hatcher went there, and to the Italian-American Club, to the Elks, to the VFW. He went everywhere and lost.

"Phil?" Margaret whispered. "Why don't you take some time off?"

But he whirled on her as on anyone, full of his complaint. "From what? From losing?"

Her eyes hardened, filmed over. "Yes," she said. "From losing."

"Christ, that doesn't make any sense. Quit when I'm losing! What's the goddamn point of *that*? Quit and what chance have I got?"

"You made some back, didn't you?"

"That's nothing to do with it." He could not tell her that most of that had gone. "Sure, sure. But what's the point in taking myself out of action now. Listen—tell you what." She waited. "What I need is a change of luck. Tomorrow's Saturday—and opening day at Monmouth. You come down with me."

"Oh," she shrugged, her voice falling. "Oh, I don't know."

"Come *on!*" he barked, suddenly convinced that this was a solution. "Like before. We'll get a table up on the turn, out on the grass, and have a good time and drink gin and tonics and make a few bets. Be the best thing for both of us. Get you out of the place—loosen me up. What do you say?"

What could she have said, but yes? But though the next day was hot and dry, though there were people sitting out at the shaded tables on the very green grass drinking gin and tonic, Philip and Margaret were not among them. He had decided that he could not follow the odds' changing closely enough out there or see how they ran in the stretch. So at first they got seats on the second floor of the grandstand well down from the wire—for

136

the first five losers. Then he tired of the seats and of the dead tickets littering the floor beneath them and of the tension in her face when he came back with another handful before each race was off.

So they ended standing down on the first floor, backed in under the stands away from the track and the crowd and the horses. It was the eighth race, and he had thirty dollars left. Margaret was tired, but he had a horse.

"Carr Bairn?" she asked.

"Right. Carr Bairn." It was the horse's first start of the year in America, but he had been here before. "See those races at Woodbine? I know some of those horses, and they're not bad. See this one? Shit he's one of the best sprinters up there. And look at his workout. He's got to beat these pigs. He's dropping way down."

He went and bet this thirty dollars, and in the four minutes remaining before post time, Carr Bairn dropped from seven to one to even money. "God damn it," Hatcher complained, "look at the goddamn bottom drop out." But at least, he thought, the horse was alive.

From the number-two post Carr Bairn broke very slowly, and the boy slapped him hard with the whip, sending him up quickly along the rail and into the lead. Hatcher watched through his glasses as the jockey seemed to try to ease the horse on the turn, to give him a breather, but he had been going too strongly for that. With a sixteenth of a mile to go in the stretch he shortened stride abruptly, twitching his tail, and all the other horses came up on him.

It was all Hatcher could do not to hurl his binoculars to the ground. "God damn it!" he shouted. "Thieves!" He flung his *Telegraph* away, narrowly missing a large Negro who looked at him stonily. Margaret looked away from him out over the crowd. "All right," he said roughly. "We can go now. You get your wish."

She looked at him surprised, then shrugged. He turned from

her toward the exit, and she followed. "Bad start? Bad luck?"

"Yeah," he sneered. "Bad *luck,* yeah." It was worse than bad. Carr Bairn was to win five of his next six starts, and a year later he was holding his own with the best turf horses in the country, going a mile and over all on the lead.

Margaret caught him up as he reached the gate. "Bad luck," he was muttering, kicking at a public handicapper's card, Jack's Little Green Card—Jack, Better Known As Chas. Busey, Who Never Misrepresents. "God damn it, that was a boat race if I ever saw one. That horse never broke that bad in his life."

"Maybe there was something wrong with him—or something happened."

"Something happened all right. Christ sake, don't be as big a sucker as the rest of these sheep." They were out in the bus-parking lot now, and some of the engines were turning to power the air conditioning for the drivers and riders who had already lost what they had. Orange dust rose from the strip of clay beyond the railroad tracks, where the special trains came in. Mutuel tickets, yellow with varicolored borders, spotted the asphalt.

"I don't understand," she said, her reasonableness making him more angry. "If the races are fixed, why play them?"

Without word or gesture Hatcher stopped walking; the corners of his mouth twisted. As if in some paralysis at that question he merely looked at her, at the back of her head and neck, and she, perhaps unaware of the power of her question, walked on for three steps. As she noticed he was not beside her, she turned; an old man, in a heavy gray overcoat in that heat, shuffled by them toward the race-track gate, free admission, and the ninth race.

"Hey, buddy. Have your program?" He paused with his hand out for a few long seconds. When Hatcher did not look at him, he shrugged as if he had expected nothing more and walked on.

"That's it," he said to her. "You just don't get it, do you? You just don't get it."

But Margaret only watched him, palms up three steps away in a pose of questioning. "No. What is there to get? I don't understand *you,* Phil. You always say that people saying the races are fixed are only crying because they lost. Or that if some are fixed, a good player can guess at which ones they'll be. But if you can't do that, it—it doesn't make any sense to play them. It's just what you said."

He was furious at her throwing his own old arguments around him—arguments perhaps true enough at a time, but mounted for the moment and serving chiefly to keep him in action. He was out of money now and out of words, and she was taking advantage of him. "You really turned out to be a result player after all, didn't you?" Two loud men passed by them, shouting at each other. One was jabbing his finger over and over at a place in his folded *Telegraph.*

"No. Look, Phil. What is it? Is it the only game in town, or what? Or did you say that just because you were mad for a minute? Just tell me what you're doing, that's all."

Hatcher was ashamed. It probably had been bad racing luck; he should not have screamed *fix* with the rest of the small-time Charlies anyway, even if there had been one. He thought that she knew this, but was using it to get him to stop playing horses, or to force him into an even worse corner.

"That's right. You're a front-runner, too. It's not gambling you don't like; it's *losing*— a few bad breaks and you cut right back on everything; you want to quit. Well, you can go ahead. But *I'm* not quitting."

Margaret's hands were clenched now at her sides, and she nodded her head slowly and savagely. "You'd say that to *me,*" she said. "To *me,* after all——"

"What," he crowed. "After all you've put up with? All you've taken? Hah! You were all right, don't worry! When I was winning!"

As he shouted at her, one of the parked buses had swung out of line, anticipating the return of its tired passengers. Its driver, who had bet his last six dollars on a horse that had not tried, was the more grimly efficient. He was not about to back and wheel around the two figures in his way and blew his horn loudly. Through the great square windshield the woman started at the sound. The man turned, jaw jutting. The driver could see that he was furious and smiled to himself while he tried to look business-like. The man's lips moved deliberately and slowly, so that they could be read: "Son—of—a—*bitch.*"

Then the bus driver grinned outright and shaped some words with his own mouth: "Fuck—you!" He nodded vigorously and worked his mouth again through his windshield: "Fuck—*you!*" The man outside turned deliberately, moving at the front of the bus, and the driver grinned again and shifted gears and eased the heavy, blank front of it toward him. The woman stepped quickly forward and around him, her face worried. She held up her hand at the driver, and he stopped. Then, with her back to the halted bus, her head tilted to the side, she spoke rapidly. She put her hand on the man's arm, and he jerked himself away from it, turning as he did toward the main parking lot. A man who had been sleeping in one of the forward seats of the bus had awakened and watched the woman catch up to the man who looked and walked rigidly ahead.

"What the hell was that all about?"

"Just some asshole," the happy driver said. "Some sore loser. But the broad wasn't bad."

"She ain't, is she?" said the other, settling back into his seat with tomorrow's entries.

Hatcher and his wife were silent in their car as they passed through Oceanport, then by Fort Monmouth with its scattered, aimless figures in olive drab. As they approached their turn across the railroad tracks in the town called Little Silver, Hatcher saw the usual trooper directing the traffic, rotating his arm and hand casually below his belt. He shifted and speeded, signaling for his turn, and the policeman suddenly raised his hand, palm out. Hatcher braked hard and swore. Through the windshield he made a series of abrupt and mysterious gestures at the trooper— left, right, up, down. The tightly uniformed man glared from twenty feet away. "You just sit there for a while," he called.

Hatcher heard him all right. Still he leaned out the window. "What?"

With a grand wave at another line of cars, the trooper stalked over. "Just sit there for a while," he repeated. "Didn't you see my signal?"

"Yeah, I saw a signal, but it was goddamn hard to make it out. How do I know what you're doing?"

The policeman stared hard, as if considering, but then said again, "Just sit there for a while, then."

"Just as long as *you* want," Hatcher said. "I've got all night."

"O.K., *mister.*"

They sat, and the traffic piled up behind them, all waiting for the left turn on County 13, and when he decided they had all suffered enough, the director of traffic jabbed his finger, first at them and then up their road. Hatcher waved at him in mock gratitude as they passed.

Margaret groaned wearily. "I don't see why—" she began, but he looked at her quickly, nodding quickly as if he expected it, and she turned away to stare through her window. They were in the horse country now and saw the signs. High, clean, white board fences bounded the green fields and were broken occasionally by a high hedge with the house rearing richly behind it, or by an open expanse of lawn greener than the fields with its house low and spreading at the back.

On some of the fences the post-tops were painted light blue, yellow, dark blue, perhaps the racing colors of the farm. The fields and fences, the houses, the colors, the lettered signs naming the farms and the horses at stud—all of it seemed the mark of a hold on life both graceful and certain. Hatcher passed through this country often, though it was a few miles out of his way to the track, and felt, too, what any horseplayer, no matter how broke or far down, will feel—his tie with some exclusive world. It is not the money or the imagined women or even all that undoubted land that attracts them, but the horses, owning horses with names—Accordant, Scotch Bull, Rasper II—with names and solid histories and styles of running that one might predict even from the names. Any bettor may feel momentarily that he owns the horse that has won for him and certainly will feel possession if the horse wins for him more than once. Sooner or later every one of them gets from his bets what he wants from the horse country itself, and becomes for a short time the king of some kingdom, his own self-made aristocrat, without the need of great good luck or prohibitive cost or thieving or even legislation.

But when Margaret pointed at some new foals standing stupid and pretty near a fence, Hatcher only grunted and stared at his road, as if to punish her by not looking at them. He was full of his bad racing luck, of horses that would not win, of the schemes of trainers and riders, of all the world he could not penetrate. But he knew, too, that he wanted to go on, chasing it. So he did not know what to say to his wife to justify his feelings, and he pretended she was severer than she was, judging him like all the wives of all the gamblers. He sat grim and face front, and Margaret's mouth-corners tightened while she looked fixedly away from him, and after a while they were through the horse country and past the intersection at Colt's Neck and back on the gray highways again. Perhaps because they did not speak, or because they had lost, it seemed a long way from those pastures in Monmouth County to the asphalt lot of their apartment building.

When they got through their door, Margaret kept walking, out into the center of the living room, and then stood with her back to him. He closed the door, and she turned. "What are we going to do?"

"What do you mean?"

"I mean what are we going to do? We're both having a miserable time. *All* you do is gamble; *all* I do is sit here waiting—waiting—"

"I'm sorry about what I said, Margaret. I shouldn't have dragged you into it. I was just hot about that horse—"

At that she bristled. "How could you—after—"

Hatcher sat down on the couch and stared at the floor. "I know. You've been good about it. I shouldn't have said that."

"I don't want to be good about it. What you said isn't even the point. The point is you would have said anything. You're pretty far gone, Philip."

Hatcher smiled bitterly, still to the floor. "You think so?"

"Don't you?"

He fell back, slumping down into the cushions. "Oh, sure, I guess so."

"You *know* you are. Now what are we going to do?"

He was stricken with the question. If nothing else had to do with gambling, why should gambling be joined with everything outside it? He did know what he could do about her, about their marriage, first because he did not think he should have to do anything. What had they to do with it?

The posed alternative was an outrage. One or the other must stop, she was saying, gambling—or everything else. But beneath his indignation lay the real motive for his silence. He was frightened, more frightened than ever, though he had been afraid ever since Paradise Island—afraid that he would be required to stop. It frightened him most because he did not think he could do it. The return to life, to the blank days themselves, seemed impossible. All the small acts and thoughts of an ordinary day, that fill and may seem to vary an ordinary life, were no longer available to him. A second cup of coffee, a movie, a new tie, papers to grade, conversations—all were the same, with no separate existence for him at all. All flowed together into a sea of what they were not; they were not the racing form waiting at the stands, nor three bookmakers' telephone numbers in his wallet, nor the sound of a new deck being shuffled and dealt. They were not action.

As he sat there on the couch and Margaret stood apparently waiting for an answer, he could only continue looking at the floor and shake his head. He could see no way out of the conversation. He could not do what he could not do.

Margaret came over then and, standing by, laid a narrow hand on the back of his neck. "Come on," she said. "You started it, you can stop it."

"Yeah," he said downward, grieving the words. "Yeah, I'm about broke anyway." He looked up at her then. "Started it? I never started it."

Chapter 13

There had not been a remembered beginning. The day that Hatcher sometimes thought of as his first gamble was not it. It was merely his first day alone at the races, when the money in his pocket and the risking of it were his alone. The ten dollars that he bet that day on the daily double was fabulous, especially since he was only guessing, he thought, at the first race. Then that horse had won in a photograph—her name was Dear Mother—and he had been so sure of Leap Year Maid in the second that he had gone upstairs to the bar to watch on television. He had a beer and a green cigar that he did not want except as the signs of something: not of the big time or the insider's life, but of another sort of success—of judgment, of the fact that Leap Year Maid was never headed and won by six lengths as the beer and the green cigar said she would. He remembered, too, that he had been seventeen at the time and had got no other winners that day.

But it would have been no more true to call that day the first time than to assign corresponding importance to the nickel black-jack games when he was twelve, or to the poker in the high-school parking lot a year or two later, or to the college crap games for fantastic stakes that were never paid. Because gambling was natural. Hatcher assumed it as he assumed that money need not even be involved, any more than cards or horses or any other furnishings.

It was the childhood teetering high on a pile of waste lumber in the yard of a factory, feeling the almost liquid pieces slide beneath his feet as he and the rest of them scrambled. They searched for anything and played any game that would fit, all to justify their precarious crucial movement. In the same way, like any child he had climbed trees, or burst with his friends through the thick hedge that surrounded the race track—Hialeah, where they never saw a horse or a pari-mutuel ticket nor wanted to. What they wanted was to cheat the pay telescopes of their dimes.

On the way to school he had stopped ritually at a candy store to steal a handful of banana taffy blocks. At times, too, he did not get that far, but retired all day beneath the bridge over the canal to fish for bream. He made doughball bait out of one sandwich and ate the other, and he threw the fish back. For one thing the school was too slow. The teachers said he was deficient in self-control, consideration for others, citizenship.

Less than a year later he and his friends had nearly filled an old construction shack with their stolen goods: with fishing lures they had to cut from their deep pockets, with stacks and rows of bright useless quantities of model airplane lacquer, with packages of small silver confection BBs—cake decorations. They made no use of these things, though they took pleasure in the knowledge that they were there, stored away. Nor was it the practical chance of being caught as they stole that thrilled them. Rather it was the simple breaking of the rule, the freedom of the moment of its breaking. Then, as his friends were, he was at last caught. The first time was at the hands of an understanding Hialeah store owner who apparently had been a boy himself and only made him empty his pockets, and so was held in contempt from then on. But the second time was in a downtown Miami department store. Through the tears that the decrepit floor manager appeared to expect he learned his lesson: that these rules were not worth breaking. Luckily, about that time, the family moved.

They had always moved. His grandfather's arrival in America as a small boy only initiated the series. He, the grandfather, was an amateur wrestler, and he ran five miles a day and ate white onions raw like apples because he thought, perhaps by some analogy of color or texture, that they were good for the lungs. At fourteen he was foreman in a shopful of men, some of them three times his age. Yet, by the time of Hatcher's own boyhood he had trickled his strength away into the kinds of inventions one could manufacture in a machine shop with a drill press and a lathe, cutting torches and files and ball peen hammers. There was finally some irony in that. Not in the inventing, for that in its confident dissatisfaction with established forms was—like coming to America itself—obviously gambling. The joke and the bitterness lay in the fact that the last, most unsuccessful and costly gadget the grandfather made, before his three sons had to leave him to make their own money to live on, was an automatic governor for cars and trucks which, when the speed rose above some limit, simply turned the offending engine off. An automatic governor it would have been, Hatcher thought when he was a graduate student, an external, mechanical, and, so, reliable conscience—as if the old man had seen beyond the sudden stroke that killed him, a few years after he had given up inventing, and sought to provide his descendants with a lesson.

That lesson, if it was recognized, did not take. Hatcher's father, too, made a life of trying to pass limits, not of machines this time, but of money and whatever lines depended on it. With an un- relieved and square-eyed intensity he fastened on it as upon a sign from his past, the only recognizable sign of achievement and power. He went from machinist to foreman to salesman to sales manager, in a process as relentlessly allotropic as the money itself. Every year the family had a little more of it; every two or three their clothes, their habits of eating, their style of life changed; and almost as often they moved.

The moving, a simple relocating in space perhaps, was impor- tant, and probably most important, he was to think later, because it placed him, after he had been caught stealing, so early in the series, out of even the smallest town or development, far out at the end of Flagler Street, in what was nearly the Everglades.

There he could take a garden rake and go down to the canal with its thick water grass growing almost to the middle, leaving there only a narrow, sliding strip of black fluid. He thrust the rake down into the grass and twisted, twisting and pulling out onto the bank a ball of dripping, yellow-green fibers, which, as he parted them, erupted in trapped and jumping iridescent fish. All different, as it seemed then, all new. He used them for bait.

He dropped his line from the bridge into the sluggish current between the grass as if into another world. Anything could happen, an anything only touched by a list of the fishes there: largemouth bass, green and black and smelling like licorice, snook whose sea-run silverness was anomalous in that thick water, and alligator gars, mudfish, snapping turtles. He once caught a turtle almost three feet across covered with gray mud and leeches. Out in the middle of the crosscurrent where his two canals met there were rolling backs, which people said were tarpon, though he never caught one.

In that way the years passed, as if black backs out of water were always hypnotizing him on, and what he caught and fixed lost its power and became the mere bait for a life still submerged. That was enough, and he never thought then—of course did not need to think—of the acts that are officially called gambling. He never knew, for instance, why he had been awakened late, embarrassed and eye-knuckling in thin cotton shorts, and set down before a long gray cardboard box filled with a long red lobster, the first he had ever seen. Though he knew enough to eat at it while his father and mother stood over and looked at him and each other with curiously brighter eyes. He might have suspected something a year or so later when the Christmas-promised bicycle came not then but in March. As he stood taken with its red and white glitter in the limestone driveway, he could have heard the explanation: it was something about jai alai. Five years later it was clearer; gambling appeared to him unambiguously in an effect. He and his father built a skiff, solid, with an oak stem and stern and mahogany sides, and they called it the Lasting Treat II, for that had been the name of the horse that paid for the lumber.

But gambling fathers or families do not necessarily have gambling sons. More often it goes, by reaction, the other way. Are gamblers born, then? Most children, as Hatcher had been, are gamblers, and yet all men are not, so perhaps he had not grown up. Perhaps, too, the gambler is one who refuses to let childhood die, one who demands that the conditions of it—the very life of it—continue. Put it any way, and it is not satisfying; no more so than the facts of the case: that after three years of work and nearly that of marriage, Philip Hatcher found himself with enough money, with introductions to poker clubs, and in geographical proximity to five race tracks, and he began to play gambling games without relief.

What his course suggests is that any man may be waiting so, for his opportunity—that what men actually do or say or explain is nothing to some brooding, cooking desire that is not recognized and may never be unless opportunity comes. But who can credit the spontaneous convert? Who can believe that one might say, suddenly, when some new and unforeseen occasion comes, "This is me. This at last is what I want"? It is far more soothing to think of causes and effects, and psychological histories, and to see life reasonably, than to admit that given just a minor chance a man may spring out of the self that everyone has seen and knows. Yet so it seems to happen.

Margaret felt sorry for him, for what seemed his helplessness. "Of course you don't have to stop."

"No?"

"No. Just ease up on yourself. On me."

But the prospect of controlling his course was more threatening for the moment than a complete break. "No. I'm going to quit for a while. It won't hurt me. I'll see where I am, and then we'll see."

"You know. We didn't need that money anyway."

"I'll think it out. Then we'll see. Maybe—"

But however saddened and worried she was, Margaret did not want to be caught in a new web of plans. She stepped backward from him abruptly. "Good. How about a movie after dinner?"

Hatcher thumped a hand down on the sofa arm, blew out his breath, and rose. "O.K. What do you want to drink?"

In that way they began their worst time. He made his appearances at the college and went through occasional attentive motions to his wife, but anyone could see that he was empty. Every night he went out for the *Telegraph*. He studied it vengefully, looking for sure things. In a new notebook he kept his schedule of mind bets: "Two hundred to win on Spicy Living—minus two hundred"; "One hundred win on Lamb Chop—plus one twenty"; "Two hundred Impressive—plus one forty"; "Two hundred Pia Star—minus two hundred." After three pages of that notebook he gave it up. It was so much trouble, and he seemed only to come out even. So then he would only sit, dreaming with the paper in his lap, then switch on the radio for results and check his paper, and resume gazing at nothing. Margaret endured it, and when he saw that her patience was stretched, he took a walk—before she told him to—out to see Frankie, to lean against the change shack and watch the boys file in and out and listen to the horse talk.

"Hey," Frankie said. "Looka this." Down the street toward them weaved a tall, broad, putty-faced man, talking to himself loudly. He stopped unsteadily at the booth, and Frank said, "Hey Al."

"Frank—Frankie," the man staggered and drooled. "Hey. Frank. Len' me, lemme a—couple—" His face went blank and astonished. Then he smiled abruptly and stuck out his large hand. Frank took it, winking at Hatcher.

"How ya doin', Al?"

"A couple—*bucks!*" Al blurted, spraying spittle. "I—gotta

eat." His neck suddenly went slack, and his chin bounced on his chest. He weaved backward again, but he still held Frankie's hand, and he did not fall.

"Whatever you want, Al, you know that." Frankie winked again and dug into his pocket and came up with a few crumpled singles, tucking them into the man's pants.

"That's—buddy. 'Member—"

"Sure, I remember, you big stiff. Go home and sleep, Al."

"Gonna! Gonna sleep. Right after I bet me this doub—double. Maricia's Mis—I dunno. Somethin'. You gimme—"

"No daily double, you son of a bitch. Go home." The big man drooled heavily from his slack mouth, uncertain. "O—K! I'm gon' home now." He blinked, and suddenly he seemed to see Hatcher watching him. He reached over and gripped his shoulder. He was strong. "You wan hear Vaw Moror?" Hatcher did not get it.

"What did he say?"

"Vaughn Monroe," Frankie said. "He imitates 'im. Yeah, Al, give us a little of that." The man's mouth snapped suddenly open and round. With his hand still on Hatcher's shoulder, he sang.

" 'Acing with the moo—moon, f'out—upon the mi—night blooo—" Each slurred line ended with a breaking lift of voice, a little yodel and squeak, while he looked steadily into Hatcher's face. Frankie grimaced over his shoulder and broke in.

"God damn it, you're just as good as ever, Al. Ain't he, Phil?"

"That's real good," Hatcher said, turning slightly so that the hand fell away.

"Good, huh? 'K., Frank. S'long, Frank." He stumbled away, down the street.

"Nice, huh?" Frankie said. "The son of a bitch. I shoulda taken his action. He only puts it in somewhere else, poor bastard. We was in the army, in California, together. What a tough bastard he was then." He told Hatcher a long story of a crooked dice game run by himself, and how Al had saved him when he had been caught.

"What happened to him?"

"What do you think! He's a goddamn *drunk*."

"Sure. But how come?"

"How *come?*" Frankie tilted his hat back and paused for some seconds. "How come. I dunno. Horse-fucked, I guess."

"I'll tell you why you can't beat the horses," he said. Sal squatted monkeylike atop the only chair in the change booth. His face was like a boy's face carved in stone and eroded. He grimaced and scrubbed both hands through his brown, curly hair, front to back. "I will tell you," he said to them, "why you cannot beat the horses."

"What's that, Sal?" Frank asked. He was leaning on the punch clock, his hat slanted as usual over his open mind. With Sal's friend Jimmy the milkman there too it was crowded, and Hatcher was propped in the doorway.

Sal looked down, inspecting his hands as if reading the palm lines. "Ego," he said.

"*Ego!* Yeah, I know."

"Ego." He raised himself in the chair until he sat on the edge of its back, and he looked at them all and nodded, as if the sight confirmed it. He nodded at Hatcher. "He's a professor. He's gonna tell you the same thing. It's ego, Phil. Am I right?"

"Absolutely."

"Well, what do *you* think. Tell this yap." He jerked his head at his brother.

"Get off the shit," Frankie said. "He goes along with you because he knows you're jerked off anyway."

"Yeah. Jerked off. Me. *I'm* jerked off." He kept nodding his head and looking out the window in the other door to the little house, held shut with a rusty fork for a padlock. It appeared that, since he knew so much, he would not tell them more.

"What is it, Sal?" the milkman asked earnestly, at which Frank snorted in disgust.

He looked back at them contemptuously, but kept nodding. "You play round robins," he declared. "Parlays, doubles—"

"He wants to bet flat money," Frankie interrupted. "I know." Sal shut his mouth firmly then, shaking his head, and would not continue.

"Come on, *Sal,*" the milkman pleaded.

"*He* knows everything," Sal gestured at Frank again. But he rose on the chair. "All right. You go down. You see this horse in the paper, and it's a sure pop and you go down. And before the race comes up, the race you're supposed to bet, you're broke. Tapioca, for Christ sake, before you even start. You know why you do that? And look at the guy," he said more loudly, waving his hands in the air, "look at the guy who's way up after the DD, and comes home with nuthin'. Look at him."

"Which is right," Frank said. "You can-not score bettin' deuces."

"Wrong. Look at the guys that go every day, play every race, tryin' to make every winner. All that," Sal instructed them, "is ego." He slumped down and back against the chair, nodding resentfully at them now, as if it all were their fault. For a moment he was silent. Then, again looking into his own hands, he said, "Ego. All us young guys got it."

"Wait a minute." Frankie turned up the volume on the Philadelphia station that had been buzzing behind their conversation. "Here's the sixth." They all bent closer to the small red radio as the disc jockey made another joke about bookmakers. "Smart ass," Frank said. Then the voice read off the names, glibly, casually, for the sixth at Bowie: the winner was Lord Birchfield— twelve forty, six twenty, four even. Sal shrieked. He leaped from the chair and ran arms waving out into the lot, kicking the tires of the cars, pounding fenders, and finally springing at the brick wall, scraping his fingers and climbing.

"I dint get it in!" he shouted, his hands full of his hair. "I did not get it in! Five hundred bananas!"

The milkman, large and smooth-faced under his grimy red leather hunting cap, confirmed. "He's right," he grinned, showing shiny buck teeth. "He wanted to put that Birchfield in a round robin, but the guy wouldn't take it. Said he owed him too much now, how far could he go, you know. He only took the ten-win parlay with Dave's Boy and that chalk." They had heard the results of those races, too. Dave's Boy had paid ten twenty, and Sal's third horse in his unconsummated three-way parlay had won at Aqueduct at even money.

"Five hundred bananas," Sal keened, coming back to the booth with hair flying. "I *had* it. Dint I, Jim?" The milkman nodded, suppressing a smile. "I got it written right here." He took out a scrap of paper tracked with scratch-sheet numbers and a totaled column of figures, his bets and losses of the week. "And that son of a bitch wouldn't take it. I gotta get 'im."

"What do you think," Frankie said. "Some bookmaker is gonna feel sorry fer you? You owe him, he cuts your action. You beat him, and he cries. They're all the same." He turned away in disgust. "I don't wanna hear it."

"Five hundred bananas," Sal said, "is five hundred bananas." He motioned to Jim and stumped off to his three-year-old Cadillac that was almost paid for. The milkman followed his simian figure, walking backward, smiling at them and shrugging.

"Which he is right," Frank said. "He is in bad shape. Bent."

"How in hell does he get in so deep?"

"Aw. He's a little wild, yeah, but he ain't a bad kid, you know. Don't ever think he isn't."

"At least he's in action. I ain't even bettin' at all. I'm really——"

"Huh! I guess I been winnin', huh? Yeah. Fifty today, eighty yesterday, two *hunnert* Monday. Yeah. I been winnin'." He ceased for a moment. "I have told you, Phil, a thousand times, there is one way, *one way,* to beat them horses. And that is when they are in the barn. *In the barn.*"

Hatcher had indeed heard it before. All bookmakers were thieves, enemies rather than conveniences, and when Frankie put himself to it, he attacked a bookie singlemindedly, unremittingly, and with all the tricks. One of those was to use what he called the service, any of a number of wire services that specialized in giving out the results of a race just as the horses crossed the finish line. The best way was to use two phones, one open to the service —"Hello," Frankie said, "this is Spade," and on a good day he would hear, "They are seven minutes ahead, and they are *running,* hold on"—and one phone open to the bookmaker. For Frank the routine was a classic pattern, and he had devised countless variations for slipping in the horse that had already won with other, legitimate bets. But the horses had to run earlier than the scratch sheet, the bookie's almanac, said they would, and for that, usually, the weather had to be bad. In addition, the "live one," the winner already being cooled down back at the barn, had to be combined with some other, later horse in a parlay. Even the most naïve and greedy bookmaker was wary of large, single win bets when it was close to post time. It was a complicated and taxing business, and with the wire services now defunct, as far as he knew—and who knew so well—Frankie had not made his favorite move for a long time. But he was ready now.

"Phil. I'm in bad shape. Lend me a yard."

"Yeah," Hatcher shrugged. "And where do I get it?"

"I know. Listen. It's s'posed to rain tomorrow. They got them kanellas at Bowie." A car came into the lot, and he punched a ticket and got rid of it.

"Quinellas, you mean."

"Same thing. We can nail two in one race. No gamblin'."

"What do we get on quinellas? My man only takes ten."

"I know 'im. He's as hungry as the rest of them bastards. He can be hit, that Joey. Ten ain't enough? He gives thirty to one, don't he?" Hatcher nodded. "That's perfick. We give him three kanellas. One is the live one, and we tie up the winner of the fifth with some other stuff. We could make five hunnert."

"We have to make that much apiece. Or it isn't worth it. And then we hit him for a thousand, and I have to find myself another man."

"What's the difference? We gotta hit 'im for fifteen, anyway. We need another guy. My brother. He needs the help."

"Sal? I don't know. That's a long way, down there."

"It's s'posed to rain good," Frankie said. "It's our best shot, Phil."

"I dunno. I got a class tomorrow. Maybe I'll just wait them out awhile more. I can beat them legit." Even as he said it, he thought how often in the past, before Margaret had heard it, he had screamed "stiff" and "boat race," convinced he was bucking a conspiracy of insiders so fixed as to leave no chance to anyone else. He saw again a short-priced stretch runner running on the lead where he had never been before and collapsing with a sixteenth to go. Or a speed horse who could have been rated from wire to wire breaking suddenly away from the pack after an unexplainably slow start and ripping off a twenty-one-second quarter mile and then stopping to a walk. He saw jockeys jumping off their horses when the gates opened and horses steadying on the rail for no reason until they had nowhere to go and horses rushing boldly down the stretch after they had no chance to get up. Through it all he heard a bleary voice crooning to him, "Racing with the moon."

For that while Frankie was muttering and snorting. "Legit! Yeah. Legit. You're gonna beat the horses. I don't wanta hear it." When he saw that Hatcher was listening again, he said, "Listen. I ain't even talkin' about that. Don't you unnerstan', Phil? I'm talkin' about *bookmakers*? Do they beat *you* legit? Them bastards. When you get a hungry one, he's gotta be nailed. You have to hit him to protect yourself."

157

"All right. I'll call off the class. We'll take a ride." As he had considered it, Frankie's scheme had begun to mesh with a new strategy of his own. Past-posting was the way to take off the pressure—pressure from lack of money, from himself, from his wife. Instead of waiting for some race that he knew he could win, with Frankie and Sal he would find a race that had already been won. He would be set up again. In no way did he see the cheating as a compromise of his usual course and attitudes. He could get out of trouble, he was sure, by waiting, by beginning again in the old way, though it would take longer, and he would have to stay away from the races more often. This was better. It would open things up. And that was what he said to Margaret.

"I've never heard anything like it," she said. "You mean a bookie will *take* those bets? But why?"

"Because they're greedy—they want the action. Besides I've been—we've been dealing with this guy for a long time. He won't even suspect, at first. Well. What do you think? It isn't gambling, is it?" He was very earnest, and she laughed.

"No, it isn't, is it?"

"So I think I'll go along."

"Sure," she said. "You need the change. And I'll be glad to see you doing something."

"I don't blame you," Hatcher said.

He did the driving to the outskirts of Baltimore. They plotted on the way, establishing the signals, and who would phone and who would carry the message. The enterprise expanded as they went, and they decided to past-post two races and two different bookies, arguing which horses to combine with their live ones while Frankie assured them that his man Norton was easy to nail. Hatcher and Frank came up with the same bets, sure shots in the seventh at Jersey and the eighth at New York, but Sal said, "Screw them favorites. We're gonna get something that'll pay." The idea was fine, but he had no horses they could agree on, and so they would settle, Frankie said, for the chalk.

The track lay away from the highways within a pine forest. It looked old and country, the paint on the fences peeling, the running surface thick and loamy, sweeping by just a few feet from the crowd. But the tote board flashed and glittered as usual, and the ticket windows, under the old and barnlike roof of the grandstand, were decked out in shiny panels. They had all but finished their work before they arrived, driving the old roads to find the nearest telephone, outside a roadhouse three quarters of a mile away. They had driven to the track again from there, timing.

"Christ," Sal said. "It's over two minutes."

"What's the difference. Believe me." Frank looked up at the rain that, as advertised, had begun to drizzle down, and at the lowering mist. "By the fifth they could be fifteen minutes early."

They drove through the gate and into the parking lot, ignoring the gestures of the attendants, and coasted up to a man standing guard on the lot nearest the turnstiles of the grandstand.

"Listen," Hatcher said. "I may have to get out in a hurry. To meet a guy for some information. I want to park close, and if I leave, I want the spot saved." He pushed through the window a folded five-dollar bill.

"Man," the attendant said. "I'll wait out here with a helicopter if you want it."

"We don't need it, today."

"Wait a minute," Frankie said. "How much for that?"

Inside they ate some clam chowder and bet their doubles. Hatcher had carelessly picked the winner of the first at thirty-one dollars, and with the second choice going in the second race he kept stretching and looking for the horse, but it never got a call. With the third race they started.

Hatcher drove Frank out to the roadhouse and came back, parking in his reserved spot and trying to avoid the seemingly curious and self-important looks of the track police. Sal stood about fifty yards away, up a slight incline and behind a cyclone fence. Then he heard over the loudspeaker system that they were off, four minutes early.

Sal's back was to him, but Hatcher watched it, and almost at

159

once an arm lifted into the air and then descended. It seemed that everyone must be watching that arm; Hatcher fidgeted and tried to concentrate. Then it rose and fell rapidly, once, twice, five times. He put the car in gear, seeing off to the side the loose and unconcerned figure of Sal sauntering away from the fence. He slid on the gravel into the first stop at the lot gate and checked his papers. Number five on his program was Lilliokulani. One more stop street and there she was, in the Armstrong, in bookmaker's numbers, six.

When he slewed around the corner to the roadhouse, the phone booth was empty. He swore to himself and burst into the dim and quiet barroom. "Have you seen an old guy, black jacket and hat?" The barman pointed silently to a telephone booth Hatcher had not seen, tucked back in a corner of the place. He went up to it and saw Frankie gabbing away to Norton, occasionally reading off a small bet, laughing at some joke, on the con. Hatcher held up six fingers against the glass.

"Yeah, yeah, ain't it," Frankie said. "Not only that—hey—listen. Here's one I almost forgot. Ain't that sothin'? What could I tell the guy, then? In the third at Maryland. What? Well what time's post? Too late? Yeah. Well I been gabbin' too long with you and forgot about it, Nort. We musta been talkin' for ten minutes. What? Na-aw, the hell with it. I just give it back to him, that's all. Yeah, well he is good action, but screw 'im. We don't need him. You gotta run—what?" The bookie had said to give it to him, and Frankie did. "That's right. Third at Maryland. Number six. Seventh at Jersey number three; eighth at New York, number five. Ten win round robin, ten place round robin. Yeah. And. Third at Maryland number six, sixth at Maryland number eleven. Twenty win parlay. And that's it." He hung up quickly.

That was it. The number eleven horse in the sixth at Maryland was, as they knew, a late scratch, and the "parlay" money would simply become a flat bet to win on the winner. It was one way of betting the horse in the barn alone without arousing suspicions.

Frankie strutted out of the booth. "How do you like *that* son of a bitch. What a story he gives me! Too late! Hah, *hah!*" he cackled. "You liked that con I give 'im, didn't you? 'Oh, *yeah,* Norton—the guy's good action!' " Then he became indignant. "Too late! They always think you're cheatin' 'em, the bastards."

When they got back to the track, Frankie said to watch this and made a long face as he went up to Sal. "Shit."

"What?" Sal cried. "I called that pig when they made the turn. Eighteen even! He wouldn't take it?"

"What do *you* think?"

Sal's eager face collapsed. "You didn't get it in?" he wailed. Then he was sure. "You didn't get it in. I knew it. That's the way I gotta go. I knew you wouldn't."

Frankie laughed again his rising laugh, punching Sal on the arm. He sputtered to Hatcher, "We didn't get it *in.* Hah hah!"

Sal's face changed again. "You did? You got it in! He took it!"

Frankie became austere. "Why, certainly he took it! What do *you* think? Twenty win parlay with the scratch, which is one eighty and a ten win, ten place ribbon with them two chalks."

"You got it in," Sal said, charmed.

"Why, *certainly!*" Frankie said, and turned to Hatcher. "Did you see his face?"

Before the fifth race, Frankie drove Hatcher out to the road-house. "Get on that phone early," he said. "There are a lot of son of a bitches around calling. That's why I hadda go in there." Post time had been marked on the lighted board as three twenty-two, eight minutes early. "You should get him no later than—three twenty-four. That's six up on the sheet." Hatcher said O.K., and Frank drove back to get the signals from Sal, waving in the wind against the fence, with the entire track population looking on amused.

Hatcher camped in the outside booth, spreading his change on the tin shelf, and waited. When anyone seemed to be approaching the booth, he put the dead phone to his ear and began nodding and speaking. He checked through the list of small bets he would give Joey to stall him and looked more carefully through the others. There were three quinellas, combining the first two horses under the wire. Two of them had the top space blank, and one had no names written in at all, open, ready for the live ones. Then there was a round robin, with one of its three possibilities open for the winner; then a forty-dollar win parlay with the late scratch in the sixth; and then a small reverse bet, six if twelve, the open space with a longshot in the ninth at New Jersey. At three twenty-five he called the number.

"And operator? Listen. Don't interrupt this call if I go over. That's right. I'll signal. Right." The circuit was open. "Joe? Hey. Phil. How goes? No kidding, bad day, huh? Well, you'll get it all back from me, anyway, ha ha. Yeah. Well, I'm runnin' a little hard luck." He was already looking, anxious for the front of the car around the corner, though it was too soon. "Yeah. Well." He could think of nothing more. "What? Oh. Yeah. I got something for you." He began, slowly, to reel off the trivial bets. "These are for a friend of mine. He might be a good customer for you. Nothing big." When he had finished them, Frank still had not shown. "An' you can make your own arrangements with him later, right? What? Oh—yeah! I got somethin' for myself." His throat was tight, and he rolled his eyes up to the rain falling harder on the glass and from the side saw Frankie wrench the car around the corner. "Yeah, I got something. Here it is."

Frank pushed the marked program through the door of the booth. Great Error was marked with a "1"; Nanny's Pride with a "2".

"Fifth at Bowie. Quinella. Great Error and White Way; Great Error and Heilo—Helioball; Great Error and Nanny's Pride. All for ten. What? Yeah, well I tried you earlier but you were busy. You must be gettin' rich, huh? Yeah. Here's some more." He rattled through all the bets, plugging in Great Error every time.

"Set?" Frankie asked.

"Perfect."

"Did he sing?"

"A little. He said it was close, but that he had been busy. He took it all, all right."

"What a lulu! They're all the same." They went back and picked up Sal and left, laughing all the way up the Maryland and Delaware and Jersey Turnpikes. They stopped and swaggered into a roadside restaurant and then went on again. At six thirty they turned on the results. All the other horses but one had won.

"That's it," Frankie said. "You get a sure one and they all fall in. Funny how that works. What is it?"

Hatcher was calculating. "We hit your man for five twenty," he said, "less the eighty we bet. Four forty there. And the quinella was limit. Seven, no, eight. Eight ten. And a twenty win parlay: a five-dollar horse and a six-dollar horse—what's that?"

"One fifty," Frankie said quickly.

"And a forty win parlay with the scratch is forty to win on a six-dollar horse—is nine forty plus that—it comes to about a gee, and the reverse bet." Frankie figured on his program with a heavy-leaded track pencil.

"I make it eleven hunnert," he declared solemnly. "It's over eleven hunnert." Sal bounced in the back seat.

"Ah, hah hah! We *got* 'em!"

"Why, certainly," Frank tossed over his shoulder. Then he punched Hatcher's arm. "Pretty nice, huh, Phil? Pretty nice. You just stick with the old man. Plenty money. Back in action, right Phil?"

Hatcher smiled, drumming on the steering wheel, passing a truck. "Back in action," he said.

Chapter 15

When Frank Buono got home that night to Bow Street at the
edge of a Negro section of the town, the lights were on. He cursed
softly, easing himself in, at the money wasted on the "electric,"
and at what might be coming. He crept through the kitchen into
the living room, where the color television was working, and
where, in the dimness, a ghostly figure loomed at him from the
sofa.

"Where you been, Frank." Her voice was oddly flat, tired and
with just the overtone of a whine.

Frankie's eyes shifted behind the heavy glasses, and he grunted,
VFW." Then he took the offensive as usual. "Where's the kids?
How is it you ain't in bed, Vi? How is that?" He gestured at the
television. "What's all this?"

"I called there twice, Frank. They said you wasn't there all
night."

"Hah!" he cried. "What do *you* think. Think I want everybody
callin' me up there? I was in and out anyway—playin' a little
pinochle—right—but I tol' 'em to say I wasn't there. There's too
many guys tryin' to put the arm on me—"

Her level, nearly patient voice broke across his own. "But I
told them it was me, Frank, and they said you weren't there."

"Naw, naw, you couldn't of. Naw, you didn't. They'd of called me then. Naw. You must not a said it was you. They'd a called me all right. I dunno, though. Maybe they didn't think—"

Violet laid her head against the back of the couch and looked up at him. "I'm tired of this, Frank. I'm gonna go to Lily."

Frankie was not alarmed; she had threatened flights to her sister's house and taken them before. They had been married a long time. "Well, that might be good fer ya, Vi," he said. "A little rest, change. You don' hafta worry about the kids or anythin'. I can get little Vi to school and all that. That might be *very* good."

"I'm not coming back, Frank." Amid her lifetime of uncertainty, she felt once again that she was taking a stand at last, showing him at last how the real world was and how it would no longer tolerate him.

"Hah!" he shouted. "*I* know. *I* know yer not! I know."

"Well," she breathed, hand to her hair. "I'll need some money, then, Frank."

He nodded at this matter of course. "How much?"

"The dentist bill alone is over a hundred dollars, Frank, and I'll have to give Lily *something,* and for groceries."

Frankie was already reaching into his pocket. "Here's three hunnert then." A languid hand rose to take the crackling bills. "I can't go for more now." He thought the money would last her until she came back. "I gotta sleep now, Vi," he said as he turned from her.

"All right," she said, in that same, too even tone. "I'm gonna watch awhile. Good night, Frank."

"What do ya think a that?" Frankie complained to Hatcher two days later. "Not comin' back! Hah! What's she gonna do? We been married almost twenty-three *years,* for Christ sake, and she says she's not comin' back. That asshole. That son of a bitch. What do I need that for?" He shook his head in puzzlement, then abruptly rapped the ticket-punching clock. "So what do *I* do," he cocked his head appealing. "I call the dentist this mornin'! What do you think that bill is?" He paused dramatically. "Thirty-four dollars!" Hatcher shook his head, puzzled now himself.

"Don't you unnerstan'?" Frank cried. "That was the *bullshit!* She's robbin' me! All I know she's been robbin' me right *along.*" Hatcher shook his head again, laughing. "So I call over there this mornin' and hit her with this, you know. What does she say? She says she wants five hunnert now and a half a yard a week!" Frankie had begun to splutter, at a loss. "I mean. I do not *under-stand* that, Phil. I do not under-stand what she's doin'." He spread his upturned palms in front of him, jabbing them at the asphalt. "I mean, she's gone *crazy* or sothin', ain't she? What do you think?" But Hatcher could not say.

"That's it," Frankie confirmed himself. "I think she's gone crazy. Anyway. I need money."

"We just collected yesterday."

"I bet a lot of that out—what *she* left me. So," he said more quietly, "we gotta get this guy again."

"Twice in one week?"

"What's the difference? He took it on his back the first time, din't he? Why, certainly twice in one week!"

So the next day Hatcher sat in a cab at Aqueduct and waited until Frankie came trotting out of the exit at the end of the grandstand and up to the cyclone fence and held up seven fingers. "That's it," he said to the driver. "We can go." The taxi wheeled around the planted circle and accelerated along the treelined way toward the main gate.

"Comin' back in," the cabbie said to the attendant, and they cut across traffic and stopped in front of the coffee shop and its telephone booths.

"Hey, Joey, this is Phil. *Phil.* Yeah, I guess we got a bad connection here. Listen, in the fifth at New York I want—what? Well, I couldn't get you sooner, Joey. First you were busy—and I work, too, you know. Yeah. Well. It *is* up to you—you want the bet or not. Huh? Yeah. Then take this."

"Make out O.K.?" the cabbie asked as he crawled in.

"O.K." Hatcher extended a five-dollar bill across the back of the seat. "Thanks for your trouble."

"Anytime."

"That goddamn horse only pays seven dollars," Frankie said inside the track.

"He was fifth choice on the sheet."

"The cutie pies got into him and knocked him down. How in Christ are we gonna make money?" That night they learned that the horse they had tied up with the winner had run second, and they had made only fifty-five dollars apiece, and so, as Frankie said, they had no choice but to do it again.

The next day, when it was cloudy and threatening, post time for the sixth at Aqueduct was ten minutes earlier than scratch-sheet time. "Joey? Phil. Listen—a round robin. Two of 'em. Thirty win, thirty place. Well, I made a little hit yesterday, didn't I? Yeah, yeah. Gimme the sixth at New York, Prince Tiki. With the seventh at Maryland, Disintegrate, and the ninth at New York, Palermo." The late scratch board said that Palermo was not running, and Disintegrate, Frankie said, was a lock.

"Stiff," Frank said through the door of the other phone booth. He was on the line to his brother, who was working his own bookie. But the next day his glee had vanished. "Sal's man give him a time bet," he said. "We get nothin' there." Maybe, Hatcher thought. He knew that he was very far down on the list of potential suckers for what Frankie called his moves, but still he was on it. There was no one who was not. Sal and Frankie could have been splitting two ways rather than three. But Disintegrate had only made second anyway, and he said nothing.

"We gotta get 'im again."

"How can we?"

"Dint they get us? Every piece of action I sat on last week hit. I lose two hunnert. Then we PP *that* son of a bitch, so we got money comin', and don't I lose my PC on that?"

"Your what?"

"My PC—percentage! Twenty-five per cent of what Norton wins from these yo-yos is supposed to be *mine.*"

"What do you want—a piece of everything, right?"

"Phil! Certainly." So the next day they tried again, this time on the daily double at Aqueduct. Hatcher watched the race, ran out to telephone Frank, and Frank called Norton five minutes late, coupling the winner with three horses in the second, and seeding the bets through the small action he pretended to have picked up at the parking lot. The bookmaker did not want the late bets, but Frankie wheedled and conned, and he took them at the last. Then there was trouble.

"You know what that ass-hole did? He comes down and says, 'You past-posted me.' Just like that. 'You past-posted me.' And I say, 'Aw, what're you talkin' about, Norton. We been doing business for years. If I'm PPin' ya,' I says to 'im, 'do I call it in seven minutes late?' 'No,' he says, 'you're givin' it to me.' So I say I stopped that shit a long time ago when the service in Delaware went dead, and he says, 'No, you're always cryin' foul. You're a two-bit chiseler and I'm through with you.' Then the son of a bitch throws the money on the ground."

"Did you pick it up?"

"Certainly. But how do you like that ass-hole sayin' that? I wish I get him good."

"You didn't do bad. An eight-dollar DD on the limit. Four-eight-eight, right?"

"Yeah. But you gotta consider my expenses. No PC this week either, now. Huh! No PC any *more.*" His eyes swam behind his glasses.

"I'll consider them," Hatcher said. "You give me my half now, and I'll consider them."

"Would I cheat you?" Frankie scowled at him, but Hatcher waited him out, and finally he reached into his pocket for the money with one hand and thumped Hatcher's shoulder with the other. "Old Phil. Atta boy, Phil."

It became a comfortable life. The mornings were spent not with the past performances but scanning the weather reports north and south. When conditions favored, and at times even when they did not, he spent a harried hour or two making arrangements, scheduling and synchronizing calls and post times, fabricating some red-herring chatter, and trying to line up new bookmakers. The afternoons were no longer punctuated every thirty minutes or so with tense gambles. They grew warmer. When the call was made, he could stand around the track immune to whatever was going on among the trainers or the riders. Or he could go home and sleep until poker time, or take Margaret for a drive down into Pennsylvania and stop for dinner along the river. It was all a separate business in his mind, and although the money counted, what he was doing did not. But then he called Joey two minutes late with a bet, and when he named the race he wanted, the bookie refused.

"Phil. It ain't that I think you're tryin' to pull something."

"It ain't, huh?"

"Naw, naw. You wouldn't past-post me, I know that. But the bet is late, Phil. Why is everything right on post with you?"

"Forget it, Joe. The horse don't have to win." He had not named the horse anyway, and was not caught.

"No hard feelings, Phil."

Not at all. Two days later, with two phone booths and a newfound "service," they did it again. Frank took the winners on one phone, as Hatcher argued with Joey about where they stood for the week and asked about scratches, weights, odds. Until at last Frankie held up his marked sheet.

"*Who's* on the three horse? Well, that's easy then 'cause I never bet that kid. So take this down. In the first at Monmouth—well *sure* it's late *now*. We been bullshitin' for ten minutes or more! Didn't we go through this the other day? Well, it must be that you think I *am* cheatin' ya. Goddamn right! Don't give me that time-bet shit, Joey. That just means I got no bet now, and you know it. What? No hard feelins, huh? I'll tell you what: the minute I get another man, you're dead, Joe. I'm packin' you up! Huh? Good customer, huh? Well just remember what I said!" Hatcher hung up.

"You didn't mention no horses names, did you?" Frankie asked.

"I'm not *that* stupid."

"And he said——"

"You know. That I was a good customer, and he'd hate to lose me, but that he'd have to give me time from now on——"

"But he didn't catch ya. So we went for the forty for the service, but you did just right. We can get him again."

Hatcher blinked. "How for Christ sake? We gotta get another man."

"There ain't another one no more! We been through all we're gonna get. The rest of 'em got a little too much larry."

"Larry?"

"Larceny, larceny! They got more than you or me! Naw. We can get this kid again. I'm gonna start givin' him small stuff this week. I got an idea we haven't tried yet."

It worked. They set up in two booths again with Hatcher on the line to the service in Baltimore and Frankie calling the bookmaker. First he asked in broken English mixed with Italian for the Electric Company, insisting that he had the right number until he was hung up on, and then calling again. Then he called as himself, spinning off a slow string of small bets, asking for odds, making mistakes. Hatcher got two winners—the first at Bowie and the second at Aqueduct. He signaled Frank and began dialing as Frank hung up. When the bookmaker answered, Hatcher ranted and complained about the busy line. Joey apologized and took the bet. The net profit was over nine hundred.

When Joey paid off the next day, he told Hatcher that he no longer wanted his action. Hatcher laughed as he told Margaret the story. "You are going to get killed," she said.

"Baloney," he said. "The bookie is his own protection in this. He's a thief himself, and he's on his own. He can always refuse the bet. But if he takes it, he's the sucker, and he's got to pay." He sucked at his beer, and chuckled again. "Get killed! The only thing you can get hurt for is not paying. He took *my* bet, and he

170

knew he had to pay. And he knew he'd been had, too. Packed me up."

"You don't mean he thought you would somehow get *him,* do you?"

"Mag! What am I, some goddamn mobster? Christ. This is just a little past-posting. Christ," he admonished his beer.

"Well, I don't know, do I? You tell me these stories, how do I know what they mean?"

"Come on, Margaret! You know *me* better than that, don't you? It's very simple. We need the money, and we get it. There's no reason to feel scared or guilty. Or anything else. It's a game, that's all. Frankie and I beat 'em at it straight." She shook her head quickly, as if to clear it or avoid an insect. Hatcher was going on. "Besides, we're all through now. We ran out of bookmakers."

"What did you get? What now?"

"Over fifteen hundred. That's what I wanted to tell you about. I've got some capital now. I'm going to treat it like an investment. I'll wait for spots—strictly class, good horses, good races—and then I'll send it in." He sat back satisfied.

"O.K."

"I'm going to be *careful.*"

"O.K. What about school?"

"School is almost over. Besides, I've been putting in my time."

"Then O.K."

"Well. What else?"

"Nothing. Nothing else. Except you and me."

"Aw, come on!" He got up and went to her, sitting on a footstool. "Betting horses doesn't change *that.* This is a start. In a few days I'll be rolling, and everything will be different. We can do anything we want. We—" But Margaret was not listening. When his voice ceased, she looked up and smiled firmly.

She raised her glass. "Good luck to us."

The profits from past-posting lasted Hatcher a week and a half. He went looking for good, sound, dependable horses, in allowance races, and ignored "sucker bets"—everything else. But it was not merely in the interests of safety. In fact he was looking for occasions where he might bet a lot of money, occasions where he would not spread himself over eight or nine races but concentrate on one, and put himself, as he said, on the line. It was very probably the right impulse. On the first horse he discovered, he bet two hundred, and won two eighty. On the next three he bet four hundred. The first of these was prepping for a stakes race at a longer distance, and did not try to win. The other two lost in photo finishes.

"Just bad fuckin' luck," he said to Frankie. "That Tumiga had to go three wide and then misses a nose. And they let him go off at two to one."

Frank gazed back owlishly. "Phil, you don't *have* to run lucky. You shouldn't be bettin' them kina horses anyway." Any horse race that was likely to be largely honest was too risky for Frank. "Screw this gamblin'. We gotta find us a good poker game." He had urged this before, and besides his other talents Frankie could handle cards. But Hatcher insisted, as Frankie himself had done before, that there was no such good game, only the house poker with its own dealers and a 5-per-cent cut.

"You're right," Frankie said. "They all know me, anyway. We never get away with it. Still, if you got a good game——"

"Frank—"

"I know, I know. Just look at this a minute." On the hood of a parked car he spread an old limp deck of cards, then gathered them seemingly at random. Very quickly he appeared to shuffle old style, one hand working and mixing the cards into the other. He beamed up at Hatcher. "This is what is known as the rundown. These are already stacked, you know." Hatcher laughed and laughed louder and admiringly when the hand dealt in front of him, one of five laid out on the car, contained three kings.

"How's that? Ever see anybody better? How'd you like to start with that kina edge, eh?"

"You're the best, Frank. But there ain't no game."

"Well, I don't say there is. But this is nice to know, right? You watch you don't get cheated."

Coincidentally, when Hatcher was trying to lengthen his short bankroll three nights later at the Italian-American Club, Bingo the dealer suddenly decided to count the cards. They totaled fifty, and Bingo said, "Oh-oh," and raised his eyebrows at Sullivan the boss. Sullivan came over and laid a hand on the shoulder of a young player named Billy, and they went out to the kitchen. A new deck was put in the game. Bingo winked at Hatcher. A few minutes later Billy ambled past the table and out the door.

"At it again," growled Big John from the other end of the table, shaking his head.

"What's that?"

"Aw, Teacher," John said, chewing the plastic tip of his cigar. "Sometimes that punk holds back cards." Hatcher looked quickly at Bingo, who laughed.

"It ain't anythin'," he said. "You just have to watch him a little, is all. He ain't a bad kid."

Hatcher made a diamond flush early in the next hand. There were three players with him, and one bet and another raised, and so he only called. But on the last card two of them checked; Big John bet then, and Hatcher raised. The others dropped, and John said, "Teacher, you got me *again*. Go ahead. Give it to me. I call."

"I got diamonds, John."

"Oh, Teacher," sang John, his two gold-capped teeth glinting, "you are the best."

On the next hand both he and John dropped out early, and from the other end John tipped his head at the door, but Hatcher did not know what he wanted. They had needled each other before, and he thought that the squat, bullish man somehow liked him, perhaps for being what he called him, "Teacher," but they had no other connection.

Still, on the next hand, John called bantering to him again. "The teacher and me can do some biz-ness—we got some biz-ness, Teacher." When Hatcher laughed at him he squeezed his eyes together, nodding urgently toward the door.

Hatcher was curious, and tired anyway. He picked up the

thirty dollars he was ahead and said good-night to the boys. He waited outside until Big John swaggered through the door lighting a fresh plastic-tipped cigar. "C'mon, Professor," he said. "Get us some caw-fee."

At the diner they gossiped for ten minutes or more, and Hatcher was puzzled. John might have heard about the past-posting, and want in. Or that he was a good handicapper, maybe, and want a tip or two. Or know of a bigger poker game for them to be partners in.

"Ya know, Teacher, I like your moves a little. Yeah. I think we can do some biz-ness."

"What business?"

"Well, Phil, this is it. I been havin' a little hard luck, ya know. I mean—I just can't seem to get lucky, an' put two together. I can't hit that parlay. Las' mont' I had a little cash—me'n some guys did all right, but where did it go? I just can't get lucky oncet. We made a little score down Mar'land, but what've I got for it?"

"Down Bowie?"

"Naw. Not Bowie. There was three of us cut up forty gees, Teacher. But I can't make two moves back to back, and now I'm bent again."

"Forty thousand. That's some bet, John. Where at? Timonium?"

John removed his cigar and measured him for a moment; his small, close-set eyes did not blink. Then his forehead wrinkled again, his eyebrows went up, and he put the plastic tip back in his mouth. He shook his head. "Naw, Phil. We didn't make no bet. To tell you da truth—well, to tell you da trut', Teacher, we knocked over a safe."

"Oh. Yeah."

"Yeah. We come away clean."

"Lucky."

"Lucky? What good is it? I had a good start, but I could not score! But here's the thing. You're tap, I know, too, and scratchin' around—"

"Where'd you hear—" John patted the air above the formica table top and nodded slowly.

"Just say, I know you could use some help, plus I like your style. Now. I know some people. They—these people—ain't gamblers. But once in a while they get a piece. When they do, the pig is there. Believe me, Teacher. There ain't no gamblin' involved. You know what I mean?"

"Fixin' races."

"Well! Yeah, you could say that." John waved him off and fell silent as the waitress brought more coffee. "Teacher, they got one comin' up. Could be this week I get the office. This ain't no chalk, either. One last week at Jersey pay eleven sothin', anudder at Mar'land eighteen, no chalk. A course, these people will want part of our action—we gotta bet a little sothin' fer them, you unnerstan'—"

"How much?"

John waved his cigar. "Half. But what's the difference. It's only right, ain't it? And there *ain't no gamblin' involved.*" He blinked solemnly out of his doglike, froglike face. "Now. But you'll do sothin' fer me—a favor. These people are friends of mine, and so we get the live ones for half, an' I bring you in 'cause you're all right with me and I know you can use the paper, right? But I'd 'preciate it if you give a man I know a little action. Nuthin' big. I mean if you got a friend, maybe bets small, maybe you steer him to this guy. The guy is good, Teacher, an' he's tryin' to get started, an' he don't want nuthin' big. An' we just help him out a little, is all." John leaned back, and seemed to be satisfied with himself. "That's all. O.K.? Teacher?"

"Yeah," Hatcher said. "I guess so."

"That's good." John waved for the check.

"Yeah, I need something like this," Hatcher said. In the morning he said the same thing to Margaret.

"Now you are going to end up in jail."

"Hah." He finished his coffee with a flourish. "You said the same thing about past-posting. How is it illegal to cheat a book-maker?"

"Fixing races is a little different."

"How? How can it cut back on me? I'm still just a bettor, aren't I?"

"And all you have to do for this is make bets with——"

"Right. With this other bookmaker. That Joey, Norton—none of 'em are any good anymore, anyway. So I'll give the new guy everything but the live ones—I can get them off. Ha. Maybe I'll even past-post *him*."

"I still don't see what this—John—what he needs you for."

Hatcher shrugged vigorously. "Who cares? How do I know what he thinks? Maybe he thinks I know a lotta guys that bet—"

"Do you?"

"I know a few, yeah. Or maybe he just likes me."

"Sure."

"Well, what difference does it make? The point is I had some bad luck on some good horses, and this can get me back into them."

Margaret rose abruptly and went into the kitchen. From there a moment later she said, "You know, I think I'll take that job."

"What job?"

"I *told* you," she said in the doorway. "An old friend from school called—"

"You didn't tell me. What old friend?" Hatcher was merely trying to generate interest, to show that for the moment he could.

"I guess you weren't listening. I told you that Tommy called —last week."

"*Him?* What? The guy you were living—"

"Oh, that has nothing to do with it. I told you all about it."

He remembered nothing. "Little more than an old friend, I'd say." He grinned sourly, teasing, pretending to be hurt and jealous. But he was irritated, annoyed at this evidence of her independent life rising to the surface, or perhaps at her going away from his gambling.

Margaret looked at him coolly. "No. Just an old friend. He asked me if I was still interested in music."

"Oh. I see. Music." He had rocked back on the sofa with his hands clasped around one knee, smiling. She carried on.

"Yes. He's producing records now with a little company. I can have a job there if I want."

"Doing what?"

"Mostly auditioning groups, scouting, things like that. I could work my own hours. Part-time, if I want."

"How did he know where you were?"

"Mutual friends, I guess. What do you think?"

He did not know what he thought. His mind sifted through possibilities—his irritation, jealousy, regret—until he came to the one that felt right: relief. "You don't have to take any job, you know. Not for money."

"Not for money. Even if it would take some pressure off. It's for me. All I'm doing now is hanging around here. That isn't any good for me or you; it doesn't help what you're doing—"

"It doesn't matter. It—"

"No. Come on. Besides this is just something until you can— until we get straightened out."

"Oh, you don't have to worry about that." But she was not interested in that confidence. No more was he interested in persuading her. He was relieved at the prospect of being alone and free in what, despite all the compromises, he still dreamed of as the temple of fortune.

"No—"

"Oh, maybe you're right," he said. "So. Say. You want to go out for dinner tonight?"

"Why, sure. It'll be a nice change."

Chapter 16

On Thursday of that week, the call came. "Teacher? Me. Yeah. I just got the office. We gonna take a little ride today."

When they got to the race track, John would not tell him which race or horse it was. Not that he did not trust him, he said, but it was better to take no chances on spreading it around; they did not want to drive the price down. Still, it was a lovely day at Monmouth, hot in the sun and cool down under the grandstand seats, and Hatcher wandered comfortably around, betting five here and ten there, and only returned to Big John on the second floor after each race to see if the next one was it. In the meantime he did his handicapping and was looking forward to the seventh race and a horse named Dancer's Gal.

After the sixth he found John still leaning on the metal rail behind the seats, staring fixedly out at the track. He did not turn his head as Hatcher came up, but spoke out of the side of his mouth. "This is it," he said. "This is the one they're goin' with."

"Oh-oh. There's a horse I like in this race."

"Yeah?" John continued to chew another plastic tip and stare into the flowers in the infield. "Which?"

"The six horse—Dancer's Gal."

John now turned his jowly face slowly to him. "Well, Teacher," he said, "that's the baby."

Hatcher strolled out the back of the grandstand and signaled a waiting cab. "I need a phone for a minute. Wherever you think."

"I unnerstan'." The driver took him to a bowling alley in Oceanport. "Leon? This is Phil—Phil the Professor—Jim the Greek give me your number. Did he speak to you? Good. By the week on Mondays. Good. Now listen, Leon. I got one in the seventh at Jersey."

"Don't tell me," Leon said. "There's a hot horse in that race."

"The one I want is that Dancer's Gal."

"That's the hot one," Leon said. "I'm loaded with that horse already. I can't take much, Phil. How much you want?"

"Shit, I dunno. A hundred to win?"

"I dunno—well, maybe I can get it off. As a favor to a new customer, O.K.?"

"Thanks, Leon."

The cabdriver had thought about the phone call and Hatcher's assurance, and he inquired gently, "Got anything good?"

"Maybe," Hatcher said, musing. "I'm not s'posed to give it away, though."

"Ya can't, ya can't," the older man said over his shoulder. "But listen." They swung back through the track gate and up to the main entrance. "You ever need a cab again, I'm right over there, by them flowers."

"Good." He took the escalator up to the second floor, looking for his partner. He saw that the odds board was now changing and that some horse was an early heavy favorite at six to five. Then he looked again, unbelieving, because it was number six, Dancer's Gal. Just then, at the wall between the grandstand and the clubhouse, opposite the hundred-dollar windows, he saw John talking with a tall, thin man in a dark suit and hat. He stationed himself a few yards behind them until John turned.

"Set, Professor?"

"I don't get it, John. In the first place, that horse is hot in town—"

"Yeah," John broke in. "Yeah, I just heard dat. Ain't that a bitch. Somebody musta give it out."

"Yeah? And looka this six to five shit here."

"I don' know what's goin' on," John said. "How much did you get down on it?"

"The man would only take a hundred."

"Yeah. Well, sothin's wrong. Brant won't like the price much."

"You mean he won't go with the horse?"

"Don' misunnerstan', Teacher! *Our* money's in, ain't it? Just that now I don' know what the jock'll do, is all. No. Far as *we're* concerned, it's goin'. But look at the price. Somebody threw a couple hunnert in early here, and that's what happens—some small time."

But this was not what Hatcher had expected for race fixing. Everything that should have been locked away, it seemed, was wide open. "Look, John, do I bet the horse or not?"

"A *course!* Ain't I gonna bet five hunnert myself? It's just that it's too bad the price ain't there, that's all." So Hatcher went to the hundred-dollar window and got three tickets. Before the race went Dancer's Gal climbed gradually to two to one, and that was where she was when the gates opened. As was usual in her form, she broke very slowly.

"I'm a little worried," John growled sidewise, "about that three horse." Over in the backstretch, Dancer's Gal had begun to lengthen stride, rallying smoothly from last. "That's the only thing I'm worried about."

"How come?" She was passing the stragglers now, coming up swiftly on the horses bunched on the lead. "Is the fix in, or not?" Hatcher was not so worried as that sounded. He had picked the horse, and it appeared she would win it, anyway.

"I dunno," John said, "whether they got to this kid on the three or not." Two of the leaders were tiring. Dancer's Gal ranged past one, and then the other. She was going well, but then, suddenly and for no reason, she seemed to steady and settle behind the front-runner, number three, who now drew off by three or four lengths as they turned for home. In the stretch Dancer's Gal made a fine run, but it was too little and too late. She missed the win by half a length.

"God damn it," John whispered, and threw his cigar to the ground. "That was the only thing we had to worry about, too." He turned to Hatcher and nodded, tight-lipped and rueful. "Couple black cats, Teacher. That pig has to pick today to break bad."

Hatcher would not look at him, staring at the horses trotting back. "She's no pig, John. That's a good filly. You ever look at the *Telegraph?*"

"Huh?"

"That filly never broke better than two horses from last in her life, even goin' a mile and an eighth, and usually worse than that. What happened comin' into the stretch, John?"

"I dint see that. What?"

"Brant pulled her, is what." Hatcher turned away and went to get himself a hot dog, and John went off again somewhere. In ten minutes he was back, and they walked out to Hatcher's car in the parking lot.

"Yeah, Brant tol' me. He says, 'John, when I see them odds, I'm sick. But I know the money is in, right? I mean—I know we gotta go,' he says, 'but them odds did make me sick. And we was comin' good,' he says. 'We was there it hadn't been for that start.' "

"The bullshit."

"Naw, Phil. You're wrong. This kid is a hunnert per cent. Listen to me. Look. I just got this. They got another one on Saturday. We get it all back. You O.K. for paper?"

"I get paid on Friday," Hatcher said through tightened lips.

"Well, O.K. Don' worry about nuthin'."

"I never heard," Margaret said at home, "of a fixed race where the horse didn't win."

"Well. It looked to me like some kind of double cross," Hatcher said. "I don't know."

"Well, you're not going to fool with him anymore, are you?"

"Oh, I'll take one more shot with him, I guess. But I won't bet much. Check this out once and for all." It sounded very cautious and sensible, but in fact he had no choice; he had to get some money.

"O.K. Oh. I start work tomorrow."

"On a *Friday?*"

"Might as well."

"I guess so."

Two days later Polyglow won the fifth at Monmouth and paid five twenty. John had said that the fix was in, and Hatcher had bet sixty dollars. "Christ!" John said on his stool at the Dunkin' Donuts. "Sixty bucks."

"Wait a minute, John. I don't wanta hear that shit. You blame me for bein' gun-shy, after Thursday?"

"Oh, I see that! But how you gonna get it back bettin' sixties? I *tol'* you, Teacher. That other one was a bad break. That shit don't happen. But what do I tell my friends? Sixty bucks! Jesus, Teacher!"

Hatcher became ashamed. "Make it on the next one."

"Next one. I hope. Otherwise there ain't no next one. Awright. I get ya, though. Listen. How ya doin' with my man? Awright?"

"Well, I ain't beatin' him," Hatcher laughed. "I'm checking a couple of guys I know today. They might give him a little action."

"Nuthin' big!"

"No."

"Good. You'll hear from me, Teacher." He left three quarters on the counter and walked lightly out.

In the next week, Hatcher weaved as usual through his two days of classes, teaching novels on the basis of a page or two and poets from their shortest poems, inventing arguments and quibbles on the moment, retailing what literary gossip he could remember from graduate school, doing anything to get past the fifty minutes. He read the *Telegraph* constantly, but he did not bet much, and he did not play poker at all. He waited and held his money for the next live one.

Margaret left for the New York bus every day at quarter of eight, and came home at seven, or later. For a few days he would ask her what she was doing, and she would tell him excitedly about the group she was personally promoting or how well a new record was going. Once she called to say that she would be late because they all were going to a club to hear a performance. Once when he came home from the track, she was there talking gaily into the phone. She had hung up after another moment, and Hatcher had thought nothing about it.

That week also he talked horses over coffee as usual with a graduate student he knew and who appeared to admire him, and as usual he gave him a tip or two. "And by the way, Marty. If you ever want to get anything in, you know, and I'm not around, you can. I got a number for you."

"That's great," said the young man. "Easy."

Hatcher slid him the slip of paper. "Just use your own name —first name. It's all O.K.'d. I told him you were a friend of mine."

"Thanks, Phil."

"In fact, there's a double that looks pretty good today. You can take a shot with it if you want."

"What is it?" Marty asked.

With Frankie he took a different tack. "We might be able to PP this guy."

"Who is he? I *must* know 'im."

"Naw, I think he's new here, Frank."

"Well, what's his outfit, his partners?"

"Naw. A guy I know down the track told me about him, so I put in a few with him. I figured I'd O.K. you with him too, then, and we could get him both ways."

"Yeah, maybe," Frankie said, and began feeding some of his own bets to Big John's friend.

On Friday another of John's piece horses won. He won by five lengths and paid six sixty. Hatcher had scraped up four hundred to bet on him.

"Not *too* bad, hey, Teacher?" John scowled at his cards as

Hatcher handed over behind the table four hundred and sixty dollars for the friends.

"Can't it get better, John?"

The other laughed. "Teacher! Don' worry. It will. That's rummy." He laid down his cards, and Hatcher threw him three wadded singles. "Yeah. The next one should be a price."

In the morning, while Hatcher was taking his wife, for the change, to her bus, a beefy man in a gray plaid jacket and gray trousers shouldered himself irritably by the janitor of the Harrison Street School across from Frankie Buono's parking lot. He tramped along the corridors, carrying his black brief-case, and stopped before a classroom door. Behind the door could be heard a shrill hubbub of voices. The man raised his hand to knock, hesitated, reddened, and wrenched abruptly at the doorknob.

The boys and girls were crying: "I know, Miss Hawkins"—"Me, Miss Hawkins"—"Oh, Miss Hawkins!" A light-haired boy in the back of the room had apparently been holding up his arm so long that now he needed his other arm to support it at the elbow; he looked glum and resigned. Another was shaking his hand frantically, as if there were a wasp on it. Little girls were bouncing in their seats and crying out answers. All fell silent when they saw this red-faced man. Miss Hawkins, sadly elegant and henna-haired, moved from behind her desk to meet him.

"You are the lieutenant?" she drawled in a whisper.

"Yes. Ma'am." He stood there stiff, holding his case out away from his side. Once he glanced quickly around at the children. It was Miss Hawkins who finally broke that silence.

"You—where would you—"

"Oh!" the man said. A little girl giggled. "Anywhere—anywhere in the back. On the street." Miss Hawkins nodded graciously and with the back of one hand touched her wrinkled, drooping cheek. The man turned, quick and awkward, and clumped to the back. Young eyes rolled on him all the way.

"Now," Miss Hawkins said. "This man has some work to do in our room for a while, and we mustn't bother him—Roy! Turn *around* please, Roy. Thank *you.*" But Roy at least had seen the man lift from the bag a gray machine, although he did not know it was a moving-picture camera until he, and all the rest of them, heard the intermittent whirring and clicking behind them that lasted until history was over and they were into arithmetic.

"Now then," Miss Hawkins beamed at them showily. "Who can tell me who it was who *really* discovered America?"

Down below, in the lot, Hatcher walked easily up to the change shack. Frankie scowled and seemed to speak sharply, then laughed. From inside the booth he hauled a newspaper and folded it over and pointed in it while Hatcher looked on grinning and careless. In the schoolroom, an incautious voice cried, "Columbus did!" Immediately four or five children played the results, hooting and jeering while Miss Hawkins shook her smiling face. Another tried to cover more of the field and mumbled, "Italians." The camera rattled softly on.

"Well, how ya been doin', Phil?"

"Not bad, Frank. Pretty good. Guy was giving me some horses. Most of 'em stood up."

"Who was givin' ya?"

"Oh, that John. Big John they call him."

"You mean Froggy? John the Frog?"

"Is that him?"

"You watch it with those people, Phil. I don't wanna see you get involved."

"They're nothin' to me, Frank. The horses have been there." He ticked off the names and the prices.

"Yeah?" Frank said, dubious. "I didn't hear nuthin' on them. Far as I know, there wasn't nuthin' out on them horses."

"Well, these people are careful."

"Those are all *figure* horses, too. Yeah. An' he tol' you those races were good? What? Stiffed?"

"Well—yeah."

"Yeah. You be careful, Phil. Don't go too heavy on them horses."

"Why not? They're winnin', ain't they?"

"Yeah. They're winnin'. But how do you know they *have* to win?"

Hatcher laughed smugly. "O.K., Frank." But Frankie became more severe, giving the lesson he had suddenly become convinced of.

"They could be *toutin'*, fer Christ sake—with horses they're *handicappin'!*"

"I thought of that," Hatcher said. "But how much could it get 'em? Why in hell would somebody hustle *me?*"

Frankie snorted and turned away to stare down at the punching clock, shaking his head. Then he seemed to relent and faced Hatcher again. "Phil, let me tell you suthin' about the con. The first thing they look for—it ain't how much you got. It's how *easy* you are. You gotta unnerstan'. If they think you're easy enough, they don' have to *know*. They wait an' see. Naw. They don't even care. If a guy is easy enough, they'll get him for four bits. What's the difference? You be careful."

"Don't worry about it, Frank."

"Sometimes, Phil, you're too soft."

"Hah! O.K. I'll remember that the next time you hit me for a half a yard."

"Well. Now that you mention it, Phil," Frankie beamed, "I am a little short—"

Hatcher's amusement had disappeared by the time he reached his office in the English building. He sat, as he always did, with the door closed and locked reading the *Telegraph* carefully. Once he heard a familiar voice outside and stiffened, but it passed.

Minutes later there was a soft, hesitant knocking. Hatcher folded up the paper and slid it into the waiting, open drawer, and waited. The knocking repeated. He kicked the drawer shut loudly and opened the door.

At first he saw no one, but when he pushed his head out he saw the figure leaning against the wall as if melting into it. "Mr. Lindt," he said.

"Oh, hi, Mr. Hatcher." The greeting seemed almost too much for him. "Can I bother you for a second?"

"I guess so." Hatcher waved him in. When they were seated, the long, pale boy said nothing; there was the suggestion of some enervated partnership. But Hatcher thought he knew the game and kept silent himself, so that at last the student averted his gaze to the door and spoke.

"I came by yesterday. You weren't here."

"Did I miss anything?"

"Well, you know, I was supposed to have those papers—yeah." He gave a low, muttering snicker. "But. I'm going to be frank with you, sir, about why I haven't done them."

"Wait a minute," Hatcher began to say. "I don't—"

"Oh, I mean a lot of guys would make up a story, you know. But I just don't see the point. You know. What the hell. You know."

"Mr. Lindt, I don't *care*—"

"No, I'm going to be honest with you. I wasn't sick or anything —I was *stoned.*" He paused, staring resolutely at his teacher. "I mean I was *turned on.*" He paused again, seeming to reflect. Then he mumbled, "Whole weekend," and subsided.

"So?"

"*So?*"

"So what?"

"Well, the fact is, sir—the fact is that I can't hack this. I mean, what is it, anyway. Just a grade hassle all the time—so that in four years—"

"I have one question," Hatcher interrupted.

"Huh?"

"What made you think that *I* would be interested in any of this?"

"*Well*—I mean, it is your thing; isn't it; it's what you do—"

"No. I don't care about drugs. And this isn't my thing, Mr. Lindt—"

"Call me Barry."

"This isn't my thing; it's my job. Just like it's your job to do the papers. But that doesn't mean that we have to *do* our jobs."

"No?" He seemed hopeful.

"Hell, no! I don't do mine, I get fired. You don't do yours, you leave school."

"Sure. That's easy. The goddamn army."

"Well, then do the papers. It's simple."

"It isn't, though. Not if you think of all—"

But Hatcher was tired of it and cut him off. "I'll say it again: why should I be interested? I'm just your sophomore English teacher—"

"But it's human beings!" The long face had become paler; the eyes narrowed. "Just one human being talking to another. I think that's enough."

"You do."

"Sure! Don't you?"

Hatcher considered, not his answer but the idea of answering. "No," he said. "Even if you mean it, I don't. Human being has nothing to do with it. Do something. Don't ask anybody to be interested in the sight of you treading water. Do something."

The boy got up. "I'll do the papers," he said wearily. "I just thought——"

"I know," Hatcher said. "You thought I was a bigger sucker than I am."

Lindt grinned slackly. With his hand on the doorknob he

began again, "Is there any chance you———"

"No chance. You owe all of the papers for the whole course. You have to do them; I have to read them."

He nodded glumly. "Well, I appreciate your talking straight with me." The doorknob turned from the other side, and the student jumped back startled.

"It's all right, Mr. Lindt." As the student's wavering form went out, another came in—shorter, straight and brisk, the chairman. He stroked his silver hair, half-turned, and stared at Barry Lindt's receding back. He turned again and smiled at Hatcher, shaking his head.

"Hello, Phil. A moment?"

"Sure. Sure! Sit down." Clough did so, crossing his legs to expose a long stretch of smooth black stocking.

"Well, Phil, I'm happy to say that your colleagues have acted favorably on my request that we promote you to the rank of Associate Professor, to a permanent place in the department." Hatcher nodded slowly, shocked: how could they have? "It's not effective immediately. What we did was extend your Assistant Professorship another three years, with the understanding that as soon as your book is accepted you'll be given tenure immediately, all other things being equal. But they had no doubt of the quality of what they'd seen of your book, and, of course, I explained that you were finishing up on it."

Hatcher was thinking, another three years, and he said, "I see. That's fine. Thank you, Phil."

"Not at all. That was right, wasn't it? I mean, I didn't overstep my—"

Hatcher took a breath. "I've been meaning to come and speak to you about it." Clough's lips appeared to compress slightly, but his gray eyes still glittered, as if amused or confident. "The idea of the book," Hatcher went on, "about art working to upset knowledge, to unstabilize patterns of experience rather than establish them—" He heard the words again that were there on the pages in the desk drawer, and it seemed he would never stop saying them. Clough heard the weariness in his voice.

"There's more than one idea there, Phil."

"Well, I guess so—sure. But it boils down to that. And I still stand by that."

"Just as you should, Phil. But really. Don't worry about how it—'boils down.' It's a new idea, Phil. People should hear about it."

Nothing to Hatcher could have been less new. Still, he had his opening, his excuse, now. "Still—I want to make it as good as it could be. And that may take more time than I'd thought. It seems to me it needs a lot of filling out."

"You mean *major* changes, Phil?"

"I'm afraid so. Much more than I'd assumed." He was looking at the litter on his desk top, seeing in it, in the chairman's announcement, in his very confidence, a future of obligation and compromise.

"O.K., Phil. You've got time." Clough still seemed satisfied, and rocked back in his chair.

"No—it might be better if I took time off."

"Oh, I don't know," Clough said, his voice more brittle. "It's late to ask for any sort of grant. It's *possible* that you could get a semester's leave. I might try to work on it."

"No, no. I'm not asking for any money, but I do need the time. I was thinking in terms of a leave of absence."

"I *see.*" Clough was looking at him steadily now, sharp and cautious. "I wouldn't have thought that necessary. But."

Hatcher shrugged. "I may be wrong. The way it looks to me at this point."

The chairman became businesslike. "Well it's not too late to get a temporary replacement for you, of course. If you really want a leave. I'd have to know soon."

"Let's make it definite now."

"You've decided." The chairman clapped his hands on his knees and rose. "All right. I'll arrange it. Perhaps your book will be the better for it."

"I appreciate—" But Clough shook his head shortly and frowned, and let himself out. Hatcher turned and gazed at the expanse of wall above his desk.

"Why should I put up with that shit?" he said to Margaret. "They want to keep their eye on me and make sure that I come along. They must really think I'm a live one."

"But isn't that more or less standard procedure? In a way it's what you worked to get to."

"Yeah, and I made a mistake doing it, too. But I'm not going to send good after bad. What I'd like to do is get hold of some of those people—my old teachers—'Sure! Teaching is great. You'll like it.' I mean, they must have *known*. Why did they say that?"

"Maybe they really liked it, and thought you would."

"I don't believe it. Who likes it? No. No, I've had it. What do I need that job for, anyway? I could never get out that way." Hatcher paused, so intent upon noting the effects of his speech on her that he did not catch its significance himself. And she was taking the news more calmly than he had expected, so to make his victory clearer, more emphatic, to her, he falsified it. "So I just quit. Clough told me that I hadn't been promoted, and I quit. Money's not a problem. I can get out with this John—where you going?"

"Wash the dishes."

That irritated him. He felt he had been telling something both important and surprising, but she was careless about his plans. "*You're* taking this all pretty easy," he barked.

Margaret turned, "Well, why shouldn't I?"

"Well," he threw up his hands, waiting for her to interrupt. She did not. "No reason, I suppose."

"Why," Margaret said, "should I start telling you what to do, now?"

She said the same thing the next day to Tommy who slumped on his sofa. His hands were clasped behind his neck, his legs stretched out easily to the floor. "And he just quit?"

"That's what he said."

Tommy laughed. "What a character. He's something."

Margaret turned back toward him from looking out the window, twitching her long cigarette in her fingers. "I used to think so."

"I know you did, Marge. I couldn't figure it out then, and I can't now." He grinned at her and rubbed the side of his blond head rapidly with his knuckles. "It was always supposed to be something different, with him."

"No, not that. It wasn't just that—not just a lot of things. I don't know. At the time—for a long time—it was fun being with someone who—who nothing really mattered to, nothing that most people care about. When we were—when you were with him, there was nothing but you and him. Nothing beyond you, over you. Nothing you had to depend on. He wouldn't allow it —or admit it, or something—"

"And now what, Margie?"

She looked up, held her hands out at her sides, and let them fall. "Now? Now he's just a gambler."

"Right."

"No, you don't see. You couldn't believe it. You can't imagine the way he does it."

"I can see that he's treating you lousy," Tom said. He was leaning forward in his seat now and seemed very earnest.

"Huh! He's not treating me at all." She looked at him. "Do you really want to talk about this?"

"Only if you do."

"Old Tommy," Margaret said smiling at him. She walked to

him and laid a hand on his shoulder. "To the rescue."

"I haven't done any rescuing yet," he said, looking at the backs of his hands. "No chance."

"I'm sorry, Tom. I'm not teasing you. I don't know what I'm doing."

"Why then, I'll wait, baby. I'll wait till you do."

It sounded so honest and sad that Margaret was very sorry she had left him years ago for someone she was thinking now of leaving. How could she just take up with him again, as if she had made him wait three years for her to get over a mistake? "Old Tommy," she said, and bent and kissed him on the mouth.

"Are you crazy, Phil?" Frankie howled. "What're you, crazy or sothin'?"

"Get off it!" Hatcher shouted back. "What do I need that shit for? I *packed 'em up.*"

"Yeah. Yeah, you packed 'em up. Now, what'll ya do? Tell me that. What do you think, anyway?" Frankie's head rocked from side to side on each word. "What do you think? You think you can past-post forever? Then what? *Gamble?* You can't have little hard luck? Then where are ya?" He shook his head more slowly and solemnly, turning his back to punch a ticket. "Naw, Phil," he said, spreading his hands on the low shelf of the booth and drooping his head. "Naw, you are one hunnert per cent wrong. One hunnert per cent."

Hatcher nodded repeatedly in irritation. "O.K., Frank. I'm wrong. Sure. O.K."

"What? Yer not? Well, what happened to me yesterday, tell me that? What happened to me?"

"What do you mean?"

"What happened to me? I got *nailed,* that's what—fer bookin', fer Christ sake!"

"*What?*"

"What do *you* think?" Frankie shouted. "Them cutie pies have got me right on film—a hundred and fifty feet of it. Hah!" His tone was both outraged and satisfied. "Next week," he nodded his head in tragic acquiescence, "next week I go up before the gran' jury."

"Jesus Christ."

"Well, that's what I'm sayin'. That's what I'm just tellin' ya. There are a lotta ways you can go in this business. Naw, Phil. You're wrong."

Hatcher did not think so even though his decision had been much less emphatic than he had made it seem in his various tellings. He especially did not think so when, a day later, he got his call from John.

"O.K., Teacher."

"Yeah?"

"This is the one. They got one comin' up that ain't no chalk. This is where you—where we all get out."

"That's good, John."

"Yeah, believe me. On'y thing, it's tamorra."

"All the better."

"Yeah. But these people want this one bet good—no more deuces and treys."

"I dunno. I can get about six together."

"See, Teacher, that's still only a trey for them."

"Yeah. Sure. What do you figure the horse'll pay?"

"Well, Professor," John's voice came confidentially, and he paused some seconds. "The word I got," again the pause, "is *fourteen dollars minimum.*"

"Christ."

"You like it, huh?"

"What do you think? But God damn it. Every time I get—"

"Well, Teacher," John interrupted. "But if it's just a question of time, I could scrape some up for you."

"Yeah?"

"Aw, I got a few connections would help you out. I'd lend ya myself, ya know, 'cept I gotta put money down, too. But I can get ya some money."

"How much can you get?" Whatever it would be would be on the horse and multiplied by six.

"We'd have to pay it back."

"So what?" That was no problem, at fourteen dollars for two.

"O.K., Teacher. How much do ya want?"

"A thousand too much?" The very difficulty of the situation had become somehow its promise, drawing him on.

"A gee? Na-aw. I could get two if you want it."

"Get two."

The horse's name was Money Honey. She was running in the third race at Monmouth—six furlongs, two-year-old maiden fillies, $6500 claiming. This was her first race ever. Hatcher bet as much as he could on her with Leon, and at the track he left John and for twenty minutes as instructed paid his two thousand dollars carefully into the machines, twenty here and fifty there, moving from window to window, trying to keep the odds up. They stayed. When the horses broke and the ticket machines locked, Money Honey was thirteen to one.

"All the better," he crowed to John.

"Yeah. Ain't it."

In her first start Money Honey ran relatively well. From a slow start and seventh position she made up three or four lengths on the turn, settled for the drive in fifth, and came evenly down the stretch to be fourth. Hatcher watched unbelieving, waiting for the horse to move, or for the others to back up, or for whatever was to happen to happen. He was still waiting, hanging, empty, starved for the needed result, when the race was over. Then, when he at last knew it was over, irreversible, he turned on John, his mouth open and silent. The other stared at the track, as if disbelieving.

"Don't ask me what happened, Teacher," he said coldly. "I know I'm gonna get to the bottom of *this!* Somebody's gonna be sorry, I know *that.*" He turned and walked quickly away through the crowd. Hatcher watched his squat, broad figure disappear, then sat distractedly down on one of the green benches that were set on the littered blacktop before the grandstand. On the result board the prices flashed; the favorite had won, and the crowd cheered her and the jockey as she stood blowing in the winner's circle. Beside him on the bench a boy and a girl shouted happily at their victory and kissed. Hatcher folded his arms on his thighs, hunched, and stared between his shoes, as if thinking.

"Yeah, that was the swindle, Professor." When John had returned only a few minutes after he had walked away through the
crowd, he said nothing. He jerked his head, and Hatcher followed
him, numbly, out to the parking lot. Now, while Hatcher drove
them back, John opened up. "That boy run out on us."

"Who, Dankin?"

"Naw! That kid Brown on the winner! What happened, when
Dankin sees him jump out on that lead, he knew he couldn' catch
'im, and he knew there's no good runnin' second or third for the
price next time, so he took back. So we can still get the price."

"The horse still ran fourth—"

"Ah, that won't do nuthin'. Believe me." John sat back and
narrowed his close-set eyes through the window. Then he patted
his pockets irritably. "Christ! No fuckin' cigars. I didn't think to
buy 'em. That's how I gotta go."

"Yeah. Rough."

"No, listen, Teacher. That kid is gonna be sorry. I person'ly
guarantee it. He should know better."

"Why? Has he done business with you before?"

"With *me?* Oh, you mean with these people. Certainly! Do you
think they'd set this up without checkin' him out? He was *in* all

right. He just thought he'd look out fer himself a little. He's in trouble now—bastard."

"What good is it?"

"Well, you're right there, Professor. A hunnert per cent. It don't get our paper back, does it?" He was talking as if to himself, gazing out the side window. "I borrowed myself to get into this horse, you know. An' now I gotta get it up, an' where—but I guess I don't have to cry to you. You're in for two big ones yourself."

"Yeah." He knew what was coming.

"Yeah. Well, my connections can wait a couple weeks, maybe even a mont'. They're gettin' vig on the paper, they can wait."

Hatcher did not reply until they had stopped for the traffic light in Lincroft. Across the street the cars of the day's winners had begun to fill the parking lot of a restaurant, as if directed by the two little red-coated, plaster statues that flanked the driveway. "How much is the interest, John?"

"The usual. Six for five. What else?"

"Yeah. Right."

Margaret was not home when he unlocked the apartment door, but he hardly noticed. He walked into the bedroom, scuffed off his shoes, and let himself down on the bed. Seven hours later, the slamming door awakened him.

"Phil?"

He grunted and rolled over, and his wife came in smiling. "What you doing?"

"Oh, I had dinner with Tom and some people. We worked a little late with one bunch, and I thought you'd be late too, and it'd be O. K."

"Sure it's O. K. What time is it?"

"Almost ten thirty."

"I gotta get goin'," Hatcher said, crouching on the bed's edge and yawning. "South River."

"Oh. You're playing cards tonight?"

"Yup. I need some money."

"Did you and that John do anything today?"

"Naw. Nothing."

Margaret began to undress, and Hatcher put on his shoes, patted her in the small of the back, and said good-night. He took his car up the street to the candy store and cashed a check there for thirty dollars that he knew would bounce. Then he turned around and came back down past the apartment building, heading for South River.

All the boys were surprised, even glad, to see him, and they said he must have something nice going to stay away so long. He asked them smiling what did they think, and they rolled their eyes and said was he the Professor or not? It seemed a homecoming, and he almost forgot, when he sat down laughing to play, just how far behind he was.

Hatcher was careful and remained unlucky. When Ray came in and greeted him about twelve thirty, he had seven dollars and some quarters left in front of him. He drew a pair of kings as his hole cards and then, with an ace showing, bet three on the first round and four on the second, trying to push the others out and to get as much as he could for his cards at the same time. But the players knew he was easy, and two of them chased him with small pairs. At the end of it he had two pairs, kings up, and three fours won the pot. Hatcher tipped back in his chair and signaled to Ray, mouthing a silent and interrogative "Fifty?" across the room.

Ray nodded, strolled over, and laid five tens in the trough in front of him. "How you been doin', Professor? Long time."

"Yeah, Ray. The horses got me. Thanks."

"They'll do it to you. Think nothin' of it."

By three in the morning Hatcher had lost, carefully, angrily, all on good cards, two hundred and thirty-five. The two hundred was borrowed. "Listen, Ray," he said at the door, "would you mind waitin' a little for that?"

The man's face was serious, but he did not hesitate. "You don' have to worry about it," he said. "An' don't hesitate to come by an' play, you know, Professor. You can owe me. Anybody can get caught speedin'."

"Thanks." He ran down the stairs and drove fast over the deserted roads back to Jimmy's place. There were still five stern-faced, tired players left there. Hatcher sat down and drank a cup of Greek coffee and looked the game over. It was fast; in fifteen minutes he saw two pots of over a hundred dollars. He had to get into it.

"There's a seat open if you want it, Pheel," Jimmy said.

"I'm tap, Jim."

The Greek shrugged, and drew from his jacket pocket a wad of bills. He spread five twenties out on the stained surface of the table. With his 5 per cent of every pot that was played and six players in the game, he could get that hundred back in three hours, and still he would have it coming on loan. But Hatcher knew also that he was being friendly.

It was just the freewheeling play he thought he needed, a strong game, the players good enough to press their cards but not good enough to respect anyone else's. There were three of them who called every pot right to the end. But none of that matters if the cards do not come. Hatcher played tight for an hour and lost twenty in antes. Then he lost his patience, excusing it with the notion that he had to get into the swing of the game to win, and flew along with the rest, hoping that for him, too, the single pairs and busted straights would stand up.

The game was loose enough so that for a while they did. Then there was a big hand with much raising. He had a flush and stayed to the finish. He lost to four of a kind, but he considered that a fluke and waved to Jimmy for more money. The player who had won the hand, however, had got enough. He said that that was all and pushed back. His buddy, next to Hatcher, shrugged and got up too. They had most of the money. Hatcher would have continued playing four-handed against the losers, but Jimmy did not even answer his silent request. "O.K., boys," he said wearily, "we play again tonight." The day closed down.

At the Esperance Club the next night he was good for a hundred more, and when he asked to make it a hundred and fifty, Ray could only shrug, sheepish and helpless. "Phil. I know you'll stand up for it. But I got a little too much out." The next night he borrowed another hundred from Jimmy, who, after Hatcher had lost it, declared that any other time but now. At the Italian-American Club and the other joints he had no hope, but he tried all the same and was refused. It was a week before his next pay check from the college, and he was really broke. He did not consider that he was, counting it up, some ten thousand dollars in debt, not even that he would be a long time getting even. The point was that there were cards being dealt and horses running, but for him they presented no chance at all. His time was dead, and he was out of action.

But he would not see the end. He borrowed fifty dollars from Frankie Buono, who said he could not go for more because his trial was coming up. The money went in three races. With the fourth impending—with a horse in it Hatcher was sure would win —he approached first his handicapping cronies and then bare acquaintances, men he had seen once or twice at the parking lot or even on the race track bus. Some of them expected it, and some were surprised. All of them said they wished to hell they could, and turned their palms up. When the horse he wanted to bet in that race lost, however, Hatcher became paradoxically more frantic. That meant, he was sure, that he would catch the next one. It then seemed to him that he liked number three in the fifth race very much indeed. After all, what they call the law of averages was with him. He made his rounds again, hoping to find someone cashing a bet, flush. He talked his horse up to anyone who would listen, for even if he could not bet, when the horse won someone might be grateful and stake him.

The sky had clouded earlier, and now there was a burst of rain. In minutes there were standing pools of water on the track. Hatcher was the more desperate because his horse, Princess Gigi, was an excellent mudder. But when the gates sprang open, he had no bet; Princess Gigi ran a close third. Then he saw Big John.

John may have seen him too, but he appeared to turn more directly toward his friends and only turned again when Hatcher came up. "Hey. Teacher."

"Hey, John. How is it I haven't heard from you?"

"Aw. Nuthin' much doin', Professor. An' I know you're tap. I been havin' trouble myself, makin' it."

"No more pieces, huh."

"Yeah. Oh, yeah! They had a couple." John nodded in earnest, as if to affirm his personal bad luck. "Yeah, they paid some prices, too. An' you know how much *I* had on 'em—*nuthin'!*" He sighed noisily and flapped his short arms at his sides. "Yeah, Teacher. They got me over the barrel again."

"Listen. John. Lend me a double?"

"Gee, you know me, Phil. You could have anythin' I got—you know that. But that's just it. I ain't *got it!* A mont' ago I was handlin' fifteen big ones, and here I am scratchin' around with fins!" Hatcher was not listening. He did not want to hear the details of the refusal and was already numbly looking for another source. "No, listen," John said. "I just see a guy I know, always has plenty paper. Lemme go see what I can do. I can use some myself anyway, Christ." He stumped away.

Because Hatcher did not really expect to see John again that afternoon, he only waited there fifteen minutes, until the race he had wanted to bet went off. His horse was pulled up, lame on the turn. He began to walk the grandstand, as if searching still, but he approached no one. On a return circuit, casting vaguely, he hesitated, stopped, and stood stiffly among the people pressing toward the windows. His face lost its tension; his mouth twisted in disgust; and he moved quickly toward the down escalator. The loudspeaker voice said that the horses were on the track for the sixth.

For three days he did not play at all. In fact, he did nothing. He appeared at his classes only to cancel them, pleading an excess of paper-grading, and his students went happily out unquestioning. He saw his wife three times, in the evening of each day. She did not see that he was any worse than usual. On the morning of the fourth day, Hatcher was sitting, staring at his office wall. The *Telegraph* lay unopened in its original, neat folds on his desk; he had no hope of finding any money, and he was sick of mind bets. When the telephone rang, he let it. After it had kept on a while, he slowly rolled his chair over to the filing cabinet and picked it up.

"Teacher!" It was John. It had to be about the money. But Hatcher was surprised as the other growled along into small talk. He was encouraged to interrupt it.

"Hey, John. I could use a little information. I'm short now, but once I get out—" The other end of the line was silent, and he thought that John might be considering.

"Naw, naw, Teacher. No dice. You know, as well as me, with these people it is strictly business. They give it out, they want their PC. You know that." There was a pause. "They're not worried about the other money, a course, but how far can they go?"

"You mean it's *their* money I borrowed to bet that stiff?"

"Listen, Professor. That horse was no stiff. The kid did cop a sneak. But the horse was there. She win next time out, ya know."

"Yeah?"

"Certainly. But like I said. I can't give you no more. It wouldn't be right. You see that."

"Maybe I'm just as well off."

"Yeah? Naw. Naw, that time was bad luck. But, listen Teacher, I unnerstan' you made the movies. Haw haw."

"What?"

John continued his unbroken, gargling chuckle. "Yeah, just like Hollywood around this town now. Naw. You know. You know that guy Buono? Frank, it is, idn't it? Down the parking lot? Well. They been takin' pictures a him takin' action.

They got him dead. It's just that I know you're in the pictures yourself."

Hatcher thought that John was trying to scare him, and bristled. "So what?"

"Nuthin'! Matter of fact, I personally know for a fact that you won't even be called to testify. Funny though, ain't it. Makin' the pictures—the Teacher."

"I know I won't be called, John. Because he's gotta be gettin' fucked. They must have somebody really singin'. He's no *bookmaker,* for Christ sake!"

John's voice came softly. "Does he take action, Teacher?"

"Ha! Sure. Action. About twelve dollars a day! Small stuff from friends that he either calls in or sits on. You call that takin' action, huh?"

"Oh, I saw what ya mean. Yeah. Well listen, Teach. I gotta go. Keep in touch, huh?"

"Sure. Keep in touch." Hatcher replaced the phone, blew out his breath, and opened the *Telegraph.*

He spent the afternoon hanging around the change booth, arguing for this horse and that, listening for results. Once he thought a horse looked so good that he asked Frankie to put it in and trust him for it, but the other said he could go no more on the arm. Hatcher said that he understood and waited still. Near the parking lot's closing time, they were listening for the results of the eighth at Monmouth. When he heard them, Frankie crowed, "*That's* me!"

"You hit?"

The old man shook his head to the rhythm of his sentences, happy and outraged at the same time. "Just a four if eight and reverse, six win, six place parlay, is all! I told that Jimmy, 'That Guy is a cinch today.' I played 'im against a four to five shot." That Guy paid fourteen sixty; the other half of the bet had been the winner of the sixth at Aqueduct at eight dollars even. "I needed this," Frankie said earnestly, "for my trial."

"How is that, anyway?" Hatcher pretended his interest.

Frankie looked over his shoulder and back. "Well, Phil, I'm pleadin' guilty. To *lottery*. In other words, *I* think I could beat it, but my lawyer says this is the best way to go. This way it costs me a few hunnert and that's that. The other way —well, I do think I could beat it—but if I don't, it's a thousand minimum plus I lose this job, plus probation, prob'ly. I don't *need* that."

"Lottery?"

Frankie's eyes swam impatiently behind the glasses. "We plead guilty," he spaced his words, "to takin' numbers! We are makin' a *deal!*"

"They'll reduce the charge?"

Frankie punched a ticket and swaggered out to attend a car. "Certainly," he called over his shoulder as he went. " 'Duce the charge." He dawdled over some joke with the car's driver and returned. "In other words, Phil," he said confidentially, out of the side of his mouth, savoring the sentence, "I am coppin' a plea."

On that day Frank worked late at his lot, and Hatcher ate with him when he broke for supper at five. Afterward there seemed to be nothing to do but go home. He was about to pull out into the street when Frankie waved for him to wait and came over. Through the car window he thrust three wrinkled tens. "Here for Christ sake," he growled. "I know you're tap."

"Hey, Frank! Thanks! The thirty dollars was so much to him that that night it stayed in his pocket. On the way home he bought six cans of beer, and when his wife came in around ten all but one were gone. Hatcher was dozing before a horror movie. He awakened enough to greet her, and she was bright and offhanded, moving around the apartment to gather papers and clothes, emptying ashtrays, disposing of the standing beer cans. Hatcher was offended by this and sank again into a sleep.

He awoke four hours later to the television's test pattern at first sheepish and then irritated. He made more noise than was necessary getting into bed, glaring as he did at his wife's form curled against the other wall. When he awoke again at the telephone's ringing, she was, of course, gone. It was Big John inviting him to coffee at the Dunkin' Donuts.

John was sitting squat at the counter, thrusting half a jelly donut into his mouth, when Hatcher came up to him. "Hey, Teacher," he said, expelling a small cloud of powdered sugar. "What'll it be?"

"Just coffee." Hatcher looked pointedly at the crumbs and spots of red jelly on the counter. "I don't want to cut into your supply of those things."

"Yeah. They got nice ones here. Well, Professor. How's it goin'?"

"What do you think?"

"Yeah. I know. When you need it, it just ain't there. Never can seem to score when you have to."

Hatcher added quickly, "But I got a few things goin' about gettin' that money up."

"Aw, I ain't worried about the paper. Fact, we might be able to do sonthin' with that. You know this guy, don't ya—the one they got hung up for bookin'?"

"Who?"

"*You* know. Haw. I even forgot his name. That, uh—Buono."

"Shit, yes, I know him, John. You *know* I know him. You were just telling me they had me on film with him."

"Don't misunnerstan' me," John blinked lazily. "They're not gonna bother you about it. They got plenny on that guy already."

"Shit. What they got—some yap that says he took one-dollar DD's? Get off it."

"Yeah? Well, but if *you* was to testify against the guy—"

"*Against* him—"

"Naw, you gotta unnerstan', Teacher. The thing is this. This guy *has* been takin' action, with no PC comin' back—to my friends. This guy is *independent,* for Christ sake!" John popped his eyes in showy outrage, nodded once sharply, then leaned over to slurp at his coffee. Hatcher could not make it out.

"John, are you tellin' me that this guy is cuttin' into somebody's action? Am I *that* big a sucker? The guy wasn't takin' twenty bucks a day!"

John wiped his mouth with a paper napkin and let it fall to the floor. He turned slowly and once again his eyelids slid sluggishly down and then snapped up and open like window shades. "Yeah," he muttered. "Course, I was kiddin' about that. It's for sonthin' else they're gonna nail him."

"What, for instance?"

"Look. Professor. Why do you have to worry about it? I dint think this was a bad deal for ya. Fact is, I suggested it to my friends. They said they really didn't need anythin' more on the guy, but there was no harm in insurance, since I said you were O.K. with me. I said there was no harm in givin' you a break, since you hit the couple pieces that went bad. So don't worry about it.

"Look. Less just say that this guy—this Buono—he's in a—*package.* You unnerstan' that? Sure. The cops got him on film, dead. They got a lot a guys dead, some of 'em friends of mine. It's just a question of who they wanna go after, for their quota. So they use him instead of one of my friends. Besides, he's easy. The other people they might know about would be a little tougher. So we help *them* out and put him in. You help us do it, we forget the bill. Simple. What you do, you don't go out for the sheet tomorrow till after eleven, that's all."

"I still don't believe it."

"That's it. They forget all about it."

Hatcher went away confused. Why anyone should be so interested in Frankie's case was clearer. But Buono would not even be tried for booking horses, but for taking numbers bets and selling sweepstakes tickets. Then Hatcher began to think that it was he that they were after; he was the real object of the scheme. But then what more could they get from him? It was not complicated; it was pointless.

At quarter to eleven the next morning the apartment doorbell rang, and when Hatcher opened it expecting John he was confronted by a tall, beaky man in a light blue suit. "Philip Hatcher?" He nodded, and the man thrust at him—and almost dropped— a piece of folded parchment. It was a formal invitation to Frankie's trial. Hatcher went out to get the scratch sheet.

After he had used his thirty dollars to bet his doubles—four six-dollar doubles, two horses in the first with two in the second —with Shoemaker John, he wandered over to the parking lot.

"Where you been, *ass*hole?"

"Go *fuck* yourself!"

"Naw. How ya doin', Phil?"

"O.K., Frank." The morning sun was warm, and Frankie sat, his hands clasped between his knees, in the open doorway of the shack while Hatcher propped himself against the outside wall and drummed one heel against the wood. They remained that way for five minutes or so.

Then without looking up Frankie muttered toward the asphalt, "You makin' a move?"

"With what?"

"What?" the other barked. "What? Dint I give you three saws yesterday? 'What,' he says!"

"What do you think? I *bet* that out already. Soon as I hit the DD, plenty money."

Frankie shook his head wearily. Then he looked up and laughed. "Old Phil. I will say one thing for you, Phil. You do like your action. You'd bet your last *dime*, wouldn't ya?" Hatcher said nothing, but smiled as Frankie cackled at him, shook his head, and resumed his contemplation of the ground. "Well," he muttered, "I hope ya hit it, that's all."

"If I do, take tomorrow off. We'll go down."

"I need the money, too. But I *can't*, Phil! I gotta go to *court* next Monday—maybe Tuesday too. I can't take no time off."

"You think it'll take more than one day?"

"I dunno. I know we're gonna fight it. My lawyer says he can beat it."

"No. I thought you were coppin' the plea."

"Naw!" Frank was indignant at that idea. "We are gonna fight it now. We can beat it. I know that."

"When did you decide this?" A car swung in, and Frank waved Hatcher off, tended it, and strutted back.

"I wanted to do this *all along,*" he cried. "All along! Why should I go for *any* kina fine. Hah! What, was I born yesterday or sothin'?"

"Yeah. But I thought it was all decided."

"Naw. I been tryin' to convince that guy all along, an' I was talkin' to 'im again about it las' night, and he give me the O.K."

"I see."

"It was my idea all along."

"Yeah. Listen, listen up for the DD from New York, will ya? I'm tryin' to get out with it. I'm goin' for a sandwich— you want anything?"

"Well, yeah," Frankie said, ambling out toward another entering car. "You could bring me a coffee."

In the restaurant on the corner of Harrison Street Hatcher ruminated over pasty cheesecake and coffee. He wanted to suppose it coincidence—the subpoena against Frankie's change of plea and plan. He wanted still to imagine that it was he himself, somehow, who was the focus of an involved and incompetent plot. Besides, he had to testify now, anyway. He would see how things went. If Frank were obviously going to be convicted—and John had said it was a cinch—then his own testimony would not matter. And they would write off what he owed them. He had to testify anyway. He took out his scratch sheet, perusing the daily doubles he had already played, trying to remember what details had persuaded him to those horses.

He was about halfway down the block toward the lot again when Frankie shouted up at him. "Hey! Handicapper! How'd you come up with *them* horses?"

"What horses?" Hatcher was innocent, trying rigidly not to let his spirits rise too soon.

"Didn't you play one and seven today—at New York?"

Though he knew that he had, he pulled the sheet from his hip pocket again to check the numbers and names. "Yeah. Arab Tornado and Fuzzie King. One and seven. Yeah—"

Frank had been shaking his head, as if sadly, and interrupted. "Well, I don' know how you come up with them. I don' see it, Phil." Behind his greasy lenses he seemed to be amused. He said then, just audibly, "They were there, though."

"Huh?"

"Well, you dint expec' pigs like that to win fer ya, did ya? Listen Phil. I told you once, I told you a hunnert times: the longer they are, the longer it takes them to come in!"

"Shit!" Hatcher was still not sure what had happened, but he had expected the worst. He turned and kicked savagely at the well-dented trash can beside the booth. "Shit. God damn it. Shit!"

"Hey!" Frank cried. "That's city property. You want to lose me my job?" He chuckled more softly. "That's my mistake, Phil. I shouldn' do that to ya. I know you're hurtin'. Naw. Them horses did stand up. The DD is limit. Stood up like a tree."

Hatcher was still grim against the good news. "What did it pay at the track?"

"What difference does it make with a bookmaker, *ass*hole? It's his limit! You can only get three sixty-six. You can't get no more."

Hatcher did not speak for a moment, full of gratitude to his friend—not for the money to bet, but for giving the news, whence his new freedom and fluidness, and his vindication. It was the first bet he had cashed in a long time, the first time in a long time he had been right. It seemed to prove that he had been right all along. He was grinning at Frankie, who became stern.

"Sure. That's all right. Just remember the old man, that's all, Phil. Just don't forget my PC."

Hatcher broke, laughed sharply. "Whatever you want, Frank! Listen. Tomorrow we're goin' down. I don' wanna hear anything else."

Buono removed his vinyl cap and poked at his grizzled wave. "Aw, I'd like to, Phil. I would like to. But this trial—well—I'll see." But he did not go. Hatcher went home that day and slept through the afternoon. He awoke once, saw that it was only seven thirty and too early for the *Telegraph*, and lay quietly while the summer sun fell. He was first in line at the newsstand that night, and by the time Margaret came home the paper was covered with red ink, and he had decided that Monmouth Park was the best bet.

"Picking any winners?"

"Some."

"You want something to eat?"

He looked up from his paper. "I had a sandwich waiting for this. Didn't you eat?"

"Oh, yes. *I* did." She stopped behind him and put a hand on his shoulder, but he was back into his work. She lifted both arms high and stretched on tiptoe. "Wow! I don't know how I get so tired! I think I'd better go to bed."

"I'll be going down tomorrow," he said without looking up.

"Good luck," she replied from the hallway.

Hatcher worked so late at his handicapping that he slept soundly through the night and awoke just after the *Armstrong* had appeared on the stands. He picked it up, and he stopped at the shoemaker's to collect, and at the lot, where Frankie said he couldn't make it, and he was on his way. He had a lot of time and drove slowly trying to decide how to play the double—what horses to combine with the one he liked in the first race.

That horse's name was Beau's Boy. He had done almost nothing for ten races that year and was dropping down in class again. Yet his last race revealed Hatcher's favorite clue: he had moved sharply on the stretch turn, from seven lengths out of it to a head away. From that effort he had flattened out and finished sixth, but Hatcher did not care about that. Perhaps the horse had been short of breath and conditioning. He was a long shot today. Hatcher decided to play him with four horses in the second race.

At the track he changed his mind. It was now or never for the horse, he said to himself, and after all, he had the money. Why not take a shot? He wheeled Beau's Boy with ten-dollar tickets, coupling him with every horse in the second half of the daily double. There were ten, and so the bet cost him one hundred dollars of his three and a half. That in itself satisfied him; he must not be afraid to bet.

It was a long race, and when at last they turned into the stretch, four horses were spread wide like a wall, and Beau's Boy seemed lagging and sluggish four lengths behind them. That was it, Hatcher thought: Get a little start and then plunge on a stiff. How stupid was that? Why couldn't he have waited for something surer? And then the wall of horses shifted coming down toward him. He saw at once a small opening on the rail and his horse, his green and white silks, driving through it, sprinting out suddenly to lead by a length and straining for the wire and the favorite making a rush so far on the outside he could not watch both horses. The photo sign went up.

A burly man hurried up to him as he leaned on the rail and puffed his breath in his cheeks. "The chalk get it? The outside horse? You see it?"

"Naw," Hatcher said, not looking at him. He spit thinly into the dirt of the track. "Naw, I don't think so. The other one got it about a neck. That long shot."

"Shit!" the man said. "I thought it was the other one." He stomped away.

The rest of it was numbers. Beau's Boy paid thirty-one eighty for a two-dollar win ticket. Hatcher had no win money but every horse going in the double. It was Dee Dee Lux, the only filly in the race, that won the second, paying twenty-seven even. He did

212

not care. He had not cared from the moment they had come around the stretch turn, when he had seen that all the horses in contention were long shots. The crowd booed when the eight-to-five favorite skittered sweating in to be unsaddled, and someone screamed, "Stiff! You stiff, Nelson! Pull in the oars!" The daily double that day at Monmouth paid four hundred and fifty-six dollars and eighty cents. Hatcher's ten-dollar ticket was therefore worth two thousand, two hundred, eighty-four.

Chapter 18

Hatcher caught two short-priced winners in three more races and decided that, that day, he did not need any more. With his money in his pocket he returned by way of the parking lot.

"What? Tap out already?" Frankie snorted. "You are the best!"

"Naw. I caught the double." That was all he said for a while, until the red radio informed Frankie what that double had paid. The older man leaned over the punching clock, hung his head between his shoulders, and shook it laughing softly. "You son of a bitch, Phil," he said.

The next day Hatcher taught his class, because it was an early morning class and did not conflict, the next-to-last class of the year before the examination reading period. They were Freshmen, and they sat glumly—demoralized, he guessed, from his absences. He prodded them about a Hemingway novel that he knew almost by heart. He was not surprised when they did not answer, but continued as always his unhopeful questions. But then someone said that the life in the book was realistic, because it was corrupt, and with apparent logic and Hatcher's genuine relief the discussion shifted. At the end of it they were talking about the shaving of points by pro quarterbacks, the possibility of fixing a World Series, of some prospect of universal slick dealing. They were still arguing among themselves as they went out, and Hatcher felt a little guilty to see how interested they could be in the right things. They could have talked that way all year, he supposed, for a moment.

He won all that week. In the days at the track, and at the poker clubs less fabulously, but steadily—the cards never really cold and something usually possible and the hands falling out according to his own set of probabilities. He coasted, collected, paid debts—at least the ones that he could pay all at once, without struggle or patience—and boasted to his wife when he saw her of how well he was doing and how it had only been a matter of time anyway. On Thursday night, in a fit of fresh attention to her, he even suggested that she wouldn't have to work for much longer, but Margaret said that she did not mind it that much.

John called on Friday night, and Hatcher had been waiting for him. "Hi ya, Teacher!" He seemed happy, but his voice deepened and slowed when Hatcher said that he had been wanting to see him.

"Yeah? What about?"

"Some of our business arrangements," Hatcher said, pleasing himself with his imitation of the other's euphemisms.

"Oh. Yeah. Well, I guess we should nail everythin' down before Monday—O.K.—tamorra—"

"Better tonight." The twenty-four hundred dollars that he had kept hidden for the last few days in a rolled pair of socks had been bothering him. He wanted to get rid of it, and to get rid of John, himself.

"I dunno. I *guess* I could tonight. I gotta see some people, but —awright. Meet me down the Italian–American, 'bout nine."

"Nine thirty. I want to get the *Telly.*"

"Yeah, yeah, awright. Nine thirty. See ya, Teacher."

John's heavy face hung over a solitaire layout as Hatcher went in. His brows were knitted, and his cigar was steady in the middle of his teeth in concentration at the game. In the other corner some eager players were having a four-handed poker game. They shouted to Hatcher to join them, and he cursed them amiably.

"Siddown, Professor."

"Why ain't you in the game, John?"

"Aw. That's only a hobby a mine, ya know."

"Yeah." But now he saw the beetling man from another angle, as if because of his sitting alone, playing solitaire in the same room with a poker game going on, John had never been a gambler at all.

"Well. I got your paper." Hatcher stretched and leaned over in the chair, so as to get at his pocket.

"Jesus Christ, Teacher!" John's eyes bulged irritably. "Not here. In the back for Christ sake."

He followed the shorter man back into the kitchen, which was shut off from the longer room by a partition with a waiter's window. Cases of soda bottles were stacked around the two refrigerators, and the old espresso machine was hissing steam as they stood, hidden, behind it.

"What's this?"

Without speaking Hatcher extended the folded wad, and John, still irritated, stripped the hundred-dollar bills from it, counting. "Eighteen, nineteen—what kina score did *you* make, for Christ sake?"

"Cashed a bet."

"Yeah." He finished and sighed heavily. "*Yeah.* But the count isn't there, Phil." Hatcher did not answer. He seemed not to have heard. The smile on his face was rigid. "I said," John repeated, "you're a little short here."

"You better count it again, John. It's there all right."

"Naw, naw. I don't count it again. I don't *make* that mistake. You're short, Teacher. There's only twenty-four hunnert here."

The smile on Hatcher's face had not relaxed. "So what did I borrow, John? Ten thousand? So we're square. That does it."

"I don't unnerstan' you, Teacher. Is this some gag or sonthin'? I said *twenty-four!* Now I guess *you* know how much you owe. Lessee. Now this is the third week, right? Well, then that comes to thirty-two. Is that right? Lessee. Right! Thirty-two."

"The third week? Wait a minute, John. What kind of interest am I payin' here—"

"Come *on*, Professor! What do you think? Was it the *bank* you was borrowin' from? Standard rate. Six for five per."

"Per week, that is."

"Why certainly! What else?"

"Yeah."

"Certainly."

Hatcher nodded, thinking. He could make up the other eight hundred, but it would leave him with a short bankroll. He was going too good for that; he did not want to jeopardize his action. "O.K. Suppose I just give you this now. I'll have the rest easy in a couple weeks at the outside—even at six for five a week on it."

"Teacher," John muttered, his short arms hanging out slightly from his sides. "That wasn't exactly the deal. If you had it all before, that's one thing. Or even now. But that trial is Monday awready. They're all set."

"Are you telling me you won't take this?"

"Come on, Phil. It ain't that *I* won't take it. You gotta unnerstan'."

"Look. Monday morning, then. I'll have it all Monday morning."

John shook his head once. "Phil. It's like I said. We made a deal. My friends are countin' on it now. Look what they're willin' to forget! Thirty-two—no, it'll be thirty-six next week, plus what is it you owe my bookin' friend—"

"Three seventy is all."

"Plus three seventy! They just forget about it!"

"In other words my money's no good? And I have to nail this Buono for you?"

"Teacher. I don' see why you gotta look at it that way." Hatcher held out his hand for the money, turned without speaking again, and left.

The next day, Saturday, he could not think about it. He hit the double at Aqueduct—not a big double but he had two ten-dollar tickets. He was ahead about six hundred, and he ran on, catching the next four races in a row. He scanned the past performances quickly, without a pencil, ignoring speed ratings and fractional times and all the rest of it. Instead, he played the horses off against each other in his imagination, name against name—the names calling up their style of running, and the company they could keep, and the distances they could go. Perhaps because he was so loose, perhaps because he so avoided the usual traps, or perhaps merely because he was running lucky again, he went on collecting. For the feature of the day he bet five hundred on the favorite who looked especially good. When the horse ran a close second, Hatcher only clucked, and looked again at the paper and nodded seriously to himself. The winner had figured, he thought; he had made a mistake. He walked out of the track hands in his pockets, whistling.

He played poker Saturday night and on into Sunday. He won, and he went happily to bed at four o'clock Sunday afternoon. On Monday morning the telephone awakened him. He snatched at it, looked at it, and spoke into it.

"Mr. Hatcher?"

"Uh?"

"Mr. Hatcher this is Frank Krauss. I'm the County Prosecutor, right downtown here."

"Yuh?" Hatcher was very groggy. It was a great effort to speak, and even to listen.

"I was wondering if you could come down a little early this morning, Mr. Hatcher. The trial's at eleven—say, ten?"

"What's the trouble?"

"Oh, no trouble. We just want to talk to you about your testimony, so we can make full use of what you have to say."

Hatcher was coming more awake now. He propped on one elbow, frowning. A single drop of sweat ran quickly down over his ribs, and he tucked the sheet up into his armpit.

"Mr. Hatcher?"

"I—uh—I don't—"

"It's just that I won't be there. My assistant Bob Brown is trying the case. We want it to go smoothly for him."

"I see. Well, I did have an appointment at ten—" He was thinking rapidly now, at the thought of having to decide so soon. "Why, you think I'm going to surprise you?"

"No-o. Well. You should have been told—"

"By who? John didn't—"

"That's all right, Mr. Hatcher," Krauss interrupted. "We can drop it. Hatcher heard him sigh audibly over the phone. "It's not *that* important that you come early. I guess we understand each other anyway."

"Oh sure," Hatcher said quickly, relieved.

"So long as you know what you're going to say, and you're not nervous, are you?"

"No, not nervous."

"O.K. Good enough."

"Right."

"Good-bye, then."

"So long."

Hatcher paused for a moment, frowned, and rose. He walked to his dresser, and then stood before it with his head tilted to the side. Absently, he picked up the folded money lying there and riffled the edges of the bills. Then, seeing the money, he counted it. He clucked contemptuously to himself. Moving to the closet, he pulled out his gray suit, shaking his head.

He was surprised by the seeming newness of the courtroom, all the more evident because it was almost empty. When he got there at ten forty-five, there were only a short, fat guard with some sort of badge and a pronounced sour smell, two solemn figures who looked like army men out of uniform, and, at the other end of the room, a white-haired, bland-faced guard who was holding cheerful conversation with jury members through an open door. Hatcher sat down in a back row. After a moment, Frankie came in with his lawyer.

Buono was dressed in a cheap blue, almost black, suit, and looked strange in it. When he came over and sat down chortling confidentially with Hatcher, patches of very white skin appeared between his short purple socks and the trouser cuffs.

"Come to see how the old man makes out, huh, Phil? Don't worry about a thing."

"Oh yeah?" Hatcher said. "I gotta testify. I'm in those movies too."

"They speenaed ya?"

"Yeah. Last minute."

"Bastards! But hell, that's all the better—now I *know* we beat it." His lawyer approached in blue pinstripe. His small, white mustache bristled as he walked slowly with his chin on his chest. Buono introduced his friend.

"A character witness?" the lawyer joked.

"*They* don't think so, I guess," Hatcher replied. "It's for the other side."

"Ah. I see." He nodded wisely, chin in hand.

Frankie rose laughing. "What's that? What you see?" He clapped his lawyer on the shoulder. "Come on, Muley! Don't worry about nothin'!" The two men walked up through the low swinging gate to their long table. Frankie was talking continually into the older man's nodding profile.

The guard at the other end of the room opened wide the large doors, and the jurors filed in. A man in light gray entered through another door. He said, "Please remain seated." The judge came in. He nodded to the room in what seemed to be a friendly way and sat down on his perch at the top of the interconnected, geometric cluster of benches and desks at the front of the room. A man whom Hatcher had not noticed talking to the two ex-sergeants got up nodding assurances and walked to the opposite end of the long table from Frankie. His face was ruddy and heavily pockmarked; his suit was teal-green and tightly wrinkled between his shoulders; his neck bulged over a curling collar, in which the necktie was slightly askew. He sat down for a moment, shuffled through some papers, rose again, and began to speak.

"You have been advised," he said to the jury, "that this is a criminal case involving gambling on horses. In the vernacular, 'making book' on horses—taking bets on the running of horses, mares, and geldings." He paused heavily, with Hatcher thinking of colts and fillies, too. "In violation—in violation of New Jersey Statute 2A: 112–3. The state will show that the defendant"—he turned and waved a hand—"Frank Buono, while under surveillance for a period of five days, between May 21 and May 26, was observed taking bets on horse racing, and that he did so willfully and wrongly, and that he was therefore guilty of crimes against the state during this period of time." He seemed then to relax, to fall away from this pitch of mechanicalness. "This," he sighed loudly, "is a simple case. But that does not mean that it is not a serious case—" He appeared about to say something more, but instead clapped his jaws together, turned, and stumped to his chair.

The defense attorney, Mr. Muller, then rose. He stood for a moment, theatrically in thought. His hands were buried in his pockets, his chin on his chest. He raised his eyes very slowly, until they rested on the jury. "I represent Frank Buono," he said.

"Frank Buono. Frank works for the city. He has worked for the city for nine years. He works a fifty-two hour week, and he has been a regular attender at his job. I am not going to deny that Frank Buono is interested in horses"—Frankie chuckled audibly, and Muller frowned at this—"he likes horses, and he makes a bet when he can. But he is not a bookmaker." Stroking his mustache, he turned from them and paced back to the rail, leaning in front of Hatcher. "Let me tell you something," he continued, "about reasonable doubt. In Scotland you know, there is a *three*-way system. There it is guilty, or innocent, or not proved. *Not proved.* Now in this country, many verdicts of *not guilty* are actually *not proved.* What that means is this: if you have any doubts whatever about the case against Frank Buono being proved"—he had been pacing, head down, describing circles in the air with one hand, but now he stopped sharply—"*even if you suspect him,* you *must* find him innocent. I know that you will be convinced that this case against him has not been proved—beyond a reasonable doubt." Muller walked slowly back to the table and sat down. Apparently he was finished. Hatcher shifted on the hard bench; it seemed a lame beginning.

The prosecutor rose again, spoke a name. The bailiff echoed, "Call Detective Wojac." One of the two men sitting across from Hatcher went straight-faced to the witness stand. He carried a cardboard file case, and he placed it, as he sat down, squarely in front of him. The prosecutor then informed the jury that this man had been a member of the gambling squad for five years, and he asked Wojac to relate the events of May 21 to 26. The detective took from his case a sheaf of papers; he began reading off items in a monotone. Muller objected, and the judge told the witness that he might only use his notes to aid his recollection. For a few moments then the detective answered extemporaneously, but stumbled and hesitated, and soon he was back reading, and again the judge cautioned him. This occurred repeatedly thoughout his testimony.

He ground on through dates and times, remarking that at one time the defendant was seen reading the scratch sheet, or at another, people were seen to approach the booth, read the racing paper or the sheet, and leave. Usually, he said, these people were walking; they had no "parking business" at the lot. He read off some license numbers: "look up" had revealed that the numbers belonged to these persons, who stopped at the lot frequently, often more than once a day. All these details were strung out dramatically, as if with each one the evidence against Frankie was mounting. In the main it was a story of people coming and reading and talking and going. Once an old black man was observed with the defendant; he wrote something on a paper and put the paper in his cap. Later he returned with a brown paper bag, handing it to the defendant. So it went, and the court recessed for lunch.

In a bar a block south of the courthouse, Hatcher asked for a hamburger and a beer, then changed the order to scotch and soda. He had three of those while he studied the scratch sheet without result. He had been going to call the bookie, but he could not arrange his bets. The heavy print of the Armstrong seemed even darker; the lines of it closer and blurring into one another. Finally he stopped trying, and with the sheet laid out in front of him, let himself worry. Because there seemed to him to be nothing in the case, no evidence, and because John had lied about it. He would have to convict Frankie by himself. Still, he thought, maybe the proof was all in the movies. It had to be.

After lunch Wojac was asked to summarize his testimony. To Hatcher it sounded like a chant: "Observed people coming and going—not parking—reading—ten or twelve people—something changed hands—looked at the scratch sheet—gave something to Buono—look up revealed the car belonged to Salvatore Buono, 127 Jensen Street—some kind of action—changed hands—betting slips—reached in his pocket—slips—action—action." The last word seemed to stick oddly, again and again, in the detective's mouth. When the men on the jury heard it, as when they had heard about the sheet, the slips, even the brown paper bag, a few of them smiled knowingly at each other. But the women there only sat, their frowns stiffening with each "action." The detective went on saying it and the rest, and Frankie's lawyer did not seem to be listening.

He began his cross-examination by asking how the surveillance had been carried out. At this the detective appeared to become more sullen.

"In a vehicle."

"Vehicle?"

"Truck." Wojac shifted his buttocks and tightened his lips. It was not clear what was bothering him.

"And did you take those reels of film from that truck?"

"Right."

"All of them?"

"Right. All—but the first ones."

"And those?"

"I took 'em from the school across the street," Wojac mumbled, his face reddening.

"*The Harrison Street School?*"

"Right, yeah. That's right."

"That's a *grammar* school, isn't it?"

"First through sixth grades," the detective muttered.

"Again?"

"First through sixth grades! This was in the fourth—"

"*I see,*" Muller said, scanning the jury, a few of whom were looking grimly at the detective. One of them chuckled. The prosecutor objected to the entire line of questioning, and Muller put his chin in his hand, walked away, turned, and took another tack.

"You say that one of the people who frequented the parking lot was Salvatore Buono?" A nod. "Do you know his relation to the defendant?"

"Brother."

"Then are you suggesting that Frank Buono was making book for his *brother?*"

Again the state objected. Muller waved his hand in the air carelessly. He paced some more and stopped at a new place in the room. "These—these *betting slips* that you keep referring to. What are they?"

"Well. They're slips of paper. With writing on them." Wojac seeemed to have recovered himself, or to have liked his answer to that question.

"You mean horses' names?"

"Numbers. Scratch-sheet numbers."

"But how do you know they're scratch-sheet numbers. They're just numbers, aren't they—"

"On the basis of my experience——"

"But isn't it usual, in cases like this, to conduct a raid on the person or place suspected?"

"Yes."

"And isn't it a fact that no such raid was made on the defendant?"

"Right."

"So isn't it a fact that you are in no position to know *what* was exchanged between Frank Buono and these other people, or what these alleged 'betting slips' were?"

"No."

"What?"

"No, it isn't a fact. I am in a position. We, Detective Loos and myself, investigated Buono's car—white Pontiac four-door, SSV 539. In the glove compartment we found three betting slips. A raid wasn't necessary."

"Ah. So you did. It wasn't." But Muller seemed surprised at this. "Betting slips. Papers with numbers on them."

"Parking lot ticket stubs," Wojac said deliberately, "with numbers—and letters—on them."

"Letters?"

"To show what track it was."

Later it came time for the movies. Muller had delayed and quibbled before as to how the reels of film were to be referred to before they were placed in evidence, and so Hatcher half-expected him to question their actual introduction. It was not a total surprise when he did not. With his continual false starts, his stagey allusiveness, his apparent confusion, Muller seemed a good match for the prosecution's own fragmentary case.

Yet Hatcher listened hard to both sides trying to distill from the erratic argument his plan for his own testimony. At the times when Muller fumbled, Hatcher was relieved, thinking that the state might be satisfied without demanding that he himself turn Frankie over to them. But then it would become clear that beyond Muller's mistakes the prosecution had no case. So when Frankie looked innocent, as if he would get off, Hatcher worried most. In that way he alternated, through the afternoon, and now he sat tense and straight, eyes fixed on the back of the bench before him as the lights dimmed. The machine whirred. The usual occult marks flashed though, and then there was Frankie.

In the changing light and inept focus of the pictures he strutted and looked suspicious, as relentless as always in the pursuit of payoffs and funny stories. And always when cronies had gone or the cars were not coming in, he was back in the booth, elbows on knees, with the sheet or the *Telegraph* or the current issue of *Turf.* Most often that picture was in silhouette, with the light fading behind, so that it seemed to be evening. But then a frame would jump and brighten glaringly, and Frankie would be hunched at a car window, engrossed in talk. Hatcher had seen him talk just as earnestly with old ladies about their dogs in the back seat. Occasionally in the film he held out his hand, and occasionally something was put into it. The old black man, Hatcher knew, was delivering the *Armstrong* with coffee. He knew also, of course, that the others were at times making bets, but there was nothing in the film to show it. No one wrote anything down. No money was ever seen.

Three times the lights flicked on again, and people rubbed their eyes while the other detective threaded the next reel patiently, an old hand at this. By the last one Hatcher was tired of seeing Frankie, himself laughing, and the other people he knew well enough. Still he did not want it to end, for he had seen no real evidence in it, and he knew now that he would have to make all the case. When it was finished, the judge asked in his soft, southern voice whether Mr. Muller would like to examine the detectives on the making of the film. The lawyer waved that off. Hatcher was called.

He gave his name and was asked where he worked and how. "I'm an Assistant Professor of English, at the college."

"A *Professor of English?*"

"Right."

"Well, sir." The prosecutor's gaze, as it had often been through the day, was oblique and downward. "How well do you know the defendant, Frank Buono?"

From the side Hatcher saw Frankie grin. "Pretty well. I've known him for about three years."

"And how did you come to know him?"

"I don't know—he's not a hard man to get acquainted with."

"Yes," said the prosecutor, with fingers probing between neck and collar. "Yes, we've had evidence of that. It seems to be good for business." Muller looked up at that, but tolerantly, and then went back to studying some notes with much concentration. "But can you remember anything specific?"

"Oh, I think one day he saw a *Telegraph* in my car, and we talked horses. Something like that."

The prosecutor looked meaningfully around. "Yes. Now, Mr. Hatcher—Dr. Hatcher—let me advise you about something. Under the law of this state, a man who bets with a bookmaker is not subject to any prosecution by the law. You understand that?" Hatcher nodded stiffly. He did not like the sound of it, as if he were somehow taking a cheap shot at his friend, when he had said nothing at all yet. "But that—for that reason, of course—he may be held in contempt of court if he refuses to speak about his— activities." That was worse. Hatcher looked over at the jury, then out into the court. The two detectives were smiling, and one of them leaned and whispered to the other.

"Now evidence has been given that this man, Frank Buono, was engaged in a crime against the state—for taking bets on horses is just that: a crime. We have heard an experienced member of the city gambling squad testify that there was action of this type going on around Frank Buono's booth at the parking lot, action——" The word resonated in Hatcher's mind, sounding strange and stiff in the prosecutor's mouth, falling from it like a bad coin dropped on the honest pavement.

"——You: can you corroborate that evidence?" Hatcher did not answer. Jurymen moved in their seats. The Assistant Prosecutor repeated the request patiently. Corroborate. But what was there, beyond side-mouthed implications: "book-making," "crime," "action"? Name-calling that they wanted him to do too.

The square, red, rough-surfaced face before him seemed to inflate irritatingly, reminding him of other faces he had thought just as inescapable, faces ballooning in eagerness for the story he was supposed to tell, that Big John, and Krauss—and for all he knew now Frankie's own lawyer—expected him to tell. That he had to tell now because none of the evidence—the suspicious behavior in the movie, the betting slips not from Frankie's pocket but the glove compartment of his car—none of it would stand up, unless he stood for it.

"The question—isn't quite clear to me."

"Why just tell what you know about Frank Buono, Mr. Hatcher. That's all there is to it," Brown said shortly. Hatcher had his head cocked, his brows angled upward. He was looking out over the prosecutor's head, as if thinking.

"Your honor?"

The judge leaned over and in his drawl told Hatcher to answer. "I'd like a specific question," Hatcher said, trying to sound reasonable, begging time.

"Mr. Brown? Would you phrase your question more pointedly?"

Brown began to shake a forefinger regularly back and forth in the air before his shoulder. "What I'm asking, sir, as you may know, is whether you are in a position to know if Frank Buono, the defendant, was making book, taking action on horses!"

"Oh." Hatcher shrank, imagining his own classroom questions, with their pre-prepared answers.

"I said are you in a position—" Position. As if the word meant something, as if he were somewhere, or they were putting him somewhere. Or as if he was with them, along with them. He had never agreed to say that. He was not like them at all. He looked at the jury. He was a gambler, and that was different.

"No."

"What's that? You mean you won't—you mean this—Buono was *not* making book?"

"I mean I'm in no position to say that."

"Do you not know people who in *fact* bet with him every day?"

"I know a lot of people who like to talk horses with him. I do myself," Hatcher blurted. "He's good at it. He knows horses—" He lost his thread and fell silent, chewing the inside of his cheek.

The assistant prosecutor turned and clumped deliberately back to his seat before the long table. He turned, staring for a moment at his witness, then leaned over and picked from the surface of the table a small square of orange cardboard. He walked to the bench and held it up for the judge to see, murmuring a formula for placing it in evidence. Hatcher knew what it was. Brown turned to him and smiled.

"All right then, Mr. Hatcher. Do you recognize this?"

"It's a parking ticket—a ticket from a parking lot."

"Very good. At least that's what it says here on the front. But I'll ask you to look at the other side of this 'parking ticket.'" Hatcher took it and turned it over, seeing what he expected scrawled lightly in pencil there:

$$\left.\begin{array}{l} 3A-4 \\ 4A-7 \end{array}\right\} \quad 10 \text{ if } 20$$

$$\left.\begin{array}{l} 1A-4 \\ 2A-1 \end{array}\right\} \quad 6dd\ 6pp$$

$$7A-8 \quad 40W$$

$$\left.\begin{array}{l} 3A-2 \\ 6J-2 \\ 7J-5 \end{array}\right\} \quad 2wrr\ 2prr$$

"Do you know what those are, Mr. Hatcher?"

"It looks like a list of bets," Hatcher said shortly. There seemed to be no harm in admitting that. Muller had appeared to surrender the point, and, besides, if he lied here he might be easily, foolishly caught.

"I think that's a pretty good guess. It is a list of bets, a list found in the glove compartment of Frank Buono's car, as Detective Wojac testified." He paused, glancing at the jury as his audience.

"Do you *recognize* these bets, Mr. Hatcher?"

"Recognize? They're not my bets."

"But you do know what they mean. The first one, for instance?"

Hatcher was happy to display this kind of knowledge, the one kind, he thought, that mattered to him. "It's an if bet."

"An *if* bet?"

"If the first horse wins, you take some of the winnings and put them on the second horse. In this case, twenty dollars of the money you won on the first one."

"And the second?"

"That's a daily double, with a place parlay on the same horses." Hatcher was caught in the rhythm of this game now. From the table Muller watched him with a little smile. Frankie was listening very closely, as if for a mistake.

The assistant prosecutor seemed satisfied. "Yes, good. And how about this last one—what does 'rr' mean?"

"Round robin. A round robin is where you pick three horses, and then make a win parlay on all of them, two at a time. In this case two dollars goes on horse number two in the third race, and if he wins it all goes on number two in the sixth. And you've got two more going on number two in the sixth parlayed on number five in the seventh and two——" Brown waved impatiently.

"It's just three two-horse parlays on three horses," Hatcher explained, gesturing. "If two of the horses win, you win."

"Thank you, Mr. Hatcher. Thank you very much. Right. An *if bet,* a *parlay,* a *round robin.* Now. Would you like to change your answer to my question about Frank Buono's business at the parking lot?"

Hatcher smiled. "No. Why?"

The prosecutor was still confident. "No? Well, in light of what you've just told us about these bets—"

"Anyone could see they're bets, Mr. Brown," Hatcher said. "I'm afraid I don't understand—"

"What *I* understand by them is that Frank Buono is a bookmaker!"

"Perhaps *you* do," Hatcher was shaking his head. "But all of these bets can be made at a racetrack. They're probably bets he was taking down, or giving someone to take down for him—"

"Come on, Professor! You mean someone's going to go to the races and bet three two-horse parlays on three horses—"

"Oh," Hatcher agreed, "it's a sucker bet all right. But betting with a bookmaker, you get into the habit. A lot of guys go down just to bet gimmicks like that."

"Then how do you explain this: '3J dash 2'? You know what the 'J' stands for."

"Probably 'Jersey'—the A would be Aqueduct."

"And could you tell us how Frank Buono or one of his friends could manage to be at two tracks on the same afternoon?"

"I could tell you how some people manage to get to *three* in one day, counting the trotters at night. Besides, he might have been going to put in one bet with a bookie and take the others down, or—how do we know? Maybe he was betting it all with his own bookie. There are plenty of them around."

"You mean to say he would write down his own bets?"

Hatcher shrugged, feeling safer and better as the exchange went on, on his own ground. "That's standard," he said. "Lots of people even write on the scratch sheet, the *Armstrong,* even though they say that's evidence of booking. Some people do that."

"Yes. Especially people who *are* bookmakers."

Hatcher leaned forward, reached, and pulled from his hip pocket his folded scratch sheet, scribbled over with his unmade bets. He shook out the paper like a piece of cloth and held it out in front of him. Automatically, the prosecutor took it from his extended hand. "For instance," Hatcher said. "Those are my bets. I couldn't put them in because of this trial. Probably they'll all win now." He grinned at the jury. Down to his right he heard Frankie laugh.

Brown turned away, back to his table. He tossed the *Armstrong* carelessly onto its surface, turned again, and folded his arms tightly over his chest. He began nodding his head, so abruptly and repeatedly that it seemed to be vibrating.

"Yes," he said. "They'll win. Just like everybody who bets with bookmakers like Frank Buono—bets his if bets and his parlays —sick people who keep criminals——"

"*Sick!*" Hatcher snorted. "Betting is more natural than—" He could not find a strong enough comparison and fell silent, glaring contemptuously at the assistant prosecutor, who seemed happier for his witness's anger.

"Certainly. Natural even for teachers of English. But the point, Mr. Hatcher, is not whether it's natural, but whether it is *legal,* Mr. Hatcher. *Taking* bets on horses is a crime. No one can do anything for the bettors. If they can't help themselves, the law won't help them. No, it's the people that feed on this sickness—"

Brown broke off his lecture, seeing his tight-lipped witness shake his head shortly from side to side. "All right, Mr. Hatcher," he said, loudly for the jury to hear, looking at them, "I'll ask you a last time: in your knowledge is not Frank Buono a bookmaker?"

Hatcher swung his gaze from the assistant prosecutor to the jurymen, imagining then their reaction to "crime" and "sickness," as to "round robin" and "parlay." They were the suckers, he thought, like a chorus of suckers, waiting to be led in sentimental and indignant outcry by the ones who rigged their lives. It was as if Big John himself had suddenly appeared at the back of the room, shaking his fat fist in the air and shouting in a duet with the state's attorney, "Gambling! Crime! Sickness!"

He hiked himself up in his chair. "Frank is anything but a bookmaker. He's a player, and a player is the opposite of a bookie. Bookmakers think their players are sick too, just like"—he was seeing the connection he wanted, seeing what he should have known all along and been waiting to say. The prosecutor was looking appealingly at the judge, who nodded but said nothing yet, and Hatcher was going on as if hypnotized. "Frank Buono is a gambler, not a bookmaker. They're opposites just like the gambler and the law are opposites. Just like the law keeps the bookmakers in business—"

"Yes. That's enough on that line," the judge interrupted smoothly and suddenly. "Mr. Brown? Anything else?"

Brown unfolded his arms and shrugged with his hands gesturing outward. At Hatcher he wrinkled one side of his face slightly, contemptuously, as he said, "No more questions."

Hatcher stared back and remained in his seat. Because there was more, much more, that he wanted to say, to make clear—a universal moral fraud to expose. He tried to hold on to his high sense of it, but through his certainties he heard Frankie's lawyer say, "Oh, *I* have no questions for this witness." Then he was stepping down. Court was adjourned.

Hatcher thought nothing had happened. The accusations had been made, the right words used, but nothing, not he, had supported them. Yet, though he did not know it then and was beginning at once to be anxious over his broken deal with John, those words had been enough. The litany that began with "action" and "parlay" and "sickness" became, the next day, complete.

Frankie did not take the stand, and so the defense presented no case of its own. Hatcher supposed that was because the state's own evidence was so weak, and because now Frankie's sly talk might harm his chances. Frankie himself seemed to be satisfied. At any rate he sprawled relaxed in his chair, muttering at times to his lawyer as Brown summarized for the prosecution, chuckling to himself as Muller walked around the room for his final speech, reminding the jury of the laws of Scotland. Then the panel was out for not more than forty minutes, which, as Hatcher saw it, was merely to be expected. The verdict followed very quickly: guilty.

Even from his seat in the room itself, while the judge set the sentencing for two weeks from that day, Hatcher did not believe it. The jury could not have been bought, he was thinking, remembering the looks of the women on it, and yet there was no other way what had happened could have happened. But then his disbelief became suddenly contemptuous understanding—both of the verdict itself and of himself trying to read that verdict, trying as always to read the world itself, for a design. Because nothing had happened, and yet Big John had been right about the trial. They had not needed his testimony, any more proof, because they had been able to count on the jury, on any jury of twelve solid Americans hearing key phrases and seeing a magical movie. That had been enough—that and all the stories they had ever heard of wives and children deserted and homes broken and men ruined. Whatever little evidence there had been, Hatcher thought, had been enough, it had summoned up all their outrage and their tightness and their certain slogans.

He leaned over, slouching toward his knees, sickened that none of his own plans and worries had mattered. Again hands and horses that should have won had lost through the same falling together of stupidity, incompetence, anxiousness, all pushing the tight-sprung door shut. He looked at the complacent faces of the jury members as they straggled out. It could always happen when you played with stiffs, he thought, the accident could always happen: everything that you figured and dared could fail. He rose quickly, not waiting to wave as Frankie was led out a different door, but hurrying to get away, to another chance, to get out to the track.

Chapter 19

When Hatcher went down to South River that night, the game was closed. Ray and the two regular dealers and one lonely, still hopeful player sat round the kidney-shaped, green table playing pinochle. He drank a cup of coffee and left, but it was the same at all the clubs he tried. The FBI was around, they told him, chasing counterfeit money. But the shutdown was only temporary, and what it meant was that he saw his wife in the morning.

"Well," she said. "I guess you're doing better."

He twitched his mouth over the instant coffee. "How come?"

Margaret had a hand mirror out and was scrutinizing her face. "Well," she said into it, "here you are. It's a record. And obviously you aren't as low as you were."

"I wasn't low. I was just losing. All the games were closed last night. FBI." He could have explained, but it sounded more dramatic this way.

"I should have known." She rose and looked down. "You and your crooked friends." But she was smiling.

"There's nothing wrong with crooks. Oh. Yeah. They nailed Frankie."

"But I thought you said they wouldn't?"

He shrugged. "They were too honest for anyone."

"Well. I'm off."

"I'll take you to the bus."

"You don't have to."

"I'm going up to school anyway, aren't I?"

"For a change?"

"Last class."

When he dropped her at the bus stop, he leaned across the front seat. "You know, I am winning now—pretty good. You can stop this crap if you want."

"It isn't crap."

"O.K., it isn't. I mean all the traveling—well, keep on, if you like it so——"

"That's all right." The big red and silver bus hissed its brakes behind the car. Hatcher waved hurriedly and went to school.

"It's the last day," he grinned at his sophomores. There were some halfhearted, whimpering cheers. "We don't have to talk much. Let's just listen to some of this." From the novel he read them a long and giddy, high-tensioned dialogue about drinking and foreign cities and unbought stuffed dogs, one of his favorites. When he finished, they were silent. One or two looked at each other with lifted brows.

"Nice, isn't it? That's writing."

Still no one spoke. Someone mumbled then, from the back, "What kind?"

Encouraged, a smart boy named Canelli shrugged, as if he could not help himself. "But I think it stinks." There were nods and irritated mutterings of assent.

Hatcher was surprised; he backed and filled. "Why? Why do you say that?"

The student's voice became higher pitched. "Well what's it about? It isn't about anything. Just like the rest of the book. Everybody goes drinking and has a good time except nobody has a good time or goes anywhere. Meanwhile they have these conversations."

"But that's just the point. Aren't conversations like this a sign of how much these people are trying to deal with and avoid at the same time?"

"You can't deal with something and avoid it too."

"Well, then take them at face value. They're fun, aren't they? Look at this one." He read them the exchange between Jake and Bill by the river, about utilizing the fruits of the earth, not inquiring into nature's mysteries, and about who went to Austin Business College with whom. Again they rolled their eyes up.

"You don't think that's funny? Don't you see the way it moves, how these guys keep juggling and moving?"

"It's silly," Canelli said.

"Yeah," squeaked Flannigan. "What do they amount to? They're not doing anything—"

"They're trying to stay alive," Hatcher said.

"They're not going anywhere."

"That's the way it's done."

"Baloney."

"This stinks."

"Yeah."

"Well," Hatcher said. "O.K. It stinks. That's O.K. That covers it. I guess you've had enough for one year. I think I have." The boys did not know what he meant. They had only been sitting there for twenty minutes. He made it clear by heading for the door.

But it was not until he was driving back from Monmouth that evening that he realized he was really finished with it. All his classes were staff courses with the directors making up the examinations. All that he had to do was wait and grade them. And that would be all. He turned on the car radio to a rock music station and beat the time heavily on the steering wheel. He had won a hundred and twenty dollars.

He expected his streak would level off some time. But he thought that he was far enough ahead to handle that. He had never really doubted his handicapping anyway, he thought: it was just a matter of knowing how to bet, of not running scared and tight—just a matter of knowing that you could stay in action.

He decided to play less poker. How much, after all, could you win there? Unless the cards were hot, the chances broke down—

if one was careful—to about even money, and he had to sit and wait for hours. He could not continue to lose the rest. It was necessary to stay sharp for his racing. He was talking about that, staying sharp, the following Monday, with a stocky, graying man who sat next to him at the track.

When he had got the paper Saturday night, he had known that Monday would be good. It seemed that he knew the history of every horse running. He was not surprised when he hit three of the first four. But the man in the next seat was.

"Looks like you know your horses," he had said. Beneath his seat were scattered dead tickets—green-edged fifties and brown-edged hundreds.

Hatcher was pleased at the recognition. "I follow them pretty close," he laughed. "But I need a little luck, too."

"Yeah?" the man said skeptically. Hatcher looked at him. In the fleshy face the eyes were grayish green with one focused slightly off center. He thought it was glass. "Well, I guess we all need that. My name's Ira. Blagman." They shook hands and then went back to their separate study of the past performances.

"What do you think of Molly B. in this race?" Blagman asked after a few moments.

"She's not a *bad* filly. I like this High Tail."

"Why?"

Hatcher stared at him again and saw that it was a real question. "Well. She used to have some class. Last—no, two years ago. She won't run to that, but she's got a little edge on this kind when she's in shape. And see this move she made at the half last time? I'll play her off of that."

The other rubbed at his good eye. "Christ she's eight to one on the morning line."

"I don't think we'll get that much. Besides, she doesn't *have* to win." But she did, by three long lengths, to pay ten sixty.

"God damn it! That's more like it!" Hatcher's new friend plucked from a pocket inside the jacket of his gray silk suit two one-hundred-dollar tickets on the winner.

"If I'd known you were going that heavy," Hatcher said, "I'd have been afraid to give you the horse."

"I always bet this way. Let's get a drink."

At the crowded, stand-up bar at their end of the grandstand Blagman paid for two bourbons. "Christ!" he said. "I can't stand all these creeps over here."

"Why don't you go to the Clubhouse? You can afford it."

"Too many people I know over there, you know what I mean."

"Oh."

"Besides, you can see the finish better over here."

"That's why I like it."

"Would you mind telling me what do you do for a living?"

"No. I was a teacher. I gave it up."

"For what?"

Hatcher sipped his drink, proud and happy. "Gambling, I guess."

"Gambling! Not for a living!"

"Why not? It's just a question of keeping sharp. That's the hard part—and handling the money right."

"No, no kidding. You gamble all the time?"

"Yeah. Horses—some poker. Right now I've got a little streak going."

"Yeah. It looks like you do. What kind of a poker player are you? How about another drink?"

"O.K." Hatcher was sure of his bets for the later races anyway, how could it hurt him? "What kinds are there? I play fairly tight, try to take a shot when I think I've got an edge. I'm fair, I guess. Not one of the best."

"No? That horse didn't have to win, either."

"Ha. That's different." Hatcher laughed.

Ira laughed, too. "Maybe we can do each other some good," he said.

Margaret came home early that night. Hatcher showed her six new hundred-dollar bills and then told her about Ira Blagman. "So he wants me to play for him in this weekly game he goes to."

"Why you?"

"I gave him a couple horses today—two stood up. Then we were talking, and I told him that I was a teacher turned gambler. Maybe he thinks I'm a mathematical genius."

"What does this—man do?"

"He just said he was an investor. I guess he doesn't have anything to worry about."

Margaret sniffed. "But you do. How can you just jump in with someone like that? What if——"

"For Christ sake! Give me some credit! Obviously the first thing I thought was that it was some kind of con. What else do you expect? But this guy is not sharp, believe me. He looks like a sucker in fact. He went heavy on the horses I gave him. He said he liked to gamble, but he couldn't pick winners, and he couldn't play poker. These guys at his game have apparently been banging him for more than a year."

"What kind of game is it?"

"*That's* what I tried to find out right away. He says it's no limit, table stakes, and that they're all amateurs. That sounded too good, so I told him, 'If you want me to play for you, this is it: you supply the money. You don't play. I play. We split any winnings, fifty-fifty."

"And?"

"Well, I never thought he'd go for it at all. And he snapped it up. Said that he just wanted to get into these people for a change, and that he'd have to sit in, but he'd keep folding. No gambler would do that. But like I say, he's not a gambler. He's a stiff."

Margaret expelled her breath impatiently. "I don't see how you can get involved with these people."

But Hatcher was too cocky. "I'm not involved with them. I'm handicapping them," he laughed.

"You were doing all right by yourself."

"Sure! I was. Does that mean I can't take a bigger shot?"

"How did the last one work? What about that—John?"

Hatcher pushed away from the table annoyed and walked out

into the living room and turned. "What about it? I got caught, is all. Can't I learn?"

"I just don't see why you have to get so involved."

"I don't *have* to. And gambling is the only place you don't. Involved! Yeah. You're pretty involved yourself, aren't you?"

"That's different," Margaret said, looking at him.

"I don't doubt it. So why not let me go my way?"

She went out to the kitchen. The dishes banged in the sink. "Your way," she said over the running water, "is always the same."

That seemed so obviously false to him that he became easier and more reasonable. "Come on, Maggie. I'm just trying to keep alive, that's all. When I make a good hit, I'll ease up. When you win, you don't have to play so much, you know that." But that was the wrong tack, and they fell silent, both thinking of Paradise Island.

Margaret's feeling that she was working on a new life for herself did nothing to allay her sense of how wronged she had been. She had, after all, been forced to do something. But Hatcher felt forced too. What right had she to rule his way out?

Admittedly there was some guilt playing on both sides. They looked at one another, with nothing more to say, each convinced that he knew all about the other. In their remaining days they confronted each other in these intense and theatrical exchanges with the resulting conflict or caricatures the only sign to tell them that the other was still there. After so long a silence this may have been something of an achievement for them. In a way—in relation to Hatcher's progress—it was the most satisfactory arrangement, since it was so obviously phony. Gambling then seemed all the more the center of his real life.

The new game was Wednesday. Blagman picked him up in a big car, and they drove up into the Watchung Mountains, weaving among the large and scattered houses and coming to rest before a low, long brick house set into a hillside.

"O.K."

"How do we work it?"

"Nothing to work." Light from the house glinted on the fixed, glass eye. "I'll just explain who you are. Then we sit down, and after a little while I'll quit and wait. Don't worry. My credit is number one here."

The door to the house was not locked, and once through it Blagman turned sharply and went down a lighted stairway. Hatcher followed, heard voices, and then stepped out behind his guide into a long room with a bar along one side and an elaborate, eight-sided poker table at the far end. A small, leathery-faced man got up from the table, in the midst of a sentence, and shook hands with Blagman and then with his friend.

"Glad to know you, Phil. Any friend of Ira's is all right here. Come on and meet the boys." The boys: a tall, heavy auctioneer who slicked his gray hair down, a happy Cadillac dealer named Pruett, Al the stockbroker, and another Al—the junkman—an immense Russian with close-set eyes. Hatcher and Blagman took the open seats.

"We can start," their host Gabe, a doctor of medicine, said. He talked to Hatcher. "It's five or seven, stud, your choice, table stakes, pot limit, no limit on raises, check and raise is O.K. Dealer antes ten bucks. A thousand to start. O.K.?"

Hatcher puffed his cheeks. "O.K."

He laid ten of Blagman's hundreds on the table before him and looked around, thinking how different it was from what people thought, what his wife thought. Always the same, sure, but always different. He was happy and frightened, at the high stakes, of course, but mainly at the new game itself, another game. When the junkman had dealt one up and one down, his hands trembled slightly as he handled his cards. A queen on top, and he peered and stopped trembling at once, a queen on the bottom. Pruett was ace high and bet five. The stockbroker laughed and dropped out. Hatcher called. Gabe dropped; Ira folded the six of diamonds; the next two called; and the junkman dealt again. Two more aces showed on the round; no kings. Pruett said that he guessed he was still high, and bet twenty-five. Hatcher called again. The Russian called with ace, nine, showing; the auctioneer folded. Three players left, and the cards spun out. The fourth ace, case ace, fluttered down in front of Hatcher, and still no kings had shown. The car salesman swore at the card's missing him. Hatcher was high, with ace, queen, six, and he checked. Al the junkman snorted and bet a hundred on a dead ace, a nine, and a five. Pruett called. Hatcher hesitated, prayed against kings, and raised three hundred.

The game became quiet, and more decorous. "I call that," said the junk dealer.

"You can have him," Pruett said, turning his cards over.

The junkman dealt for the last time—to Hatcher a deuce, to himself an eight. Quickly Hatcher bet five hundred, as if bluffing. Al squinted his tiny eyes at his cards, started to fold them, and then with a sharp look at Hatcher changed his mind.

"Call! Pair nines."

"Queens," Hatcher said, apologetically, and he had a cushion. The others squinted at him, and one asked Blagman if his friend were a sharpie. They all laughed at the idea, and in the next half hour Hatcher, only half deliberately, gave them back the thousand he had won. On one hand, with an ace in the hole and none out, he called a hundred hoping to catch, and he missed. On another he thought he was beaten, a pair of eights to possible jacks, but he called anyway, two hundred, and lost. One more like that, worse than that, and his winnings were almost gone. But it seemed to be worth something, and so he called it strategy. The rest of them had relaxed now, talking as they must have before he had been there, directing old stories of their game to his new ear. Blagman was laughing loudly, playing loose but staying even.

For an hour then Hatcher anted away, played a cheap card or two, and folded his cards. When he bet he did so loudly, both feeling and pretending reckless relief at being able to play part of a hand. He went out of turn once and once misread his cards—all, he thought, just in case. And once between hands and again just in case, he slipped another two thousand, all of Blagman's stake money, under his stack on the table.

"You're in teaching, that right, Phil?" That was from the stockbroker on his right.

"Uh-huh."

"Yeah. That's a tough racket these days, right?"

"Well, it's not poker." They laughed and changed the subject.

On the next deal—five-card stud again—Hatcher began with a five up and a five down, wired, and called ten dollars. Everyone, all seven of them, called ten dollars. His next card was the jack of diamonds, but there were no pairs and no fives out, and so he called twenty more. The cards slipped around again, and the auctioneer called them out: "Ira's queen—four for Al—*pair* of fives—three clubs to the king—seven eight nine—Ira gets a ten —queen for the dealer. Fives bet." Hatcher bet what he hoped looked like an automatic and harmless fifty. The doctor called, and the next two players folded, Blagman reluctantly. The auctioneer, showing queen, ten, seven, smoothed his already smooth, gray hair and raised two hundred. Hatcher thought, pair of queens, as Pruett dropped and the stockbroker called with his ace showing.

He said, "I have to play." Behind him, the doctor threw his money in.

"No help to the ace; no help the fives; king gets a nine; no help; no help to the dealer. Fives again, fives bet." Hatcher tried to look cautiously around the board, pretended hesitation, checked. Immediately Gabe checked along behind him.

"Checks in the bank," muttered the auctioneer. "Three."

The stockbroker quickly, and as Hatcher had expected or at least hoped, sprung his trap: "I'll raise five hundred."

"You son of a bitch," the auctioneer said. "So you had the aces!"

While they were crying loudly back and forth, Hatcher counted his money. Deliberately then, he checked the hands on the table again, but there were no open pairs but his. He could not possibly lose. "Play," he said, "for an even two." He laid the twenty hundreds beside the other money in the pot, so there would be no mistake. Ira's glass eye glittered across the board. Gabe shouted a burst of laughter and turned his cards down. The rest of them were silent.

"Geez Christ," the auctioneer whispered. "Out."

Al the stockbroker gazed through his glasses at the new bettor and smiled, as if fraternally. Hatcher, thinking that it was at last over, smiled back. "I guess I better call that," Al said.

Hatcher kept smiling. "O.K."

"Oh, I call all right. I got aces. You got the three?"

Hatcher nodded, flipped his hole card. Gabe muttered something on his left. Pruett looked at Ira and raised his eyebrows. Hatcher waited while his caller counted twelve hundred more into the middle and then reached slowly for it. There was about five thousand there.

Al got up. "You're too good for me tonight. See you next week?"

Everyone nodded, Hatcher vigorously, and then waited for him to get out. When they resumed, Hatcher won the next hand easily, a pair of aces wired from the beginning, his luck running. The other players had folded early, and it was a small pot, but after that the cards kept on coming, and he loosened, playing anything, confident that it would improve and usually it did.

"You lucky bistid," the junkman said. "You can be lucky. Me."

"Yeah, I guess I'm getting some cards," Hatcher said.

"You *guess?*" Pruett said. "*I* raise this time."

"Call. Tens up."

"Son of a bitch nines up. You're too goddamn much." He rose.

Hatcher was looking at Ira, who at last pushed his chair back. "My stomach is killin' me," he said. "I'll sit out a while, too."

Gabe laughed, as if embarrassed. "I'd better stop. They're not getting any better. You men want to play three handed?"

Hatcher did not answer, but the auctioneer did immediately.

245

"No. We'll see you next week, anyway, hey Phil?" Hatcher looked at him. "Give us a chance at our money, you know," he shrugged.

Hatcher laughed. "Oh. Certainly. But I should probably take this and run."

"Yeah," blustered the Russian. "Maybe *I'm* luck next week, hah?"

"Right."

Then they were all saying good-night, and Hatcher apologizing to Gabe for the doctor's bad luck. Gabe turned down his mouth corners and smiled at the same time. "Aren't you entitled to make a hit, Phil?" he said softly. "I'll see you next week." With Blagman he climbed out to the car.

"O.K.? I saw you were doing good. So I played it careful. Right?"

"Could you have got out a little sooner?"

"Oh. I dunno. It didn't make much difference, did it?"

"No, I guess not."

They pulled away over the crunching gravel of the road's shoulder. "Well, how'd we do, partner?"

Hatcher took out his lump of bills and counted methodically. "Good. We split over eight. With your original three you get seven. No. Seventy-two."

The dashboard lights glinted in Blagman's smile. "Pretty nice. Soft game, huh?"

Hatcher stretched and thrust his four thousand deep into his pocket. "A couple of good hands. Then, I was lucky. Yeah. They call a little too much."

"Uh-huh. You're probably lucky all the time."

Hatcher did not reply to that. He was already beyond the game, past its results, restless and whetted. By the time Blagman dropped him at the apartment-house corner, he had decided to visit the Italian-American club, just to see who was there. But his four thousand dollars, though mostly hundreds, was too heavy in his pocket. He crept into the apartment with it, tiptoeing in the light shining in from the courtyard toward some hiding place. He decided on a book and scattered thirty-five bills through his thick one-volume edition of Shakespeare. He went out then, easing the door to behind him. His wife did not seem to have awakened.

But whatever he had expected at Sullivan's place was not there. The proprietor's own dark face hung over the racing form at one of the tables; at another, three young men were playing knock rummy for quarters and halves. They halloed him when he came in and cried that now they could all play poker. Hatcher shook them off. He had not come to play, or certainly not to play two-dollar limit four-handed. He got himself a cup of espresso from the kitchen and sat down across from Sullivan, who grunted at him.

After a moment of reading the back of the other's paper, Hatcher asked, "John been around?"

"John? Which John? You mean Froggy?" His uncertainty seemed theatrical. He circled a horse's name in red marking-ink and turned to the next race. "Lessee now. No, Phil. I ain't seen John for a while." They talked horses for a few more minutes. Hatcher told him that he thought his selection in the sixth at New York was a good bet. After that there seemed nothing to wait for. He said that he would see them all and went out through the set of doors, closing each carefully behind him in routine, and into the dark street. Across it, an old man reeled and muttered. Hatcher had begun to walk the thirty yards to his car when, in front of him, out of the shadows of a tenement doorway, a small, thin man appeared.

"What's the time anyway, Mac?" Hatcher told him it was two thirty, made to step around him. He heard footsteps and turned. From beyond the door to the club a heavy, blond figure walked quickly toward them. He wore a quilted vest, the lining from some coat, over an undershirt, and the ankle-high, laced boots that construction workers wear. In back of Hatcher now the little one said, "How was the game, Mac?" He flipped open a wallet, flashing something metal.

Hatcher laughed. "You mean the rummy game? What's going on?"

The big one spit on arrival. "Don't give us that shit," he said, inexplicably angry. "You give us shit, I'll stomp your ass for you. Come up with it, you bastard."

"I don't get it," Hatcher began, and the man's heavy hand swatted him high on the cheek, a left-handed, open-handed swing that he had not seen, knocking him toward the steps of a building. He let himself fall all the way down.

"No reason to get hurt, Charley." The small man tugged at the lapels of his sport jacket. "We take the dough, is all. For evidence."

"Oh," Hatcher said, his right ear ringing. He got to his feet and reached back for his wallet, starting the punch from there. It all seemed then to go very slowly, the arm coming around, almost overhand and as if disembodied, agonizingly slow as if it would never get there, never land. It could not hurt anyone, he thought. Then he felt his knuckles in the big one's teeth, saw the lip split. Just as slowly, he made a jump for his car. He even gained the door, knowing then it was no use because, of course, he had locked it. He looked down between the buildings, then along the darkened street. They were about four blocks away from the center of town, from lights, from anyone. He turned to face the others as they came up, the blond man grinning at him with a bloody mouth. The left hand seemed to be coming again, and Hatcher threw up his arm and ducked and was hit, with the other hand, in the throat. It made no sound at all, and he fell to his knees, coughing and squawking.

"Come up!" Hatcher threw the wallet down in front of him and retched.

"Cutie bastard," muttered the big man. "You'll figure who to mess with. I'm gonna stomp you good, Cutie, so you don't cross——"

"Shut up, Eddie!" the other said sharply. He measured it out, "All that we want is the money." He took it from the wallet.

"Gimme that!" The thick hands ripped at the cards, licenses, papers, and then tore the old leather itself. He flung the remains away from him, kicking at the same time at a knee, and Hatcher fell heavily on his side. The blond drew back his leg again, bent at the knee like a football place-kicker's, and as Hatcher felt the shock of it, he heard a shout that seemed long and drawn and saw the door to Sullivan's swinging open in slow motion. He heard running footsteps but did not trust them and stayed where he was, propped and sagging on one arm.

"Christ!" Sullivan said. "O.K.?"

Hatcher croaked at him, nodding, and the other repeated himself. "Christ, boy." And the next day he said, "Nobody pulls that on my customers outside my own joint. John told me to tell you he took care of those punks."

"Yeah?" Hatcher whispered. "You saw John about it?" There were purplish bruises on his cheek, and his neck under his chin was red and sore.

"Sure. John got some connections," Sullivan said. "This is what they had on them. He threw down on the table a small stack of bills, it looked like a hundred and fifty or so, short five hundred. "John said to tell you he'd take care of them all right. They won't be back."

"Where from?"

"Down south somewhere. Maybe Trenton. Say, I don't like that crap with my customers, you know."

"No."

"No, when some outside guys mess with my guys, it isn't right." Sullivan went on, his thick, growling voice insisting that it should not have happened, that people should live and let live. He was a man who spoke, ordinarily, less than fifty words a day. So among his other suspicions, Hatcher wondered at that production.

On the same morning he talked to Frankie about it, though he could not tell him what he suspected most. "Why certainly," said Buono, "they mighta been put onto you."

"Nobody could figure I'd have five or six hundred on me, though."

"Not unless you was talkin'. Naw. It musta been somethin' else. You been fuckin' around with them guys down there, or what?"

"Get off the shit, Frank. I know that John down there, I told you."

"Phil, I tol' *you,* those people are all right for a card game once in a while, you wanna take a shot. But it's no good gettin' involved with 'em. They are no good."

Hatcher did not answer, turning his mottled face and pretending to watch a pretty black girl swagger past the change booth. "Besides," Frankie went on, "who are you s'posta be, anyway? What are you s'posta do when they put the arm on you like that?" Hatcher looked at him. "You give 'em the *money!* You hand it right over! You got no business in the world swingin', you know that Phil."

Again Hatcher resisted telling him that he thought the money had been beside the point. "I guess I was groggy. From being hit. They hit me first."

"But *before* that. And it makes no difference. You're layin' on the ground. You throw the money and get the hell out. You *take off."* It sounded like a horseplayer's neat theory.

"I guess you're right."

"Why, certainly I'm right. But listen. I gotta get some money. I'm sentenced on Tuesday. We makin' a move today, or what?"

But Hatcher begged off, and so there was no hurry, that day, for either of them. Frank began the story of his own suspicions: how his lawyer had sold him out, and there had been no evidence anyway, and the detectives who had said they would go easy had gone hard. "The only guy who stood up fer me was *you!"*

"There's no question you got fucked," Hatcher said. "The question is by who."

"Yeah. That's it, ain't it?" And after a moment, as his friend was turning away, he repeated it. "By who. Yeah. That's always it, ain't it?"

At home Hatcher lay back on the couch with the *Tele-graph*, the scratch sheet, and an ice bag for his face and neck. Every half hour or so the radio gave the race results. He listened and studied and made three calls. When in the evening Margaret's key clinked in the lock, he was asleep, the radio station had played the Star-Spangled Banner and gone off the air, and the ice in the bag was melted.

She walked past the couch into the middle of the room before she noticed he was there. She came and stood over him, and her mouth twitched nervously until she grimaced it straight. Hatcher's eyes cracked open.

"Jesus."

"That bad?" His grin was stiff and pursy in favor of the split lip. The flesh over one cheekbone was now swollen and purple, and his eye on that side almost closed. But it was none of that, nor the way he hauled himself upright using his arms, nor his fingering of his ribs, that bothered her most; it was his reedy, squawking voice. She was furious.

"Well. You've really done it, haven't you? You finally made it."

He was embarrassed, and like anyone who has taken a beating he was faintly proud. "Just a little misunderstanding," he said, grinning again. Then he told her everything, thinking perhaps that he had paid for the privilege, expecting even to be praised for not turning Frankie in, for the pains that, he was now sure, had resulted from his equivocal defiance of John and his people and, of course, for his newest success at cards, his intrepid discovery of a goldmine. All of it came out in the same, strained whisper.

"How could it go this far?" Margaret was still standing over him, becoming as he talked more and more angry, both at what he had done and for her latest ignorance of its happening. His discolored face, the fat back of the Shakespeare book that he pointed to, the croaking voice—all—declared she had been left out. She had not known, had not mattered in any of it. She became aware then that she had already given him up and became even angrier that she had somehow been excluded even from her own decision.

She saw him sitting there grinning crookedly, beside him on the cushions a racing form and the lukewarm ice bag. This, apparently, was what he had called with glowing eyes "action." Action. It was only another name for an interminable series of hypocrisies, positions undercut, rules betrayed. But she did not talk to this because it was foregone. She merely wanted to get out and so tried to insult him. "It's no wonder you almost turned that Frank in."

"What're you talking about?"

"With you there are no rules at all. With anything new the rules change. You just do what you want."

Hatcher was outraged. What did he love if it were not rules— the rules of games? Who could tell him about them? "I don't have to hear this," he cried, and his voice cracked.

"No. You don't want to hear it. A piece of cake. No question. A lock. Have you ever listened to yourself *talk?* Action!"

"Yeah, O.K. What I say is all of a sudden pretty important, huh?" He was embittered to discover that she seemed to have been eavesdropping, spying on him from some moral height as if she did not know what it all meant for him. "Because that's all you see—all you can see. What you say to your little buddy at the music box is different, I guess. *That* isn't going through the motions! *Everybody* bullshits each other, and gets lovey-dovey, and makes money, but I'm the one who's wrong. What gets me is how you and the rest kid yourselves that you're doing anything besides hustling like anybody else!"

"Ha. That sounds just like your life to me."

"Well. It would. I misjudged you, Margaret. You're just a stiff like the rest, aren't you?"

"Sure. Because according to you everyone in the country, in the world, is a 'stiff.' You're the only one alive."

Hatcher smiled in bitter self-pity. "There are a few of us," he said. "In a tomb."

252

"You mean here? With me? Is that it?"

He had not meant that, but he would not deny it now. "Your choice. *You're* on the sell like the rest. You're on the bullshit. You want that, then good. Take it."

"I guess I will."

Hatcher had not thought he was describing an alternative, had not expected, anyway, such readiness in her. As always when at a loss, he moved, rising. "Then leave me alone." He walked slowly, gingerly toward the door, imagining what his halting form looked like and expecting to be called back. But Margaret said nothing, and he had to keep going. He drove off in his car to look for friends. When he returned very early the next morning, she was gone.

For three days Hatcher merely waited for his wife to come back, at night sitting before the television set with a racing paper in his lap and in the day reading science fiction until it was time to go out—to eat something, to a movie, anywhere. He did not want to gamble. It would be bad for his game, he thought, to play while his attention was so divided. And he wanted to be ready when she called, to bring the situation to a head. It was like waiting for a race to be over. On Monday he found the note in the mailbox. She was staying with friends, she said, in New York. She would not come back, the way things were.

Hatcher thought she was demanding a moral reform and scorned the idea at first, though after a while it only made him impatient. As a gambler he was accustomed, he thought, to more crucial tests than this, trials not merely conventional, but trials with higher stakes. How could anyone who knew him expect him to jump through old hoops? In his imagination the weight of such right routines hung like a shroud. He became the more convinced that he had been wrong about his wife, that she had been a mistake.

He sat on the couch for an hour or more with the note crumpled in his fist; he was not thinking, but only making ready. Then he began to wander through the apartment. He peered into the sink, at its etched stains, and he thought how often they had had to fix the crumbling plaster around the kitchen radiator. He looked at the furniture drawn up in the living room, in what lately had seemed the best way. That was what they had to show for their life together: nothing more than arrangements and rearrangements. All the fixtures that they had wrestled into place and then approved in the days after—a leather-covered chair, a new phonograph, the beds side by side—all now seemed oddly immovable. Nothing more could be changed here for him; it had to be left.

He went out and bought two large trunks, dragging them back through the door propped open for the last time. The clothes that Margaret had left he laid carefully in one of them. In the other he packed all his suits but one, all his white shirts, ties, shoes, flinging them in quickly as into a hole in the ground. He called moving and storage companies, one after another, until the voice of a little-known firm said that if he insisted they would come right away. He asked for terms and costs, so that when they came through the open door with their dollies and checklists, he had the money waiting. To move everything out did not take them long. He stored everything in Margaret's name, paid the bill for a year and kept the lists of goods aside to send her later. On his single suitcase in a bare corner he set his raincoat and his binoculars and waited for the men to leave.

Hatcher locked himself out of the room and went quickly downstairs, prepared even to pay up the remaining three months of the lease, but the large, affable woman said she thought it was not necessary. The apartments were in demand, though she was sorry that he was leaving. Then outside in the cement courtyard he looked back to the wide window barred with its blinds, standing with his case in hand in the sun of early summer. For a short moment he hung there, though he could now go anywhere. There was no threat to the place now; it seemed very little to run away from. But he was not running, he thought. He had places to go. He looked at his watch and saw that if he made good time he could catch the fifth at Monmouth, where he had some horses going.

The fifth race perfecta at Monmouth Park that Monday at the end of June was Correggio and Robie J. C., and Hatcher had it, as he told his friend Frankie, cold. Colder if it had not been for Frankie, whom he had found up on the second floor, chewing a hot dog with his loosening teeth and awaiting sentence. Instead of a sixty-dollar, one-way bet, he bet twenty of it with Frank's combination. Still he collected three hundred, and while he stood in the cashier's line, Frankie complained that there had been a tangle at the start. After the ninth—they had got no more winners —they rode home together.

"Where you been, Phil? Don't need the old man anymore, huh?"

"I found a good game." He told about Blagman's weekly party, omitting details of names and location.

"Get *me* into that game."

"Naw, Frank. You don't need to cheat these guys."

"I don' wanna hear that," Frank snorted. "What's the matter with a little edge? You mean you don't have to move as long as you're runnin' lucky. I know." When Hatcher did not reply, he asked sharply, "Who plays in this game, kids?"

"Business guys. Nobody you know."

"Why that's perfick," Frankie said as they drove obliquely off the turnpike. "They won't let me play around here."

"It's cake. Why should I cheat? Besides," Hatcher said, imitating the other's bluster, "ain't I one of the best myself?"

Frankie turned away disgusted, cranking down the window to pay the toll just as Hatcher reached to his own pocket. "Pretty fuckin' slow," he growled. "Little arthur-itls or sothin'? Yeah," he said to the toll-taker. "How ya doin', Jzzra?" The name he only pretended to know dissolved in an anonymous mutter.

Frank sat staring glumly ahead for a moment. "Phil. You are not gonna win all the time." Then he was silent again. "Hah!" he

255

barked, as if to himself. "You know I could lose my job over this rap? I mean, who the hell's gonna hire *me?* Naw! You know what I'd do? Hatcher smiled faintly and nodded, braking at the main intersection before the town. "I'd be a bookmaker! A real bookmaker. Plenty money. They never catch me this time."

When Frankie eased himself grunting from the front seat, he said, "Now I gotta make up sothin' to tell the wife, ya know."

"What? She back?"

"She come back *two weeks ago,*" Frank growled. "Just after my trial."

"Oh."

"Yeah. Be seein' ya, Phil."

"Good luck tomorrow."

Two blocks away from Buono's house was the only big hotel in town. Hatcher checked into it. His room smelled of dry, hot wool, and he opened all the windows and sat down on the bed. There was nothing now until tomorrow, when there would be more horses, and then the next day Ira's poker game. He had discovered that he was all by himself, and it made him irritable and restless. From his seat on the rustling mattress he imagined another routine, he would go to a tavern he knew and have a drink and a sandwich. It would be about nine by then. The television set's gray face looked back at him reassuringly.

When he went down to his car, the air smelled damp and fresh. There were few people on the sidewalks. Hatcher walked slowly, with a curious impulse to look behind and around him for someone, perhaps, that he could nod to or inform of his day's success.

That at least was what he tried on the bartender who he knew was interested in horses. But the bar was busy, and he had to wait to ask, "How ya hittin, 'em?" Then the trouble was that the man had almost hit the Big Exacta at the trotters two days before, and he did not ask Hatcher how *he* was hitting them until he had told the story up and down the bar, in fragments, for half an hour. And finally, when Hatcher replied provocatively, "Oh I been runnin' a little lucky," the large-eared man merely slapped about with his wet towel, said, "No kiddin'," and moved away again.

Hatcher chewed the steak sandwich rapidly. He had become angry with his wife once more. Why did she have to go this far? She could at least have left a phone number so that they could talk anyway. He wanted to tell her how the day had gone, how well he might do tomorrow. By this time the bar was filling, and through the entry the tables in the dining room were crowded. The bourbon soaked into him, and, feeling numbed and more and more isolated, he began to turn his head when he heard some secretary's off-duty laugh. Each time the front door opened, he swiveled and stared with the rest of the boys at the bar. After a while three girls came in, shiny and tightly packed into their clothes. One of them was tall with heavy breasts, an odd, flattened face, a big mouth. Hatcher decided to go into New York.

That was the ticket. He eased through the turnpike entrance and asked the attendant how he was doing and then stepped on it. He was drunk enough, and the green and white signs for the exits appeared rapidly out of the dark, one by one. He liked the Holland Tunnel, but the Lincoln was better for midtown, where he had to go. He drove uptown and then east on Fifty-sixth Street, and his lips tingled with the drinks he had had. He thought he might have another. But then he turned down on Broadway, slowing, and looked for a parking place across from a flashy restaurant selling hamburgers, and there they were.

Once on a vacation from college he had seen them in the same place. He had been walking all the way down from a movie house on upper Broadway, and he had seen clustered on that corner four or five black girls. Four had studied his walk, or so it seemed, with their jaws jutting. The best one had not. He had supposed they might be whores but was not sure; they seemed too withdrawn, even exclusive. Especially the one who had not looked at him at all, and who was something. He was tall, and heavier then, but she was almost as tall and looked as strong. She had stood very straight. Her breasts seemed hard as rocks, and her hams bunched thickly as she shifted her weight as she waited. Hatcher had gone up to her.

"You lookin' for somethin', *Tom?*" Her face had smoked at him, under the shiny, piled up hair.

"What's happenin'?" he had asked stupidly, smiling.

"Hah!" she snorted. *"Nuthin's* happenin'!" She turned away. Hatcher had remained there for a moment, confused, about to approach again, fantasies failing. But her shoulder confronted him, and she tapped one foot. He had felt the others watching, smiling. He pulled out with an embarrassed, careless shrug, walking on. When he got to the next corner he made to cross the street so that he could look back without craning. She was at the curb bent over and laughing into the window of a big white car. He had hurried on west and did not see whether she got in or not.

Here they were; here he was, again. Amid the sidewalk press he sorted them out—only two or three that he was sure of, that looked calculating enough, alone enough. They, as he looked more closely, were all right, but he had time and would try for something better. As one jerked her head, beckoning, he rightangled away and began to walk.

He walked for hours, stopping twice for drinks, hurrying out again to resume the search. At first he had gone all the way down Broadway to Forty-fifth, and then over to Sixth Avenue, and up past the Americana where the best ones were supposed to be. He did not see many, and most of those were lean and tough-looking. He saw a white girl, too, but did not trust white streetwalkers. Besides, he did not want, somehow, to have to pay for a white girl.

He did not notice how long he walked, covering all the cross streets between Broadway and Sixth, looking, feeling his sexual itch, his freedom, the money in his pocket. There was always another street to turn into, another corner to round. Who could know what he might find? Occasionally he would pass a covey of them in a dark doorway, and their chant would rise and fall.

"Hey, baby. Want some pussy?"

"Baby you *never* had—"

"Hey Tom-m-m."

"*Shit!*" said another. "He don't want nothin'!" When Hatcher laughed at that, her eyes rolled, as if threatening. "*I* know, baby."

He had kept on around another corner, slowing and speeding his pace, after their slowly moving, watchful backs. But in two hours more the hookers had thinned. As he walked, he saw the same faces on different streets, uptown and down, and they recognized him, too—some with irritation because he was just wasting time, others skeptically, thinking perhaps that he was a cop in plain clothes. He kept walking even then. He made two more circuits and saw, twice, a bitter woman who glared at him hands on hips. He puffed his cheeks then, on the corner of Forty-seventh and Broadway, blew out his breath. His mouth tasted of metal from his exercise in the city air. Tucking up his *Telegraph* under his arm, he strode off more rapidly, uptown toward his car. In a way, he thought, he had enjoyed himself.

When his hangover awakened him early, he twisted in the light and tried to sleep on. But he only lay there, sodden, for two more hours, feeling the aching of his legs and feet, occasionally reaching under the light blanket to explore a broken blister on his heel. The only satisfaction he had from the night was that he had done nothing and so did not have to worry about catching a disease. But what it came to was that he arrived at Monmouth thick-headed and tired, without having reviewed the horses, and he handled his money clumsily. With three winners and two of them good ones, he lost seven dollars.

He was so unhappy about that that he did not go on Wednesday, killing the time until dinner with bookmaker bets. He met

Blagman at nine in a roadhouse on U.S. Route One. On a stage in the center of the circular bar a thin blonde was jerking and twitching to music. Ira turned from her to Hatcher; he smiled, small-toothed, and his glass eye stared out over Hatcher's shoulder. "What do you *say*, tiger? Eat 'em up again?" When Hatcher nodded tensely and sat down, the other laughed. "All business, huh? Re*lax!* How about a drink? How much you think we're worth tonight?"

"Depends on how they run. We can lose, too, you know."

"I don't see that. Drink, huh?" He drank a bourbon quickly, just cool over the unmelted ice, and they left.

On the road into the mountains Blagman made a few false starts at conversation, and then, hesitantly, he said that he guessed he might play a little more tonight than he had last week.

"Yeah? What for?"

"*Well.* Why not? And I don't want them to think you're trying to lean on the game. They think you're a friend of mine, that's all."

"You think so?"

"Sure. Don't you?"

Hatcher sighed. "Get into it, then, if you think it looks better. It's your money. But when I bet, get out."

"Right. Unless I have something good, huh?"

Hatcher looked straight ahead through the windshield and took another noisy breath. "No. I'll usually know what you have. Just get out. I won't be gambling. I can figure the betting better when I know what you'll do."

"Oh. I get you. Right." He did not get it well enough. That night cards ran to Hatcher better than they ever had. He tried constantly to underplay them, betting small and erratically, trying to draw in the others. But twice Blagman raised clumsily in the middle of the hand, driving out the cautious ones: the stockbroker, Gabe, and the auctioneer. So usually it was only Al the junkman and Pruett left to laugh with sour disbelief when Hatcher turned over, again and again, three of a kind, flush, full house. Still at times the others were in. How could they not be? Not only was such a streak against their abstracted notions of probability, it outraged their sense of themselves. What about *me,* they would scream inwardly. Where are *my* cards? How can *I* be shut out? They would not allow it to be so and put their money in the pot. After three hours of this Hatcher was more than nine thousand ahead. The car salesman and the stockbroker were gone, and the junkman was glued to his seat, losing steadily. Yet even he was gun-shy now, bludgeoned into some sense of how the cards were running, and so Hatcher tried a bluff. At the end of a hand of seven card with an open pair of aces and none showing anywhere else on the board, he made a small, as if sucking, bet: three hundred. Gabe waited for just a moment and then turned his hand down. The Russian was next, and he swore gutturally as to how he had not made one straight or flush that night and ripped his hole cards in pieces. But Blagman, with two small pair, called and won.

It worked, as it happened, for the best. The others had seen the bluff, and Hatcher knew it and was far enough ahead to turn down the screw on his game once more. He played only his best cards, trying not to gamble at all, and the others—at least one of them—called him now every time he bet. That night, when he counted in the two thousand that Blagman had lost, the net was thirteen thousand. but on the way back to town he remembered the other's face when calling and beating the open aces.

"You made a mistake."

"What are you talking about?" He knew. "Forget it. Sixty-five apiece."

"It could have been different. We should have made more on a couple of hands where you raised. We were lucky tonight."

"What's the difference? You keep winning, don't you?"

"What about the times when it won't be so easy?"

"I'm not worried." But Hatcher was. What of all the other games? What of what learning and guarding his play had cost him before, had cost him all his life? He did not want Blagman in it, compromising it, except with his money.

"Another time it could hurt us."

"Listen. For Christ sake! Don't you think I like to play? We're doing all right, and I like to play, too. What do I get, for Christ sake?"

"You don't think I like to play? You think this is fun, watching it all the time? It's tough enough without supporting your goddamn good time, Ira. I sweat it out, and you piss it away?" It was an exaggeration all around, but Hatcher thought that next week it might not be.

"Hell, I didn't lose much tonight. I'm getting on to it." He drove his heavy car in silence for a moment. "So there's no reason we both can't have some action."

"No, huh?"

"All right, all right." He said nothing for a moment, and then, "Suppose we play each for himself next week, then. We can get back partners later." Hatcher smiled and saw it. Blagman had ready money now, even enough to play his kind of game for a while. But Hatcher had money, too. He, too, had got what he wanted; they were alike enough.

"Maybe that's a good idea."

"Now. No hard feelings."

"No. Drop me in the middle of town." They glided up to the newsstand. "O.K.," he said with his hand on the door, looking down into the car. "Next week. Across the table."

"Right," Blagman laughed, and the car hissed away.

Hatcher paid for the *Telegraph* and a local paper, exchanging greetings with the old man who sold them. When he reached his room, he went to bed and read the papers with the television on, alternating between past performances and rooms for rent and the old movie. When he thought he had found what he wanted in both papers, he switched off the set and the light.

Thursday he strutted around early with two wads of money in his pockets. There was nothing he could not do with it, nothing too high or too low. He imagined himself sitting in a diner eating a chili dog with six thousand in his pocket. Or what if he wanted to fly to Vegas that afternoon? Or to Saratoga in August, first class, all the best? He thought of himself so circulating, rich but better than rich, not counting his money. And so because he could do anything he wanted, and perhaps because of some counter-thrust of asceticism or gambler's misgiving, he rented himself the cheap room he had chosen the night before.

It was in an old and swayed, tall frame house, on a narrow back street only a block or so from newsstands and trains and buses. His single room covered the entire third floor. By the window the stuffed chair was sagging and grayish, and the floor was covered with jagged-edged red linoleum. Still the creaking bed was large, and the water gushed heavily from the tap. He mopped around with wet paper towels for a while, and went out, returning with a steady metal writing table and an expensive lamp; he had gone through three office furniture stores to find just what he wanted. He spread the *Telegraph* on the table and sat down to work until the bus to Monmouth.

But still he felt the pressure of his money against his legs. Spring Double was running and looked a cinch, but betting him for four or five hundred did not seem to jibe with hanging in the grandstand with all that money. He had to do something with it. His attention had gone from the horses, and he sat back looking out the single window toward the back of a Chinese restaurant.

To deposit it could make it liable to taxes. Then it seemed a good idea just to exchange the rolls of crumpled, soiled bills for new hundreds. But he imagined the cashier officiously calling some manager for advice on the transaction. He decided instead to pay off his debts.

On the way to Home Finance he called Leon and bet Spring Double five hundred to win. Then he spent the afternoon driving from bank to finance company to university credit union, paying most of them off in cash, folding the canceled notes into his breast pocket. About four o'clock in his room the money in his pocket was nicely reduced to sixteen one-hundred-dollar bills and some change. He hauled out his file box and cleaned out the loan file, tearing up all the old papers. As he filed the canceled notes—some

264

of them dried and discolored with their age—the sight of Margaret's co-signature on them made him wistful. He began to remember where they had been when he had borrowed each sum of money and how each borrowing had been the projected last, enough to straighten them out at last, and never had. The trouble, he thought, had been beginning in debt; that was everybody's trouble. Now Hatcher missed his wife again, and if he had known how to reach her, he would have phoned. He even thought to write a letter and began it until he saw that it was almost five. He went out and made his call.

"Yeah, Leon. Phil. How'd that Spring Double make out?"

"He win fer ya. Four sixty, Lucky."

"Thanks." When he returned to his room he was all right again.

On Saturday he found another letter at the post office. Margaret said she had sublet a furnished apartment; she was still working at the record place; she had made some new friends. She did not ask him about his plans, and for that he was both injured and grateful. He sent her, along with the storage receipts and some money, flowers. There was no time to compose a message to go with them, he had to get off to the races.

He had three good horses that day at Belmont, and all three ran third. Hatcher was so confident now that this performance only amused him. He clucked to himself about what he thought was a bad start or a bad ride. Wasn't the game at Gabe's coming, so soon, again? But Frankie, when Hatcher drove by the lot the following Tuesday, saw things differently. He had been fired from his job as of that day; he was broke; he wanted Hatcher to send some money in to the service so that they could past-post. "Besides," he said. "I'm goin' to jail."

Hatcher was incredulous. *"Jail!* How, for Christ sake!"

Frank was calmer. "They gimme one to two, is how. That means I gotta stay in at least eight months. I *tol'* you I could go, Phil."

"I never believed it. What a rough deal that is."

"Hah! I guess they're makin' a zample of me." His tone softened. "But the only thing, Phil, is I hate to go in the summer, with the season just startin'. All right, if I gotta do time, but why not in the winter? My lawyer says for about five C's I can get a postpone for a couple months."

"You gonna do it?"

"I hate to go to jail now. Monmouth is just gettin' good. But I'm bent."

"Shit I can loan you the money!"

"Na-ah. You'd never get paid. I hate to pay that anyway, I know they're grabbin' me—"

"What a fuckin' you got."

Frankie leaned for a moment, pensive, with arms propped on the punch clock. "How you doin', Phil?"

"Good, Frank. That game is pumpin' me up."

"Well, maybe you got a good thing there. But you watch it." He took off his cloudy glasses and rubbed the bridge of his nose. Hatcher hesitated, took two steps back from the booth, then stopped.

"You broke?"

"Aw, I'm all right, Phil. I'll see ya before I go in."

"Come on! I can easy let you have a bean or two."

"Two beans? Like I say, I dunno when I could get it up."

Hatcher stuck out some folded bills between two fingers. "Here, for Christ sake. Don't worry about it."

"Hey! I 'preciate that, Phil."

"I'll see ya."

The next night he drove out to the game in his own car. Now on his own money, he was tight, trying once again not to get involved. His cards were poor, and he did not chase possibilities, but he thought that with the high stakes he did not have to, and waited. Twice in the first hour and a half his two pair, kings up, stood. He was ahead about six hundred, and he sat half-listening to the table talk and scraped and squeezed.

The junkman was winning, and he was laughing and thumping

shoulders and telling stories. The others were more or less even, except for Blagman, whose eye stared furiously in contrast to his droning whine about his luck as he played and lost hand after hand. The complaining and losing went on another hour. Pruett was made a small winner, too, and Al the broker started a streak. Hatcher waited. It was near midnight when Gabe dealt out a hand of five-card stud—one up, one down—and both Hatcher's cards were aces.

"A hundred," he called quickly and loudly. Then, surprised, he saw the rest of them follow the bet. The doctor was first showing a king, and he waited a few seconds before putting in the money. Then the junkman, whose little eyes glittered at his jack of clubs. When it got to Ira, he raised two hundred on an open queen. Al dropped. Hatcher, peering closely at his hole card, called the raise, and so did the rest of them.

Gabe dealt again, and no pairs showed. "Still the ace."

"Check to the raiser."

"Check along, then," Gabe said.

"Hah!" said the Russian. "I guess you check now! *I* bet!" He threw four mangled hundreds in front of him short of the pot. Pruett showed seven and ten, and Hatcher was figuring him for paired sevens when the other turned his cards down.

"Oh, I'll play along," Ira said. Hatcher called, and heard Gabe mutter and saw his money go in.

Again the cards slipped around, and again there were no obvious improvements. Hatcher checked again, then Gabe, and the junkman bet again, the same bet as before. Blagman looked at his hole card, hesitated for a long moment, and called. "Go ahead," Hatcher blew out his breath. "I'll play."

"Call," said the doctor, and dealt out the last round. When he had finished, there were still no pairs showing, and Hatcher relaxed. He checked once more, Gabe following, and Al the junkman made the same bet as before, shouting it.

Ira Blagman leaned forward, ostentatiously scanning the board; then he tilted back, with a little smile. "I'll raise," he said, and counted another thousand into the middle.

"Gottam *sind*bagger!" the Russian cried.

Hatcher had figured the hand that far, but now he had to gamble on the doctor. "Call," he said.

"Call?" said Gabe. "Too late for calling, Phil. I have to raise. Up two more." Hatcher puffed his cheeks again.

"Jesus Christ," breathed the stockbroker.

"Sonofabitches!" Al bellowed. "All of a sudden, bistids!" He crumpled his cards in one hand and flung them out into the room.

"What is this?" cried Ira. "Now everybody's got 'em? All of a sudden is right! I *got* to call!" And he put it in.

Hatcher had been counting himself, at the top of his dream. He wished he had brought more to the game. With what there was of the night's careful winnings in front of him, it totaled about six thousand. As soon as Blagman's money was in he said, "Raise four."

"Jesus *Christ*," the stockbroker whispered again.

Gabe had watched, hard-eyed, as Hatcher had reached and counted. Now he, too, seemed to relax, and smiled as if contemptuous. He nodded slowly. "So you did have 'em," he said evenly, "and checked all that time. You *are* a son of a bitch—some son of a bitch. You got your action. Out." He turned his hand down.

"Out! Had what? He had shit!" Blagman cried. "You gonna let 'im steal it? Not me. I'll *see* that bet."

Hatcher waited, his eyes cast down toward the table, until that money was in too. Then using one ace as a lever, he flipped up the other in the hole.

"God *damn* it! *God* damn it!" Blagman jerked away from the table hurling his pair of queens into the money at the center and stalked across the room to the toilet.

"Jesus aces all the while," said the stockbroker, as Hatcher took the money. "Kings, Gabe?"

The doctor shrugged. "Yeah," Al said. "What else."

"What you guys think? You think *I* play with shit?" the junkman bellowed. "Who dils?"

They were in the middle of the next hand when Ira came back to the table and waved Gabe away from it. Hatcher supposed he was trying to borrow some money and was surprised he hadn't been approached. After that, when they had all resumed, the game limped. Ira turned over every hand early, and no one else, even the junkman, wanted to bet. When after a half hour of this Pruett suggested quitting, there were enough grunts and nods. They began to straggle out, silent. Hatcher stood still facing the table and counted his money. He turned to look at Gabe, who approached from the foot of the stairway. Gabe was smiling, and Hatcher grinned back.

"Sorry to get you in the middle."

The doctor laughed. "Oh, I got out of it cheap, considering. But not as cheap as I wanted." He shook his head. "You know, I had you *figured* for aces—I mean what the hell else could you have had—but you just sat and *sat*—"

"Right," Hatcher broke in. The strategy did not sound like much, now.

"But listen, friend. We've got a problem." Hatcher waited, unworried.

"You're a professor, right? What do you teach, math?"

"English."

"Oh. Now Phil, there's no hard feelings, buddy, but Ira's trying to blow the whistle on you. He says he just found out you're a pro."

"A *what?*"

"He says you play all the time, all around."

"Well, sure I play! That could just make me a bigger fish, too, couldn't it? I also teach English. What's on your mind, Gabe?" But he knew well enough.

"Now listen, Phil. These people come over here once a week, and, sure, they've got money to play out. But we both know that you're a little sharper——"

"You mean I can't lose?"

"Wait. Just wait. I know what you're saying. But you do have a little edge."

"I paid a lot of tuition for whatever edge I've got, Gabe. And I could still pay." But the other could only shrug apologetically, waiting, and Hatcher gave up. "O.K. Forget it. It's simple, you don't want me here, I won't come. It's your game."

"It's not *me*. But I have to keep the boys happy. Listen, this game has been pretty good to me, too, you know."

"I figured *that.*"

"No, it's not that, not at all. I'd *like* to have another decent player here—somebody I could know what he was doing, and not tearing cards and crying. But this bunch——"

"So Ira says I'm a pro, huh?"

"Yeah. Oh, you don't have to tell me what your setup was— I had an idea after the first night. But I figured live and let live, long as I knew what was what. And I know what Ira's doing now, too. But it isn't what he says to me, but what he might say to the others, and do to the game.

"No, wait. I wouldn't give you a dime for him. I'd a lot rather see you here. Listen. Why don't you leave a number, so I can get you when he either cools off or goes broke."

But Hatcher wanted no more hanging deals. "No, Gabe. Thanks. Maybe we'll run into each other."

"If that's the way you want it. Take it easy, buddy. By the way, how'd you do?"

"Tonight?" Hatcher said, mounting the stairs. "About fifteen thousand."

"Is that bad?" the doctor asked of his retreating back.

That, in some version, was to become the story: wrinkling foreheads, apologies, and all the oblique references to some inner circle that had to be preserved. The better the stakes, the more it seemed that the men who played for them gambled by choice only together. Their games were fixed and social arrangements where they won and lost among themselves, passing the money back and forth. But Hatcher appeared as a potential drain on that closed economy. They did not care how good he was. All that mattered was that he was not an obvious sucker, which they usually discovered, despite his efforts, on the first night. And through it all the source of greatest irritation remained: he knew that, like anyone else, he could lose, that these people misjudged him. He did not want to misjudge himself, and so he kept looking, up and down and across New Jersey, for a high stakes game—not so much for the money, but to find a hand in which fixed caution, self-control, ruthlessness, and all the other little negatives would not be enough, where there were higher secrets he could discover.

But either there were no such secrets, or those who had them were not talking. All that he found were cheaters. He made shifting friends at the tracks, giving horses out when they were wanted. A few of these returned the favor with an invitation to some kitchen or basement, where a small man with pink, soft hair and eyelashes shuffled quickly and passed them for the cut, and Hatcher, losing, squinted at the deck, saw its halves pressing slightly away from each other, and rose and marked off another source. Or in a living room with blinds drawn, where all eight players stayed, and the deck diminished too soon, short. There was no point in remarking this, or the way that, when he was involved in a hand, there was much noise and betting, and players holding nothing raised each other relentlessly; but when he did not play, the game became a series of "checks" and "no-bets." He would just sit out the next hand then, finish his coffee or beer, and leave. At the old clubs the housemen and the dealers still liked him. He was after all their own discovery and invention. They could remember when he had appeared fresh from somewhere, and how loose he had played then. Besides, when there was no action, he would sit and talk, commiserating over wandering children, cackling over meaningless games of rummy and pinochle, shouting in arguments about who the best horse ever was. There was no question that it was Kelso.

The regular players would make up stories about Hatcher, and a few others, when they were not there, glamorizing the simplest maneuvers, seeing in small kinds of control some power to compose the cards, as if Hatcher had willed himself three queens when another had three tens, as if he had not been waiting night after night for the cards and the opportunity. They would repeat over and over a story of how he cut to pieces some poor fish, as if it were a feat, or chortle at the way hours of slow losing funneled down to one, rich, decisive hand of vindication. But for all that he had to be absent. When he was there, the games were quiet and duller. They knew he would gain them little, since it was not likely he would be beaten for any considerable money, yet he was there, waiting, for them.

Still he made his opportunities for action, out of his own little imagined stable of horses, for instance, horses that he knew were always good at their right distances, or horses that were the best of their divisions, or horses that would only be sent to win in certain spots at certain times. He pored over the *Telegraph* day by day looking for additions to the group, though for the bets he made, they could be made simply from the listed entries in any newspaper. All that he needed were the names, tilted against each other.

He took satisfaction in thinking he had become one of a union of gamblers, a member of an austere fraternity, separate from all those who asked him for tips or suggested a partnership at cards, and certainly from all the rest who did not gamble but worked or stole for their living. There were only a few, he thought, who could judge him, and even in them he had little stake, finally distrusting anyone's conception of his way of living but his own. His acquaintances melted away gradually, or, like Frankie, they left abruptly.

One night in mid-July, waiting as the freshly arrived *Telegraphs* were doled out, he saw Frankie for the last time. He was leaning against the streetlamp at the corner in front of the soft ice-cream stand. He tapped a racing paper slowly against his leg —Hatcher supposed he had somehow got the first one off the pile

—and scrutinized the traffic, until Hatcher swatted his shoulder with his own paper.

"Hey!"

"Hey! Phil! Where you been?"

"All around. What's up?"

"I'm going in, is what. Tomorra!"

"I thought——"

"Na-aw. I'm not feedin' them bas-tards any more money. If I'm goin', I'm goin'."

"You should've let me know." A black and white car pulled up in front of them. One of Buono's brothers leaned in the seat and waved. Frankie stepped off the curb.

"I didn't know where you were, Phil. Besides, it wouldn't have made no difference."

"We could've gone down a few times," Hatcher said.

"Yeah. Yeah, we coulda. Well. You come and see me, Phil. I'll put you on my visitin' list. Have your wife make me a cake."

"Yeah." As the other reached the car door, Hatcher cried out suddenly, laughing. "If you're going to Trenton tomorrow, what the fuck you doin' with a goddamn *Telly?*"

Frank looked at the paper in his hand, as if thinking. "Hah!" he said then. "That's right, ain't it? Naw, what? You don't think there's action in there? Don't worry about the old man, Phil. You come and see me."

"So long, Frank. Good luck down there." He stood to watch the car recede up the slight incline away from the newsstand, and then he walked back to his room.

Once again it was not what he had expected—a narrower, duller, more severe life. But he stayed with it, he told himself, not because of lucky streaks or gambling buddies or confidence in his great success. He stayed with it because of what it was not: not punching a clock, or conning the boss, or stealing, or being made a sucker of in all the countless ways it could happen. He took satisfaction in avoiding, as he had said to himself before, various kinds of death.

The schedule was established. There was always the call to the bookie around noon—Leon had not failed to pay yet—and then an excursion to one race track or another. There was some kind of poker every night if he wanted it. Then, though his room was bare and suited for sleeping, he would have trouble. When he had won that day, he would be yet excited, concentrated, imagining good races or hands for the next day. Then he did not sleep but did not mind, no more than he minded the waiting through parts of any day, before and after winners. But losing caused him to reflect. Even though the same, faint neon glare filtered through the same single window, though the buses and the papers and the games and the races and all his life surrounded him, he would lie staring, and feel the slight swaying of the bedsprings. He might wonder then what he was doing, and remember his wife with the distant affection one might have for a daughter gone off suddenly to her own life. Yet when he speculated for long upon that life, his vague jealousy would dissolve into a vision of what he himself no longer had to do: men calling cabs and ordering dinners, walking slowly and awkwardly solicitous down the aisles of theaters, talking and arranging in all the ways that were necessary. He would imagine one of them to stand aside woodenly at the entrance to an elevator, and he might almost be asleep.

But usually his fantasies were not so specific. Curled on his side in the paling darkness, he might suddenly open his eyes wide, roll over, and stare up into the same old nightmare of paralysis, where losing would remind him of what he was, of what he had wanted and got. Then he would think again of childhood, sorrowing for missed chances, possibilities that kept dissolving as he lived, lost yet never-existing moments. How much better yesterday had been than today, as today was better than tomorrow, when other steps would be taken, and the choices become fewer.

But he always awakened with a feeling of slight shame over what were only, after all, night thoughts. It would always be almost time for the scratch sheet, and he would dress quickly, trotting quietly down the stairs, perhaps greeting one of the two old sisters who rented him his room. With each day and night so much like another the summer passed. Once every two weeks or so he thought he would visit Frankie in jail. But he put it off because by now he would have been moved out to one of the state farms, and Hatcher did not know which one. Besides, it was difficult to establish when he could go since he only knew a day in advance what horses would run. He thought he could surely make it in the autumn. He had a good meeting at Atlantic City.

When he had a very good day, he would send something to his wife—a gift, flowers, money. He saw himself at those times as a remote and romantic provider with none of the obligations. Or at least he did so until late September when the horses were about to return to Garden State, and he received a letter with a long legal heading. The stated grounds were extreme cruelty, and the enclosed arrangement contained no request for money. Then, winning or not, he had to write her a letter.

I don't know what you want with a divorce, though, I guess, you can have one if you want it.

But I've learned a lot since you left. At least maybe you'll be glad to know the results: we're out of debt; I've been free and clear for months, with money in the bank. When did we ever have money in the bank? Of course I don't know what your plans are, or how serious you are about this. All I want to say is that I'm going well, and not to worry. Not that I'm so good at it. *I* think I am, but that's not the point. It's a good life, Maggie. You cut yourself out of everything everybody else is stuck in. You're free and you can have the best without thinking who you owe for it. But I guess I can't expect you to believe that now. You'd have to see that what you went through were just the early stages that anyone has who tries it. I'm sorry for that, but I'm way beyond now getting involved the way I used to.

But I was right about it; it *can* be done right, and it's just what we wanted. Every day's brand new, a fresh start, with it all going. I can see why you didn't think so before, but you see it was just a matter of time. I'm trying to say that things have changed. I'll be going down to Maryland soon, and from there to Florida—Tropical, Hialeah, and

Gulfstream. And everyone says that Delaware is good in the spring. I'm going to get a new car (maybe a Cadillac! but you can have your choice if you want it). I'd like to have you with me on this trip and the rest of them. And don't worry, I've got thousands in the bank, and no losing streak can hurt us. We'd be safe. We could have the kind of life we've wanted—the one I used to talk about.

He signed it with love and waited for her answer. He expected that she might accept, but he was sure she would at least reply. Yet before he knew it was mid-October, and the horses had gone from everywhere but New York where the track was muddy every day and the fields short. On the day that he had four winners and the longest payoff he got was five eighty, Hatcher decided to leave.

He was surprised that night, when he tried New York City information again, to find they had a listing for her. "Hello. This is Phil."

"Oh. Hello."

"Maybe you didn't get my note?"

"No. I got it."

"Ah. Well, how've you been?"

"O.K.—"

"Can't we have a talk?"

"Yes. I want to."

Hatcher fell in love again with that clear, straight phrase. He was suddenly full of hope and excitement. He would show her things. "Can you meet me tomorrow?"

"Sure. Are you coming in?"

"Meet me at the corner of Fifty-sixth and Broadway—O.K.— about eleven?"

"Why there?"

"See you then, O.K.?"

"All right, Phil." He hung up smiling at her goodness to agree to meet and the easy way she did it, at the swell surprise he was planning, and at their long, wandering future.

When she had hung up, Tommy said, "That was him, huh?"

"That was him."

"Did he sign it yet?"

"I don't think he did."

"You've got to get him to, tomorrow." Margaret nodded but said nothing, still sitting on the bench by the telephone. "You will, won't you Marge?"

She looked across at him and said gently, "What for, Tommy? What would that give you that you haven't got?"

"Give me?" He paced quickly into the kitchen, and she heard him snap the top from a can of beer. In the doorway now he pointed with it. "It would give me what I don't have, that's what. We're right where we were three years ago, Margaret. Why do I have to think you're still hooked on this guy?"

"I'm not hooked, Tom."

"Then——"

"I don't know. I'll see what he says. He's so sad with all his plans—crazy—"

"So let him be crazy!" Tommy cried. "You don't have to look out for him."

But Margaret was still talking, softly, to herself. "Maybe that's always been it. Like a little boy wanting to shoot the moon."

Tommy set down his beer and walked over to her. He leaned down and took hold of her shoulders. "Look, Marge. You've got to get the divorce. Otherwise—otherwise I have to do something else."

Margaret lifted her head at him. "All right, Tommy. I'll see about it."

There was no one waiting for her on that corner. Across the street, north, was a church, behind to the south some kind of restaurant. Then she heard her name called, and she looked and saw Hatcher beckoning from across Broadway.

He stretched out his hand to her, and she took it. "You look great," he said.

"You too," she said. "I didn't see you."

"Oh," Hatcher said, a hand on her elbow, turning her. "I was waiting inside." He smirked and watched her from the corners of his eyes as the sales manager held the heavy glass doors for them, smiling. Four shining cars sat on the showroom floor.

"Which one do you like?"

Margaret stopped and turned at him, first nodding as if she should have known, and then shaking her head slowly. She broke into laughter, sputtering, "Phil, Phil—"

Hatcher smiled broadly, and she saw that his face seemed longer than before, his jaw sharper. His eyes were bright and liquid. "No, no, now. Come on. Which one?"

"Phil. I don't want you to buy——"

"You don't have to think about that. Just which one do you like—to settle a bet?"

Of that there was no question. Margaret pointed to a long, dark blue convertible with a white top. Hatcher winked at the manager, who had been standing quietly a few yards away. "Just as you said, sir."

"Yes. That's the one, all right. Is there anything more to sign?"

"No, sir. But I'll need the name of your bank."

"I'm going to pay cash."

"Oh. If you wish, sir. Very good. Check——?"

"Cash. Can you have it ready in an hour?"

"Of course."

As they went out Margaret turned and looked again at the car. "Don't worry," he said. "You'll be seeing a lot of it."

Out on the sidewalk she stopped him. "No, Philip."

"Huh?"

"I like to look at it, and I like to think of you in it. But it makes me scared."

"Scared? Of what? Of being rich?"

"No," Margaret said. "Of being broke again."

"C'mon, for Christ sake. Let's get a drink."

Two blocks south on Broadway there was a large empty bar that still smelled faintly of last night's whiskey and perfume. They had martinis.

"It wouldn't be any good. I couldn't think about it without remembering how it was—to lose, to see you lose, what happened when you lost."

"I had to *learn,* Mag! Everybody has to learn. It wouldn't ever be like that again."

"You could get me to believe you now," she said, "but I'd still remember it, and all the winning in the world wouldn't be any good."

Hatcher looked at her and in a little boy's tone said, "You like the car, don't you?"

"I *love* the car. It's big and vulgar and beautiful. But someday I'd look at it and wonder when you were going to tell me you had to sell it."

"Maggie—you know I really am smarter than I was. I'm a good gambler. Sure I can lose at times, but I don't see myself getting hurt." His eyebrows were raised, forehead wrinkled.

"I *know* you're good. You have to be. How else could you have paid all those debts? No, I know that, Phil. It's just what has already happened. You got through it, but I didn't. As long as you're gambling, I'd always expect it again."

"But that doesn't make sense!" he cried. Margaret reached out a hand to him.

"I know it doesn't."

"You could handle it, Mag," he bluffed.

"No. No I couldn't." For some time then they were silent, until Margaret brightened and said, a little too loudly, "Let's have another. Tell me what you're going to do."

Hatcher began to talk about his plans, and as he gathered momentum, spinning out the dates of the race meetings and pictures of the country and the different cities, Margaret watched him and nodded and smiled. After a while he thought that he might be persuading her, despite what she had said, especially as they walked up the sidewalk toward the midnight blue convertible parked at the curb two blocks away.

"It's a pretty way to go South," Margaret said, when they reached it.

"So we'll all go."

"Phil, I couldn't do it."

He leaned against the front door of his car and folded his arms. "Do you want that paper signed?"

"That isn't what I've been talking about."

"I know. But do you?"

"Do you want to sign it?"

"No. Do you want me to?"

"No."

"But you won't go with me?"

"No."

He lifted his arms out to the sides and let them fall, slapping. He frowned at her. Her face puckered into a strained, quizzical smile. For a moment she thought she would cry, but it passed and her smile widened.

Hatcher looked at her confused. "What can I say?"

"Well," Margaret said. "You can say, 'Wish me luck!' "

He still could not understand it or believe it, and he propped his chin in his hand and looked at her. She took a step backward, and then another. "Good-bye," she said. "Good luck, Phil. Write me about the winners."

Hatcher said nothing, but watched her still, and with another step she turned and walked rapidly away. Her face was angled so he could see nothing of how she looked. He watched her, his eyes misting, and she reached the next corner and rounded it and was gone. Still he stood there until he saw beyond the showroom window the salesman looking at him. He came away from the car. As he pushed through the glass door he counted out the money.

Later the engine of the new car hummed and the scent of the white leather seats filled his head. Hatcher leaned over the wheel, driving straight as on a track for the end of one turnpike and the beginning of another. With the brown landscape flowing past him, he stared fixedly out at the limits of the road.

00750541 6

Guetti
  Action.   c. 2